BLEEDING ROSES

APRIL SAVAGE

Copyright © 2024 April Savage

All rights reserved.

No part of this publication may be reproduced, distributed, or transmitted in any form or by any means, including photocopying, recording, or other electronic or mechanical methods, without the prior written permission of the publisher, except as permitted by U.S. copyright law. For permission requests, contact Splash Tide Publishing, L.L.C. or April Savage

This is a work of Historical Fantasy.

The story, characters, and incidents portrayed in this production are fictitious. No identification with actual persons (living or deceased), places, buildings, and products is intended or should be inferred.

Book Cover by MiblArt

Map by Stardust Book Services

"The Dacians say there is a monster at the river. It comes to feed on man's flesh in the Carpathian Mountains. It lurks by the black sea. The Greeks call the monster Vanagandr. My people of the west call it Mahigan. The Romans call him Lycanthrope, the man-eater."

-Matunaga, Scribe and linguist for the Prior elite under Axius, commander of the Roman army.

Contents

The Beast Eater Is Taken   1

Fullpage image   5

1. Southern Pannonia Plain, 20 years later   6
2. Rome   8
3. The Hunter Comes   11
4. Titus's Vengeance   14
5. Kilian's Warning   17
6. The Games of Fear   21
7. A Reckoning is Coming   34
8. Rome Goes to Bleed   43
9. Nestor's Abode   52
10. Nestor's Fate   63
11. Kilian's Grievance   80
12. Dacia Calling   83
13. The Mercenaries   90
14. When the Darkness Comes   112
15. The Deceit   125
16. The Hunters Become the Hunted   127

17.	The Quest Begins	137
18.	When the Beasts Come	146
19.	Pannonia	161
20.	The Grieving Hate	167
21.	Kilian's One Chance	174
22.	The Heirs are Found	178
23.	The Danube	186
24.	Honus's Punishment	195
25.	The Library of Reckoning	203
26.	Lupescu Rising	208
27.	The Hunt for the Heirs	223
28.	The Library of Deceit	237
29.	Diana's Pain	241
30.	The Stubborn Heart	244
31.	The Horde	254
32.	The Warning	260
33.	Vezina's Warning	266
34.	The Reckoning	275
35.	The Wolves of Dacia	283
36.	Darkness likes to Follow	289
37.	The Beasts at the River	295
38.	The Romans Face the Beasts	314
39.	The Dacian Wolves Retribution	329
40.	Where the Heart Breathes	339

41.	Where Grief Finds Them	346
42.	Oltenia Comes	362
43.	The Survivors	366
44.	Manius forces the Senate's Hand	375
45.	Roman Wolves	385
46.	The Hope of War	395
47.	Domitia's Power	399
48.	The Desperate Hour	411
49.	Retribution	419
50.	The Arrival	425
51.	6 months later	434

The Beast Eater Is Taken

Commander Artgus pulled on the reigns, his eyes craning over the Danube River. The rocky plateaus rolled around them as Autumn bit the Roman Army roaring behind him for miles on the rolling plain. He craned his neck from the choppy waters to acknowledge Omitus lunging behind him on horseback. Omitus sighed, his red cloak flowing over his bulky shoulders.

His brown eyes sparkled in precision over a clean-shaven face of determination, his shaved head shadowing his resolve. "Commander." He nodded.

Artgus huffed at him, smiling. The forest moved on the plateaus, and shadows from the trees fingered the waters in darkness. As the shadows stretched toward them, Artgus turned to glare at the army bustling to leave the Pannonia Plain.

"Did you find them?" Artgus wondered, eying Omitus.

Omitus smiled. "Found them. One will be of great interest to us in time."

"Very well. Let me see it." Artgus turned to follow him along the shoreline.

They rode for a mile until they reached a tented settlement along the river. The Romans gathered around fires while others packed up their belongings. Their red capes filled the plains like the lands had bled out, but there was no war. Omitus smiled as Freya met them, bowing to Artgus.

She dressed in furs from Dacian tribes, but she was Roman. Her black hair spilled down her back, her blue eyes as bright as her smile. "Commander Artgus. Come!"

They slid from their horses and followed her into a tent, where a scrappy black-headed ten-year-old boy stood dressed in rags. He turned to face them, his lip bloodied. His eyes were bright and wide. His skin was dark, his black hair was chopped to form spikes on his little head. His tunic had been torn off his lengthy arms, and Artgus narrowed his brows, noticing the blue swirling tattoos. The tattoos were intricate, racing up his arms to his neck and over his chest across his upper back.

"Oh my." Artgus gasped.

Omitus smiled and gripped the scrawny boy on his shoulder. "This is Lupescu. He comes with me. I will bring him into my family."

Artgus bent on one knee to get on Lupescu's eye level. Lupescu eyed this Roman Commander's Lorica Segmentata armor, the silver accentuating the firmness of his clenched face. Artgus huffed, pressing a firm hand on his knee and clenching his fist to look over the boy.

"Why do you bleed, son?" He asked, eying Lupescu's bloody lip.

"I pull my front tooth," Lupescu remarked, his thick south-eastern dialect echoing.

Artgus craned to stare at Omitus, who shrugged his shoulders and eyed the middle-aged Freya. He looked at Lupescu again. "Why would you do that?" Artgus questioned him.

"I am dead." Lupescu belted out, his thin face clenched. "I am dead to them."

Artgus leaned back when he said that. "I see. Do you want to live in Rome?"

Lupescu nodded, his eyes growing wider.

"You will live with Omitus and his family. He has a daughter around your age. You will grow up together. It will be crucial to Rome that you protect her. Understand?" Artgus commanded him.

Lupescu nodded. "Important. Yes."

Artgus patted Lupescu on his arm and stood up, towering over him. "Very well, brave Lupescu."

Omitus followed him out, leaving Freya alone with the boy. Artgus sighed as they marched back to their horses. "You realize he must come as an enslaved person. You can make him a freeman in time, but it must look official to Rome first."

Omitus nodded. "Understood."

As Artgus jumped on his horse, he turned to his old friend. "Ensure you leave with him today. You will have a Roman escort. We must get him out of here straight away. For Rome, of course."

Omitus agreed. "We leave within the hour, commander."

Artgus waved him off as he turned his back to him. "Name him something else!" He hollered back. "To protect him!"

Omitus lunged back into the tent to face Freya and Lupescu. "Ready him. We leave momentarily."

Lupescu swallowed, turning his head to Freya. "They come for me. We leave now?"

Omitus froze at the entrance, his face drawn and hard. "What."

Lupescu met his stare. "We leave now?"

Omitus walked to him and bent on one knee at his eye level, his long blue robes cascading down to his boots under his cloak. "Who comes for you, son?"

Lupescu swallowed again, his eyes shimmering in amber. Omitus leaned away from him as he noticed his eyes glowing inside like a fire had lit him up. He held his breath, his heart skipping a beat.

"What comes for you, Lupescu?" Omitus whispered.

"The beasts." Lupescu clenched his jaws, his amber eyes hard as stone.

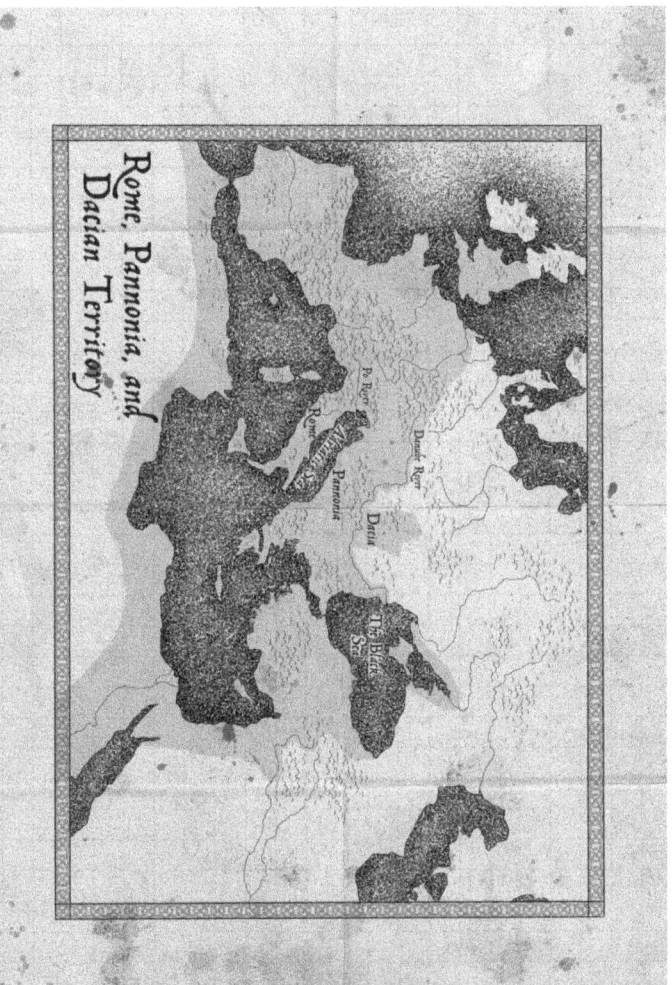

1

Southern Pannonia Plain, 20 years later

Dante crept over wet Oak leaves, grunting with the strain in his knees on the sloping knoll that seemed to crawl into the heavens. The breaking dawn sang in crimsons with hues of pink like the dogwood blossoms in early spring. The twelve-year-old pushed his thin frame to the top through the embankment engulfed in Spruce towers. He rustled through a trail, one knee up to his chest to grapple a hold with his leather-wrapped feet on the ledge.

He held his breath as the air sucked out of him. Behind him, his father grasped the rope to their donkey. It pulled a small carriage full of leeks, garlic, onions, and driftwood for the market. It was a two-day trek by foot, but worth it. They would find wildflowers, and Dante would make crowns for the ladies to sell. His father would carve the region's gods into the wood with his carving knife and tie them with jute for the travelers coming through.

They made an honest living traveling along the river, but this morning was different. By the campfire last night, they heard echoes. Shouts. The shouts filtered screams through the night air.

It sounded like the world had folded in on itself, and humans got caught in the middle. Then something else showed up that was not man. Dante's father doused the fire in desperation, and they sheltered against the mountain base. Through a glen of Evergreen's, they shivered in the darkness, listening to roars and screams of rage.

At breaking dawn with no sleep, they gathered their cloaks with their cart and headed into the daylight.

As he stood there, Dante's brown eyes were wide as he stared ahead. His long hair blew wisps around his thin head. He pulled his wool cloak tighter to his chest as sudden chills slithered up his spine. He swallowed down fears when he heard his father's echo behind him, worried.

"What do you see, my son?" The older man wondered, as still as he could handle his son's rigid body language.

Dante turned to face him as the color drained from his face. His lips froze before the words came out, "I see death, papa." Dante's voice broke as his lips shivered.

His father grew stiff and huffed in silence. Dante turned his head back to face the carnage on the open plains, his knees weaker since he climbed the knoll. This was a sight he had never seen before.

Ahead of him for miles were bodies riddled in silence, a rolling plain drenched in blood. He immediately recognized the red capes and helmets, although many body parts and heads were missing. The rising sun cast reflections off the dented body armor and elongated shields, shadowing the red and black pools of blood. In the middle of the plain were poles with an insignia wafting on a bloody flag and a body impaled.

This Roman legion was slaughtered, and the body of the man impaled high over the army had been a commander.

2

Rome

Axius dug his sandals in, flexing his naked arms to lunge forward; his Gladius sheared under the hot mid-day sun. His eyes tinged with splashes of yellow, sweat rolling down his naked back to the torn tunic hanging at his waist to ward off the heat. He rounded his comrade in silence, smiling. Titus laughed him off, pressing into him with his own Gladius.

"Lupa bids you farewell demon!" Axius goaded him.

Axius lunged at his midsection just as Titus leaned away, the blade slicing the fibers at his belly on the already worn-out tunic. He froze, blocking Axius's attack in silence, riveting his blade off his hilt and cutting a gash on his knuckles. Laughing, Titus pulls away as Axius jumps back.

"Ah, yes! Yet Artemis has shown me favor! Surrender now or die." Titus toyed with him, smiling.

Axius stood upright, scowling at the blood dripping from his knuckle and sighing. His commander, Titus, was a formidable warrior. His blonde hair was dripping in sweat, and a firm brow line that reminded him never to cross his leader. Instead, he learned from him. Titus was thinner and taller than Axius but just as fast.

Axius tossed his sword into his other palm, the dimple on his left side beaming as if this was a horrendous game to him. "If Artemis shows you favor, then Leto, the wolf goddess, controls mine!"

"Lies! All lies, foolish Roman." Titus taunted him.

They stood each other off, rounding about each other, sizing each other up for a final attack.

"You laughed at my swordsman skills when you taught me?" Axius questioned, huffing.

"I laugh at you talking too much and wasting my time, fool." Titus laughed at him.

Axius lunged into Titus's stomach, but Titus blocked him, pinning his head in a lock between his sweaty armpit. He smacked Axius's backside with the side of his blade. His laughter was thunderous, his grip an assault on Axius's fighting skills. Axius nicked his ankle with his blade, and Titus released him in pain. Axius twisted his hilt into Titus's ankle, pulling forward until his commander fell flat.

Titus looked up in shock to see a tanned, scruffy face beaming down at him. Axius's emerald eyes sparkled in mischief as his cool blade pressed against his throat. Axius slid Titus's sword away from his grasp, where it met the foothold of another Roman standing at the entrance.

"Which god favors me now, commander?" Axius laughed.

"Veni, vidi, vici," Titus whispered.

Axius rolled his eyes, pulling away to lend him a hand. "No, I did. You lost."

Titus smiled as he took his subordinate's hand and then turned to Micah, the Centurion. His fist clasped around a parchment in silence as he stared at them both in the courtyard.

"I see Titus won again." Micah nodded. His crisp robes of white and pale blues were a stark contrast to the dirty warriors before him, covered in pride.

Axius huffed. "I get no respect at all."

"Micah! Are you well?" Titus asked, taking his Gladius and sheathing it at his side.

"I am well commander." Micah leaned into Titus's chest, plastering a battering hand against his back in a hug, dust rising around his dirty frocks.

"I bring news from the emperor. The legionnaires Aurelian sent to colonize Dacian territory..." He handed Titus the parchment, the seal still fresh.

Titus tore the seal. "A tribe of ancient relics, no more. Simple-minded fools with a vast territory Rome will colonize..."

Micah leaned back from him; his eyes screamed another story, and Titus turned to stone as he read the parchment. Axius froze in the forum, the pillars rising around him like a bloody parliament of doom. They had sent four thousand months ago. The messages received were vague and lifeless, and there was nothing until now. Titus eyed Axius, knowing what this would mean if it was true.

Axius swallowed. He could read truths on his commander's face like no one else. Besides his father, the Roman commander practically raised him as his own.

"They are dead," Axius whispers, restless pain growing deep inside him.

Titus turned his face to his second in command, his eyes bright in terror as if facing a mountain of pain. "They are all dead."

3
The Hunter Comes

The Tiber River flowed like a goddess of silk curtains under the Aemilius. The bridge glistened under dawn's caress of tangerine kisses against the running waters. To Kilian, it was a monstrosity of evils in a territory he should never have ventured back into. He sulked in silence across the bridge for moments on Tiberine Island. As he ventured out in the open to cross the bridge, the city beyond its limits rose. Illuminations from flickering torches spilled shadows in dark crevasses the rising dawn had not touched yet.

He pulled his pale frocks over his bald head and small frame and marched what he had left of his pride across the bridge into the city. The robes were a necessary evil to blend into Roman society. The sandals were comfortable, but itched his ankles. He gripped a side sheath that was not there, sighing as he pulled his shaking hands to grab his front cloaks. At least grabbing something in his palm would keep him from looking suspicious.

Inside his chest folds rested two parchments. One would get him in the presence of Senator Manius, and the other had a seal the Romans would kill him for. He meandered like an innocent visitor across the bridge in silence, admiring the rising sun blasting the city with warmth and light.

He emerged on the other side of the bridge and headed south of the Colosseum to Caelian Hill. It was there he was commanded to go as quickly as possible. The Roman elite would be starting their games midday, and fewer patrols of the city would make him stand out more. He would need the senator's blessing and an escort to return to the island in one peace.

Rome allowed visitors, bringing in more revenue for the empire and business owners. The city's wealth was apparent to him as he walked into it. The streets were full of families and guards meandering about, talking and laughing about the day's events coming or making plans with family. That was one good thing he could say about these people. They seemed to love their family.

Romans were out and about early, heading to market with their goods to sell. He felt vibrations underfoot from the army convening, patrolling the city's innards. He smelled the pungent stench from animals hauled in for the games. He hated that. He felt like a caged animal wandering streets of uncertain doom, waiting to get caught and die himself.

He pulled the parchment out for the senator and slowed, nodding to women with their children making their way to the markets. He bit his tongue the closer he came to Caelian Hill, the tangled trees melting around him overhead like claws waiting to dig in his back.

"Ecclesia! In Ecclesia adest."

Kilian had heard Latin many times before, but it did not end well for the one speaking it. He turned a corner and saw the rising columns of a church. The woman acted as if they had gotten lost and finally found the church. The steps towered before him in a silent haven, and he wanted to go inside. It reeked of a haven for him. The woman with her husband eyed him cautiously and walked up the steps as he walked deeper into Caelian Hill.

Kilian froze when the next voice sounded behind him. He knew the air of authority, so he bowed slowly, swallowing his bitterness in solidarity. The Roman guard approached him slowly but did not pull his gladius. It was a good sign for Kilian that he looked the part as a visitor to the city at least.

"Hic Liber Adferat?" The guard demands.

What brings you here, Freeman? He asked in Latin. Kilian narrowed his brows in confusion as he was confident he did not look like a previous enslaved person.

He was never enslaved, especially to any man. He raised and handed the parchment to the guard. The soldier eyed him up and down with a twinkle in his dark eyes. The Roman was clean-shaven, with a riveted body of muscle, and every inch of him was armed. His red cape spilled down his back like reams of blood, but he was not wearing his helmet.

"Et cum senatori habere conventum M '. Hic es meus papers." *I have a meeting with Senator Manius. Here are my papers*. He knew Latin well, which was why he was the one always sent to deliver messages. It seemed they were more like warnings these days.

The Roman took the parchment and eyed the seal as the color drained from his face. He pushed it back into Kilian's hands and motioned for him to follow. Kilian knew what that meant. He caught himself eyeing the seal again as the Roman marched him past the churches and under a grove of twisty trees to a manor atop the rolling knoll.

When they stopped before the steps, the roman nodded to him, his jaws clenched. Kilian understood. After all, he would also be disturbed by a stranger in his land bearing the seal from the commander and his legion killed in Dacian territory.

4
Titus's Vengeance

Titus stood stroking his stallion's mane under the cover of the stable's archway. Silence surrounded him, gnawing at his bones while the streets became more packed. The games would start soon, a reprieve from the worries that had plagued him since news of the legion and commander's death in Dacian territory. He stopped brushing her mane, raising his head to a dark figure looming at the entrance.

"I know you are there, Axius."

Axius marched to him from the cover of darkness. "I see Adonis is treating you well." He admired the horse, who nudged his hand at the carrot he brought her.

Titus smiled, leaning his forehead into her back. "She is a loyal friend."

Titus turned away from him, rubbing Adonis's muzzle as she gnawed on the carrot. "In all the history of Rome…" He paused as Axius met his stare. A severe indention between his eyes told him he knew what he would say, and it disturbed him.

"A whole legion slaughtered Axius, many fathers and sons. Strong soldiers. Just slaughtered like animals." He huffed.

"We will kill them and take Dacia as Aurelian commands…" Axius stopped talking when Titus pressed a firm hand on his shoulder, meeting him eye to eye.

"You are staying here to command. I am taking my legion in."

"No." Axius defied him.

"Axius. You know Rome. We bleed for her. We live and die for her. I am going. All will be well." He promised, but Axius tossed the order away from his mind.

"Today, we eat, rest, and enjoy games. Tomorrow, we leave for Dacia." Titus informed him, changing the subject.

Axius wanted to tell him no again, to fight against him.

All he could do was nod at him. "Ready for the race?"

"Always ready," Titus affirmed.

"The senator. Is he coming?" Titus asked as Axius turned to head toward his horse back into the stable.

Axius turned. "He always comes! You know my father." He walked away from him, shouting: "He made certain the hunt would be exciting for us, though!"

From a side stable, another man emerged. He was shorter than Axius but just as feisty. He pulled his horse, his red sash sagging down to his buttocks. Axius stopped in mid-gait, eyeing him from the side.

"Nestor! You ready to be the champion today?" He boasted.

Nestor nodded, his unshaven face accentuating his pitch-black hair chopped so short it stood up all over his head. The sides of his head were shaved and added to his barbarism. He was missing a front tooth but ferocious in battle. His arms bore white slashing scars, but nothing deterred this small fighter with the blue ribboned tattoos swirling up his arms and kissing his neck.

He was in this game to win and win it big. The last time he won the games was just last year, and the three of them left very wealthy, with the senators supporting them in big wins themselves. He was a champion for a reason, and Axius meant to keep it that way. It gave them great favor with the senate and the emperor and benefits for their families.

"I was the one who secured our winnings last run." Nestor toyed.

"Come here." Axius yanked Nestor by his arm and twisted him around so he faced his horse's mouth. He attached the red shawl around his chest and backside, fastening it into his armor.

"By the gods, I think you let a child demon dress you at times instead of the son of a Titan you are," Axius complained.

Nestor smiled. "I think of my daughters as I dress myself, yes."

Titus laughed from the entrance, shaking his head at Nestor. "Good father, Nestor. Bad judgement of attire."

Nestor narrowed his brows. "Lupa looks at the heart. My wolf heart. Not the outward appearance. I have never failed you at the games, my lord, nor in battle." He gloated as Axius finished buckling his armor.

It is a blessing, Axius thought.

Titus turned his horse to walk to the entrance with them. "My friend, you are not a wolf. You are correct, though…"

Axius and Nestor turned to look at their commander.

"The heart does matter. Now, let us go." Titus turned away from them and disappeared past the entrance.

5
Kilian's Warning

The creatures were getting closer. Kilian could smell them. He stood silently, peering at this tall, thin, bald senator. Though he noticed as he read the parchment, his shoulders slumped in defeat. Yet a silent defeat, where the man's title meant more than showing emotion. Senator Manius set the scroll on his desk, turning his back to Kilian in silence as he glanced at his lavish gardens in full bloom.

The fish fountains spilled into an array of silky fronds, caressing the water line with scruffy shrubs. Kilian smelled peppermint and cloves, and the aroma calmed him only slightly. The walls rose around him in the hall, painted with murals of gardens and birds dancing across the ceilings like mischief had just been set loose.

The private courtyard was surrounded by the house, rounded in pillars of ivory and trumpet vines of crimson caressing the waters below. A wind blew the stench of the wild animals lurking in cages at the city center, waiting for the dreaded hunt, bothering this serene moment for Kilian after his long travels.

The senator turned his face to him, his big hands clasped behind the small of his back in silence, thinking. "Do you know of the tribe who killed them?" He asked, his cheeks clenched.

"I do," Kilian said.

Kilian would not dare hurt this famed senator, but he could. He could kill him, even before the Romans stationed at his manor could stop him. Kilian would not do that and jeopardize this mission. It was vital to his survival. As if he knew what Kilian was thinking, Manius turned to face him behind the desk in the center of the expansive room. Pillars in rows on either side of him spilled into the gardens. His ivory robes sunk around his muscular frame, and rivets of gold hemmed into the sashes.

"This pressing news of our beloved commander comes at a most inopportune time." Manius glanced back down to the parchment.

"Aurelian is most displeased to have gotten word of the demise of our men. The news of the murders has given him too many sleepless nights as it is. We were hoping to brighten his mood with the games today." Manius sighed.

"Ah. The circus." Kilian mumbled.

Kilian froze. He huffed, watching Manius grovel back and forth from the parchment. "Yet if I tarry too long with this particular news, he may slay me alive. I will go to the emperor myself with these findings. You will join me at the games as my guest first…" He put his hand up to silence Kilian's protest.

"Until news from the emperor," Manius ordered him.

"I cannot stay," Kilian warned him, his eyes as wide as figs.

Manius sighed. "Your queen demands it, eh?"

Kilian scowled. "She demands. I serve. She will want to know I am alive."

Manius pressed his sweaty palms behind his back, thinking. "I will need you to accompany the armies back into Dacia. The emperor will proclaim war after this final news of the murders of the army." He commanded. "We already planned to go back in tomorrow. Regardless, war is here."

Silence filled Kilian like a blood wound never mending.

"You cannot send another legion senator. The territory will be expecting that now." Kilian warned him, his eyes like fire.

Manius huffed at him, a dimple on his left cheek dancing a mischievous warning. "One tribe cannot kill twenty thousand Kilian. Surely, your queen knows this. You know this. Dacia must be Romanized!"

Kilian defied him, a growl rising in the pits of his guts. "They will be slaughtered just the same!" He fretted, his face pale.

Manius froze, his eyes a blue thunder of penetration, another mountain to climb in Kilian's eyes. "Then we shall send in more! And more! Twenty thousand Romans will persevere and not die, not again. That is a fool's assumption."

Kilian shook his head, wringing his hands at his sides. Again, he had no sheath to hold a weapon. He missed his weapons. "You do not know what killed them. Please…" He begged.

"Did you even read how they got ripped apart?" Kilian added.

Manius sighed, dropping his palms atop his desk, hoovering over the splayed-out parchment. He froze when he noticed splotches of red dots. Blood. How long had it been there?

"The emperor will make the right decision, a tactical embrace to assert Roman rule in Dacia, and we shall praise it." He confirmed.

"Numbers matter not to the beasts of Dacia, Senator," Killian warned him.

"Roman rule over folklore Kilian. Rome wins." Manius added.

Kilian closed his eyes. He pressed a firm palm into his chest, his fingers grasping the rivets of fabric hanging loose. The other parchment was still in there, protected. He felt his heart beat against it, pinging an ancient relic of hate through his feral bones.

His queen ordered him to wait until after the emperor's proclamation before he revealed it. It seemed he may be giving that one up too soon as well. It may cost him his life anyway because he was going to be staying longer than he needed to. His queen would be most displeased with him. He could not risk bringing the wrath of his kind upon Rome also.

Kilian dropped his head to the floor, his reflection a sour dream of mass proportions. Manius clapped his hands, and servants appeared from the side rooms off the pillars with fruit and meat trays. Kilian smelled the meat as if it were sugar in his veins. He wanted the whole tray. His mouth watered. Deer flesh, his favorite.

"Eat, my friend! For after we dine, we go to the games!" Kilian followed them to a table in the center of the gardens and sat down to eat.

He piled his plate high with meat and bread, his body famished from the journey. He noticed Manius glanced around and that Roman guards lingered throughout the manor. The vast halls disappeared into the hillside in a labyrinth of luxury gardens and rooms for them.

Kilian knew they were not alone. Other senator families often visited, and guards remained watchful of the premises. Manius seemed to grit his jaws while he smiled, putting on a good show. Kilian knew it would be his demise eventually. He hoped the famed senator would wise up and listen to him before the war started.

A breeze blasted in, and trees caressed the manor roof, scratching eerie pains against the tiles. The clawing sounds sent chills up Kilian's spine, causing his hair to stand on his neck. He craned his neck to another sound that hit him hard in the guts.

He stopped chewing and drinking wine long enough to hear the parchment slide across the desk and hit the ink well. His heart ached inside. He knew what it said. He remembered it well, but would Rome understand what they were up against?

6

The Games of Fear

Circus Maximus rose around the players like a stone doom of mass proportions. Human heads bobbed up and down in the stadium, wisps of pale garments billowed around the families' finding seats. Axius loomed at the entrance with Titus, glaring in silence, his heart beating faster and faster in excitement. Above him, clouds blew in shards of black rivets, threatening the games with a midday shower.

"Augh! Get on with it." Nestor emerged from the dark entrance behind them, startling Titus. They both turned to eye their small friend, shaking their heads at his sudden outburst.

"We should win by default." Nestor smiled.

Titus narrowed his brow at him. "Entitlement is of fools, Nestor. I trained you better."

Axius pressed a hand on Titus's shoulder, smiling, but pulled away when his commander marched away from them to the chariots.

"I meant no offense. I am in a good mood." Nestor worried.

Axius sighed. "It is not you, my friend. It is not you. Let us go."

They walked Nestor to the chariot, side by side with the other former gladiators on his team, the twelve Andalusians in rows of four for each one. Axius shot Titus a stare but then nodded, stuffing his worry for his commander somewhere deep inside that was not supposed to show itself. Not on this day, anyway.

After all, the red team were champions. A wealthy asset for Rome, and it would stay that way. Wealth and power came with the circus winnings, and Axius was ready to play.

"I will not fail you, commander," Nestor assured Titus as the corridor became engulfed with Roman soldiers.

Titus nodded. "I know this. Win. Sed salvum maneat."

Axius agreed. *Win, but stay safe.* Titus always told the team that before a race. Nestor and his two comrades would go out with the competing teams for seven laps. Sometimes one, or two laps would leave a victor because of accidents with the horses. He was curious to see what happened today, but a part of him wished it over with. Titus was not his usual sarcastic, proud self today.

Titus watched Nestor emerge onto the track from under the corridor, and the crowd erupted in cheers. "Nestor! Nestor! Nestor!"

He raised a bulging, naked arm in the air, pulling the reigns back on his horses, smiling. His red cape flowed behind him, melting on his small frame. His white tunic was engraved in golden folds of fabric, glistening under the sun. The thousands upon thousands of heads bobbing up and down became more hysterical with long arms and whistles high in the air.

Titus laughed at the crowds, turning his head to Axius as the corridor filled behind them with guards and Senators giving them blessings and taking bets before heading into the stadium. Aside from Nestor came the opposing teams, which were blue, green, and white. Their four horse-drawn chariots filled the dirt road before the middle stadium.

"The crowds are eager today," Axius mumbled.

Titus agreed. "Yes. Cupidi." Very eager, he thought.

"Higher stakes today for the senate reelection," Axius recalled.

Titus smiled. "Ah. Et vincere Manius."

Axius smiled. "Yes, my father will win, no doubt. He has spared great expense today for the games and the hunt."

"Speaking of which, where is he?" Titus wondered, glaring around the corridors over the heads of the guards spilling in to watch the games.

Axius followed Titus' glances around, unaware of where his father was today. A pang in his gut hit his insides suddenly.

Kilian walked beside Manius into the busy streets toward the circus, followed behind by a fully armed Roman guard. Kilian noticed the roads were busy in certain sections but empty in others. He smelled the sweet aromas of bread and steamed meats. He had eaten his fill at the senator's fine mansion but could eat again if offered.

Kilian noticed Manius eyeing him from the side, pushing through the crowds to get to the games. "Feasting my friend. We feast, we play, we get rich." He laughed.

"You bet on the games?" Kilian wondered. Such strange customs here, he thought.

"Ah, more than that! I sponsor them. Today, we have special events after the racing." Manius gloated.

"You pay for the games? For Rome?" Kilian pondered, eyeing a turkey leg fresh from the butcher. The steamed flesh ate at his nostrils, and he meandered to the table.

Manius tossed the vendor a gold coin, and Kilian backed away, catching himself before he made a fool of himself in front of everyone. "Eat! Take your fill. You are my guest, enjoy!"

Kilian took the pheasant leg and savored a juicy bite, noticing the vendor gawking at the gold coin as if he had won a fortune. Manius strolled away from him, turning back to make sure he was still following. Joining him side by side, Kilian froze as they veered around a corner to a massive street lined with cages.

"Ah! Here we are! The sed pars Maxime!"

Kilian froze, his arm limp at his side, the half-eaten leg dangling by his fingertips. "The best part yet? I do not understand."

He followed Manius to the cages, and urine drenched the air in his mouth. The stench of rotted straw played with his dry throat. Still fresh on his tongue, the meat turned into a lumpy mass. He recognized the leopards immediately. There were three cages of them. They appeared devoid of life, as a spark had died in their eyes. The scars on their snouts and chests showed riveted lines of missing fur.

Kilian had no choice but to follow the senator and his guard down this path, even though a part of him was howling inside for retribution. "I do not feel this is a good idea..." Kilian mumbled, but Manius laughed.

"They are animals and caged at that! They have a purpose for the games today. Rome demands entertainment. I give it to them." Manius cheered.

Kilian wanted to turn and run, but the guard behind him was fully armed, and he had to stay on course as his queen demanded. He must stay neutral. Cautious. As he followed Manius gawking into the cages, the hair on the back of Kilian's neck sent a shock down his spine.

He turned his ear to their desperate hearts beating, their fears playing a melody through his chest. All of a sudden, fear fled from him. The animals perked up once Kilian came into view. They backed away from him, barring fanged teeth. They foamed at the mouth, their eyes black as coal. They followed him with their faces, saliva pouring from their fangs like hot anger. Their fur made a ridgeline up and down their backs as they dug their claws into the wooden floors.

They hissed at him. Manius turned his confused glare to the Roman soldier, who watched the beasts, confused himself. "Perhaps they are mad." The soldier wondered, pulling his sword.

Manius froze in the street, a sudden fear shooting through him. Kilian walked past the cages, the street filling with Roman guards from the commotion of the leopard's screams. The handlers started prodding at them with spears from the other side to get them to silence and calm down. They did not. They became more hysteric to get out.

"Perhaps they are mad." Manius wondered, eyeing his soldier with confusion.

The last cage was silent as Kilian marched past it to the end of the street. His heart beat like fine music playing. He could not be around these animals. He was forbidden but forced to stay on course for the mission of Dacia.

As Manius and the guard joined him at the last cage, Kilian turned one last time to look into it. Frozen in silence, he felt eyes on him like a seared mark from a poker at a campfire. It was a mark that never went away but still hurt over time.

The brown bear, more than double Kilian's height, pushed itself against the bars on the other side. It was stiff, its black eyes wide and unwavering at him as he passed. It did not growl. It continued to follow him with his eyes without moving its head. A cautious resolution dawned in the way its eyes followed Kilian.

The bear's calm demeanor met his face with a hollowed-out retribution coming that made pangs splice Kilian's guts up inside.

"What is the meaning of this?" Manius turned to glare at the handlers filling the street behind them.

"They are mad!" The guard wondered, sheathing his weapon back in his holster as guards filled the street.

Kilian watched the animals again, whispering to himself. "No. They are not mad. They sense the hunter."

As Kilian turned to follow Manius and the guard out of the street toward the Circus, the hair on his neck stood up, and he turned his ear. He hears the bear grunt while the handlers are calming the Leopards and the plank wood cracking on the floor in the cage. He could not go back or do anything to stop it. The guards would not allow him anyway.

All of a sudden, the games became clear. It would not end well for Rome today, especially since he was here.

The battlefield in Dacia would be even worse. Kilian held his breath and swallowed his worries, following Manius through the now-crowded streets.

Nestor played dirty. He always did, even in battle. Nestor played to win, and it did not matter how. He turned the reigns against his wrist, and the horses veered left, their legs dancing against each other like music. In the middle of Circus Maximus, tall pillars made a platform like a median for guards to stand and watch the races. The game counters placed their eggs on riveted palettes to keep scores.

Right now, Nestor was on lap three. A restlessness in him was pleading to get this lap over with early. He pushed his chariot into the wheel of the white team, and they catapulted off his side, spinning into the median wall. Nestor left them behind, laughing into the black clouds forming overhead as he pressed between the green and blue teams' neck to neck.

He clipped the back wheel of the blue chariot to the right, sending them charging into the wall. The rider lunged out of the chariot, dragging along the track. Dust beat his face as his helmet made rivets on the road. Nestor turned his head one last time to see the rider cut the reigns off his wrist and free himself as his body lay prostrate against the wall.

At least he was still alive. Nestor laughed again. This time, it was the green chariot's turn. He pushed his horses side by side with the rider, a toothless smile invading his arrogant face. The rider pulled away from him out to the front. They were on lap five now, two more to go.

"You cannot run from Nestor!" He screamed, whipping his horse's behinds and catapulting his chariot side by side again on the final laps.

The crowds were screaming his name again. Shreds of red garments blanketed the arena skies like snakes dancing in the breeze. His fans tossed red rose petals over their heads, splitting the races open in blankets of blood.

Kilian meandered in silence aside Manius as they entered the arena. Screams of joy and debate echoed through the city at the animal's cages. He caught a whiff of sweat and fear as they marched in through rows of Roman soldiers laughing and talking amongst one another as if they were enjoying the festivities. Manius led him through the tunnel, where they would find seating on top.

The Circus was an abomination of sports to him. The annoyance of the masses from Romans screaming for more sport above his head smelled of revelry, which bothered Kilian. It was the smell of fear.

Kilian put his nose in the air, stopping as Manius raised his hand to a tall, blonde-haired Roman. Kilian noticed the way this human stood, which screamed authority. He equipped himself with weapons and swords hanging from his sheaths, his body armor glowing among the soldiers not wearing theirs today. Kilian met his blue eyes that screamed wisdom and caution with a malice bred of a trained killer.

This man reeked of fear, which made him more ruthless. Kilian caught himself holding his breath as he gazed at him.

"Titus! Welcome commander! Welcome!" Manius praised him.

Titus leaned in to give him a battering hug. He smiled but dropped the happy look as he noticed Kilian eyeing him from behind. Manius picked up on his confusion and laughed.

"Ah, yes! Kilian is a servant to the Dacian queen. Kilian, this is Titus, our commander." Manius smiled at Titus, but Kilian felt a sense of urgency in the senator.

"Dacian messenger, eh?" Titus questioned.

"Where is my son? That sniveling man who continues to defy the gods?" Manius changed the subject, glancing around the busy arena underbelly.

Titus huffed. "Where do you think, senator? Already getting drunk on his winnings!"

Manius rolled his eyes. "Ah, of course."

Titus nodded. "Come! I was waiting for you. Axius was worried."

Kilian followed them through the crowds up winding corridors of steps, with Roman guards closely behind him. He felt the hair rise on the back of his neck and froze, a chill darting up his spine. He hurried behind them as the Romans pushed him along to get seating, but his guts were burning inside. Titus led them through rows of seats and stopped at a section of silence with a perfect view of the racing.

Kilian froze, gazing at the petite, brave warrior who seemed quite mad as he raced round and round alongside another chariot. The warrior would raise his arm and shout, and Kilian saw he was missing a front tooth. He saw the slashed marks over his body. Scars. Lots of them.

"Have you never been to a game Kilian?" Manius asked him.

Kilian turned to him, still standing, and pressed against the wall to look at this little warrior who was winning. He felt the prying hunger of rage eat at him from Titus's eyes and backed away to sit beside them.

"Never. The small hunter is winning." Kilian pointed several horses ahead of the last chariot, and that one was still trying to catch up with him.

Titus glared at him. "How do you know he was a hunter."

Kilian bit his tongue. "The scars."

Manius sat rigid in his chair. "He was no hunter."

Kilian narrowed his eyes to look closer at Nestor, his breath breathing in this chariot-racing warrior's courage. "No. He was a hunter when your people took him. Look how he crouches in the chariot. The way he studies the stadium, the road, and the humans surrounding him? He sees everything. He will win today."

"Fascinating! Did your low land queen teach you that trick Dacian?" Titus goaded him, his face a stern glare.

Kilian turned his head to face the small chariot racer, his stomach churning in anger then dissipating. "She taught me everything." He whispered.

Manius stood up and marched to the railing as shouts turned into screams of slaughter. Titus stood beside him and watched, his eyes melting all over the arena. When Kilian noticed it, he was not surprised. The bear had warned him. He stayed in his seat as panic ensued around him, and the populace erupted into a force of confusion mingled with excitement.

The chariot warrior made the bend on the final lap by himself. Three leopards stopped the chariot that remained. They stalked the rider on the track and lunged. The man was pulled from his horses and ripped to shreds before the Romans. His horses hit the wall, screeching cries of fear and rage echoing through the stadium.

The leopards tore into the helpless horses and lunged at the scorekeepers in the middle podium. They lashed into the five of them, along with the Roman guards keeping watch in seconds, slicing them open with cries of rage. Blood spilled down the walls.

Kilian sighed inside. He could not get involved. He leaned in his chair as he noticed a lone Roman soldier had rushed into the arena on horseback with his weapons drawn. He knew other Romans would follow to help him hunt and kill the beasts.

Yet Manius sweated and cursed under his breath. Titus veered away from him to join the Romans in the arena to fight the leopards and protect the chariot warrior. The lone rider on horseback slung a blade that lodged through the guts of one of the leopards. Kilian was impressed.

He did not sense fear in this human, or either of them. The chariot racer crossed the finish line and turned his horses toward the remaining leopards stalking him from the podium. Kilian stood to watch him, a sudden realization dawning on him.

He joined Manius at the edge, the crowd leering around them, the sky bellowing in darkness as rains swept in. Titus would command the Romans below to join him in helping these warriors kill the beasts.

"Oh, my son, be safe. Axius, be safe." Manius jeered, a crack in his voice set Kilian on edge.

"He is your son?" Kilian wondered; his eyes lit up in anticipation to watch Axius.

"Get in there!" Manius screamed at the Romans who were chasing down the steps to help Axius at this sudden, unexpected turn in events.

Axius pressed his Andalusian stallion around the bend and raced toward Nestor, who hollered at his horses to keep racing regardless of the beasts stalking them atop the podium. Axius gripped his Scutum in his left arm and released the reigns. He pulled his gladius out as his horse barreled to a stop. The leopard lunged through the air at him.

Axius shoved his gladius before him just as the blade met the leopard's throat. The leopard splayed long limbs with discharged claws into Axius's naked arms. His shrieking howl echoed through the stadium, its mouth full of loathing fangs. Its sudden weight knocked Axius off his horse as it hit the shield. Axius's back hit the dirt. He lunged his blade into the soft skin at its neck, spewing blood across his shield, forehead, and arms.

His horse screamed as it kicked in midair to fight off the last one. Axius smelled blood and feces on the jaguar as he heard a familiar voice shouting at him. He pulled the blade from the beast's throat and stood to ready his shield again as three more jaguars slithered from the corridor at the entrance of the games.

They stalked him at the entrance, writhing in a vengeful agony, slithering at the wall, growling at him.

Axius readied his gladius, dripping in blood, and took a deep breath. A sliver of a shaft catapulted past his cheek, and he froze in mid-step. The javelin struck one of them in its chest as it ran toward him and catapulted back against the wall.

Nestor lunged toward Axius on the road, pushing his steeds into the remaining ones. Axius stood his ground as the leopards cried, their bones breaking under the horses as they were trampled.

He turned behind to see Titus in the ring with him, another javelin in his hand. He pointed to the podium. "One more!" He hollered.

Axius gripped his gladius until his knuckles went white and lurked toward the podium to kill the final one. With Titus in the ring with him now and the other leopards dead, the last one remaining would die a quick death against these three. Titus lured it off the podium, taunting it with the end of his spear. Axius meandered around it, his bloodied arms dripping to his fingertips.

The leopard hunched down, glaring back at Axius, its fur at its backbone raised in a ridge standing up. It pressed into the dirt on the road at Titus, gawking back to watch Axius near it closer. Axius froze when it hissed at him, its fangs dripping with blood and saliva. Axius scowled at it, his eyes narrowed, his cheeks clenched.

Titus lunged the spear into it, but it grazed its backside just as it turned on Axius.

"Damnit!" Titus cursed to himself, pulling his own Gladius to chase after it.

Axius pulled his arm out of his shield and flung it into the leopard, the pointy end lodging into the chest. The leopard shrieked in pain and paused the attack, giving Axius enough time to pivot his Gladius like a pole vault. He slivered it through the air into the leopard's head. Titus reached it, lunged down, and sliced its head off.

The crowd's cheers made the echoes ache in Kilian's head, but it seemed Manius was relieved now. "Thank the gods!" He cheered, his face more colorful.

Kilian stood still beside the senator. He had watched the leopards enter the ring with full intentions of killing all in their paths. He smelled their rage and sensed their pain. Done with living, this was their final hunt. He watched as Axius faced the beasts and killed them with no remorse. He watched as Nestor protected him and used tactics and his resources to kill two of them at one time under the horses.

Those two were great warriors. He smelled no fear in them.

Titus disturbed him, however. Kilian growled inside, snarling his face into a scowl as he watched the commander fling his javelin into the chest of a leopard. He watched him hunt the final one with Axius and Nestor and the cold, methodical way he lured the final beast out into Axius's sword.

Tomorrow, Kilian would escort the Roman army into Dacian territory as their guide and introduce the commander to his queen. Chills raced up his arms. The Romans were doomed.

7

A Reckoning is Coming

Manius paced in front of his desk, clasping his hands behind the small of his back, huffing. Kilian stood at the doorway, the rain washing the stench of the animals from the air, clearing his airways to smell other more sinister things. He watched Manius eye Axius and Titus, even as his face clenched in a nightmare of mass proportions.

"In the morning, I must appease the senate about the games that went wrong!" He sneered.

But then his sneer matriculated into a devilish laugh.

"Went in my favor. The senators thought we planned this! Can you believe this nonsense? How the hell did those beasts get out!" He stopped pacing and glared at Axius, searching for answers.

Axius allowed the healers to wash his arm cuts and wipe them with a salve before wrapping them, the scent easing his headache. He shook his head and stared at Titus, who leaned against the post nearest the desk at Manius's left. He was doused with blood slivers across his forehead but was not injured. Kilian noticed that the small warrior who had won the race was nowhere to be seen.

"I do not know by the gods how they got out unless someone let them. There is no other explanation." Titus rolled his eyes, wiping the sweat from his brow.

"And the bear? What of it?" Manius fretted.

Kilian stepped closer to Axius's back, peering at them with intent and worry. Axius felt his shadow lingering at the door and turned a bloody face to him, motioning him to come closer with a bloody finger.

"You there, Dacian, come here. Never step as a shadow behind a Roman. We can smell you." Axius commanded.

Kilian obeyed him, but not because he told him to come. It was because there was something about this Roman war leader that beckoned him. It was why he was here and why he had come. He had to get Titus out of the picture as soon as possible.

"You have beasts in your land? Like the bear?" Axius asked, his deep eyes piercing every inch of Kilian's face in a hunting graze. Kilian swallowed; his eyes shifted to Titus for a moment. Titus crossed his arms over his chest and narrowed his eyes at him. Kilian was in enemy territory and had to choose his words wisely.

"We have bigger beasts. Worse ones." He warned them.

Titus laughed. "Bigger beasts than the bear? Liar. That bear was the biggest one in all of Rome I captured last fall."

Manius did not laugh. He leaned his palms atop his desk and gazed down at the parchment Kilian had brought.

"The bear will not bring you harm. It is far from here by now." Kilian assured them.

"How the hell do you know that?!" Titus commanded him, pushing himself off the pillar and stepping closer to Kilian.

Axius glared at Titus for a moment and then back to Kilian, his butt firmly planted atop the bench. "Go on. Kilian…" Axius assured him, still beckoning him to come closer.

"We will not bite. Titus might, perhaps. Nonetheless, I promise we will not harm you." Axius once again assured him, so Kilian stepped within arm's reach of Axius.

"Kilian, tell me of the beasts of your land." Axius goaded him, half smiling.

Kilian felt his heart go stiff and his spine straighten. He took a deep breath and stared at Titus again. His mouth opened like he wanted to say something, but he stood there shaking his head. Axius turned his stare to Titus, who was still scowling at the Dacian with a contempt that bothered Manius deep inside.

"Enough! Kilian brought news from the Dacian queen about the demise of our men." Manius stood upright, grabbing the parchment.

"We received word as well, Manius." Titus barked.

"No. Not this one. It is from the hand of the commander himself." Manius handed it to Titus, sighing.

"This Dacian brought this to you? How convenient." Titus cursed as he unwrapped it and started reading.

Axius stood up when the color drained from Titus's face. A red hotness grew in Titus's cheeks as he flung the parchment to the desk before Manius. Kilian lunged out of the way, but Titus pressed into his shoulder, his height overpowering Kilian.

"All Dacians will die for this." Titus moaned.

Kilian held his breath, pushing down his anger. Titus bolted past them into the rain, his fury casting shadows down the halls through the stormy night. Kilian heard the commander march through the rain, his boots slamming into muddy puddles, the downpour spilling down his blonde hair and angry face. The deep hatred of Titus ate him from the inside out.

Manius handed the parchment to Axius. "Commander Titus. Cunning, brutal. You see why he is our chosen. I had him train you for a reason, Axius. Trained by the best, our elite."

Manius watched his son's back grow tense and muscles flex in his arms, his knuckles going white. Kilian studied Axius's face while he read it. This Roman did not overreact. Axius read the writing, his brain processing the content of the text in silence. When he finished, Axius cleared his throat and gazed at Kilian, who stood against the pillar beside the one Titus leaned against.

"You will not go with Titus in the morning," Axius told him. "You shall accompany me instead."

Manius huffed. "He must go, Axius. He is the only scout familiar with the territory and the only one who keeps coming back alive. Do you know how hard I have worked with Aurelian to get into it?"

"What of the last scout then? Was he killed, too?" Axius beamed, looking at Kilian.

"You know, don't you?" Axius ordered, his black brows creased a wrinkle across his forehead.

Manius threw his arms in the air. "Everything I have worked for will be gone if you do not cooperate, Axius." He complained. "My arrogant son and his vicious questions."

"No, but he knows father…" Axius raised the parchment to Kilian's face, coming a hair from breathing on him, his shadow towering over Kilian in a dreaded silence.

"I know that writing. Commander Artgus penned it. You know it too, do you not?" Axius breathed on him.

Kilian raised his face to meet his, not breathing. "I do."

"It says here the beasts are black as night, taller than our biggest bear. Here…" Axius opened the parchment and pointed to the blood drops. "…they feed on man's flesh!"

Manius bit his tongue. "Axius…"

"No, father! Enough games. We lost legions! We lost good men…" Axius lunged into Kilian, picked him up by his chest, and pressed him against the pillar. He leaned into his face, clenching his teeth.

"What are they, Dacian? You will tell me." Axius's eyes cut through Kilian's stare like blackness filling pools of blood.

He could not blame him, as they wanted answers. Kilian was not sure if they could handle it. He felt the surge of strength from Axius's grasp pulling at him but did not get angry. It was never good when Kilian got angry. He liked this Roman enough to let him play with him for a bit, but now it was time to end this.

Kilian beamed into Axius, his dark eyes a power of dominance into his face. "We call it Vanagandr. The monster of the river."

Axius studied Kilian's face and stared into his eyes.

Manius sneered. "Release him, Axius, and step away. The last thing I need is a war between me and the Dacian queen over harassing her famed scout."

Axius released him slowly and stepped away. "We are already at war. And you are no scout, are you, Dacian?"

Kilian straightened his tunic, his face going pale.

"I know the legends. You think this is the first time we have seen these writings, Dacian?" Axius beamed at him, then glared at Manius.

"Axius, please," Manius warned.

"No, father. You are sending my commander into certain death by morning. This Dacian will not be going with them." Axius warned, his voice cold.

"I must go. My queen..." Kilian fretted.

"You honestly think Titus will let you live that long? He craves to slit your throat Dacian. I am saving your life." Axius warned.

Kilian paused.

"You know this is true. Search yourself, Kilian. Titus will use you to gain entrance into Dacia before your queen and then kill you. If not him, our guards surely will." Axius boasted. "I love him like a father. I do. But he will kill you."

"He can try," Kilian whispered. Axius heard the mumble, his face lighting up at Kilian's eyes.

"Axius enough!" Manius yelled at him, slamming his hand atop the desk.

"Yet you came anyway. You come for another reason and not to ride into Dacia with our commander." Axius goaded him.

"Enough!" Manius ordered him.

Axius ignored his father, glaring at Kilian. "You will take me there."

"No, he will not! He will lead the army into Dacia under Titus's command as Aurelian proclaimed Rome to colonize that territory. End of story." Manius glared at Axius as they faced one another, the silence overwhelming them as Kilian watched. Father and son. A battle of the wills.

"Are we not to avenge the deaths of our men? Our brothers who now leave their wives widows and children orphans?!" Axius wondered, his face a solemn hate. "Mother died of fever when I was young, but we are privileged. These families left behind, not so."

Manius met his son's stare, leaning into his hands atop the table, his face flushed with anger. "We are sending in twenty thousand Axius. Our men slaughtered were only four thousand, barely a legion! Twenty thousand Romans trained in battle will succeed against whatever the hell this enemy is. Mark my words. Beast or no."

Axius shook his head, huffing. "Are you okay with this, Dacian?" He turned his face to glare at Kilian.

"No. That is why you must come with me. You and that small warrior who won the race." Kilian told him.

"What?!" Manius complained. "Stop. Both of you…"

Manius continued. "I cannot stop Aurelian from sending the legion. I do not have enough power to stop his plans to colonize Dacia, which **will** be Romanized. Titus is the commander now, and you know he will do well. He is a formidable leader and killer but succeeds in battle when many have failed."

Axius nodded, pursing his lips, agreeing with his father. "He does."

"I cannot send you in with Titus, Axius. If Titus fails, then it is on you."

Silence filled the room.

"I must send Kilian with Titus because we have a peace treaty with the queen of Dacia to return him safely, or there will be another war," Manius warned.

"You mean another war besides the man-eaters killing Romans?" Axius clenched his jaws.

Manius sighed, tossing his arms in the air and turning his back to Axius, thinking. He closed his eyes and swallowed. "I know what you want to do, son. I cannot let you go." He turned back around to face them.

"If you want Rome to survive in Dacia, you will send me. Nestor will come, too; he is as quick on his feet as his blade. His memories of that place can help us." Axius chimed.

"He *is* a brave hunter." Kilian nodded.

"Why must you go? Why Axius?" Manius fretted.

Axius took a deep breath, his red cape blowing behind him as the wind sucked it toward the door. His armor had blood smears, and his sheaths pinged against his sides with his swords. His black hair spiked atop his head; his scruffy face needed a shave. He had rings under his hazel eyes, but it was not from being tired. Kilian recognized that look.

"They were my brothers. Their families are my family. No man or beast hunts Rome and gets away with it. I will avenge my fallen and hunt these beasts." He purred, his eyes teary.

Manius scowled, his mouth dropping open like he wanted to scream at his son, but the only thing he could say was, "Everything is a hunt to you. If only you hunted women the way you do battles, then I would have grandchildren instead of fretting if you are coming back alive!" Manius worried.

Axius sighed, turned his head to look at Kilian, and shook his head, glaring back over at Manius.

"Oh, and another thing, father..." Axius added in.

Kilian held his breath, his eyes wide, staring at his boldness. This Roman soldier was unafraid to defy authority and slew jaguars with his blade and shield. Kilian smelled no fear in him as Axius was brave and cunning.

"We will not be going in as Romans. Do you agree, Dacian?" Axius commanded.

Kilian nodded at Axius, agreeing with him.

"No! No! You are a fool, Axius!" Manius sneered at him.

Axius leaned down, slammed his hand atop the mahogany table, and glared into his father's face. "The enemy is expecting Roman's father. The enemy will be looking for us. If we will hunt this enemy, we need to blend in. I hardly think twenty thousand will blend into the territory with our armor and weapons on horseback." Axius warned.

"They will not blend in." Kilian agreed. "They will die."

"See? Kilian agrees." Axius confirmed.

"Why do the gods torment me with a son who craves blood? Why?" Manius whined.

"Titus trained me. Blame him. Now, father, about this plan of yours to colonize Dacia..." Axius purred.

Manius plopped his head down his shoulders and leaned into his arms atop his desk. He raised his face to stare at his son with contempt. Kilian could tell Manius was worried for Axius. He was not smiling.

Axius, however, leaned over the desk into his father's face and informed him: "We will need falxes, javelins, and short swords, father. Nestor and I will take bows."

Killian smiled.

8

Rome Goes to Bleed

In the morning, Kilian stood watching the Roman army in rows as thousands of Roman soldiers lined the road. The crimson cloaks and crests of feathers atop their helmets roared like a wound had bled out. He stood aside Manius and Axius while Micah emerged from under the pillars to bid them farewell. When Titus marched out behind him, Kilian grew rigid and bit his jaw.

Axius turned to face Kilian, whispering. "I do not doubt your ability to stay alive."

Axius paused, his eyes narrowing.

Kilian looked over Axius's shoulder to Manius, gabbing with Titus. He turned his glare back to Axius and whispered: "Quamquam ipse iustus vigilate. Et dabo vobis misericordiam."

Just the same, though, stay alert.

Kilian clenched his jaws. "Non minus quam reverti sustinet Vasiliki vivere Romanos."

Vasiliki will tolerate no less from me than to come back alive, Roman.

Axius's face lit up when the Dacian spoke fluent Latin. Kilian lunged into his front folds of fabric, pressing a rolled-up parchment half the size into his palm. He met Axius's eyes in a heated embrace of desperation. Axius grasped it fervently, pressing it down at his side. He slid it under his chest armor with his back to everyone while shielding the Dacian.

"Do not read it until the army is gone from this city. You must do as it asks. Time is now of the essence." Kilian warned him, pausing as the men talking and laughing around them became louder.

Axius widened his eyes. "Vasiliki. So that is her name."

Kilian nodded as Titus barged over to Axius, battering him with a pestering pat on his shoulder to bid him farewell. Axius smiled at Titus and returned the embrace, but his eyes melted back to Kilian. The Dacian refused the horse Manius brought to him. The horse snorted at him and pulled away, and Kilian stepped away.

Titus huffed. "Let the scout walk on foot. The Dacians are primitive. They are used to walking."

Kilian agreed with Titus and nodded in respect, but inside, he wanted to tear the commander to shreds and eat his heart out. Yet he feared his time was coming regardless. Axius pushed Titus away from Manius and Kilian, pressing into him with frustration.

"Why do you taunt him so? He will be your lifeline in Dacia, getting in, getting out. You know this. Yet you continue to anger the gods." Axius warned him.

Titus pulled away from him, sighing. "I have killed my soldiers for defying me with less rebellion, Axius. Just because you are a Senator's son does not save you."

"I am also a Tribunis of the elite. Therefore, I am bringing this caution to your attention, my lord. I want you to come back alive. You know you are like a father to me." Axius warned him, his spine rigid, his eyes hard into Titus's face.

Titus took a deep breath, turning his back to Axius while rubbing his hand down his stallion's snout. He turned his head to look at him again and nodded. Axius felt a cold shiver rush up his spine as Titus walked away.

Axius put his palm over the hilt of his gladius, watching Kilian take the lead on foot. The road looked long and hot, the steam pestering the army as their armor glistened under the rising sun at dawn. Manius met him beside Micah, and together, they watched the army embrace the lines like a fluid forged from steel.

The Signifier waived the insignia flag before Titus and his Primi centurion. Behind them on horses rode the Legatus, who commanded five thousand men in each legion. The emperor was sending in four legions, twenty thousand Pilus. Axius glared up the wall as Aurelius stood flanked by his guard, and Senators watched the army go. The air was heavy as Romans riddled the horizon in muscled silence, the legions swarming together like fingers.

Axius did not question the bravery of his men or any Roman. He stood aside his father, pride swelling from his guts that dissipated into a sweltering frustration. Titus refused to say goodbye to him, and he had not been himself in days since the news of the slaughter. Axius was busting at the seams to read the parchment Kilian had given him in haste as if the Dacian was desperate to tell him something more but was forbidden.

Axius feared Kilian was right. The Romans were going to die.

Micah leaned into Axius, pressing into his shoulder. Axius turned his head to glare at him, questioning his motives, until the scribe's face lit up with a mischievous dimple.

"My all-seeing eyes advise me you have something of utmost importance on you I must read," Micah whispered.

Axius rolled his eyes, ignoring his father's loud clapping as the city joined them in saluting the army off. "Damnit," Axius complained.

"One condition," Axius warned him.

"No conditions, Axius. You know I am within my legal standing to take it from you now. What you hold could start or stop wars, which is of great expense to Rome." Micah warned him.

Axius opened his mouth to speak, but Manius plopped his hand on his shoulder, smiling ear to ear. "The whole city watches us. Please smile very big, son, and let us take a nice stroll back to the villa. Risus magna. Felicem agere." *Smile big. Act happy.*

Axius smiled so big that his eyes teared up. His father was tactful but manipulative, and Micah was no different. They were in positions of power, and he should have known Micah would watch the Dacian closely.

Micah raised his arms to bid the army farewell and marched out with Axius and Manius, smiling big. As Axius realized what they were doing, he smiled bigger, angry inside.

"Filii Eride, et vestrum." *Sons of Eris. Both of you.*

Micah met his remark with an open mouth and a "tsk." "That's not nice."

But Manius just battered his back with his palm, pushing Axius through the crowd away from the populace.

Axius sat on the stool at Manius's desk, yanking the parchment from his armor. Micah and Manius allowed him the pleasure of reading it first, although Axius knew they had the power to condemn him for hiding it. He questioned Kilian's method in giving this to him the way he did, but when he opened it, his eyes grazed it in silence, and then he sighed.

"You cannot read the language." Micah fretted, crossing his hands at his groin. Manius stood with a cup of coffee in his hand, the steam contorting his face into a scowl. Axius rolled his eyes, plunging his arm to Micah, who took it like a giddy child.

He read the first lines: "Est autem traditor in atrio Aurelius.

Longis auidum saturasset non quasi hominibus." He froze, narrowing his eyes into a fearful blast from his face.

"What," Axius commanded, pouring coffee.

"This is Albanian. This Dacian queen you spoke of, Manius, is she truly from Dacia?" Micah worried.

Axius perked up, stopping mid-sip of his hot brew to watch his father's face lose color. "What does it say, Micah." He commanded.

"There is another language here. I cannot read it. But…"

Axius became impatient, sighing. "What does it say? Read what you do know."

Micah swallowed. "It says there is a traitor in the court of Aurelius. It bleeds like man."

Silence.

"There is more here I *can* understand." Micah gazed over the language.

"Prisoners." Micah stopped reading, thinking. "Dacian prisoners here. She is demanding their release." He gazed at Manius.

It dawned on Axius, and his hair stood up on his arms. "Captured from a previous battle? She wants her people returned, eh?" Axius informed, thinking.

Micah kept reading. "She wants you to bring her people to Dacia. And the mercenaries. She will meet you at Lupa's village on the edge of the Danube River…"

"Mercenaries." Axius grew excited. "Mercenaries are cunning warriors and very skilled. We have no mercenaries here."

Manius grew rigid, plopping his cup atop his desk where the black liquid soaked the manuscripts he had been working on for the senate. "We do." He applied.

Micah swallowed. "Forgive me, senator, but on my advisory to the emperor, we had only Dacians, simple villagers with primitive weapons we imprisoned. If memory serves, we have only kept them alive this long to sway the queen to give up Dacia."

Manius crossed his arms over his chest and glared at them, the lines between his eyes a severe indentation of processing truths from lies. Axius stepped closer to him. The silence filled the men like worry, eating a backbone from the inside out.

"Rome was not only built by Romans. We also had and still have, although few, an elite source of barbarism. The ones I have managed to keep alive are also hidden from the empire, educated in more subtle arts, if you will." Manius told them, sitting at his desk as if his knees had given out on him.

Axius bit his lip. "Your version of subtle arts is up for interpretation, father."

Micah smiled, his face lighting up. "Please tell." He poured himself a cup of coffee, smiling through the hot steam.

Axius did not worry about private matters with Micah. The scribe was an elite scholar and writer for Rome. His specialty was keeping secrets and spilling them only if it benefited the lives of Roman citizens. He was revered by the emperor as trusted, an expert of Indigenous tribes, and a master linguist. Rome sought delicacies like Micah but were few and hard to find.

"I cannot tell you. I could never describe it." Manius stood up, sighing. "I will have to show you, and we will have to journey to Mount Circeo. We leave straight away, and you both are coming with me. Senator Opiter's villa journey will not take as long traveling from Nestor's."

Micah handed the parchment to Manius, who pushed it into his robes. "Manius, what about the prisoners the queen demands to be freed?"

Manius met his stare and then looked at Axius. "If I am going to send you and Nestor into Dacia with those damn monsters, we cannot get the prisoners freed until you see for yourself what I mean. I am going to take you to him first. You will need his interpretation of the remaining language there. He knows this folklore. Although I will admit, these are more like nightmares."

Axius scoffed at him.

"I was going to go anyway without your approval, father, so now you are saying I can go with your blessing?" Axius smiled, growing excited. Micah gasped.

"You must go now. I have no choice." Manius swallowed.

Axius sensed the dread in his father but stuffed it down.

"Where are we going again, and why is Opiter involved?" Micah wondered, the color draining from his face, but Manius ignored him.

Manius pulled a leather pouch and a bag of gold coins from his desk drawer. He strapped a leather belt around his robes with a gladius. He gazed at Axius's fully armed attire and nodded his approval, and then his eyes went to unarmed Micah.

He pulled a dagger from his top drawer and tossed the pretty blade embedded in a leather sheath at him. "I am no fighter."

Axius laughed at him. "No, you are not."

Micah shot Axius a look like *hey, that is rude*.

"We are taking a day's journey to the country outside of Rome. On the way out, I want you to grab Nestor. I will leave the money with his wife as an incentive to let him go. I know how she can be over his life.

Perhaps she will take the children shopping in the markets while he is away. Women love money." Manius huffed.

Axius sighed. Domitia, Nestor's wife, was very protective of him. Axius feared getting her to agree to this would be hard.

"What are you doing, father," Axius demanded, clenching his jaws.

"I am letting you go into Dacia with my chosen mercenaries," Manius warned him. "Mercenaries I know personally and have for years. Then you will deliver the prisoners to take with you as well. That will help ensure your and Nestor's survival with the queen and my intentions to believe her."

"Nestor and I only need…"

"Enough Axius!" Manius yelled at him. Micah jumped, his eyes wide as lemons.

Manius pulled the original parchment Kilian had brought and shoved it at Axius. "You listened to the truth of this. You have read all of them. Though Rome may be in denial, you know what awaits you. You are a Tribunus Laticlavius, an elite Roman senior officer, and my second in command. I had no power over sending Titus. I do have the power to send you, albeit privately. You and Nestor. I agree Kilian was correct about sending him with you." Manius warned.

"But you are also my son. I have had to come to terms that we may all bleed and die for Rome, but damn, if I am to bleed and die and my son also, we shall do this my way." Manius complained.

Micah wiped a tear from his eye.

Axius glared at his father, their eyes meeting in silence before he turned away from Manius and barged to the entrance. When he reached the steps, he turned to face them, his hand on the hilt of his Gladius.

"This was my idea, you know. Just because you are older than me does not mean you can twist it to make it seem it was your idea." He shrugged his head and marched down the steps.

Micah dropped his mouth, glaring at Manius, who flared his nostrils at Axius's backside as he went.

9
Nestor's Abode

Axius rode side by side with Manius and Micah trailing softly behind, but just enough to goad Axius into complaining about the horse's lazy stride. Manius was not surprised nor impressed with his son's bashing of the poor animal. He felt Axius did not like things lurking behind him.

Nestor's country villa was a half-day ride from Rome. It would align them with Mount Circeo to the south of Italy. That would rest the horses, and the men could sleep at Nestor's. They could get good food before their quest to Senator Opiter's villa and the transcribing of the rest of the parchment from Vasiliki.

"I can smell the olive oil from here. Delightful." Manius took a deep breath while the rolling hills lunged around them. Pecan groves and open expanses of vineyards twirled on the horizon as purple dots kissed the vines before them.

Micah straightened up on his horse and peered ahead of them, smiling. "Fascinating! How Nestor can manage these fine orchards, vineyards, and olive businesses is amazing. Blessed by the gods he is."

Axius huffed, turning his head to Micah, his long red cape flowing behind him over the horses behind. "His wife Domitia is the owner. She manages the children and the businesses. Nestor is a champion, so she prefers he focus on that for Rome."

Manius perked up. "Ah yes, lucrative money makers, smart woman, much like her father was."

Micah pursed his lips. "Now I am even more intrigued. Looking forward to making introductions with that fascinating, hard-working lady of the estate."

Axius burst out in a thick laughter. Manius smiled. "Micah, my friend, never take a paterpotestas heir for granted. Domitia is very cunning. She rules her manor like her father did before he died, under dutiful control." Manius advised.

"Then how does Nestor..." Micah paused, thinking. "...paterpostestas, so her father was powerful. When did he pass Manius?"

Manius sighed, his eyes grazing the pecan tree-laden fields riddled with paths and servants working the harvest. "Ten years, I believe, when Nestor was granted manumission and became a freeman, and Domitia was free to marry him then. He also inherited Domitia's wealth as she was the only living child."

Axius bit his tongue. "Yes, Nestor is blessed, Micah. Domitia is blessed to have him as well. You will see."

Manius scowled at Axius. "Always so hard on your god sister. You fear women because you have not had the right woman in your life."

Axius huffed, roaring out in laughter with his mouth wide open. "I fear not women, nor war or blade nor beast father. I have yet to see the right mate for me with my own eyes, that is all." He complained.

Micah chirped in. "Ah, and I was so looking forward to introducing you to someone this coming week. Pity."

Axius turned his head and glared at Micah, but all the scribe did was smile wide-eyed and blink his eyes back at him. Manius laughed at them both.

The knoll rolled onto a flat plain after the wooded pecan groves emptied into rows of vineyards. Stone towers rose behind a sprawling, pristine white manor stretched over the hillside. Behind the pitched clay roofs of the manor, sounds of grinding stone echoed in the back lot from the olive press. Laughter rolled through the air like a soft peck of hope. Wild, red flowers kissed the lane before the manor, beckoning the entrance to an even more elaborate home.

In front of the house on the other side of the lane were rows of stables. Horses neighed through the fencing as their caretakers fed them. The plain rolled into a vast expanse over a hillside as stud horses frolicked in them. Thick woods adorned the horizon past the stables on the other side of the field to the west end of the sprawling manor.

It was late, and Axius was famished after a long day of dealing with his father's nonsense. This morning, at Manius's behest, a guard had told Domitia they were coming and would arrive by late midday. That would give them time to wind down after overseeing the toiling vineyards and orchards.

Axius was looking forward to seeing Nestor's daughters, who had become his god children. He had brought the children gifts, but it was not as if they needed any more material things. However, Nestor would appreciate the sentiment coming from Axius regardless.

They arrived hours later, and servants met them to tend to the steeds. Two servants opened the double wooden doors to allow them to enter. Axius had been here dozens of times, but Micah never had, and his gawked expression showed.

"By the gods. Very pleasant to the eyes." Brilliant colors of murals of all kinds of nature and scenes filled the walls. The pillars had an elegant vine sauntering from the earth in the ground under them. The ceiling glowed in bright light under the stained glass, accentuating petite white flowers.

A servant motioned Manius past the pillars through the great hall out back to the terrace as Axius and Micah followed. Pillars surrounded the gardens, and the manor engulfed this private space. Pools of water filled the silence with a tickling tranquility. A long wooden table sat under stone pillars in the middle of the terraced garden. The canopy of twirling vines caressed the tops of them like intertwined fingers.

Statues in regal attire stood by all four corners of the pillars, watching the guests. Manius half smiled, nodding to the vast spread of delicacies and wines atop the table. Wildflowers in clay pots kissed the table in rainbows of colors. At each place setting were pots of wine and pastries adorned with fruit platters of figs, apricots, and various citrus with ramekins of olives.

The main dishes were wafting mouth-watering senses into the men with the wild boar and pheasant and seasoned mussels on platters with boiled eggs. Manius sighed heavily and breathed in the aromas, his mouth watering. The servants continued to bring out platters of all sorts of delicacies.

"Welcome, senator Manius." A slender woman stood on the pebble path between potted plants as tall as her and just as regal as if she had been watching them this whole time.

Manius drifted to her and bowed, taking her hand and kissing the top of it. She did not smile at him, but her pale skin accentuated dimples on either side of a pleasant mouth plump with a sinister gaze. Her green eyes boasted a fire thriving inside her, under a crown of black locks braided atop her head and adorned with turquoise beads.

The beads accentuated her sleeveless gown in pearls and blues that wafted down her ankles, flowing behind her on the stones. Manius smiled at her, nodding in approval. Domitia always met his approval, albeit she did not acknowledge them. She pressed her slender arms down from his kiss, and her fingers melted into one another. Her golden bracelets rang through the silence between the birds chirping in the gardens.

"Domitia, a pleasure. I see you have a feast prepared well enough to please the gods looks like." He motioned back to the table.

"Always for you, Manius." She confirmed.

"Axius." She nodded at him, and then her eyes fixed upon Micah, who nodded his respect for her.

"And you are Micah, the famed linguist and scholar." She acknowledged him, and Manius bit his tongue. "I would be honored to have you give a literature lesson to the children."

Micah perked up. "I would be honored, my lady."

"Domitia, where is Nestor?" Axius interrupted. "Let me guess, pressing olives and drinking."

Domitia met his stare with a firm glare herself. "You know him well. Please retrieve him so we can dine. The feast is ready at any moment now." She motioned to the path behind her, leading out a side gateway to the stone tower in the back lot, where roars of laughter could still be heard every few minutes.

Axius marched past her, and Micah followed. Manius watched them go. Domitia studied his face and took a deep breath. "You have not come just for dinner and a night stay, senator."

"You know me too well, daughter of Omitus, the great and wise." He huffed at her.

Domitia smiled back at him, her eyes lighting up. "When you sent word you were coming with Axius and Micah, I knew this was no normal feast. It is to get Nestor's aid in whatever you are plotting."

Manius froze, opening his mouth to speak and then saying nothing. Domitia motioned him to walk with her, and he did so. "Come, let's talk, you and I."

"I assume this bag of coin I have brought is useless to you in persuading you to let Nestor come with us?" Manius goaded her, eying her from the side. "You can shop in the markets with the children at my expense."

Domitia laughed at him. "Even a wealthy person would be a fool to turn down more wealth. I will split the money between my daughter's dowry regardless."

Manius handed her the leather pouch, and Domitia inspected it. As if her servants had been there all along, she thrust her arm out, and an elderly woman dressed in a flowing white gown kissed in violet shawls took it. The woman bowed to her.

"Dowry's," Domitia whispered. Her white braided hair shimmered as bright as her gown. "It will be so." She marched away through the gardens and back into the sprawling manor.

"How are the children?" Manius asked.

"They will dine with us, and you will see them momentarily. They are so full of love and knowledge, just like their father,"

Manius laughed. "Of course they are! Brilliant little blessings, yet I dare say they are intricate like you."

"Intricate, yes." She paused and sighed. "This brings me to a concern I want to address. The day of the games, when the beasts escaped." Her voice lowered as if she was trying to whisper.

Manius froze, stepping in synch with her, and recalled that day. "Yes. We did not anticipate them getting out. The emperor, I, and all of Rome were relieved when Nestor defeated them with Axius and Titus."

He paused. "I promise I will use all my power never to have Nestor go through that again. Forgive me."

Domitia stopped walking, meeting Manius's concerned face. "How is that your fault? Yes, it was concerning when I heard about it, but

Nestor has a way with beasts, you know this. I never doubt his abilities."

"Oh, well then." Manius blurted out, confused.

Domitia started walking again, her head going back and forth as if trying to remember something in the vat of her mind but could not place a finger on it. "My eldest twins have been telling their tutor they see a big black dog, taller than a man's shadow, at dusk. Here, across the road in the woods before the stables."

Manius swallowed, his eyes gazing past the wall surrounding the beauty of the intricate gardens. "Here? Are you certain this is not a wild dog? Perhaps the daily hunts from your archers attract one?"

"You know the children, Manius. They are not liars, and they know the penalty for lying. I work hard to keep my people content, which may breed fear. What other beasts did you have there that escaped? Is there a beast that looks like a dog taller than a man? Perhaps a black bear?"

Manius wrung his fists behind his back, chills racing up his spine. "A brown bear. That is it. Axius needs to be privy to this discussion if you do not mind." He warned.

"I am aware the discussions this evening will not be pleasant." Domitia sighed.

"Are they certain it was black? Could it have been the brown bear? In the darkness, it would look black, perhaps?"

Domitia shook her head *no*.

"Have any of your servants mentioned seeing anything?" He asked, disturbed.

"No. The tutor and I are keeping this private."

"Ah, does Nestor know then?" Manius wondered.

Domitia cleared her throat. "No. He only returned last night, and with my duties here, we have not had a moment."

"Where were the twins when they have seen this?"

"In the west end suites, in their wool spinning class. The window has a view of our woodlands there." Domitia stated. "They claim to have seen it at night."

"How often and when did this start?" Manius held his breath, his heart beating his chest to death.

"Two weeks. Only in midweek, so they have only seen it twice now."

"Twice enough to see it is real," Manius confirmed, and Domitia nodded.

"They have seen something with their own eyes, yes. I informed the tutor to watch with them, and I will join them during lessons tomorrow evening." She confirmed.

Domitia turned to start walking back to the table. Manius sighed. "Domitia, I need to discuss this with Nestor and the others. Regardless, I still require Nestor to come with us. Do I have your agreement with this?"

"I do not agree my husband does anything more for Rome other than win the games and be my love and the father of my children, and when the time comes, our daughters be privy to the wealth and freedoms we pass onto them." She boasted.

"This is not for Rome publicly. Something is happening that may spill into Rome if I do not find out the truth." Manius shook inside. "I fear it may already be here."

Silence.

"I need Nestor to go with Axius into Dacia."

Domitia gasped.

"Titus has already gone, yet you need my husband to venture there now? Tell me, Manius, how much more blood needs to be spilled for Rome?" She complained.

"Axius goes also. I will use all my resources and wealth to protect them. You have my word." He assured.

Domitia huffed. "You can spend your wealth protecting anyone but cannot control the evils in a strange land. Nestor has told me the tales. I need you to tell me the truth. I am my father's daughter, your goddaughter. I demand the truth, or you can leave."

Manius wrung his hands behind his back, turning his back to her. He gazed up to the spindly willows spilling overhead in the gardens lining up against the wall and wondered how long it had been since he had taken notice of nature's beauty.

"Beasts are hunting Romans in Dacia. Man eaters. The army was slaughtered and ripped to pieces. Titus is now going in, and I fear for them. I had no control over sending him. I need Axius and Nestor to go in hidden, albeit I will have mercenaries from Dacia going in with them to meet their queen privately. I need her to trust me if we are to discover the truth of these slayings and stop them…"

Domitia closed her eyes.

"We travel to Senator Opiter's at dawn to secure the mercenaries from him. We need to get information from his scribe about this parchment from the Dacian queen, but we cannot decipher all of it. He is the only one I know of in all of Rome that can interpret it."

Domitia huffed, clenching her jaws.

"You need Nestor because he came from there. You know he is of Dacian descent, yet you have kept it hidden from Rome, and my father still freed him regardless." She added.

Manius turned to face her again, his hands clasped behind his back. "Yes. If Nestor goes, Axius has a better chance of survival. If Nestor goes, they have a better chance of gaining access to the queen and her army. I do not believe she had anything to do with the slaughter, albeit the emperor thinks otherwise. I must get Axius and Nestor in her presence. I have been working with her scout, Killian, for some time. Something else is at play here, but I need Nestor's help to find out what."

"You want to return Nestor to the land of nightmares and bring him face to face with this queen. I will let you tell him. It will not come from me." She warned.

Manius turned his expression of pain into her as she clenched her jaws.

"Just like my father, you continue to play games with fate." She pressed a firm hand on his forearm and stared at him. "I do not want to lose any more of my family, Manius. I have had many sleepless nights with the news of this last slaughter of our Romans. I fear Rome cannot bear to lose much more."

"Already, I have assembled a committee in Rome of wealthy women leaders to help the families and children left behind. This tragedy of great loss wears us thin," She whispered.

Manius nodded his head, his eyes tearing up. Domitia was special to his heart. Maybe this was too much to ask Nestor to come, he thought. Before he could say anything more, she gripped his hand tighter.

"I have no doubt Nestor can fend for himself. He did it for many years before he was brought here by you and my father. I am grateful every day my father favored him. I love him. So, I am holding you accountable if something happens to him."

Manius pressed a shaky hand atop hers and sighed. "I cannot guarantee we will survive when these truths come to light. I can promise you that between my resources and Axius's fervor, we will do everything we can to keep him safe."

Domitia let out a pity laugh. "Oh, dear Manius, Rest assured, Nestor is the one who will keep Axius safe." She pulled him by the arm into her side, and they strolled to the table.

Manius chuckled at her.

Manius patted her hand, and they turned to meander to the feast. "I have arranged Roman soldiers to stay here to keep guard. It will not be many, as the army is awaiting commands from Titus. However, it will be substantial protection while Nestor is away. They can be here by nightfall in two days. Do you agree with this?"

Domitia shook her head. "No. I disagree with having the Romans here. That will breed fear among my businesses. We can handle it. My huntsmen are very skilled with the blade, and Nestor has trained them."

Manius sighed. "So be it."

"Now, where is my husband? I hope he did not encourage his man servants to get into the press with him drunk again." She rolled her eyes.

Manius laughed. "Ha! From the sounds of the roaring laughter coming from the yard, I would say so. Let us gather the children and get ready to feast. I am famished."

Manius walked back to the feast with Domitia, but his head was reeling with the wonders of what she had just told him. He wondered if Nestor would want to go once he found out his family may be endangered. Regardless, they needed Nestor. This quest was too pivotal not to take him. On the other hand, Manius questioned if the beasts of Dacia were already in Rome.

10

Nestor's Fate

Nestor wiped the sweat from his brow that dripped down his tanned face.

"My homeland is cursed." Nestor stuttered. "Like a bitter woman from the loins of Aphrodite, only a beast comes out, beautiful, and terrible and very hungry."

Nestor was butt naked except for the loin cloth he had tied around his privates wrapped around his midsection to hold it on. He laughed with the servants and helped them push the stone tapetum, their tanned backsides glistening in sweat together as they pressed against the pivot. The pungent aroma of smashed olives crunched under its weight and filled the mortarium's bowl. Another servant, dressed in a loin cloth to match Nestor, held a wooden bowl filled with rose buds and petals.

Nestor stood up to stretch his back and grunted as the other two men continued to push the press, the burning sun blasting through the windows over them. "Lands flowing. Mountains, fish, and beasts. Did I already say that?" He mumbled, narrowing his eyes.

The man holding the bowl of roses nodded. "No master, you did not mention beasts." He let out a roaring laughter to match Nestor's, and the men all laughed at one another.

Nestor turned his bright eyes to the man and huffed. "Ah. Well then! Let me tell you about beasts!" Nestor laughed a thunderous rage and lunged over by his servant to grab a wine bottle. He pulled it to his dry mouth and guzzled until it was dry, the dark red fluid drizzling down his sculpted chest.

He held it out to his servants, who had stopped the press while watching him and laughed with him. "Wine."

The two men glared at him. "You drank the wine, master?" They stood puzzled, staring at one another for a moment before bursting out in laughter again. Nestor glared into the vat and smirked, lunging his arm as if making an announcement.

"Did I?" Nestor made a *hmpf* sound.

"Well, where is the wine you brought for yourselves?" He asked.

The men gazed behind them at the rocky outcropping sculpted into a bench under the window, several empty clay jars lying on their sides.

Raol replied, hiccupping, "We drank those too."

Nestor blinked his eyes as if shrugging off the sweat dripping from his drenched hair. "Do your wives know you took the wine?"

The man with the roses laughed. "*Your* wife does not know."

They let the silence fill the room as a breeze simmered in, blowing the terra cotta oil lamps hanging from the beams above them into a gentle sway. Nestor fixated on the empty clay vessels, hunching his head down as if peering through a veil but seeing nothing.

"Beasts!" Nestor hollered, jerking his head back up again, startling the men. "We had beasts on the river, and if you got lucky, you could catch a week's worth of fish, and they would never know!"

"My wife is a beast. In bed!" One of the men roared out.

Nestor agreed. "Ha! All of Rome knows this truth, but a true beast hunts and kills,"

Nestor took a deep breath.

"And stalks the world before taking over, blood spilling in the streets..." he ended, speaking in a whisper, as if in deep thought.

The three male servants glanced at each other in concern before roaring in laughter again. Nestor jumped up on the edge of the stone press, his bare feet gripping like they were made to climb rock. He sighed deeply before jumping in on top of the olives, the juices and pulp smashing between his toes, splattering the men's midsections and juices across their faces.

"I am a beast. Did you know that Raol?" He pointed to the man holding the roses, who nodded in agreement, his eyes wide with confusion but too drunk to care.

"Beasts! Fish eaters! Wait, no, I am a fish eater, too. Beast eater." Nestor rubbed his sweaty forehead, glancing back down into the empty vat of wine. "I am a beast eater. The worst one." He glared at the empty wine bottle for a split second and then catapulted it out the window over his servants' heads.

The men roared in laughter, their high-pitched echoes vibrating through the building out to the road.

Axius and Micah had heard the drunken revelry from the courtyard and meandered slowly to the olive press. Micah froze as a shadow loomed at his forehead as they approached the door. Axius lunged his arm forward and caught the wine vessel in the palm of his hand before it hit Micah between the eyes.

Micah froze mid-step, his eyes as wide as the lemons in the trees lining the path behind him. They leaned on the door frame and peered their heads in. Axius was not shocked, but Micah's face froze as if in horrendous terror.

"Is he dancing naked in the olive press?"

Axius's shocked expression turned into an amused smile from one side of his face to another. "Not entirely. The cloth slides up his crack, but yes, he is nearly naked."

Axius glared at Nestor, his mouth gaping open and widening his eyes in disgust. "That is not dancing."

"Will the pits not bloody his feet?" Micah wondered.

Axius thought for a moment. "His pride will face worse once he is sober."

Nestor had his back to them, facing his servants, his buttocks a gleaming white compared to the rest of his finely tuned, tanned skin. His servants noticed Axius and Micah at the door and froze. Axius noticed the half-naked servants were splattered with fleshy chunks and oils dripping down their bodies from Nestor's frolicking in the press.

Nestor let out a roaring burp and hiccupped, his body lurching up and down as if some unrhythmic curse was controlling his extremities. He burped again before cutting an obnoxiously loud fart toward the door.

Raol sighed. "The beast has spoken."

"Agreed!" Nestor laughed. The men's laughter filled the room, and a fart echoed at the back of the press from one of the servants, who laughed even harder.

Micah opened his mouth, widened his eyes again, and coughed. "Remind me not to buy oil from them." He backed away from the door frame.

Axius burst out laughing, and Nestor turned around to face them. "Axius! The beast hunter! The killer! The slayer of, of, why are you here?"

Axius walked in, but then stepped back outside, nodding to the stench. "Your lovely wife has put on a feast, and I am to fetch you."

Micah gagged, waving his hand in front of his face. "I implore you to bathe first."

Nestor jumped down from the press, mushed olives caked between his toes, his body wet with sweat, and a pungent stench of alcohol and flatulence roaring off him. He turned to his men and nodded as if approving of them. "My friends! Go home to your families before dark."

Axius turned to go with Micah before pausing, but Nestor stopped and faced his men again. "I implore you, do not speak a word of this to anyone." Then he turned to the man holding the bowl of roses. "Raol, you can stop standing there now. The roses have not been added to the oil yet. I missed many steps today." Nestor scratched his forehead, the wrinkles forming crevasses of confusion.

Raol smiled, his thin, dark face gleaming with joy. "Many steps, my lord."

"Do not tell my wife."

Raol smiled big. "Never."

With that, Nestor turned and marched out the door past Axius and Micah toward the bath house in the back of the yard, oblivious to them.

Micah sighed, watching him go. "Instead of a mighty warrior, we have Nestor of Bacchus."

Axius shook his head and sighed, watching Nestor parade almost naked away from them, recognizing Micah was referencing the goddess of wine.

"I doubt not his abilities as a warrior. Even men have nightmares that drive them to the wine. Nestor more so than most." He patted Micah on the back, and they walked through the citrus tree-lined path for the feast.

When Axius rounded the corner to enter the courtyard feast, bursts of cackling laughter met him on the stone terrace. Three petite, dark-headed girls rushed him, catapulting into his arms and knocking him over. Micah smiled, his eyes bright and wide, fascinated by Nestor's beautiful fair-skinned children.

"Ah, my beautiful blessings!" Axius dropped to his knees and let the four- and five-year-old melt into his chest while wrapping his arms around Diana, who was seven. "You have grown! Why do you grow so fast?" He laughed.

"I have brought you each a doll from the markets. Your favorite colors!" He bragged. The girls squealed in delight.

Micah stood behind Axius, soaking in this warrior's softness. He laughed with him and then meandered around the fray to sit at the table, where Manius stood laughing at them. The two youngest led him to the table, the wafting goodness permeating his senses, making his stomach growl. Domitia waited for her girls to sit beside him, gazing behind the entrance for Nestor.

The nine-year-old eldest children, Aurora and Venus, sat next to Domitia, a perfect copy of her thinness and black hair. They had it piled atop their pretty heads in thick braids. The five girls were awash in rainbow-colored robes as if they had spilled down from heaven. Axius gazed between the girls, gazing at the eldest twins at the head of the table with their mother.

"Look at these beautiful queens!" Axius bowed to them, smiling. Aurora smiled, picking a fig from the platter and plopping it in her mouth. Axius marched over to them and kissed the tops of their heads.

Manius agreed. "Indeed. Domitia, your daughters are the most beautiful in all of Rome. We are honored to dine with you today." He craned his neck to the entrance and then huffed at Axius. "Nestor?"

Micah cleared his throat, sitting down next to Manius. "Ah, he is in the bath."

Domitia poured herself a glass of wine. "Drunk with the servants again." She sipped her wine.

Axius and Micah glanced at each other, and Manius laughed at them. "Did you think the lady of the estate would not know her husband's revelry?"

"Yes, and I must make his workers alter shifts to give him company in the press when he is home." She smirked, a slight dimple on her left cheek.

Axius looked at Domitia, who lifted a half smile at him and then filled her plate with pheasant and seasoned mussels. "Please, help yourselves. I know the girls are hungry, so we do not need to wait any longer. Nestor will come along."

Axius waited until the five girls had filled their plates, smiling at them as if they were his children. When Axius reached for the feast, Nestor popped up behind Domitia. He was clean and dressed in blue robes down to his ankles, his spikey black hair still damp.

He leaned over and picked his wife's hand up to his lips, eyeing her in pride. "Forgive me my beauty."

Domitia blushed, smiling into his face. "A man who works hard for Rome is given joy. Forgiveness is not needed, my love. Dine with us."

Nestor sat aside his wife, smiling at his girls, whose faces lit up at his presence. "My beauties, please eat! I hear Jupi has cobblers in the ovens!"

The twins looked at each other. "Strawberry? I hope?" Aurora pined. The other girls agreed.

Nestor thought a moment, filling his plate with the boar meat. "I smelled strawberry. Although, I believe there is also blackberry and peach!" He goaded them on.

The girls giggled, and Manius laughed while stuffing his face and sipping the wine. Domitia sipped her wine slowly, the silence from everyone eating filling the courtyard with clanking forks and happiness. They ate the pheasant first, the steamed carrots and leeks dripping with the broth from its juicy meat. She eyed Manius, picked a chunk of fresh bread off the fruit platter, and dipped it in her ramekin of olive oil and herbs.

Nestor cleared his throat and turned to his wife, gazing into her eyes before meeting Manius's stare. They smiled at one another while eating side by side together.

"This is unexpected, Senator. I am honored to have you. What brings you?"

Manius set his fork down and leaned into his chair while servants brought more vats of wine and another platter with piping hot bread and quinoa lined with roasted garlic and leeks. Manius waited until the servants removed the pheasant platter that was now empty to replace it with a board of goat cheese with flatbreads and grapes. He gazed at the girls and then cleared his throat again.

Nestor sensed Manius's concern and smiled. "It is okay, Senator. We have no secrets in our home. My children are wise beyond their years, trust me. Please, tell me."

The eldest twins stopped eating and watched Manius, their eyes going from him to Axius, who leaned into his chair to sip the wine.

Axius spoke before his father did. "I need you to go with me into Dacia."

Domitia set her wine glass down, staring at him. Silence took over where joyful eating once was. Nestor glared at Manius, clenching his jaws and setting his fork onto his platter. The girls watched their father, the youngest, still piling food on their plates to eat as if oblivious, although Manius knew otherwise.

Nestor poured himself a steaming cup of coffee, not wine. Axius followed and poured himself one, too, offering some to Micah, who thankfully accepted, his stomach full of food now.

Manius gazed at Axius. "I will take some of that coffee, thank you." Axius poured a cup for his father, thinking.

"If you do not go in with me, they will kill me. It was my idea, not my father's." Axius goaded.

Nestor waited until the servants brought out the various fruit cobbler deserts, and the table filled again with sweetness and hope. He lunged his hand to get a scoop of the peach cobbler and plopped it on his dessert plate. He sipped his coffee and ate the sweetness, staring around the table at everyone, even his daughters. While waiting for him to respond, the silence was like daggers in Manius's throat because the mission's success depended on him.

When Nestor had finished his bite, he turned to his daughters and smiled. "Did you get some? It is sweet." He watched his girls dig into the various flavors, conversing with themselves about playing outside, lessons, and food. The eldest twins had stopped eating.

Nestor poured more coffee on top of what he already had and cleared his throat. "Titus is already gone, and for us to go in and make good time, we would need to leave by the river, which means a boat. I hate boats. We would only be mere days ahead of the army."

"Boats are chariots for the water. You excel at racing. You will do fine." Axius smiled.

Nestor sipped his coffee, the steam slipping up his forehead to the spikes atop his hair, his jaws clenched at Axius's remark.

Manius sighed.

Axius continued. "I need you to help me gain the trust of the Dacian mercenaries we release and use them as leverage to get into the queen's presence. Rome does not know."

Nestor's face drained of color. He stopped sipping and set the cup down.

"You plot against Rome." He laughed out loud, taking another bite of his cobbler.

"And then what, brother? What will you say to the queen that she does not already know? Do you think she is ignorant of the ways of war?" Nestor goaded him.

Axius blared his nostrils. "I need to know what is happening in Dacia. Her hands have blood on them. Woman or not. Aurelian colonizes Dacia regardless and believes she is the cause of our army's demise."

"Aurelian knows nothing of Dacia besides the gold he steals from the land. You know nothing of the ways of women." Nestor taunted him.

"No woman or beast or man kills our brothers of Rome and gets away with it." Axius gritted his teeth.

"You know nothing of the beasts hunting Dacia as Rome does not. Rome is playing a fool's game." Nestor warned him.

Domitia took a deep breath, noticing the youngest children stopped eating and fidgeted at the table. She stood and directed the servants to take them in and clean them up. As the youngest left, Axius gazed at the eldest twins. Aurora, the eldest of them, met her father's eyes across him at the table.

"One of the beasts is here. Just like in the stories you told us."

The table grew silent once more, and Nestor met her stare with desperation screaming from his face. He clenched his jaws and bit his tongue, his eyes wavering at her.

"Where my love." He commanded, his eyes bright.

The youngest twin, Venus, agreed with Aurora. "Edge of the woods. At nightfall during wool lessons."

Micah spit out his coffee. "What. Here?" He glared around the courtyard.

Domitia chimed in. "Yes, they have now seen it twice, my love. You only returned from the circus late yesterday, and we did not time to speak of this."

Nestor grieved inside. "I have only gotten home to find I am summoned to go back into a land that hunts Romans, and the beasts of my land are stalking my family."

He then turned to Domitia. "Have you seen it?"

Domitia swallowed, her eyes meeting his at the table, the silence overtaking the feast. "No. I will sit with them in wool class tomorrow evening and watch."

Nestor leaned his head back from his wife, and his body grew stiff. "You are in great danger. Rome is in danger." He then turned his clenched face to Axius, but his daughter belted out before he could say anything.

"What is it, father?" Aurora pleaded. "Is it the beast of your land that has come?"

Nestor met his daughter's stare, clenching his jaws. "This beast, is it big, like a tall bear?"

Aurora agreed. "Bigger than the bear we saw last year at the circus."

"Is it spindly, not as bulky or fat as the bear? Is it thin, I mean?"

"It is thin and muscular, like you." She agreed.

Nestor closed his eyes and took a deep breath. Domitia clutched her hands in her lap under the table.

"Is it pitch black, like the darkest of night?" He asked.

"Yes, the moonlight was how we noticed it."

"Did you see its eyes?"

"They looked pale in the moonlight."

"It was looking at you?" Nestor sighed, meeting her stare.

She glanced at her sister, and Diana suddenly spoke up. "It was looking at me."

Nestor gazed upon his girls, leaning into the back of his chair. "It is known by many names, children, but it is all the same. It is a man-eater."

"So, the beasts of Dacia are coming." He whispered.

The girls jumped from the table and ran to their mother's arms. He turned to his wife. Domitia's face was pale, and she had tears in her eyes, clutching her girls. "What do we do, Nestor?" She feared.

Nestor pressed his fist atop the table and shook his head. "This is not the news I wanted today."

Axius grew chill bumps up his spine. "Here? What would one be doing here?" He turned to Manius. "Who else knows Kilian came, father?"

Nestor froze. "What name did you just say?"

Axius thought the food in his stomach was going to come back up. "Kilian."

"Damnit!" Nestor complained, slamming his fist down on the table. His plate toppled over, and the carrots spilled to the ground. He rubbed his forehead, the wine slowly wearing off, but a looming headache haunted him.

"You know of Kilian? He has been a scout for the Dacian queen for years now, Nestor. He has been bringing me messages from her. He left with Titus and the army to lead them into Dacia." Manius confirmed, concerned.

"To lead them to death! The famed Dacian queen scout, all Dacian's know of it." Nestor fretted.

Axius sipped his coffee and stared at Nestor and then Domitia, who was trying to compose herself for the girls wrapped in her arms.

"What did he bring you, Senator? I must see it." Nestor begged.

"How would you know him, Nestor? How would you know he brought something?" Axius questioned his friend.

Nestor laughed. "My father-in-law took me from Dacia, Axius!"

"Did you think I would be ignorant to the queen's scout?! I may be from Dacia, but that does not make me a fool in Rome." Nestor huffed.

Axius set the coffee down, swallowing, staring at Nestor in silence.

"Kilian is known by many names, but not in Rome. He is known as one of the greatest warriors of the Gray tribe. Vasiliki." He huffed, shaking his head. "How any of you are still alive, I do not know."

Axius narrowed his eyes. "What is he, Nestor."

Nestor huffed at him. "Did he come looking for me? Yes or no."

Axius blared his nostrils. "What is he."

"Did he come looking for me, Axius? Yes or no."

"You tell me, brother. He is no scout. Is he?" Axius goaded him, crossing his arms on the table.

They sat at the opposite ends of the table, staring at each other in silence before Nestor huffed again, biting his tongue.

"No," Nestor whispered, his eyes meeting Axius's face.

"Then what," Axius commanded.

Nestor huffed through his nose. "A killer, Axius. And yet, he let you all live and is now leading our beloved Commander Titus and our brothers there. The emperor is a fool."

Manius sighed and pulled out a parchment from his shawl pocket. "Kilian has come to Rome many times in the past for Dacia. I have never sensed any ill will on him Nestor, although, I think he may have been searching for something. Kilian was gravely concerned about Rome going back there. Albeit, he did mention his wishes you were to come into Dacia with Axius after joining me at the circus. He did not come looking *for* you. He came to warn Rome at the queen's behest."

Manius handed the parchment to Micah to hand down the table to Nestor.

"However, I will say Rome is not listening and knows nothing of this warning from the queen." He added, watching Micah pass the parchment down the table.

Micah cleared his throat, his face pale with worry. "It is in Albanian. Can you read that?"

Nestor shot him a glare, his face now on fire.

"Of course, you can." Micah leaned over the table to hand it to him.

Nestor lifted the parchment to his nose and sniffed it, closing his eyes and thinking. He opened it and read it slowly, his breathing slowing to a delicate rhythm. He bit his lip, gazed at his daughters and wife, and glared at Axius again.

"This other language at the bottom is not something I know. I recognize it may be some ancient form of Etruscan I remember seeing as a child..."

Nestor paused, glaring at the language. "We go to release the Dacian mercenaries. How many are there?" He demanded.

Everyone looked at Manius. "Thirteen."

"Trained with a bow? Trained to hunt? Skilled with the blade?" He asked.

Manius agreed. "Yes, they have continued to train these years throughout their imprisonment under a Prior elite while maintaining other studies, if you will."

Axius scoffed. "Pfft, other studies."

"From which tribe in Dacia?" Nestor demanded.

Manius cleared his throat. "Vasiliki's."

Nestor laughed. "Goooodddd." He goaded. "You are to leave five here to protect my family, the ones *I* choose, while I go into Dacia with Axius and the others."

Domitia gasped. "Nestor!"

But Nestor ignored her.

Axius felt a weight of relief come off his shoulders. Nestor was coming.

"And the prisoners, how many are you releasing once we secure the mercenaries?" Nestor demanded.

Manius sighed. "I do not know how many are left."

"You mean how many Rome has allowed to waste away? Pity. That will not go in Rome's favor with this queen." Nestor warned.

Domitia closed her eyes atop the heads of her girls and gripped them tighter, her face pale. Manius dropped his mouth open. Axius would have laughed out loud but smiled instead. Nestor was known to be a harsh negotiator and played dirty.

"The five mercenaries of my choosing will guard my family and estate. They will already know how to hunt them, to smell them, and how to kill them." Nestor warned. "I will see our most skilled hunters are available also."

"What are they, Nestor?" Micah spoke up, his hand shaking while trying to pour more coffee, but all he did was splatter the black brew atop the table.

"Growing up on the Black Sea, we were told stories about the beasts, man-eaters from the Carpathian Mountains. When I came to Rome, I heard the stories told to Roman children. Your people call it Lycanthrope." He dumped out his cold coffee and poured fresh, sipping it as if in deep thought.

"Lycanthrope!" Micah complained. "Like Fenrir, the child of Loki? Are you saying a man walks among us that walks like this wolf beast?"

Nestor nodded. "He is not the only one. There are many, many. And that, my friends, is why Rome is in danger."

Micah gasped, glaring behind him to survey the surrounding gardens and farm, his face pale. "Not the only one."

Axius narrowed his eyebrows, thinking. "Then we go in, warn Titus and the army, and kill these beasts."

Nestor sipped his coffee so fast he almost choked on it, his face turning into a rage. "You do not get it, do you, Axius. This is not a hunt where we will be in control!" He shouted, slamming his bronze goblet down.

"This is not where you survive on just your stealth or stamina! Your prestige, power, and wealth are nothing. There is no training a Roman can do to kill them. There is nothing you can do as a lowly man that will give you favor with the beasts of Dacia!"

Axius leaned back in his chair, listening, biting his tongue, his eyes narrowed. Micah grew so nervous his coffee splattered out of his goblet atop his uneaten food. Manius held his breath.

"You lie, brother. You were raised on the shores with them." Axius belted out.

Nestor turned to Domitia as the color drained from her face, and her eyes were wide and wet with tears.

"I hunt many beasts. I fight many beasts. I kill them all." Axius clenched his jaws.

Nestor leaned over his plates, still half full of food, and if he could have reached, he would have put his face into Axius's. "We do not go to hunt them in Dacia, *brother*. The moment we step foot in that cursed land, we will *be* the hunted." He gritted his jaws, his eyes a fire of torment, barring his teeth as if he had fangs to show off.

Silence pricked them all as if daggers flung through their hearts.

Nestor continued "We go to Vasiliki first. Her army will protect us until we warn Titus and get them all out."

Manius huffed. "Aurelian will not let that happen."

Nestor scoffed. "Then they will all die! Make no mistake, Senator, though our famed commander goes in with an army, and indeed he is a formidable fighter, Rome is in grave danger…" He paused. "It will be a miracle by the gods if one soul is left standing for Rome against the beasts."

Axius held his breath, the rivets from his frustration forming long lines of indentations across his forehead as he met Nestor's glare.

"By going this way without Titus's approval, we risk certain judgment by Rome." Nestor fretted. "And this time, Axius, your father's prestige or power may not save us."

Manius sighed, his eyes wavering atop the mounds of food half-eaten on the table, the steam contorting his face. Axius met Nestor's stare again, holding his breath and biting his tongue. Nestor stood, placing his palms on the table, leaning down to glare at everyone.

"A warning, if we do not succeed in getting Vasiliki's aid to Titus and the army…"

Axius stared into Nestor's dark eyes, not wavering, face clenched. He then bolted up from the chair and marched out of the courtyard back through the manor to the front gate. Nestor watched him go and took a deep breath, huffing. "Just as Titus would do."

"What are you saying, Nestor?" Manius wondered.

Nestor leaned over, grabbed his wife, and kissed her forehead, his eyes folding back to Manius.

"Man does not survive the monsters at the river." And with that, Nestor goaded his wife and children up from the table and walked them back inside to console them.

Manius sat alone with Micah, with mounds of food still piled atop the long oak table. The coffee had gotten cold, and the wine vats were still full.

11
Kilian's Grievance

Kilian smelled home getting closer, although they were still days away from Pannonia. They were riding the coast of the Adriatic Sea now and at the Po River. The army would be able to bathe, cook, and catch fish. Kilian smelled the salty ocean but would have preferred the bitter cold of the mountains he called home to this hot plain of heat. Summer was dying, and a slight bitter breeze blew in hints of Autumn coming.

They were nearing the Carpathian Mountains, where the sunrises kiss the plain, and rivers flow like jewels. It gave him hope. Titus had been silent while leading the armies on foot, with his mounted archers lingering behind for miles, filling the horizon with dread.

He was beginning to think the commander wanted to test his perseverance in leading the army into Dacia. Still, all he succeeded in was driving his patience into a deep vat from which there was no escape. He never had to lead anyone back into Dacia because Rome knew the way. Rome had fortitudes and villages built along the Pannonia plains at the base of them by the mountain.

Kilian knew they were using him to get Titus into Vasiliki's presence, and he seethed more and more as the day went on. Titus stopped his horse and dismounted, the army behind him and Kilian began to disperse to make camps for the night.

A senior officer rode up to address Titus, dismounting himself. "My lord, our scouts confirmed the village to the East of Pannonia on the Danube. The Dacian named Fenrir, who leads it, has formed an allegiance to Rome and is preparing us to rest there to meet the queen."

Kilian froze. The hairs on his neck stood up, and a low, rumbling growl belted into his throat. His eyes dilated to a pale white, ethereal like a full moon in pitch darkness, and then he blinked it away. He turned his ear to hear the conversation.

He had his back to Titus, watching the army begin to make pit fires for them to cook their grains for dinner, and some were already sitting around them talking to one another. He stood there, razor shivers chasing up his spine and listening to the officer encourage Titus to go to Fenrir's village.

"Very good! The men must rest and eat good food once we leave Pannonia to be prepared for this wench." Titus clenched his jaws.

"This Fenrir, the same tribal leader in talks with this wench queen?" Titus scoffed.

The officer agreed. "We have the parchments with her seal, and he is making arrangements with our scouts for you to get her."

Kilian clenched his fists tight in the folds of his cloak.

Titus agreed. "Good. Once we reach his village, it is ours. Then we take her, kill the rest of them."

The officer agreed. "Also, Honus is in Pannonia and awaits your command." The officer yanked off his helmet, his short black hair dripping with sweat.

"I was hoping to see him. He may not be ready for battle. If Axius were here, he would try to convince me otherwise." Titus scoffed.

The officer agreed. "You know how Axius encourages him. He is, after all, his Godfather. Do you want me to send word then? That Honus is to stay at the outpost until you arrive?"

Titus took in a deep breath. "Yes. Once I have seen his skill when we arrive, I may let him accompany me to test his abilities. Until then, he stays put."

Kilian turned to face them, his pale, unshaven face now showing stubbles of blonde, his eyes back to normal. "Surely you would not send your blood into Dacia?"

Titus ignored Kilian, breathing in the fresh air and gazing at the army. He grabbed his horse's reins and glared at him, his knuckles white. He lunged forward into Kilian's face, seething, clenching his jaws.

"You are to stay to yourself, Dacian, away from my army. You are not permitted to beg for food." Titus pulled his horse, marched away from him, and disappeared into the fray of the Romans filling the plain.

Kilian watched him go, clenching his jaws. His heart beat faster as a burning rage rose in his guts. He took a deep breath and turned his back on the army's madness and noise, gazing upon the vast, empty plain before him. Behind him, the red capes from the Romans swished through the air for miles like a river of blood had broken a dam of eternal pain.

12

Dacia Calling

That night, Nestor lay in bed naked with Domitia, their bodies intertwined under sheets of milky white. His blue wolf tattoos splayed down his shoulder to his groin like a beast had already eaten them. She lay on his chest, his muscular arm propping her head up, her long black hair spilled over the side of the mahogany bed frame. He kept the arched windows open to listen in the darkness, his head turning to peer out and watch the trees move in the gentle breezes. Their shadows bounced off the terra cotta lanterns swinging from the ceiling. Flickering red flames softened the walls of the room into an ethereal glow.

Domitia thrust her arm over his chest and squeezed tight, and he bent down and kissed the top of her head. "I do not want you to go. I fear you will not come back. I feel I only just saved you from Dacia."

Nestor sighed, wrapping his arms around her thin body. "If I do not go and help Axius, the queen will have him killed. I love him like my own flesh. She will let him live if I am there. Having the mercenaries freed will help our mission, too."

Domitia sighed. "As do I, but is this wise?"

Nestor took a deep breath. "Nothing is wise about Rome trying to take Dacia with the beasts in power."

"And then what?"

"My hope is the Dacian queen will work with us to save Titus and the army, though I know Titus will be enraged at us."

Domitia huffed. "Titus does not abandon missions; you know what he will do to you and Axius once he knows you are there. Axius has another reason for trying to warn Titus."

Nestor agreed, staring at the ceiling. "He does not want to lose him or any more of the army. Axius fears losing those he loves more than you know."

"Axius is going into Dacia to save Titus. But not to get more information for Rome from this queen?"

Nestor agreed. "Axius wants to save Rome from itself, even if it means undermining it to save Titus and the army from Dacian beasts. He wants to speak with the queen to get on her level and understand Dacia better. Axius cares for humanity but will not forsake Rome. I hope Vasiliki works with us, but I fear she will try to drive us out regardless, as she has tried to do these many months, and yet Rome is not listening."

"What if you and Axius fail?"

Nestor froze. "Then the beasts will take Rome, and there will be nothing here to return to." He gazed into her eyes as he met his, his hand caressing her face.

"Yet one is here, Nestor." She chirped.

Nestor agreed. "They will hunt us all, Domitia." He warned, whispering. "They start with a scout or two, and then they come. Someone lured them here. They do not scout areas unless they are making plans for something."

Her eyes teared up. "What do they want?"

Nestor looked up to the ceiling and watched the terra cotta lanterns sway, their shadows lingering like fiery fingers above them.

"They have come for me, my love. And they have finally found me."

Domitia swallowed, closing her eyes and gripping his chest tighter against her.

"When I was a child on the Danube, my grandfather told me stories about how the Romans annihilated the Dacians under emperor Trajan. The family that escaped were the only descendants of Fenrir. He told me they went deep into the Carpathian Mountains and made a blood oath with Loki to get their ancestor's powers."

Domitia widened her eyes.

"Loki granted the family the power of Vanagandr, the monster of the river. Yet, to live long, they must turn others to be like them and feed on man's flesh when they turn. They vowed to take Rome down."

"Vengeance?" Domitia sighed.

Nestor took a deep breath, thinking. "This is something more. I need to speak with the queen to find out what."

"How does the Dacian queen live when these beasts rule that land?" Domitia questioned.

Nestor swallowed, his eyes veering away from her back up to the ceiling lanterns. He wanted to answer, but his voice cracked, and he shook his head and sighed instead.

"I do not understand the ways of your homeland, my love, but I am thankful you have come into my life," Domitia assured him, kissing his face.

"Do you ever miss it?" She asked.

Nestor huffed. "Rome is my home now. Dacia is beautiful, but I have been away so long, and I am thankful for my lot in life. I will do all in my power to protect my family and home. I promise you."

Nestor met her kisses before pausing. "I am not leaving you or our children without protection. The mercenaries under Vasiliki are renowned and respect family. They love children. They will keep you all safe. I will come back to you."

He rolled atop her and devoured her kisses in a passionate embrace. She met his open-mouthed kisses with her tongue.

Then he stared into her eyes. "I love you, my beauty."

"I love you, my love." Domitia dove into his kisses.

Nestor lunged inside her, his mouth wide open and pressed against hers as he dove inside her. Domitia leaned her head back and held onto his muscular shoulders tight as their bodies thrust together. As they embraced one another and Domitia's moans lived within his breaths, Nestor caressed his wife until the rising sun exhausted them of strength.

At dawn, Nestor readied his horse for the journey to the Tyrrhenian Sea. The seaside villa belonged to Senator Opiter, a prominent member of the Senate. Opiter had more influence than Manius, just enough that Manius had no choice but to seek his help.

Opiter's manor held the Dacian mercenaries, and Domitia questioned his reasoning for keeping them there, of all places. Nevertheless, she trusted Nestor's decision to go into Dacia with Axius. Albeit, her heart panged a heavy burden in her chest this morning as she watched the men ready their horses and prepare their rations for the day.

Before they all left, Nestor had gone into each of the girls' suites and kissed the tops of their little heads, tucking them tighter under the wool covers. Domitia watched him survey the windows and doors and double-checked the porches and courtyards, peering through the fog and silence as if seeing something coming from miles away that refused to show itself. As he marched out front, he eyed the hunters lined up along the front road to see him off.

He slithered around each of them, inspecting their attire, their chosen weapons, and even how they had their hair tied up off their necks. "Hair gets in the way in battle. Better to tie it up or cut it off." He mumbled, agreeing with the women he had summoned to help protect his family. They had their hair tied in braids around their heads, tight and out of the way, and Nestor approved.

Domitia watched her husband goad them on and master them as if he were in the gladiator ring teaching foreigners to fight. She held her breath as she noticed Axius gripping his longsword's hilt, pulling his red cloak over his shoulders. Her eyes met his, and he swallowed. He looked away from her as if pondering the thick fog rolling in, but she knew what he was doing.

Axius was always watchful, just like Nestor. Although the men played bravery as a fine wine, she wondered if a bit of fear panged at them as it did her. Her eyes followed where he was, looking past the almond groves. The trees looked like skeleton shadows dancing as the brisk wind pelted in.

Domitia stood before the servants, both men and women, all fully armed with broad swords and bows and arrows strapped to their backs. They had daggers strapped to their leather armor and small ones poking out the sides of their sandals, the leather straps tied up in knots to their calves. She turned her gaze to them and half smiled at all thirty-six of them, and their bravery.

"Good. Remember what I have taught you all. By tomorrow evening, if I have not returned, you know what to do." Nestor warned them, his eyes like pits of fire.

Domitia watched them all nod their heads to him. His gaze then turned to her, and he marched over and pulled her tight against his chest, wrapping his arms around her. He kissed her forehead.

"You know what to do if we do not come in time." He whispered. Gather Dia and the children into the wine cellar and stay there. You must do this before nightfall."

Domitia sighed, gazing at the brave warriors. "We will."

Nestor marched away from her and mounted his stallion, nodding to Axius. Manius and Micah sat atop their steeds a few yards away, already in the middle of the road. Manius waved to Domitia.

"See you all tomorrow, God willing." He encouraged her.

Domitia raised her arm high in the air and watched them go. The fog lifted around them as the horses trotted off, and four figures transformed into eerie shadows as they disappeared. Domitia turned to the thirty-six men and women, nodding to them.

"Three by three, just as Nestor taught you. You are all family. Please be safe." They bowed to her and split up in groups of threes around the manor and farms to keep watch, disappearing into the morning silence as the sun cascaded crimson shadows over the horizon.

Dia emerged from the manor and joined Domitia on the front porch, her teal blue robes cascading down to her toes, her white hair in braids. She pulled her white shawl tighter around her shoulders to fend off the bitter wind moving in.

"Storms are coming this day." She belted out.

Domitia agreed. "Indeed. Summer has been good to us, but Fall approaches early, it seems."

"Changes are coming. Nonetheless, we continue." Dia whispered, meeting Domitia's stare.

"The lessons will be in the East wing today. No outside revelry for the children. The warriors will have food ready in the back courtyard." Dia whispered, turning to watch the road where the men trotted off.

Domitia sighed, pulling her cloak over her shoulder and folding her arms across her chest. "Thank you, my friend. You always make our people welcome; I thank you for your kindness."

Dia huffed. "I promised your mother I would care for you until my last breath, and now your family is my family, and your children my grandchildren." She leaned in and put an arm around Domitia's thin shoulders. "My family is everything."

"Now come, my dear. Let us have coffee and wait for the children to wake up. We have eggs and hot bread from the kitchen, and fresh strawberry jam waiting on us, and I am hungry." She giggled.

Domitia laughed with her. "That sounds lovely!"

"It will all be well. You shall see." Dia encouraged, smiling.

Domitia smiled at Dia, who towered over her by a few inches. "Coffee sounds wonderful."

Domitia turned to go in with her, craning her neck one last time to watch the fog engulf the road and bleed through the trees like a silent hell was coming.

The milky white fog encompassed the swirling almond groves as if torrents of spirits were gathering, and within the shadows from the woods, peering eyes watched the humans. As crackling underfoot and the smell of flesh drew nearer, the beast stepped back into the darkness away from the hunters. The only thing left behind of its presence was a sunken paw print a foot wide like an ambitious wound had started bleeding out.

13

The Mercenaries

Senator Opiters Domus sprawled out over the open countryside, its back to the falling cliffs of Mount Circeo, encircled with acres of rising stone walls as if some impenetrable ancient god had constructed the seaside villa themselves.

Opiter emerged from the elaborate door jamb columns and slid down his front steps to meet them, his golden hemmed robes glistening against the navy-blue shawls wrapped around his body to his feet. Axius watched as Manius glided off his tired horse to greet the senator. Opiter's white beard and mustache danced in the ocean breezes, his gray hair braided down his back with golden rings splayed in the knots as if the gods had kissed him.

"My friend!" Opiter rushed in to give Manius a battering hug. "Forgive me for not coming to the games. I did hear it was the best circus Rome had seen in ages." He turned to Nestor and Axius, who slid off their horses alongside Micah.

"Ah! The Champions of Rome. Let me have a good look at you." He marched over and patted Axius and Nestor on their forearms, his white teeth shining in the sun, his dark eyes glistening.

"Welcome, my friends. And, Micah, the famed scribe of the emperor, is it not?" Opiter turned to stare at the thin man with his leather pouch strapped around his bodice filled with parchments and pens.

Micah bowed to him. "It is, thank you, senator. We apologize for not informing you of our arrival."

Opiter laughed. "Oh, come on! This is no bother. It is an honor to have you, regardless of the lack of notice. Although, I will say I am intrigued by your sudden appearance." He turned back to Manius.

"What is wrong, my former pupil?" He eyed Manius, who half smiled and then swallowed.

"Many things. I have come to ask you for your help in the name of Rome. Albeit, privately, you understand." Manius advised, biting his tongue.

Opiter stopped smiling and pursed his lips. "Aha. I see. Well then." He raised an arm as servants appeared from the entrance. "Take care of these steeds for my friends."

Axius handed over the reins and watched multiple servants emerge to lead the horses into the stables, care for them, and let them rest.

"I was not expecting you, but I will have a feast made. It is a long journey back to Rome, and I assume you plan to stay the night?" Opiter turned to lead them up the steps.

Manius agreed. "Yes, indeed. We have much to discuss."

"As do I," Opiter warned Manius, eying him from the side as they entered a vestibulum sprawled out to a central hall. The walls danced to life with intricate paintings and frescos of Rome, wildlife, and nature. Multiple rooms adjoined this fabulous space. They could see straight through the home from the hall on either side. Marble pillars seemed to dance for miles, as each wall displayed a different life of painting.

Opiter led them into an atrium with an open ceiling. To the back of the wall, a patio opened into a massive flat yard laden with fruit trees, herb gardens, and flowering vines kissing pergolas. The ocean roared, beating the cliff walls. It sounded like the trickling fountains and streams Opiter had designed in his backyard were roaring waterfalls.

"This is truly splendid." Micah stood gazing at the beauty while the men sat on thick pillows on the floor in a sunken dining atrium. Servants already brought wines and coffee or their choice of teas and breads to dip in olive oil and herbs. Micah turned, smelling the hot bread, his eyes wandering to the silver platter of figs, grapes, and cheeses.

"This should refresh you. Please enjoy! We have much to discuss." Opiter encouraged them.

Axius poured himself coffee and then turned to pour Nestor a cup. "No wine for you." He chirped.

Nestor agreed. "Hope it's strong then."

Opiter laughed. "Strongest coffee in all of Rome! You will enjoy its robust flavor."

He eyed Manius while pouring his own steaming tea. "My wisest, most powerful pupil has a burden. I know it."

Manius stretched past the coffee vat and went for the teapot, plopping a slice of lemon in the teacup. "Opiter, the time has come for the mercenaries."

Opiter coughed as he sipped his tea. "Oh?"

Micah widened his eyes and stopped chewing on the figs. "Well, that was fast."

"No time to waste." Manius chimed, sipping the hot tea.

Opiter set his cup, leaning into the wall supporting his back. "And why do you need them now of all times?"

"I need to send them into Dacia with Axius and Nestor to speak with the queen. I need them because the queen will readily allow them in her presence, and we can find out what is happening in Dacia. Not one Roman or commander has been able to breach her tribe yet. And

Romans continue to be slaughtered. Although gold is still coming in from Dacia, the cost is becoming too much for Rome to bear. The emperor needs a resolution."

"Yes, the cost is too much for Rome, but you also seek vengeance. Or is it Axius seeking this?" Opiter eyed Axius, who set his coffee cup down and met his stare.

"Yes. It was my idea." Axius glared over at Manius, narrowing his eyebrows, but Manius just shook his head and flared his nostrils.

Opiter huffed. "Vasiliki has been a source of ill repute for Rome for some time. You know the emperor will succeed in taking Dacia, regardless of the lives lost. It is part of war."

Manius nodded. "Yes, however, if we could get into her presence, albeit secretly, then perhaps that would save Rome from losing more and end these wars that may cost us all more than we can continue bearing."

Axius leaned back against the wall. "We must try. We cannot lose any more men, Opiter. Rome is not making armies quick enough to justify sending them to their deaths. Vasiliki will listen to Nestor and the mercenaries."

Opiter huffed, thinking. "Though you are brave, son, you alone are not enough to stop the evils in that land, Axius. I know Manius and Titus trained you better than that. You are just one man, a strong one, yes, but just one man. And human, at that."

Nestor raised his eyes to Opiter, pausing in mid-sip of his coffee. "You know of the beasts."

Opiter met his stare, his face going pale white, his aged wrinkles riding down his face as if blades had engraved his cheeks under his eyes. "Oh yes, Nestor. Oh yes. Mere mortals going into Dacia to chase beasts cursed by the gods, going into a land that eats man."

"Yet you side with the emperor to continue sending in the flesh for them?" Nestor questioned, wrinkles indented across his forehead.

Opiter leaned into his pillow against the wall.

Manius held his breath, glancing at Axius and Nestor. "We have to try."

Opiter sipped his wine again. "Oh yes, you have no choice but to try. For Rome. For the world. For we are all in danger."

"I cannot stop the emperor in sending in more Manius, you know this. But..."

He stood up, setting his wine down and straightening his robes. "I will take you to them, but you must go through Matunaga first. He is the one who will approve you to go into their presence. If he disapproves, then your mission here is in vain."

"What's a Matunaga?" Micah asked, standing up with the others.

Manius tried to smile at them, but his face contorted into a leery contempt. "The primary reason we have come." And with that, Manius pulled the parchment from his robes and followed Opiter outside to the rising tower at the end of the property overlooking the sea.

The tower was built as a fortress house, rising round and round with never-ending steps. Between the pillars were walls of built-in stone bookcases filled with books. The walls without bookcases were painted with frescos chipped away with time.

With each floor they reached, the wind blasted in at their faces through the narrow window cracks. The pungent smell from the leather book covers hit them in their faces. Axius admired the sea life paintings stretched on the walls rising into the tower, their shadows dancing over them as if they were immersed in an underwater realm.

"What manner of place is this?" Micah whispered, his fingers grazing the book covers in a trance. His voice echoed past them into the tower, and he froze on the landing steps.

Opiter turned to him, pausing his climb. "This place is not of Rome, its ancestry, or history. You must not speak of this to anyone. Once we are gone, history will remember this place as a mystery falling into the sea."

Micah glanced back at Axius, who nodded in agreeance. "You have our word." Axius agreed.

The last landing into the tower opened into an expansive round room with ocean views. Axius froze at the man watching them from the center of this room, but the ocean's splendor enthralled the rest of them. The shimmering waves danced like diamonds stretched out for miles. They were so caught up in its beauty and power they had neglected to see the man standing behind a waist-high table, documents, and books splayed out from one end to another.

Opiter walked into the room and bowed, lifting his open palm to introduce them. "Senator Manius, Axius of the prior elite, Nestor warrior of Rome, and Micah, the elite scribe of the emperor, I introduce you to Matunaga."

The man was very tanned, darker than any Roman Axius had ever seen. He wore a sleeveless creamy-colored robe as his muscular arms leaned over the table, his dark eyes twinkling at them. His black eyebrows accentuated a firm jawline and thin lips under a clean-shaven bald head. He wore leather wrist cuffs that bore an emblem, and Nestor gazed at them to get a better look.

Matunaga meandered around the table past Opiter to gaze upon Nestor. Nestor met his eyes with curiosity, although Matunaga was an inch shorter than him.

"You are no Roman." His voice was very smooth, and Axius noticed the Italian accent.

Nestor agreed. "No. I am Dacian. You are no Roman either." He answered, staring into Matunaga's almost black eyes.

Matunaga agreed. "Correct. I am, however, a Roman citizen like you, from a prominent family, unlike you."

Nestor clenched his jaws into his face. "So. Prominence does not save a man in the heat of battle."

Matunaga backed up from him, gazing upon his attire, before retreating behind his table. His eyes lingered on a few books bound in leather, and the room was silent before he raised again to meet Nestor's aggravated stare.

"Very wise, warrior. Prominence means nothing in Dacia, as you know." He answered, lifting a book from under a pile and splaying it open on a pile of maps.

Opiter started to chime in, but Matunaga interrupted him. "The senator from Rome has brought me something to interpret. Please hand it over."

Manius walked to the desk and handed the parchment to him. As Matunaga splayed it open to read, his expression did not change, but his eyebrows narrowed. Axius wondered if he was disturbed at this revelation.

"This is an ancient form of Etruscan, a relic of Romania, where the gods cursed Fenrinsulfer." Matunaga started reading the part of the scroll without delay, and the room became as eerie as a silent pain.

"The eight tribes that form the paw of my people's curse are now together. The Free Dacians and Sarmatians are mine. The Carpi, Goths, Taifals, Bastarns, Heruli, and Pannonia joined Fenrinsulfer to take Rome and kill the mortals. I rule the heart of the paw, but Fenrir seeks it because once he has it, will be unstoppable. Dacia will fall into darkness, Rome, then the world."

Nestor leaned against a pillar, eying Axius from the side, their eyes on fire to this revelation as Matunaga continued. "There is a traitor in Rome who bleeds like man, has favor with the senate, has eyes on the lands, the estates, the country roads. It plots against Rome to undermine its sovereignty, to take its power, its wealth. It will bleed Rome from the inside out."

Axius looked at Nestor, who met his stare, clenching his jaws. "The Senate has been breached."

"The scouts are here also." Nestor chimed in.

Matunaga paused the reading to hear them and then continued. "The traitor has scouts ready. The traitor uses the emperor's seal to trade gold for war, Dacia for power, and Rome to break the curse."

Matunaga set the parchment down, leaned over the table, and pulled another book out of a pile.

Manius held his breath. "Oh, this is worse than I feared. Rome is in grave, grave danger."

Opiter's face was pale as he met Manius's glare. "Indeed. Is this why you have come?"

"It is. I had no choice. Your private scribe is the only one I know who could read this. You are the only one I can trust with this truth."

"Does anyone else in Rome know of this?" Opiter demanded.

Manius shook his head. "No."

Matunaga picked the parchment back up again. "The seal is from the queen of Dacia and is legitimate. Based on my studies based on Dacian rule and the Sarmatians, I recognize her mark. The book from Romania confiscated from the court of Vasiliki shows her warning to be true."

He turned an elongated book with painted pictures to the men, who lingered around the table to look at it. A paw print showed eight sections for eight clans, the heart of the paw being the leader, Vasiliki. For now. The language was written in Etruscan and transcribed into Latin below it, the same language on the parchment.

But then Matunaga turned the page. The men leaned back. Axius gripped the hilt to his gladius. The painted page showed a big black beast standing like a man, spilling over the page. Its eyes were a fiery white, bleeding into a mischievous yellow. It had thick black fur and an elongated snout sporting dagger fangs. It reared into the sky at night, its pointy ears fully aware of its surroundings. Its height towered over what a man is, and its claws protruded like spears.

Micah took a deep breath, freezing at this terrible portrayal. Opiter and Manius gazed upon it, their eyes fixed in horror. But Nestor and Axius leaned into it, exploring the beast and its powerful stance. Matunaga's gaze lingered on them, his eyes vibrantly relevant to their bravery.

"Is this the beast of your land?" Axius questioned.

Nestor clenched his jaws at it. "Yes."

Axius melted his eyes up to Matunaga, clenching his jaws. "Where are the Dacian mercenaries you have been training with?"

"Follow me." Matunaga turned away from them and drifted to the back of the wall behind his desk.

He pushed a stone discolored from all the rest between the floor-to-ceiling bookcases filled with books. The stone lunged forward, and the wall pivoted wide open into a circle that followed deep crevasses in the floor. It was as if a silent hand scooped down from the heavens and breached the tower wall in splendor.

Micah gasped. "Brilliant engineering!"

Axius noticed stone steps leading down, which looked as if they would fall over the cliffs. The ocean was before them as if they were ready to fly into the heavens. The salty spray kissed their faces and the smell of fresh air and pines from the forest below enthralled them with a mysterious beauty.

Matunaga turned to them all before climbing down. "Do not fear their appearance. These are heroic, dignified warriors." With that, he marched down the steps open to the elements on the cliffside. The men saw a completely hidden landscape as if Opiter had created an alternate world.

Micah gripped the railing and lunged into Axius's cloak, his fists white. Axius paused on the railing, craning to see Micah's pale face clenched. "Beasts hunting man, possible death by cliff, and now mercenaries…"

The blue tattoos snaked around the Dacian mercenary's half-naked bodies like ribbons sewn into their tanned skin. A Draco head leaned over one side of their shoulders as if the wolf was sewn into their souls, keeping guard. Axius noticed up against the wall were rows of elongated yellow shields trimmed in red with wolf heads protruding out of them, made of iron, mouths open and fangs like daggers.

Fake bodies of earth and straw were tied to posts in the middle of the yard and covered with burlap. The thirteen men stood as a force, their red skirts dancing to their knees, their wrists protected with red leather cuffs inlaid with iron rivets. The men had long brown or black hair braided down their backs, and some had beards. Three men picked up a curved hilt as long as the blade, and Axius held his breath.

The Falx was a formidable weapon for the Dacians and could cut a man in half. The Dacian mercenaries lunged into the fake bodies on the poles with their Falx, slicing them in half and shattering the poles into splinters.

The others stood in a row with their backs to the men, slinging smaller Sica's into targets on the wall. When they finished slinging their Sica's on the targets, they picked up their long bows and arrows and fired them. Axius recognized the tactics they used in training and smiled. The men were finely tuned instruments of war from head to toe.

"I am happy to see them doing well after this time, Opiter. Have they not requested to leave?" Manius questioned.

Opiter huffed. "Do you think I would still be alive if they did request to leave and I refused them? I think not. No. They have requested silence here to train and learn under Matunaga, so I am not certain they will want to go to Dacia."

"You have given them a home here, a fortress of solitude and peace." Axius wondered, watching them as they shot their arrows.

Opiter agreed. "Indeed! The way they were taken was horrible. They lost many of their warriors during that battle, and thankfully, Manius and I had the power to spare them and bring them here. My wife convinced me to spoil them into staying, and so I have. I do not regret it!"

"Indeed. It pleases me seeing them prosper here." Micah mumbled, smiling.

The three men using the Falx paused, sweat beading down their bodies, and turned to Matunaga. They pointed at Nestor and spoke amongst themselves in Thracian. Nestor recognized the language, his eyes meeting theirs in a mutual embrace. Nestor also recognized the tattoos because he had a few of them.

"A Dacian comes to us!"

Matunaga turned to Nestor and then to Axius and the others. "Gentlemen, this is Brasus, Moskin, and Tarbus. They were once generals in Vasiliki's army many years ago. The rest of these men were scouts."

They stopped walking as they noticed Axius. "Roman traitor of Dacia," Brasus complained, spitting on the ground.

Axius stood his ground, clenching his jaws, until Nestor spoke up. "This is Axius and my brother-in-arms. We have come for your help."

Brasus rubbed the wetness out of his beard and took a deep breath of morning air, his tattoos glistening in sweat. "You need our help? For what." He turned to Moskin and Tarbus, whose facial expressions changed from slight amusement to pure annoyance.

"I am going into Dacia to speak with Vasiliki. We need you to come with us so we can get in." Nestor explained. "And get out, in one peace."

"You mean to come back to Rome?" Moskin asked.

"Yes, my family is here. I love it here." Nestor agreed.

The three men exchanged sideways glances before glaring at Axius. "Why is he coming?" Brasus demanded.

"My commander is heading there, and I fear it is a trap. I must get to him in person because he will not listen otherwise." Axius informed them.

Brasus scoffed, slithering up into Axius's face. Axius held his ground and his breath. This Dacian was a couple of inches taller than him. Brasus bared his teeth into Axius's face. "We care not for your commander, the killer of Dacian's. He can rot in the field with the rest of your army."

He turned his back to walk away from Axius, but Axius pulled a dagger from his chest sheath and slung it at his head. It flew past Brasus's temple and hit the bullseye on the target between two other Dacians at the wall. The men paused, and everyone turned to look at him.

Manius gasped. "Damnit Axius."

Micah sighed. "I'm stepping back, away from the ensuing battle."

Brasus froze, turning to face Axius again, his eyes going from Matunaga to Opiter. "Did you bring this Roman fool here to die?"

Axius scoffed at him. "You are the one who could have died, seeing I had a clear target of your naked skull. Now let me ask again, Dacian, will you and your men go with us into Dacia to get us into the presence of your queen?"

Moskin and Tarbus gripped their Falx tighter, and Axius stood still, his red cape flowing behind him in the ocean breeze, his breathing deep and easy. Nestor stood beside him, watching them, waiting.

Brasus glared at him as the other Dacians joined behind him. Micah swallowed. "We are going to die."

"That was very brave of you, Roman, knowing you are outnumbered here, even with the little Dacian warrior." Brasus sneered.

"There are only thirteen of you. You are in the home of Opiter, the most powerful senator in Rome. If you kill us, you will have the Roman army in the city upon you." Axius warned. "Last I looked, you all seem pretty content here in this land at sea, ignoring the perils of your lands, forsaking your queen."

Brasus gripped his Falx hard, pointing the blade at Axius, his nose flared, gritting his teeth. "Careful Roman."

"Unless you plan to use that blade, it would be wise not to point it at me," Axius warned, his hand going to his gladius.

"But if you are going to use that blade, I challenge you to win your trust." Axius goaded them.

"No Axius!" Manius yelled at him, tossing his arms in the air.

Opiter sighed. "Axius, they do not play by the rules, son."

Nestor grimaced. "Neither do we."

Matunaga crossed his arms over his chest and stood aside Micah, standing with his back against the tower wall, his eyes wide.

Brasus laughed, raising his Falx over his head. He turned to his men, and they raised their weapons, shouting *Fight! Fight!*

"Have at it, Roman. If I win, we stay. If you win, we go with you into Dacia."

"Fine. Terms?" Axius untied his cloak and tossed it to Micah, who caught it.

"Why do you pull me into these things?" Micah pleaded.

Brasus thought a moment, gazing back at his men. "What should the punishment be for the loser? Shall he live or die?"

"No, no death. You are far too valuable for Rome to die, Dacian." Axius warned.

Brasus aimed his Falx at Axius. "Yet you are not."

"I know my worth! I also know if you do not join me in Dacia, the beasts of Fenrinsulfer will destroy everything you love there." Axius yelled at them.

"So, what's it to be Brasus!" Axius goaded him, walking out into the middle of the yard and pulling his gladius.

Brasus clenched his jaws and charged, his Falx pointed into Axius's midsection.

Brasus screamed, "Never mention the beasts of Dacia!"

Axius pinged his gladius off the Falx's blade and turned sideways, his blade dancing up Brasus's blade. The high screech of metal on metal rang in everyone's ears. When the tip of his blade reached the end of the curved Falx's, Axius turned in circles to avoid the curved blade. He yanked out a short sword from his other side and slapped the top of Brasus's hand with the flat side of his blade. Brasus let out a yelp as Axius lunged the Falx out of his hand, pulling it away from

Brasus with his gladius. He lunged the Falx hard out of Brasus's grip, and it flew behind him into the yard.

Axius aimed both blades into Brasus. "Your answer, Dacian."

Brasus stood still. "You are skilled with the blade. Impressive."

"Your answer."

Brasus smiled. "But are you skilled without blades?"

Axius stepped back, eyeing him. "You want me to put these down and fight me with no weapons?"

Brasus smiled. "No. I want to see how you fight when I take your weapons."

Axius stood his ground, watching Brasus circling him like a lion would do to prey. Axius gripped his swords tighter as the rush of an arrow pinged into the side of his hilts, knocking both swords out of his grips. He glared to his left to see Moskin had fired an arrow to free him of his weapons. Axius remembered they do not play fair.

Nestor eyed Moskin with contempt. He yanked his short sword from his side sheath and flung it between Opiter and Manius. The blade twisted around until it found its mark on Moskin's hand holding the bow. The blade catapulted the bow out of his hand. The Dacians looked at Nestor but did not do anything to stop him.

Opiter and Manius glared back at him, but Nestor huffed. "Told you we don't play fair."

"Hey!" Moskin exclaimed, seeing Nestor's sword plank into the wall behind him and his bow shattered on the ground yards away.

Brasus charged Axius in the stomach, picking him up by his legs and tossing him, slamming him down on his back into the grass. Axius held his breath, gritting his teeth, swinging his legs around to knock Brasus off his feet. But all Brasus did was jump over them. Brasus snapped his knuckles and laughed.

"Foolish Roman. You cannot fight without your weapons." He scolded him.

Axius took in deep breaths, thinking. Brasus grabbed Axius by his boot and dragged him through the yard to the target wall. Sand blew behind Axius as a dust cloud of mass proportions. The Dacians cheered him on while Nestor and the others watched. Manius sighed, but Opiter was worried.

"I can call them off. They will kill him." Opiter fretted.

Manius glared at his old mentor, huffing. "Hardly. My son is a smart ass."

Brasus picked up a rope and swung it around and around like a whip. Axius turned to see the rope aimed at his head and lunged an arm up to protect his face, where the rope entangled his forearm, pulling on his leather cuff. Axius let Brasus drag him back to him through the sand until he thought he was close enough.

Brasus laughed, dragging Axius by his feet like a limp rag doll. Axius gripped the rope tight in his palm and lunged forward into Brasus's legs. He pushed his head between his legs and knocked Brasus off his feet face-first into the sand. Axius lunged up over Brasus's backside and swung the rope around his neck, pulling hard. He pressed a firm knee into the middle of Brasus's back, yanking his arms behind him with his grip and pulling. Brasus coughed.

"I can dislocate your arms this way," Axius warned him, gritting his jaws and pulling Brasus's arms further away from his body at his back. Brasus hollered in pain.

"I can also strangle the shit out of you while I jerk your arms out of their sockets." Axius goaded, sniffling the dirt out of his nose and coughing. His pecks flexed so hard the veins were like blue ribbons down his arms.

Brasus was frozen under Axius's grip. "As I said, you are worth more alive than dead, and although you think so little of Romans, you lie by your actions because you choose to stay in a land that has taken your people and killed them in battle. You fear Dacia, as we all do. But we must stop the beasts."

Axius released the rope and stood off Brasus's back, watching him roll over and cough. Brasus pulled the rope off his neck and stretched his arms out either side of him. He sat up, turned back to his men, and sighed, coughing and rubbing his throat.

He stared at this Roman who had just bested him yet let him live. Axius sniffled, his face plastered with sand. "I need you Brasus. We need your help."

"You lie in your hand-to-hand fight. You pretend to be weak when you are not." Brasus coughed, pointing a finger toward Axius's face.

As Opiter patted Manius on the shoulder, Manius closed his eyes and sighed. "He's going to be the death of me."

Axius walked over to pick up his blades, and the Dacians parted to let him. When he had sunk them into their sheathes, he walked back to Brasus and held out a hand to help him up. Brasus accepted it, stretching his back.

"What's it to be then, Brasus of Dacia?" Axius demanded.

Moskin and Tarbus started laughing. Axius froze, listening to the Dacians burst out in laughter as the others joined. He craned his neck to look at Nestor, who rolled his eyes. Micah was still leaning into the wall, gripping Axius's cloak with terror on his face, but Manius and Opiter were glaring at Axius. Matunaga stood to the side of Micah, watching them all in silence.

When Brasus stopped laughing, he smiled at Axius's and said, "Of course, we will go with you! We were just fucking with you."

Nestor burst out in a roaring laughter, taking everyone off guard. Axius turned his face to him, blaring his nostrils, clenching his jaws as if a silent hate had eaten his face.

Manius turned to Opiter through the laughter from the men in the yard. "We will need to secure the release of the Dacian prisoners in Rome as Vasiliki demands. I need your help to approve that."

Opiter froze, his eyes meeting Manius's. "I cannot. It is too late."

"They are dead?"

Opiter shook his head. "They are not there, Manius…"

Axius marched over to them, his face lighting upon his father's, glancing at Nestor, who had stopped laughing. The courtyard became silent again, and the Dacian warriors dispersed to clean the yard.

"They are gone." Opiter sighed.

Axius cackled. "There is no way they could have escaped. Titus and I would have been first to hear about it."

"When did this happen?" Nestor asked.

"The day of the circus. The guards tracked them to the Tiber River, but with the animals that escaped and the bear loose in the city, the chaos made it worse. To this day, the bear has not been captured again, to my knowledge."

"How many Dacians were there?" Axius asked, wiping the sand off his armor.

"Three," Opiter confirmed.

"I thought there were several of them?" Manius questioned.

"There were. But my wife, a diplomat in the Senate, convinced the emperor to let most of them go to maintain relations between Rome and the tribal leaders on the Danube. It has yielded us much wealth in gold and silver, helping to fund these wars."

Axius side-eyed Nestor and raised a curious eyebrow, huffing. "She did? Very well. At least they were freed. I would say the last three followed them into the wilderness."

Opiter huffed. "Perhaps."

"Any evidence on how they escaped?" Nestor wondered.

"They did not escape. They were set free. Someone besides the guard had a master key and let them go during the chaos of the circus." Opiter worried. "There were no signs of a struggle or anything, and the guard's testimony revealed they had left only for the shift change. The shift lapse was twenty minutes."

Axius narrowed his eyebrows. "This is very concerning."

"When did your wife negotiate the other's freedom?" Axius wondered.

Opiter thought a moment, leaning his back against the wall. "Six months ago, I believe? She has been traveling with her guards and other leaders in the Senate to the outpost on the Danube to help delegate peace talks with the tribes there."

Nestor clenched his jaws.

"Where is your wife now, Opiter? Anna, is it?" Manius asked.

Opiter's face lit up in a smile. "Yes, Anna should be home in a week or two. Between my responsibilities at the Senate and her travels to the keep the peace between Rome and Dacia, we stay busy, my friend. But it is lovely to come home to this." He raised his arms and took in a deep breath.

"Very well. May I set a time for dinner for us to discuss the tribes?" Manius begged. "My villa. I am happy to host you both."

"Certainly! We will both be traveling into Rome for our duties once she returns, mind you. We will have a few days' rest, but I will see you in the Senate, and we can plan from there." Opiter cheered.

"Perfect." Manius chirped.

"Now come! I am famished, and you must all rest before traveling in the morning."

"We will be leaving tonight. We will be trading horses with your own." Nestor demanded.

The men froze and turned to look back at him. Moskin and Tarbus approached them. Opiter widened his eyes. "Of course, of course. I have some of the finest steeds in all of Rome. After this long journey, do you not want to rest?"

Nestor bit his tongue. "No. We must leave straight away."

Axius turned to Tarbus, who had joined the other Dacian warriors. "You head home to your family, Dacian?" Tarbus questioned.

Nestor started to climb the steps ahead of everyone. "The beasts are on my lands already. I need your help, you and five of your men, my brave Dacians, to guard them while I go with Axius."

Brasus turned his head to Moskin and Tarbus, their eyes following Nestor.

"The beasts are here already?" Brasus scoffed.

He turned to Tarsus. "Prepare the men. Now it is time. We

leave with Nestor and the weak Roman."

Axius scoffed at them. "Weak? Hey."

Moskin and Tarbus nodded and marched away into the fray of the Dacian warriors. They were at the back of the wall, slinging blades into bullseyes to tell them they would need to clean up quickly and ready themselves for the journey. Nestor knew he would have to wait until they were all ready.

The men followed Matunaga behind Nestor back up the cliff steps from the yard overlooking the sea. Below them in the yard, the Dacian warriors strapped their Falx's to their shields and prepared their weapons for the coming carnage. It would be a long ride to Nestor's, but this was urgent.

When they reached Matunaga's study, Axius watched him pull a leather pouch from a wall hook and start filling it with books, maps, and other things.

"You are coming?" Axius questioned. "I assumed you would remain the tower recluse." He tossed his arms in the air as if showing off the fine tower room, smiling, his eyes twinkling in mischief.

"I do not leave them behind. You may be taking the bulk of them into Dacia, but if five stay at Nestor's, I stay also. We will return once the danger has gone."

Axius glared at Nestor, but all Nestor did was roll his eyes. "If that is the price I must pay for my family's protection, so be it."

Opiter watched Matunaga pack his things. "I will leave for Rome once my wife has returned from the Danube. We will catch up then. We shall take Manius up on his offer."

Matunaga agreed with him. "Yes, that will be good. Perhaps by then, we will have more information regarding these beasts."

Axius stood beside Nestor, watching Matunaga pack strange books and more parchments. Their hearts beat wildly as a sudden urge to get out of there hit them.

An hour later, Opiter waved them goodbye from the stoop of his grand entrance. The night would be falling soon. He watched the Dacian warriors gird in their leathers and red cloaks blow behind them on his fastest stallions. Axius was in the lead with Nestor, and Manius and Micah were hunched down low on theirs to keep up, too. Matunaga's sea-blue cloaks blew behind him as if a river of hope spilled among walls of blood.

And something was coming indeed.

Axius turned his head to Nestor, the others flowing behind them. "The warriors were not released to Vasiliki."

Nestor agreed. "She penned that just last week? If they were released six months ago, Vasiliki would not be demanding their release, would she?"

"No," Axius mumbled.

"My family is in grave danger, brother," Nestor mumbled, clenching his jaws.

Axius agreed.

They raced as dusk fell and stars twinkled overhead, their hearts on Nestor's family and whatever lay in wait for them in the darkness.

14

When the Darkness Comes

Troy readied his bow, an arrow plunked against the thread, ready. He followed Mel, who held her longsword in her strong left hand and her short gladius gripped in the palm of her right. Behind them, a yard away, Liam followed. He has his bow and arrow ready and a spear shaft sticking up from his sheath on his back. They were doing as Nestor had told them, staying three by three but cautious.

The horses were getting edgy, their deep moans echoing higher the closer they approached the woods by the stables across from the estate. Nestor did not want anyone on the farm until he returned. So that meant whatever was stalking the farm would not kill innocents, hopefully.

Troy froze on the narrow wooded trail, the fog fingering his boots. He stepped in a hole and froze, pulling back out of it as he noticed the paw print.

"Stop. Shhh."

Mel joined him and glared at it, clenching the hilts tighter in her grasp. She eyed the trees, the forest, and the road and then glared through the fog back at Liam, who had stopped moving. Her eyes focused on his shadow, which seemed to loom and rise midair through the fog. When his head punctured the milky apparition, blood was spewing from his mouth, and his eyes were already rolled back in his head.

Behind him, a black shadow loomed and rose higher above the fog. Pointy ears punctured it as if black daggers had come to life. Troy turned his back to Mel and fired through Liam's body. The arrow tip made a kerplunk echo into the beast's stomach.

The beast dropped the body, growling at them, its fangs shimmering against the dusk moving in. It snarled, its white eyes melted in yellows, dagger-like fangs splayed a grimacing snarl. Mel started breathing heavily, backing up.

"Now we run." She whispered.

Troy readied another arrow and fired it, but the beast lunged at them. The arrow plunged into its shoulder and out its back, making it pause its attack on them. Troy readied another arrow and aimed.

"Too late to run!" He yelled.

The beast lunged in at them again, only this time Troy and Mel held their breaths. Mel stood aside Troy as he fired an arrow directly into its gaping mouth and then dropped the bow to pull his gladius. The beast's elongated muscular arms stretched out at them, its dagger-like claws dislodged to shred them apart. It howled a ferocious gut-punching wretch as if something ancient had awakened, made them quiver at the knees.

Mel gritted her teeth and ducked below Troy as the arrow lodged out the back of the beast's throat. She pressed into it with her longsword, slashing across its stomach and hollering, putting her weight into the blade. She felt a hard press on her leg as the flesh ripped in splits under her trousers and belted out a scream in pain. Its forceful thrust tossed her midair against the trees.

Troy was knocked back on the road as the beast flailed upon him. It ripped into his shoulder as the claws sunk in, and he hollered, pushing the gladius blade through the body at his chest. The beast stopped flailing at him and jumped off him yards away on the path, abandoning the attack. Mel pulled herself out of the trees where she had been slammed and rushed to Troy, who gritted in pain.

"You got it." He pointed at Mel's bloody long sword. She pointed at his.

"And you. It got us both." Mel gripped the bleeding slash on her upper leg and gritted her teeth.

Troy gazed at his gladius, blood dripping off it to the hilt. "I felt it stab through it. Come on, finish it off."

Mel helped pull him up, and they readied their swords, meandering closer to a wadded-up dark body on the road now lying still. The growls became more like whispers as they approached until there was silence. Where pools of dark blood had once been, the fluids changed into bright red the closer they approached it.

"What is that." Troy pointed at the human body they had gored together, an arrow still plunked through its mouth out the back of its head.

"This is worse than we feared," Mel whispered.

Mel gazed down at the naked man they had gored to death, blood dripping from their faces from scratch marks and injuries on their legs and arms. Another roar echoed through the farm, and they jerked their heads toward it past the stables. They started hearing screams and yells.

"Another one." Troy went back and picked up his bow. "Hurry!"

Mel followed him past the body on the road toward the other screams, limping on a hurt leg as fast as she could go, both desperate to get to the others.

As they left the body, the pupils rolled back into place and followed their boots as they marched away. It yanked the arrow out of its mouth and popped its jaw. It popped its neck as it stood up, snarling, its fangs protruding again. The holes in its chest and stomach healed over, sealing as if bloody fingers were pulling it back together. Its eyes glossed into a yellow aura, and its neck craned to follow the hunters in the wood.

In the almond grove, the fog had not lifted as Raoul hoped, but the sun was setting into violet crimson before him, and he relished in the beauty of this farm. He had picked the remainder of the roses and wildflowers in the fields and trudged through the gnarly tree-lined wood road in the groves.

Nestor loved the rose-flavored olive oils, and Raoul was the expert at making it for the business. The trees stretched over him like fingers, and he admired the strength and solitude of this beautiful farm he was privileged to work in and call home.

He pulled the wicker baskets tighter against his back and walked through the fog until his sandals felt sticky and wet. A strange smell ate at his innards, and he felt ill suddenly. He glared down, stopped walking, and realized he was standing in pools of blood. He froze as his eyes followed the blood trail and entrails to a tree. Above him, deep claw marks slithered down at his face. His knees became shaky.

He peered around the tree to a mass of shredded flesh that used to be a human body and dropped the baskets. He turned his head as familiar voices screamed at him to run.

Troy fired an arrow past Raoul's head, and it hit with a loud thud coming at him behind the tree. "Run Raoul!"

As he ran away from them toward the estate, the petals of flowers spilled out, mingling into the blood and blowing across the road. As he rushed past the tree where Troy fired, Mel lunged forward with her long sword and pressed into a black beast lurking.

Raoul ran through the fog toward the estate. He did not look back, but Mel's and Troy's screams rang in his ears. All he remembered seeing was a black beast towering over them, barring fangs and claws as it growled and a snout snarling in seething anger.

He remembered hearing another beast come up behind them and Troy's arrows plunking into flesh as fast as he could fire them. He heard other voices of the hunters rushing into the grove to help Mel and Troy. But the screams from them all rang in his ears, too. When he heard a third roar from another beast, his heart fluttered his chest to death.

He heard Mel and Troy holler at one another, but the others' screams drowned out their words. He hoped they were running.

Behind him, shredded to pieces, were bodies. He could not determine who they were. He remembered bows shattered along the ground and swords planked into trees. An arrow was sunk into the tree over the mass of flesh as if someone had tried to save them but could not. The tree-lined glen in the grove looked like a blood war had opened the pits of hell.

His master's wife and their children were in danger, and he had to get to them now. He should have stayed home as Nestor had warned him to.

Domitia and her five girls sat around the table in their dining room, enjoying fruit and fresh bread as an evening snack. Domitia smiled at them as each had their teapot and fancy little flowery cups, and they took turns pouring tea for each other. She had been unusually restless today and had lost her appetite. She wished Nestor was home. It had been a long day, and she was tired but could not rest.

When she thought she would have tea with her daughters, Dia barged in. "Raoul." Her eyes were wild and full of tears.

Domitia lunged up. "Aurora, Venus, watch your sisters."

Aurora and Venus stopped pouring tea and watched their mother lunge out of the room into the main hall at the front entrance.

Venus gazed out the expanse of windows and watched the fog roll in on top of the road, stretching like fingers over the rock walls. It was getting dark outside, too. As the sun set lower, the crimson tides from its aura shattered through the fog between the trees, and she saw a black shadow move within it.

Domitia froze as she rounded the corner, covering her mouth with her hands. Raoul stood shaking, blood splattered on his feet clear up to his knees, his robes ruined. He cried.

"My lady, forgive me, but I found a body, many bodies. I think it was the hunters. There is nothing left in the Almond grove."

Dia swallowed. "Oh no."

"Did you see any others?" Her voice cracked.

"Mel and Troy were fighting them. Fighting beasts! I am not sure." He wiped his face with his shaky hand. "Others were coming to their aid."

"Dia, has anyone reported in yet?"

Dia shook her head. "None. The food is not touched. I just came from there as Raoul came in."

"They should have been reporting in by now three by three." Domitia worried.

"Raoul, did you see anyone else keeping guard outside? By the mills? By the courtyard entrance?" Domitia demanded.

Raoul nodded his head and dropped it, his shoulders slumping. "No. No one. I feared for you and the children and ran here. Although

Nestor will kill me when he knows I have disobeyed his orders to stay home. Forgive me."

"They were ordered not to leave their posts, so something happened to them. Have we been watched all day?" She pondered.

Domitia huffed. "Where is your wife? Is she home?"

"She is visiting her mother with the children in Rome." Raoul shook.

"Good. You are not leaving this house! Understood? We are heading to the cellar." Domitia commanded.

Dia took Raoul by the shoulders and led him down the hall to the cellar. "Come, come with me. Hurry."

Domitia ran to the front entrance and pushed the wooden slab across the lock, pinning the double oak doors shut. She then raced into the dining room. Her daughters did not acknowledge her as stood wide-eyed, staring out the window as the fog moved in. She pressed around them to shut the right-side wooden shutter. As she began to shut the other to lock it, she paused.

"Girls, let's…" She watched the shadow linger closer through the fog and froze.

It lurked. It was something not human. It came through the darkness at the edge of the woods across the street. She heard the horses screaming in the stables. Her heart stopped beating. She glared at it, her eyes following its towering frame. As the darkness from the coming storm moved in, her girls watched in silence.

"Cellar. Now." She whispered, her voice shaking.

The creature lingered at the opening of the wood, and it was then she noticed the ears standing upright on its elongated head, and a thick, broad skull with dark eyes. The trees looked like brutalized sticks against the massive muscular body this beast portrayed.

She lunged the shutter shut and locked it, gathering her children and lugging the four-year-old in her arms. They ran down the hall to where Dia and Raoul had gone. Aurora pulled the five-year-old Clelia by her hand, and together, they ran down the long corridor until Dia met them at the bathroom entrance.

"What is it!" Dia yelled, picking Clelia up in her arms.

"Hurry!" Domitia yelled.

Raoul helped her with the children. Together, they rushed with the children past the bath hall to the back of the house, at the kitchen entrance.

"Where are the hunters?" Dia breathed hard as they reached the kitchen.

"I do not know; something is very wrong." Domitia worried. "Someone should have been back by now!"

The youngest started crying as they ran through the kitchen to get to the cellar. Luna clutched Domitia. "I want papa." She cried.

"Shh, it is okay, my darling. It is okay. Papa is on his way."

They froze in the kitchen against the long island, the open windows to the backyard blowing in screams from the woods. The three cooks stood against the ovens, clutching knives in their palms, sweat dripping down their faces.

"We've been hearing sounds, screams..." One cook stuttered. "We've locked the windows except this one, so we can see if someone needs in."

Domitia thanked them. "Good, because I have no idea if anyone out there can make it here alive. I wish Nestor were coming tonight." She bit back her tears, glaring around the expansive room.

The brick haven known as the kitchen engulfed them in a fortitude of safety, and the rounded ceiling rose above them, the wooden beams brimming with drying herbs and baskets full of bread and goodies.

Raoul pointed to the window. "Someone is coming now! Good, they made it!"

Domitia craned her neck to see two of them hobbling together, soaked in blood, their long swords drawn. "Open the door! Let them in."

She then turned to Dia and her children. "Cellar now." The cook rushed across the kitchen and pried open a two-foot-thick stone door that led down steep steps into a brick-lined cellar. The cellar opened into a vast expanse of storage space, with tables and tons of wine stacked against the walls. The stone path leading down was curved and only wide enough for one person at a time, so the beasts could not fit down there or follow them.

Dia led the children down, taking the youngest in her arms, with Raoul following behind the children. He grabbed a lantern and handed it to Venus, and Aurora also took one off the wall also to follow Dia down.

Domitia stood at the entrance, the cold blast of air blowing her dark braids loose from her head, where they spilled down her shoulders. She watched the servants open the door as two hunters barged in, falling to the floor together. The cooks slammed the door shut again and locked it. Domitia recognized Mel and Troy immediately.

"There are three of them. They are killing us in the fields. The others did not make it, did not make it." Troy breathed out, grasping at the bleeding claw marks on his leg and forearms. Domitia swallowed.

"Three of them!" Domitia feared. "Why here! Why now!"

"Get in the cellar, like Nestor said! We can fight them off from here." Mel ordered.

"Yet Nestor and the others will not be back til tomorrow." Domitia turned to head into the tunnel.

"Do you think there is anyone still…" Domitia's tears fell down her cheeks.

Troy shook his head, his blue tattoos now showing on his bloody shoulder. "No. Everyone else is dead. A few came to help us when Raoul was in the glen, but they did not…"

Troy pulled another arrow from his back sheath and readied it at the window, bracing himself on the thick brick ledge. "They will not die this way. We killed one. It came back for us. The others are the reason we are alive."

"Chop off their heads." Mel blurted in, wiping the blood off her chin. "It is only way." Her thick accent echoed.

"Can we risk getting that close to them again, two on three? We can take one, yes. But three of them on us, we are dead." Troy warned her.

He turned back to look at Domitia. His face was scratched hell, and a gash across his scalp bled down the back of his head, his thick black hair drenched with sweat and blood.

"We fought with all we have. We are not enough against these beasts, even one of them, but three, too much."

"Nestor trained you well," Domitia added, her eyes tearing up.

Mel side-eyed Troy and sighed. "We are Dacian. We have seen these beasts before. The others were trained to kill them, yes, but it was not enough. Not enough."

"Nestor will skin us alive if we let anything happen to you and the children. Go to the cellar." Troy warned her, clenching his jaws.

Domitia motioned for the three cooks to follow her. As she let them pass, they rushed down the steps, their flowing aprons swishing at their knees. Domitia turned to follow them. When she got halfway down, she turned back on the narrow steps to watch Mel push the thick door shut, grunting with all her strength. The sound of the door grinding on the stone floor clawed her nerves.

Where light had once been, Domitia was now in darkness. All she remembered was the look on Mel's face of pain and sorrow and the blood dripping from her leg injuries that needed stitches.

She turned and headed down, taking her youngest in her arms aside Dia and nodding to the others who stood restless, listening intently. The candles lit throughout the room melted a softness from the glow of the lanterns, filling the darkness of the great room with warmth.

"Mama, when is Papa coming?" Aurora asked.

Domitia placed her palm atop her head and held her face. "He is coming. Soon. Do not worry. It will be alright."

"Axius will kill them!" Diana, the seven-year-old, exclaimed. She pretended she held a sword and was killing them.

Domitia understood. She pressed her head into her little ones, closed her eyes, and prayed the men came back soon, ready to fight. She feared it would take a small army to kill these beasts, who had already killed many of her people today.

She suddenly realized she had neglected to tell them of a fourth beast lurking by the road across the manor, but it was too late because Mel would not open the door.

Mel stood against the elongated waist-high table, tightening a strip of cloth around the torn skin above her knee. She grunted in pain. Troy craned his neck back at her and sighed.

"Darkness comes. They are stronger in the darkness."

Mel agreed. They hobbled to the elongated window and peered out, the bottom of the window meeting their chins. The walls were over four feet thick and solid, but an uneasy nervousness filled the breadth of their hearts.

"Yes, and Nestor and Axius are not coming back til tomorrow. You have ideas in case the beasts come at us at once?"

Troy pulled his arrows and laid them out on the table, knocking over a bowl of apples. He had twelve left. "This is all I have. You?"

Mel pulled her long sword. "This is it for me. Lost my gladius."

Troy nodded and pulled his long gladius. "Yeah, I still have mine. If we survive this night, remind me to get Axius to raid the armory for us."

Mel scoffed. "Fuck the Roman armory. I want Dacian weapons and armor." She raked a bloody hand over her tightly braided head. Some of them had fallen loose and hung like snakes down her back.

"I'd take the curse to defeat these fuckers." She mumbled. "But then I would die, so, never mind."

Troy gasped at first but then glared down at the claw marks on his thigh, still bleeding. They had both been clawed but not bitten. He ripped a shred from his tunic and tied it around his leg, grunting in pain. A wind blew in through the window, and his eyes went up to the high ceiling and the ropes hanging down where baskets used to be.

"Stand atop the table and get the ropes down. I have an idea."

Mel glared back at him as she pulled the double-arched doors shut to the kitchen entrance and pushed the plank slab lock across both doors. The doors were a foot thick, but she questioned how pinning them all in the kitchen would stop the beasts from bursting through regardless.

Mel pulled herself atop the table and did as Troy asked, pulling down the hemp ropes from the beams with the tip of her sword. Troy gathered them in his lap, waiting on her.

"Our best chance is to stay hidden and silent until Nestor returns," Troy whispered, leaning back into the window and peering out into the silence. He glared into the darkness melting in the courtyard, the gate wide open. As the wind blew against it, it creaked and cried as if it were alive while beating against the stone wall. He noticed blood smeared on the wall to the gate.

Mel pressed her back against the wall, swallowing, blood dripping down her face. Troy met her gaze. "When they come, we must cut off their heads. We will have mere moments to do this together."

She gazed at him, clenching her jaws, nodding. Troy reached over and grabbed her hand, their blood smearing in one another's palms. "It has been an honor to serve with you, my friend, no matter what happens." His eyes roved over her face as he sighed.

Mel smiled, tears in her eyes. "An honor."

She snickered at the mounds of rope in his lap. "What are we doing with those?" She questioned, her eyes wide and bright.

Troy smiled at her, but then a roar echoed from the stables, and they heard the horses screaming. Then another one, but that one came from the almond grove. The third roar reverberated off their spines and sent chills through their soul, and Troy raised back up to peer out into the darkness.

He questioned the beasts' motives. "How long have you beasts been here, and why do you come to a Dacian?" He whispered to himself, clenching his jaws as shadows began to linger past the gate at the wall.

15

The Deceit

Opiter had watched his mercenaries race into oblivion with Axius and the others, his fist clenching the robes at his chest. The double entryway doors were still blasted open, the sea breezes pelting through his seaside estate as if silent storms burst to life. A shadow emerged from the end of the hall, lingering at first but then stopped in the darkness, gazing upon his backside.

"You did well remaining hidden, my love."

"They did not know." Anna's voice echoed.

Opiter turned to face her, smiling. "No, they did not, my love."

Anna emerged from the shadows, her curvy form kissing his brute body with her brown eyes. Opiter turned to stare at her. His wife, twenty years younger than him, was petite but full-figured and robust. Her blonde hair hung down her back, and she was only draped in a blue robe to cover her nakedness. Luring him. She was good at tempting him, and Opiter always fell for it.

"Were you successful in Dacia?" He commanded her.

"I see you were successful with the Dacians. Now they will go to him. Perfect, darling." She purred.

Anna allowed her robe at her left shoulder robe to fall, revealing milky white skin and a curvy shoulder to him. Opiter held his breath and walked closer to her. "Because we must ensure you are successful with Fen to..." He paused, watching her hand slide up his naked arm to his face, her fingers caressing his chin.

"...For the sake of Rome..." He froze.

"It's been weeks since I have kissed you." She begged.

Opiter rushed to her, pulling her close and planting a wide kiss on her mouth. "My brilliant wife." He whispered, leaving her mouth to suck on her neck.

"It's been a long journey, mere weeks, and I need to taste you." She whispered, backing up into the room aside from the entryway. "You know how I hate to be deprived of you." She ached.

Opiter followed her into the suite, anxious to slither out of his robes and get her out of hers, too. Anna smiled, biting her bottom lip, as her eyes explored his thick muscular frame under his robes. She would keep him busy in bed the next few days before they left for Rome.

She never did answer his question. She never planned to.

16

The Hunters Become the Hunted

When night came, it was pitch-out, like hope had been snuffed into an eternal darkness. This night seemed to fold in on itself, for even the moon had fled. Troy and Mel waited in the darkness, their breathing slow and steady, their bloodied bodies still aching from stitches they desperately needed. Their peering brown eyes focused on the wall at the back of the courtyard, where the gate had stopped swinging against it.

They dropped below the wall as the wind quit blowing, as if their gods and dreams had abandoned them. Troy gripped his bow with an arrow ready, waiting. Pointy tips of black ears rose through the darkness above them, and coal black eyes glistened at the window. Troy and Mel held their breaths. They had managed to stay hidden for hours, but not anymore. The beast rose past the window, breathing heavily and growling under its breath as if an ancient force had awakened from within it.

Now, it was time to face it.

Another grumble echoed through the silence, and their eyes went to the barricaded door at the end of the kitchen. It lurked down the hall at them. Its claws raked the stone floor, screeching like the sound of bats. A looming shadow paused there, stretching from under the crack in the door, prodding fingers to their boots. It stood there, breathing heavily, cornering them.

Mel gripped the rope knot she had made in her shaky palms, tied around her hands. She did not have time to eye her last-minute invention because something hit the door with immense force. The table they had pushed against it moved away from the barricade, and the foot-thick slab holding the doors shut cracked and splintered.

When it hit the door again, slivers of wood split from the slab and catapulted off like darting arrows. They jerked their heads to their left as the kitchen door heaved when a beast lunged against it. The arched window was too small for the beast to go through, so Mel sat upright and melted on one knee, staring at the kitchen door down the room. The slab split and the door gave way. A long snout sniffed the air in the room at them, snarling. Its fangs dripped saliva as it pressed its claws in at them. It belted out a roar that echoed through their heads.

Troy lunged forward as the door beside Mel gave way and smashed against the stone wall, busting into chunks of wood at them. His eyes focused on the broad, elongated head and gaping snout. As it lunged down onto Mel's head, Troy fired the arrow. It lunged into the beast's mouth and out the back of its head. It strapped it to remnants of the door against the wall.

The arrow catapulted it away from Mel, but still within paws of reaching her. It lunged a clawed fist in at her and swiped at her back. It flung her away from Troy toward the other beast that pushed its growling way in at them. Troy stood up and pulled his long gladius, gritting his teeth. He swiped at the beast's arm and cut it clean off as it pulled itself off the arrow to get him.

Just as the arrow protruding from the back of its mouth broke off, Troy lunged up and swiped at its throat, cutting its head off. The body flailed away from him at the door and melted down against the wall. But now the door was wide open, and they still had beasts to face.

Mel lost the rope grip as she flew across the kitchen in midair. She landed against the table on her back, her eyes raising to meet the beast whose eyes lighted upon her. It screamed a horrendous growl at her face, towering over her. It pressed harder against the door until its black claws pressed in, breaking the rest of the door slab in half over her.

She lunged away from it, crawling to get to the gladius she had dropped behind her. The beast belted in, pushing the rectangle table and Mel against the doors where the table lodged sideways in the kitchen against the walls. Mel pressed her foot into it, on her back facing the creature. Troy loaded another arrow and fired it, and the arrow lodged into its chest. It writhed back in pain, snarling.

It gave Mel seconds to scurry to Troy, but his eyes were now on the open door again, where the third beast beamed in at them. He did not have time to load another arrow, so he gripped his long gladius to face it. The beast at the door in front of Mel lunged in atop the table. Its black-clawed paws and fingers gripped the edge of it as if it were on a rock, climbing.

Mel dropped her sword and lunged forward at the rope she dropped, hollering as she picked it up and lunged back to the wall. She pulled on it with all her might as the beast jumped forward to get her. It screamed a howl and snarled, and Mel closed her eyes and pulled. She hollered while holding her breath against the wall.

The rope swung up from the wall and stretched straight across the kitchen wall to wall from the iron rings embedded in the stone. The beast saw the gleaming edge of a shimmering silver blade tied into the knots as it pursued her, and its head came clean off. It rolled to the door toward Troy, who readied himself, holding his breath and clenching his jaws at this beast who towered over him by several feet.

Mel opened her eyes and rushed to her gladius to help him but froze. Flickers from flame lights lit up the courtyard on the wall one by one, and suddenly, the darkness was bright again.

As the beast centered at the door, growling at them, an echo pinged outside from the courtyard. Her eye caught a shadow through the window, shooting through the air at it. She heard horses neighing and snorting outside and the familiar screams of Axius and Nestor.

Axius craned atop his horse, widening his eyes with Manius and Micah, who gasped in terror. Their faces fell to a pale white. The beast rose over the kitchen door and busted it through with one punch. Muscles riddled its body from its neck to its foot-wide paws. It stood like a man.

Axius heard Mel and Troy yelling, while another sound that was not human echoed from the kitchen and then abruptly silenced. But Mel and Troy were still yelling so that meant one beast was dead, yet it was in the house. Axius trembled for Nestor's family and the children.

Brasus and Tarbus had lit torches, and the light splattered across the wall from the front yard entrance. It warned the back of the beast in hues of reds and purples. Moskin jumped from his horse, pressing his longbow into the rocky earth, the spike securing it into the ground. He pulled the arrow back, the metal tip sparkling against the fires.

The beast froze when an arrow penetrated its stomach and came out its front. The silver tip craned open and revealed prongs like claws, so it could not tear it out unless its guts came with it. The beast turned to face its hunter as torch lights beamed, but it was too late. The rope attached to the sprawling arrow pulled the beast back out the door into the lit-up courtyard. The beast let out a bellowing howl as the shaft dragged it out. It clawed into the door frame, pulling chunks of the trim and metal hinges.

Axius watched the arrow catapult through the beast, the rope attached to it a steady line in the air. The Dacians pulled the beast out the doorway from the kitchen, where it grasped the threaded arrow at its stomach. The deployed metal prongs kept it embedded in the body. The beast howled and growled, its fangs barring a wide mouth under black eyes of malice.

Matanuga sat aside Axius, watching the terror unfold as the Dacians surrounded the beast, pulling their falxes and axes to hack it apart. Manius sat atop his horse, his eyes melting on Micah. "Beast!" Was all Micah could say, his eyes as wide as lemons. "A beast here, of all things."

Mel stood up, weakened, but Troy limped to the door and peered out. He leaned against the remainder of the door frame with Mel, relieved as Nestor had arrived with his mercenaries. The beast hurled growls at them and tried to lunge in, but the mercenaries surrounded it, taunting it before lunging in and cutting it into pieces. They took turns.

The beast would have done worse to them. Brasus pulled his long falx and reared up, slicing its head off. The body fell with a thud, black blood pouring from its missing limbs. Axius took note of its size, the hair on his arms raising. Nearly eight feet. Slender, yet muscular, just as the children had said.

But its eyes held no light, and Axius saw nothing but darkness. The claws on its paws where hands would be protruded like daggers, black and shiny. Sharp and long enough to rip a body to shreds in seconds.

The arms and legs were long, making the claws perilous and deadly. Axius held his breath, eyeing his short Gladius.

"They must all be killed." He mumbled. "With longer weapons."

Nestor agreed, lighting off his horse, his face contorted into an angry scream. "These are not the beasts of Dacia. These are smaller." He noted.

"Smaller?! What." Micah gasped.

Brasus cleaned his falx blade of blood on the back of the beast, glaring at him. "Half-bloods. These have been turned. Probably Romans."

Matunaga clenched his jaws, thinking. "So, it comes."

Mel stood aside Troy and melted into his chest, closing her eyes. He gripped her with a bloody arm, pressing his chin atop her head, and closed his eyes.

"Well done." Troy wanted to smile at her but could not. Instead, he pulled her in close to him, shaking. Mel gazed up at his eyes, tears falling. Troy kissed her forehead, and they stood there at the door in the darkness together, bleeding, their fingers still clutched to their weapons.

Nestor pushed against the massive stone door with Axius to open the cellar and screamed for his family. "My Loves!"

Axius heard the children scream, "Father! Father!" Their footsteps rushed up to meet him, but his eyes kept wandering back to the courtyard and the horrendous beast the Dacians had killed.

Nestor met his children on the steps and made them return to the cellar with him. "No, no! I am coming to you!" He turned to Axius and widened his eyes.

Axius gazed upon the bloody gore behind him. The family would need to stay there longer to clean the mess up. The bodies would need to be burned. The estate was no more than a bloody battlefield and smelled of rotting flesh.

"Axius, come!" Brasus hollered at him from the courtyard.

"Look." He pointed to the dead body, now a human.

The beasts had returned to their human form, and Axius did not recognize their faces. Anger burned inside him.

"What witchcraft is this evil," Axius mumbled.

Nestor pulled his children in his arms as Domitia cried atop them. "I came back as fast as I could, my loves!"

Aurora peered up the steps. "We heard the beast's father! We heard their howls, and then Mel and Troy fought them. They fought them!"

"They succeeded and are very brave and shall be rewarded!" Nestor smiled at his children.

Nestor stood up and pulled his wife into his arms. "Forgive me my beauty!" He kissed her, and she melted into his arms, crying.

"I feared the worst! Raoul says people are dead. Our people!" She feared.

Nestor took her face in his palms, and his eyes lit up with fire. "And the beasts will pay, I swear it."

"Mel and Troy saved us. Did you kill them all?"

"Three are dead, yes." Nestor sighed.

Domitia pushed off him, shaking her head. "There were four!" She hollered, tears falling.

Nestor craned his neck back up the steps. "Axius!"

Axius lunged down the steps, his eyes going from Raoul to the frightened cooks and then Dia. They were all petrified with terror, but the children were fierce and resilient. "Did I hear Domitia say there were four? Yet only three are dead."

Nestor growled, pulling his wife tighter into him. "Hunt it." Axius nodded, lunging back up the steps three by three.

Nestor peered over at the thin Raoul, whose face quivered in fear. "My friend, I am happy to see you alive."

"My lord, I, I saw many deaths." Raoul trembled.

"Did you see the beasts?" Nestor asked, still gripping his wife in his arms.

"I saw two, and the fighters, the fighters were losing. I ran as fast as I could to warn everyone."

Nestor sighed and closed his eyes. "Damnit."

Axius melted up the steps as Brasus met him at the edge of the wall. He leaned in, still gripping his falx, his leathers squeaking under his muscle-riddled body. "We tracked a fourth one, but it has left this place."

Axius clenched his jaws, narrowing his brows, pushing past him. "We must hunt it and kill it."

Brasus gripped Axius's shoulder and stopped him. "Moskin and Tarbus tracked it heading toward Rome."

Axius froze, glaring into his eyes. "What."

Manius entered the kitchen, sighing in disgust. Axius turned to him, who was returning to Rome with Micah in a few days, and his heart beat faster. He pushed Brasus's hand off his shoulder and turned to meet Manius at the door.

"Eh Roman!" Brasus hollered after him.

Axius craned his neck to glare back.

"The beast tracking stopped where the human tracks began, and then others joined it," Brasus warned him, glaring into Axius as if his soul was on fire.

Axius froze, a reckoning hitting him. "How many more?"

Brasus huffed. "Thirteen."

Axius thought a moment before pushing past his father. "Why do they hunt my brother from Dacia."

Brasus took a deep breath, his blue tattoos dancing around his face and neck. Manius glanced around the kitchen, sighed, and then froze as he looked at the headless bodies. "These change back to human after death, eh?"

Brasus nodded, flaring his nostrils. "Yes."

"Have they ever not changed back after death?" Manius questioned.

Brasus huffed. "Purebloods. Thank your gods these are not them."

Manius gawked at him. "Oh?"

"Pure bloods do not die unless they are beheaded. That means getting close to death yourself."

"Yes, but these were also beheaded, so what is the difference, Brasus? You must know." Manius questioned him.

Brasus gazed at the rope contraption that Mel had used to kill the beast with butcher knives tied in it, his eyes then meeting Manius's, his face clenched.

"Purebloods are bigger, more powerful, stronger, and faster. They do not pity mortals. The warriors here who defeated these were brave but were Dacian, and the gods were with them. Against a pure blood, even fifty of your best-trained Romans could not take one down."

Manius listened to Brasus and scoffed, his hands gripping his robes at this chest, thinking. "You think Rome is full of fools, Brasus?"

Brasus smirked, showing a dimple on his scruffy, tattooed face. "The purebloods do. Your emperor will keep sending men until Rome is decimated of them, and the beasts will take it."

"You think they mean to take Rome?"

Brasus slithered to Manius, gazing into his eyes at the same height, his jaws clenched. "They mean to take the world. They are already in Rome."

Manius let Brasus go by him, and then he ducked out of the kitchen to escape the stench, his heart beating his chest to death and chills rushing up his spine.

17

The Quest Begins

"It's a full day's ride to the Po River." Manius prepared his satchel while side-eyeing Axius. Nestor and Domitia had paused briefly to listen to him but then went on about filling Nestor's pack with rations and weapons. They stood as whispers in the massive dining room, as the cooks had emptied the kitchen until it could be cleaned of blood.

The gardens and properties in the groves were a mess of riddled bodies, and blood spilled on the lanes to the vineyards. All but five horses survived. Fires rose over the trees as bodies had to be burned quickly and blood cleaned up from the kitchen. Nestor made his family and the others stay in the cellar until daybreak so they could get the remains out, and wash the blood from the floors and walls with buckets filled of lemon vinegar and water.

Axius helped repair the kitchen door from the outside, fastening new hinges and planks. When it was cleaned, Domitia walked the children to a study suite upstairs, where they could play until the manor was cleaned. Dia set about bringing the children food and watching them so Domitia could be with Nestor. The cooks were once again busy in the kitchen, the roaring fires ready to feed everyone.

Manius continued. "We have an outpost there. Titus would not have traveled past it yet. He will be with his son, Honus, at the settlement before continuing to Dacia. I own multiple Liburnas at the port. They are small and fast. There will be less scrutiny of our journey there since it is so isolated."

Axius stopped and turned to face him. "You are not going old man."

Manius huffed at him. "Micah and I are joining you there and will return to Rome from there. I need to get Opiter to join me there with his wife."

Axius sighed. "Traveling alone with a Scribe while beasts are on the road, father. Do not do that." He warned.

Manius signed. "I have no choice, son. There are greater risks here than me dying on the road to Rome."

Axius wanted to yell something, but Manius kept talking.

"With the Dacian mercenaries, you will cross the Adriatic Sea at its most northern point into the Sava River. It will take you to the Danube. You will have a mere four days' head start at this route before Titus and the army reaches the plain at Vasiliki's kingdom unless he allows the army a brief rest. Knowing him, it will not be a long rest."

Nestor paused, staring at him. "By boat the whole time."

"The boat is small. You can hang your head over the side." Axius teased him.

"I hate boats," Nestor murmured.

Domitia froze. "Yet, according to our maps, Manius, they will be in enemy territory while coasting down the Danube toward the Black Sea. You know our outposts do not reach that far."

Manius stopped. "Yes. I am aware. That is where Nestor, Brasus, Moskin, and Tarbus come in. Axius will also have Dacian weapons and attire to blend in with the tribes there."

Axius turned to Manius. "Leaving the rest here to protect Nestor's family? Wise choice."

Nestor nodded. "Yes. Ten are staying here. Once Vasiliki approves of us, and she will, since we are bringing her famed generals back to her, we will send the others back if they wish once we return."

Axius grimaced.

"I do not doubt their ability to protect you both. However, attacks have always happened on land, not by water. Going by boat will be silent, much faster." Manius bragged.

Domitia took a deep breath and bit her lip. "They are still out there, yet you return to Rome." She complained at Manius. "I wish you would listen to Axius. You are not safe in Rome." She chirped.

"No soul is safe anywhere, my dear," Manius warned her.

Nestor turned to her, clenching his jaws. "No one is safe in Rome."

"I fear for you, my love," Domitia whispered.

"I have no choice. After revelations by Opiter, I must do this. Rome is in grave danger, to the brink of destruction, if these beasts continue to roam our lands."

"I know Nestor does not approve; however, I would prefer you and the children stay with me," Manius told her. "I have Rome's finest guarding my home as is. I do not want to leave you all."

"Rome's finest will die first before a Dacian lets them take them." Nestor grimaced. "Even ten Dacians will survive over a hundred Romans."

Manius clenched his jaws at him.

Nestor took her face in his palms and kissed her forehead. "We have the best Dacian warriors to protect you and our children. Troy and Mel survived, didn't they?"

Domitia signed. "Yes. They saved our lives. Yet they are the only survivors, Nestor."

"They are the only Dacians skilled in fighting the beasts. The rest were Romans. I was foolish to have left you here with so many Romans." Nestor grimaced.

Axius turned to face him, his eyes watering. "Do you think me a fool?" Axius questioned him. "Do you have no faith in Rome or our brothers who bleed for it?"

Nestor turned his face from him. "I fear for you greatly. I fear for you all. Even as skilled as Romans are with the blade. Do not take offense to me. I need you to stay alive. You will see differently once we reach Dacia, and the beasts come face to face with you."

Axius turned away from him and marched out of the room, his boots beating the long hall to the entryway. Manius watched his son go, feeling the weary contempt of his shoulders slumping in defeat. Domitia sat down in a chair, crossing her arms.

"When will you all return then?" She fretted.

Manius cleared his throat, picking up his cloak off the table. "It is a sixteen-day journey, fraught with peril. Titus will take longer to get there on foot because he goes to Honus first. It may be months, Domitia, as we are beginning Autumn. I do not want to risk them traveling the Danube in Winter. I am sorry."

Domitia sunk in the chair, thinking. "And if we are attacked again? If the ten left here with Troy and Mel are dead?"

Nestor turned to her, watching as Manius left the room, ignoring them. "If the Dacians are all dead, Rome is dead soon after. You know to gather the children and go back into the cellar til dawn, and then take the children with any survivors out of the country as fast as you can. To keep running to stay alive."

Domitia raised in the chair to accept his loving embrace, her eyes melted down the hall to where Manius had gone.

Manius marched down the hall into the entryway, pausing at the doors. They were still busted open, and shards of wood planks were strewn all over the room, so the house was wide open. Servants and carpenters worked tirelessly to clean up the manor and the grounds and rebuild the doors. The land was busy with hammers and metal experts crafting new hinges to secure the home.

Manius stepped outside and gazed at his son, who was tending his horse in the front yard. Thracian voices echoed in the morning from over the wall past the courtyard, and he knew the Dacians were preparing for another attack. He noticed one had climbed a tall olive tree and was fastening some rope contraption and a pulley between it and several other trees in the grove. There were three more on the roof above him with two ballistae, and Matunaga was working with them to secure them to the roof.

Axius did not acknowledge Manius. His red robes wafted behind him in the morning breeze, his black hair shiny and spiked atop his head. Axius turned his face to see his father walking toward him. Manius noticed the shadow of Axius's beard casting darkness across his unshaven face, and under his eyes were black rings.

Manius paused while Axius lowered his head to the saddle and slowly back up again. "We go to these beasts to save Rome and the world. Titus, who is like a father to me, is in harm's way, and yet I am told I am not strong enough to fight even one of these cursed beasts." Manius felt the deepness of his son's voice as if a dam had busted loose.

Axius turned to face him, his eyes hard, his cheekbones clenched. "I can fight bears and tigers and kill them for Rome. These beasts are no different. They are cowardly; they are still beasts. A sword and spear can kill anything living."

Manius felt chills rush up his spine. "Titus has trained you well to kill animals, yes."

Axius swallowed. "No matter their size or strength, I will kill them all. Rome will not fall." He stormed off toward the courtyard where Brasus and a few of the others were still burning bodies.

Manius watched him go, his innards beating his heart to death. "Oh, son." He mumbled.

Nestor glided up to him from the porch, eyeing Matunaga on the roof and perking his head to the carpenters securing the premises.

"I would send my family with you, Manius, but Romans are not ready to face the beasts yet. Please understand. I mean no disrespect for your position or household. I only want to see Rome survive the beasts."

Manius gripped the hems to his robes and signed, glaring at the direction Axius went. "No, Rome is not ready for this. You know how they were slaughtered at Auvergne. The beasts overtook them."

He faced Nestor and patted him on the shoulder. "I trust you to protect my son. There is no one else I trust more."

Nestor's eyes teared up. "He is my brother. He is an uncle to my children and a brother to my wife. We love him."

Manius swallowed. "Promise me you will bring him back alive. He is all that remains of my bloodline. I would so love to see him married with children one day."

Nestor huffed. "So long as he listens to me, he will remain alive. I promise you this on my life."

Manius shook his head. "You know better than that. So, I need you to keep him alive."

Nestor crossed his arms and glared at the front yard path Axius took, narrowing his eyebrows and huffing through his nose.

The Po River glistened in the twilight under a full moon. Autumn was coming. The beginnings of bitter winds were seeping in from the forest's darkness surrounding the small outpost marina. The river was engorged, and the banks overflowed to the tree lines, as Manius hoped. The river flooding would help his son and Nestor coast to the Adriatic Sea, with the tributaries seeping at the delta toward the end of the Po.

With winter soon coming after, Manius was questioning whether he would see them again until Spring. It may take them months to get into Vasiliki's presence, if they made it that far. He understood Nestor's reasoning for leaving the bulk of the Dacian mercenaries at his family's estate. The wrath of Nestor would be a rageful death for all involved if his family was harmed.

They had stopped at the outpost, boarding their horses. Axius and Nestor watched silently, along with Micah and the others, as Manius talked to the Roman caretaker. He whispered over the bar for moments before they both disappeared out the back entrance toward the river.

Moments later, Manius appeared and motioned for them to follow. They walked down a narrow path through the woods to the river, which opened to a vast expanse of a slew of ships floating tied to a long dock.

"Ah, there she is. Safe and sound." Manius pointed to the end of the dock, where an elongated shadow lingered on the water.

Nestor hopped onto it with bags in tow, tossing them atop the deck of the Bireme. The oared ship was small and long enough to hold ten men, with one set of imposed rows of oars on each side. It would achieve high speed, giving them time before Titus reached the Danube territory.

"You expect us to work the oars the whole time?" Axius scoffed.

Manius smiled, patting his son on the back. "Matunaga designed this vessel. It is a smaller replica of the Bireme's we use in war. It can be worked with ten men or less. With the winds, it will coast quickly without rowing. You will see."

Micah smiled. "Ingenious design! Matunaga never fails to impress."

Axius watched the men board the vessel and gazed at the moon before meeting his father's face in the moonlight. Manius cleared his throat.

"You will find Dacian weapons as you requested and clothing and leathers to blend in. You will look as the Dacians look, son."

Axius nodded, glaring at Micah. "You will watch him and not leave his side."

Micah nodded and bowed his head at Axius. "You have my word on my life." He promised.

"Very well. Stay safe, my friend." Axius hugged him, and Micah swallowed his tears back.

"You as well, Axius. Come back alive. I have a woman for you when you do." He smiled.

Axius scoffed. "I have yet to find a woman in Rome that could take my heart."

Micah smiled. "Oh, you will."

Manius smiled at them. "I want you to know that I am proud of you son. That your mother would have been proud of you. For all you do for Rome."

Axius took in a deep breath of air, half smiling at him. "I know, father." He leaned in and hugged Manius before jumping on the boat.

When he turned around, he boasted, "And I want you to know this was still my idea, so when we come back victorious, you know who will get credit." Axius smiled. "I love you also."

Manius widened his eyes and flared his nostrils, watching the boat sail away in the darkness under the cover of the moonlight. Micah giggled at him.

"The world may be ending, and Axius laughs at it," Micah noted.

Manius agreed. "His humor has saved him more times than I can remember. He hides great pain for the people he loves."

They stood there in silence, waving them off.

"I want my son to come back to me." Manius fretted. "I want Nestor to come back to his wife and children. They are all the family I have left in this world."

Micah agreed, his face paler since they arrived at the Po. "They are in the hands of fate now."

"Let us rest tonight. In the morning, we go back to Rome."

Micah clenched his jaws. "That is where the beasts have gone, Manius. I hoped you were kidding about returning, but here we are."

Manius pursed his lips. "Yes. I will need your subtle cunning to help me find the truth to protect Rome. We do, after all, have a traitor in the court. Which one, and how many are there?"

Micah swallowed. "Of course you will."

A long silence wafted between them before Micah spoke again. "Long gone are the days when I could read parchments of foreign languages to protect Rome. Now, all I get are perilous journeys of calamity and the torturous fear of sudden death by the beasts of Loki."

Manius patted him on the shoulder, nodding his head. "Yes. Come, it is time for wine."

Micah followed him back down the dock over the sparkling waters of the Po River. The moonlight cast their shadows like prickly fingers across the flooded sand bars as the dark shadow of a Bireme coasted further away from them toward the Adriatic Sea.

18

When the Beasts Come

Domitia had been subjected to the endless worries of her girls wondering about their father and Axius and the relentless downpour from the heavens. She sat at the table in the dining hall downstairs with Dia, her girls playing on the floor with their tea sets and dolls, and the whisper of worries dancing in their heads. Fog rolled in again, and Domitia wondered if they should return to the cellar down the hall.

The picture window gave them ample views of the farm and groves, but the rain splattering against the glass made visibility harder. Fog seeped in through the groves again, dousing the lands in a mysterious shroud of uncertain doom.

Raoul had been escorted back to his house earlier this morning, promising to stay put this time. Mel and Troy remained in the manor, and Domitia felt safer with them nearby. The carpenters had repaired the front entrance doors, barring them with thicker planks, and Domitia ordered everyone to keep it locked. Not that it would help if a beast came. If anyone needed to go into the manor, it was only accessible through the narrow kitchen door now via the courtyard.

Matanuga approached the dining hall, pausing at the entranceway to acknowledge Domitia. "I see the children are well cared for." He noted, his eyes bright.

Domitia started to say something but then froze, looking at him. He was dressed in inscribed leathers of the Dacian people, cuffs on his arms and legs, and a leather breastplate that seemed to melt into him. He had a sheath on his back and arrows protruding over his head. In his hand, he gripped a long Falx, his knuckles white. Strapped to his waist were short falxes and a long sword. The girls froze and stared up at him.

"You are a wolf!" Diana giggled.

Matunaga smiled down at the children, turning so they could see the white wolf Hyde and its head down his back. "Yes, indeed. If I pull this up on my head, do I look like a wolf?"

He pulled the skin over his head, and Domitia widened her eyes as his face melted into the face of a wolf, a long snout sticking out from his forehead, the ears upright on his head. "This skin will keep me dry in the rain."

"Wolves are bad." Aurora chimed.

Matunaga leaned down, pressing on his knees to face them. "Whether wolf or lamb, there is good and bad in everything. You will know by their actions they are evil, for they will not do what is right. Never forget this, little one." He patted her atop the head gently, standing up.

"You mean to go out there? With them." Dia marveled.

"I do. Stay close to the kitchen, little ones." He warned them. "Troy and Mel watch it, but they are still weak."

Domitia felt her heart beating faster, and she closed her eyes, wondering about Nestor. It was a long journey, and she feared for Nestor and Axius.

Matunaga wandered through the kitchen out the door, nodding to the cooks and Troy, who watched over Mel asleep on the cot. The cooks paused, gawking at him as he slithered by them, the wolf ears standing upright on his head and the elongated snout sporting fangs. They glared at one another as he exited the door, shutting it behind him and disappearing in the rain.

"Dacia has come." One of the cooks mumbled, chopping herbs.

The other cook scoffed. "As long as Dacia stays out there and does not interfere with my baking today, then we are good. I have work to do."

Matunaga pranced around the courtyard to the front yard out the gate, glaring through the rain at the Dacians left behind. He had them stay close to the manor and did not patrol the farms. They had fastened torches to the courtyard walls for light at night, and the fires were still burning off the bodies and horses of the carnage before. The rain threatened to put out the fires, so the mercenaries, ever watchful, stood under the manor's eaves surrounding the entranceways and courtyard entrances.

A ballista that could shoot three long-shafted arrows awaited to the side of the manor by the kitchen door. The pronged arrows would deploy once they hit their targets, erupting wide open and exploding limbs or organs. The Dacians had crafted these beast weapons based on Roman weapon designs.

He pulled himself up a ladder to the roof at the edge of the manor outside the entrance, where three Dacians waited in the rain. Their wolf headdresses made them look as if a pack had joined to scout out the beasts. The roof was flat except for the fireplace chimneys rising on either side of them, high enough to view over the lands in all directions. He investigated the arrow ballistas they had fashioned with the silver-pronged arrowheads, nodding in satisfaction. One was faced in each direction.

He melted his eyes behind him toward the courtyard, watching the forest. "They will come again. They want something." He whispered. "They want someone."

Troy and Mel had made cots in the kitchen and kept the fires going for the cooks. The cooks would continue to serve the family, even if they were required to stay in the house. Troy pulled lemon salve off the table again and bent down to Mel, who lay in her cot half asleep. Her head was bruised, her lip busted, but her defiance and resiliency proved to be as fierce as her fighting skills.

"Here, Mel." Troy gently pressed the salve on her forehead and then wiped the gashes on her leg. She grimaced, sighing.

"It burns." She complained, opening her weary eyes.

Troy smiled. "It is healing. It will help."

Mel watched him care for her, his face battered and bruised, too, his eyes as dark as the rings under them.

"You need sleep. Now is the time to sleep since the Dacians are here." She told him, the fire crackling behind his back and warming their achy bodies.

Mel grabbed Troy's hand, and he froze. "Promise me something. You will not let the curse take me if I am ever bitten. That you will…"

"Enough of that, Mel. Shhhh." He wiped her hand with the salve, the fragrant lemony scent tickling her nose, trying to keep her silent so the cooks did not hear her.

Mel stared at him, her eyes like fire, her jaws clenched. He put the salve back on the table and swallowed, meeting her stare.

"I promise. I will not let the curse take you." He assured.

Mel sighed. "Good. Now leave me alone and let me sleep."

Troy smiled down at her, shaking his head. He turned to face the fire, the warmth kissing his scruffy face. He closed his eyes, enjoying the solitude of the kitchen. The cooks continued chopping and cutting vegetables and making bread in silence. The rain beat on the patio and statue columns in the courtyard as if music was playing in the air. He walked to the narrow window and peered out into the fog, watching the torch fires getting snuffed out on the wall.

One of the cooks who was kneading bread froze, watching him. The others joined in silence, noticing his back growing stiff.

The torches sizzled and smoked until, one by one, it was darkness again, and all he could see was the endless fog and the outline of the courtyard wall past the patio and gardens. He gazed at the narrow kitchen door Axius had helped repair, noting the cast iron hinges were new and the strips of cast iron holding the planks were embedded into the stone wall. The planks were thicker but would only give them moments to escape if a beast burst through it again.

He turned his gaze back out the window and froze. A shadow moved through the forest past the wall on the hill. It lingered for a moment and then moved closer, its lanky form slender like the trees around it. He snarled his face and clenched his jaws, gripping the hilt of his long sword by his side.

"Here we go again." The cooks left their stations and pressed the stone door open at the cellar. Troy nodded at them as they disappeared below.

Mel opened her eyes to see Troy's backside as stiff as a board, and she slowly sat up, eyeing her weapons strewn at the end of the table. Troy turned to face her and began strapping on his leather cuffs again. Mel turned to pull the bell rope on the wall above her head, which vibrated down the hall outside and around the manor.

The Dacians stationed about the manor turned their ears as a single bell chimed, lowly and elegant, like a trickle of water in a calm pool. They turned their gaze to the wall, and their wolf headdresses pulled up to keep the rain out of their eyes. Their blue tattoos danced up their naked, bulging arms as they readied their arrows in their bows and waited in the darkness.

Matunaga and the three Dacians heard the bell warning. He stood amidst them, glaring through the rain toward the forest. "Be ready to strike. When they come, we must cut off their heads." He warned.

Three Dacians were planted high atop trees outside the courtyard walls at separate points on the farm facing the manor. The cover was enough to stay hidden, but not too much. They could still see below them on the trails through the orchards, and they were still within eyeshots of each other.

Below, as the fog covered the path, it swirled in anticipation. Heavy movement caught their attention, and they froze on the branches, waiting. Smoke filled the air, hot and heavy, as the fires from the burnings were snuffed out. They smelled rotted flesh with a tinge of malice in the air.

They noted one beast emerge from the dark of the forest. Its heavy presence slithered below them as if dancing with the rain but bringing with it cruelty. It rose above the fog with black eyes of coal. Its prickly ears stood upright on a long square head. Its snout snarled in silence as it stared at the wall. Its thin frame was accentuated by rivets of muscles running from its neck down its black, hairy back to its tail. It walked like a man, albeit spindly but tall and powerful.

The Dacians watched it snake toward the courtyard wall past the olive press. But then another one appeared from the forest under them. Followed by another. And another. They counted seven slithering together toward the wall, flanking each other in silence. The

Dacians gazed at one another from the branches, readying themselves with bows and arrows, their eyes wide.

The howling started from across the road at the horse stables. And another joined it. They counted twelve. They were surrounded. The three Dacians in the trees fired upon them from behind, the arrows plunging through the backs out the front. The ropes attached to the arrows catapulted the bodies back toward them, away from the wall they were climbing. They let out deep bellows of pain, echoing through the grove.

The pulleys yanked them straight back off the wall, jerking them in the air at the tree trunks so they were face-first with the Dacians. The metal-tipped arrows splayed on their midsections like fingers, and the gaping holes ripped them wide open. The beasts bellowed out howls, clawing at their midsections.

Two Dacians lunged around from the branches and sliced off their screaming heads with their Falxes, the bodies falling into the fog below. The third Dacian missed the first time, the beast scrambling to get a claw hold on the branches and succeeding. The Dacian gripped his Falx and swung, but the beast lunged away from the curved blade, only its fur at its chest getting slashed. The beast belted a roar and lunged into him as the Dacian twisted again to push the blade at its neck. As the Dacian plunged the Falx into its throat, it lunged forward and bit his forearm just as he sliced off its head.

The other two Dacians turned their ear to their comrade, hearing the bite, their hearts in their chest. They killed three, and the others had already crested the wall at the courtyard. They had to stop as many as possible to give Matunaga and the others a chance to use the silver-pronged arrows at them. The Falxes were long weapons, but not long enough.

Domitia stood, her knees trembling. Her girls froze on the rug. Dia dropped her goblet from her lips, her hand shaking. The howls sent shivers up her spine, and her heart felt frozen to her innards.

Troy and Mel froze when the howling started. It started as one, deep and bellowing. An oppressive hunger ate them from the inside out, like prey, knowing they were dying but had to run anyway. Troy turned to race down the hall to get Domitia and her children. They had no choice but to put them back in the cellar.

"Why do they come again," Mel whispered, following Troy down the hall.

"They are after someone." Troy feared, meeting Dia at the doorway with his sword drawn. "Nestor's family is being hunted!"

He reached the dining hall, gripping his long sword in his hand.

"Hurry. It is time!" He warned, watching Domitia pick up the youngest and gather the children around her.

They raced the family down the hall to the kitchen, the howling ringing in their ears. The howling was getting closer, and the rain beat in their hearts. They heard the Dacians yell out at the front yard by the entrance doors. The cooks yelled at the family to hurry up and join them in the cellar.

Matunaga froze atop the roof with the others, the chilling roars and spine-tingling howls growing closer as more of the beasts made themselves known. "They have us surrounded. They are hunting us." He warned.

The Dacians turned the pivot to ready the pronged arrow as the beasts began to crest the wall at the courtyard, where the kitchen door lay. They fired, and it jutted through a beast's guts and out its back.

They pulled the trolley lever until the beast was yanked on the ground through the mud and grass, straight toward the kitchen window. It roared helplessly, flailing its long limbs and clawing into the ground.

Troy watched the beast yelp, twisting and turning in pain until its face was in the window, growling at them. He readied his long sword while it pulled at the stone trim to keep from being yanked up to the roof. The children screamed as it snarled in at them. Just when Troy was going to slash its head off through the window, it was yanked upward violently away from them. It clawed the stone up to the roof, belting out its rage. It dug its claws into the clay tiles at the roof, gaping a growl at Matunaga as he met it face to face. He lunged in and shoved his Falx through its neck, severing its head.

Troy saw the legs and clawed paws stop twitching at the window, and then the head fell, followed by the body. "One down." He claimed.

Mel pushed the oldest twins down the stairs, followed by Domitia holding her youngest and pulling along Aurora.

At the front entranceway, five beasts rushed the Dacians from across the street in the woods. Matunaga watched the men fire another arrow, and they got one but did not have time to maneuver the other ballista. The Dacians would have to face them. He turned to them, the rain beating his cheeks. "Keep firing them! From both sides if you can."

He grabbed the rope left from the first pulley where he killed the beast and hoisted himself down to help the Dacians at the front entranceway. He landed on his feet, peering into the kitchen window. The children were still screaming, and Troy was trying to get them into the cellar.

"Watch the hall! They come to the entrance." He warned them and then disappeared around the bend toward the front doors.

Matunaga reached the corner of the manor toward the front entrance doors and was met with a beast lurking down at him, snarling. It lunged a long arm toward his head, snarling. Matunaga ducked, twisting around and slicing his long-curved Falx through the beast, cutting it in half. The blood and tissue splattered across his leathers and the corner of the manor, dousing the stone in black blood. The beast had shaved the hairs on the top of his wolf tunic with its long claws. Matunaga pressed over the body and met the Dacians, blocking their strikes with their long Falxes.

The Dacians were slicing into the beasts without being scathed themselves. They would lunge in at the men, and the men would follow them further away from the entrance during the attacks. Matunaga joined in fighting one, slicing its leg off, and when it landed, the Dacian cut its head off. Out of the woods, two more came throttling through together between the fighting and threw themselves into the doors, bursting them wide open.

"They have breached it!" Matunaga shouted.

Matunaga met long claws with his sword, his eyes now facing another beast, preventing him from following the two who breached the manor. Mel and Troy would be on their own again.

Five more beasts jumped over the wall, and Mel blasted over the table to grab a bow. "Here we go again." She complained.

From the courtyard, the three Dacians fired their arrows from a ballista they stationed at the corner. It shot three at a time but took time to load new ones. The arrows splayed through three of them, spreading apart like fingers and bursting their midsections into bloody pulps. As Mel was loading her bow, Troy watched the bodies fall.

"Three more down." Troy started to turn to help Mel fire upon them but froze, noticing Dia and Diana still in the kitchen. "Get down there!" He ordered them.

Dia was frozen with her back against them, grasping Diana in her arms. She shook as the beast loomed over them from the doorway, snarling and inching closer.

Mel kept firing upon them in the courtyard, the arrows and yells from the Dacians echoing outside. Troy rushed to Dia and Diana, firing an arrow over Dia's head. The arrow lodged through the beast's shoulder but did not deter it.

"Get down there now!" Troy screamed at them, gripping his long sword, tossing his bow, and pulling his Gladius.

The beast entered the kitchen, snarling at Dia, its eyes on Diana. Mel turned to see the commotion and began hollering. "No!"

She turned to fire upon it, her arrow plunking through its shoulder in the same spot Troy had hit it, not deterring it. It stepped back from the hits, but it kept coming. It snarled at them both, growling at their faces in anger, stretching its claws out of elongated black hairy fingers.

It walked upright like a man and hovered over them, its shadow stretching through the flames of the kitchen fire outside the window to the patio. Troy rushed to Dia, ignoring Domitia's screams begging them to come to the cellar. He readied himself to face it.

As he pushed to place himself between them and the beast, another beast lunged in behind it and drove itself into him. It catapulted Troy back against the kitchen wall to the door, leaving him breathless. Mel watched as if in slow motion, her heart racing. Troy pushed both swords through its head and heart as it hit him, and it lay motionless when they landed.

Mel struggled to push it off him, and the remaining beast pressed toward them again, but it was too late. The beast picked Dia up by her neck, lunging its claws into her neck so blood spewed from her mouth. Dia gasped but could not scream, her legs and arms flailing to push it off her. It snarled in her face and squeezed tighter, and Troy heard her neck snap. It tossed her away from Diana, her body landing on Mel and Troy against the door. They tried to catch her the best they could, but Dia flayed atop them, lifeless.

The beast curled its long arm around screaming Diana and turned away from them to race down the hall. Mel and Troy felt their hearts die as realization set in. Diana pushed her little arms out over the beast's neck as if trying to reach Troy, to no avail.

"No!" Troy screamed. "Diana!!!!"

Mel screamed, her eyes tearing up.

Domitia raced back up the stairs, crying. "Diana!" She turned to see Dia's body broken against Troy and Mel, her eyes lighting upon the dead beast and terror filling her guts. She saw it was dead and fell upon Dia, crying.

Mel pushed herself up from Dia, yanked out her long sword, and sliced off the beast's head. "Damnit!" She cursed.

Troy rushed past them down the hall, following the beast, his chest burning, tears coming to his eyes.

"No! Diana!" He cried, rage rising in him.

The front doors had been burst through again. He plunged down the steps, meeting Matunaga, who continued fighting against beasts with the others. They started to retreat away from them.

Troy reared up as he was running, gritting his teeth and hollering. He sliced a beast's head off as its back was turned to him as he jumped down the steps. He followed the beast as Diana's screams were still heard up the road away from them. The beasts lunged away from the Dacians, sprinting for longer strides and quicker than they could get to them.

"They are retreating!" Matunaga shouted.

"They took Diana!" Troy screamed.

They rushed to the road, weapons drawn. More Dacians joined them. They tracked them to the end of the road one by one, but the tracks disappeared in the mud. The rain wiped them away. Troy turned back to stare at the manor, cursing to himself deep inside, falling to his knees and screaming in the air.

"We cannot outrun them." One Dacian chimed in, his breathing heavy, his face and naked bulging arms swatted with blood.

"They are not killing her. If they wanted her dead, she would be dead already." Another one complained, gripping his Falx in anger.

"Cowards. Cowards! To take a child!" Another Dacian hollered.

Matunaga pulled Troy up by his armor. "Come!" He rushed with them back to the kitchen, defeated. Diana was gone. The beasts can cover territory quickly.

The howling had stopped after Diana disappeared. A horn, baritone, and bellowing sounded from the Dacians in the woods. They had killed some beasts but did not defeat them. They had all been outnumbered. Troy felt weak in the knees, tears running down his face. Dia was dead. Diana was taken. This attack meant something.

"They waited til we were weak, even with Dacians here, and then outnumbered us. They were always after one of them." Troy cried. "They waited til Nestor and Axius left."

Mel put her face in her hands and growled, teary-eyed.

Matunaga joined them in the kitchen. His face was spewed with blood, and his arms were slashed open like the rest of them. "They hunted Nestor's children. They hunted the family of a Dacian. They came in numbers to overtake us."

Domitia petted Dia's bloody head, tears pouring. Troy and Mel turned to face her. They could hear the children in the cellar with the cooks crying. Domitia sprawled out on the floor, her robes stained in blood, her posture broken by grief. Domitia raised to look at them, her eyes not as bright but weary. Her hands shook as her lips trembled.

"What do the beasts of Dacia want with my children?!" She cried.

Mel felt the hair rise on her arms. Troy swallowed, staring at her, his knuckles still white clasped to the hilts of his swords. "They will use her to sway Nestor in Dacia. There is no other reason."

Domitia confirmed. "When Nestor finds out they have our daughter, an heir of Dacia, the beasts will die."

Domitia cried atop Dia again. "They will all die!"

Hollers echoed in Thracian over the wall, and the Dacians melted away from Troy to the kitchen door and pried it open. The three from the woods rushed through the gate toward them, but Matunaga froze at the sight of them. They were holding up one together, and he gnashed his teeth in pain.

They pulled the beast's body outside to get to them. As it became human again, Troy's heart broke all over again eying the injured Dacian. "He has been bitten."

Matunaga rushed outside with the rest as the rain stopped to a gentle whisp. The Dacian moaned with the pain in his arm as black veins protruded into his neck, throbbing. The bite mark was deep and bleeding down his arm to his fingers. It spread like the curse had kissed his blood but mingled with hate.

"You must kill me. I will turn at nightfall. I will serve its darkness and the master who turned the rest of them. I will not take the curse." He cried. "I will not take the curse."

Matunaga closed his eyes and sighed. His eyes teared up. "Very well."

The Dacians left him alone, and he dropped to his knees. He gnashed his teeth from the pain of the bite. "Speak it to me." He begged.

Mel wandered out and stood by Troy, tears falling as her lips trembled. The Dacians gathered around Mantunaga, and Troy and Mel watched as they recited the ancient curse in Thracian.

The dark beast came for me.
I will not take its fate.
I will not drink blood or eat flesh.
For this fate is not my destiny.
I chose to die as my forefathers, curseless.
I refuse to take the fate of Loki, the dark one.
I will die at peace, for the curse is not taking me.

Matunaga closed his eyes and sighed. He swallowed, clasping a firm grip with both hands on his Falx. He raised his arms and swung back down on the Dacian, severing his head from his neck. Mel turned her head away and closed her eyes. She sobbed, moaning. Troy stood rigid, watching, clenching his jaws. Tears ran down his cheeks, but he was too numb to acknowledge them. He closed his eyes as his tears wet his bloody face and reached over and grasped Mel's shaking hand in his own.

Mel met his stare with quivering lips, but all they could do was stand there and cry together.

"He will be given a burial on a pyre." Matunaga moaned.

The rain had stopped to a soft whimper, and the fog was lifting well above the forest. Blood still ran through the orchards, and the cries of the children and Domitia echoed throughout the manor.

19

Pannonia

The Pannonia plains rose like pillars had formed into the heavens, kissing open fields of emerald green hope slithering into forests dripping with life. The Carpathian Mountains were now just to the north of them, and Kilian felt an endless lump continue to rise in his throat the closer they got to the Danube.

It reeked of home. But he was not coming with tidings of peace. Titus wanted his queen dead, and Kilian could not allow that. To make matters worse, Kilian was forced to lead the army to the outskirts of Pannonia on the Danube, close to where Fenrir's village lay. That was their next journey. The final one would be the open plain before Vasiliki's kingdom.

Titus roared past him on his horse through the plain, and Kilian knew his time with the Roman army was ending. He watched Titus and the other generals convene at the lead without him, plunging into a camp that smelled of seared flesh, fish, and fresh bread and grain cooking in their pots. Romans were busy walking in the street they had built. White tents and stone buildings had been engineered to make this plain look like a bustling city, albeit a small one.

Kilian noted the Roman colony thriving here. Families wandered the streets shopping and trading. As the army behind Kilian dispersed to the tents and fields for baths, rest, and food, he meandered up the road to follow Titus and the generals. At the end of the street was a stone fortress with columns attacking the inhabitants with its magnitude.

"You there, Dacian." Titus emerged from the steps of the fortress. "Follow me."

Kilian followed him up the steps into an open room overlooking the plain and the town. A tall, slender, blonde-headed man erupted from behind a pillar with the other generals. His blue eyes lighted upon Kilian, and then he froze.

Titus scoffed. "Ah, Honus, my son! This is the Dacian I spoke to you of."

Honus was a replica of his father, but Kilian did not smell fear in him. He smelled something lingering, something familiar about him. He narrowed his brows at Honus and kept silent.

"Kilian is leading us to Dacia. We go to Fen's village to gain access to this wench of a queen." Titus gloated.

Kilian bit his tongue, feeling hot anger rise within him.

"And you will take me with you this time." Honus bribed.

Titus laughed at him. "You will stay here until your fighting skills have improved. Then I will send for you."

Honus huffed, gritting his teeth. "I have been here already two years father. I am ready."

Titus turned red in the face. "You will go when I say you are ready! You are to work with Kilian on these maps for the Danube conquest into Dacia. That is your job."

Kilian watched Titus abandon his son and march away with the generals before turning back to face him. "Oh, and Honus. Keep your eye on this filthy Dacian. He has not been approved to be released from the army yet."

Kilian growled under his breath. "I am no man's slave." He muttered.

Honus grimaced at his father's back before turning to Kilian, who was inches shorter than him.

"Come, Kilian, I know you must be hungry. We shall find some food."

Kilian froze, glaring at him all wide-eyed. "What."

Honus turned to go and then paused, sighing, pointing toward the back of the fortress. "Food. You know, meat. Come."

"Oh. Yes, food would be good."

He followed Honus through the fortress into a city hall brimming with vendors and bakers selling all sorts of goods and foods. Kilian thought this reminded him of Rome. Honus walked them to a roasted meat vendor and tossed a coin to him. "Pick one." He told Kilian.

Kilian picked the venison flank and watched as Honus picked a smaller chunk. It smelled of rosemary and seared fire. It warmed his nose, and eased his heart a little. He took a bite out of it and sighed. Honus smiled at him, and they turned to walk down the hall, admiring all the other vendors and shoppers buying their goods.

"Tell me, Kilian, how did you end up in Rome's service regarding the Dacian queen," Honus asked him, taking another bite of the venison.

"She is my queen. I was sent to give warning to Senator Manius by her."

Honus stopped walking. "Manius, you know his son Axius is my godfather. Is he coming also?"

Kilian froze, staring at Honus. "Is that so."

"What. That Axius is my godfather? He is a good man." Honus bragged.

"Indeed. He is fearless." Kilian agreed.

"He is coming, is he not? I know Axius." Honus chirped. "I know he will come."

Kilian half smiled, chewing on the meat. "You know he wants to come."

"He is coming. He may not tell Rome. Nonetheless, he loves my father and will do anything to keep him safe."

Kilian stopped chewing. He was right. Axius did love Titus like a father. "He is very special to Axius, that is clear."

Kilian hoped Axius transcribed the parchment and that he and Nestor were on their way with the Dacians. He suddenly felt nervous, like a jittery pang had begun crawling up his backbone.

"My father already knows the maps. He needs me to keep you busy until he calls for you again, you know." Honus started walking again, and Kilian scoffed.

"I feared as much. I did not know Titus's son would care so much for Dacia."

They walked to the end of the market, which opened to the river, where people fished and families were having picnics by the shoreline. Kilian let the midday sun kiss his face and warm his heart before gazing across the river to the plain soaked in red. For miles and miles, as far as he could see, Roman soldiers dotted the plain. It became suddenly clear Rome wanted to decimate his queen. His heart sunk in his chest at this revelation.

"I love Dacia. I want to go, and I want you to convince my father to let me come." Honus begged, noticing Kilian's stare.

"Titus wants to kill me. He wants my people dead. I think you know this, and he wants Dacia decimated from the looks of this army."

Honus scoffed, spitting. "He can try. He will not succeed. The last scouts from Dacia he tried to keep escaped. I will not allow them to be harmed. I will continue helping them."

Kilian gazed at him. "You are the reason so many scouts made it home safely. You saved their lives, so I am in your debt."

"Indeed, they did. Well, come, Kilian. We have much to discuss, you and I. For instance, when is Axius coming? Because I need him here."

Kilian swallowed. "Why do you need him here?"

Honus huffed. "Because he is the only one who can stop my father from killing the queen. I need him here to help me stop this war. Dacia must survive." He whispered.

Kilian gawked. "What have you done, Honus?"

Honus turned to him, his eyes meeting Kilian's. "I know of the beasts of Dacia." He half smiled, pursing his lips. "I know you come from the tribe of them. My father refuses to believe in this."

Kilian gasped, gazing around them but freezing, watching the busy market and gawking at the scene around them. "You know what I am."

Honus nodded at him. "I know where you are leading them is a trap and that you risk death yourself. Vasiliki needs you back to help protect them. So, I will stow away and follow you. Once I am there, my father cannot send me away."

"Honus. No." Kilian begged him. "I do not want you coming. You are safe here."

"You will keep me safe."

"Have you ever seen one?" Kilian begged him.

"I have seen many. Under cover of darkness, when my father was not here, I and a few of my friends ventured out. Yes, I know what we face. You know we cannot win this."

Kilian leaned away from him, his face contorting into a sinister snare. "You are so much like Axius."

"So, tell me the truth, Kilian, is Axius coming, yes or no?" He demanded.

Kilian smirked at him. "I believe he does."

Honus smiled. "Good, because from the village, I need you to get him and take him to the queen. Keep him safe for me."

"I cannot enter Fenrir's village." Kilian huffed. "And you should not be staying there either."

"No, you cannot, Kilian. Fenrir will sense the killer for Vasiliki, so we cannot let that happen." Honus enticed him. "That is why you are named Kilian, right? To kill again."

Kilian swallowed, his eyes bright and firm at him. "It is."

"I will ensure you escape before we near it so the tribesmen there do not sense your presence. I need your help. Will you help me?"

"I will." He chirped. "A son of Axius the great is trustworthy for me to protect."

Honus smiled at him. They stood there gazing upon the sparkling river waters, finishing their meat. "You have much of Axius in you," Kilian mumbled, shaking his head. "I like it."

Honus smiled big, his white teeth sparkling. "Yes. Who do you think taught me these ways?"

Kilian nodded at him, but he was not smiling. Axius would not be pleased that his godson was conspiring in this way against Titus and Rome. He risked death if he got caught, and Kilian could not let him get caught.

He had no choice but to protect him. He did not like being cornered this way, but Axius would expect no less of him to watch his godson if the worst should happen. And the worst was slowly coming. They turned away from the ensuing carnage of the Roman army that filled the valley with reams of blood, meandering back through the city to talk about maps of Dacia.

20

The Grieving Hate

"Diana was named after Dia." Domitia bit her lip, her long arms a sliver against the dark robes she wore to ward off the biting cold moving in.

Matunaga stood with her alongside Troy and Mel, and they watched with the children as the Dacians lifted the body and carried her into the cavern. The family tomb site rested just outside the courtyard wall under a grove of Olive trees, lit by an ivy path.

"Nestor will be devastated to hear of this news," Domitia whispered, her heart aching.

"Will they come back for us, mama?" Aurora asked, clinging to her, along with her sisters. The twins were red-eyed, as they had cried all night for Diana.

Matunaga gazed upon the children, sighing, then meeting Domitia's stare. "Yes."

She clenched her jaws at him. "Where did the tracks lead with my daughter?"

"Rome." He answered.

"Rome is where we go. We leave straightaway. We will stay with Manius."

Troy and Mel gazed upon her, their eyes widening.

Domitia turned to the Dacians. "You are coming with me. All of you. Your task is to accompany me as free Dacians. You will protect my children. I have four children with me. I expect my children will have two Dacians guarding them. The others can disperse and help protect Manius's estate." She warned.

"I will seek my help in the Senate, privately, with my wealthy women leaders. We will deploy our messengers to the streets. I will use all my wealth and power to protect my family and Rome."

She then turned to Matunaga. "This is how it will be until we find Diana. Is this understood?"

His dark eyes sparkled at her. "To Rome then."

She then gazed upon Mel and Troy. "Both of you will accompany me. We will need the help to get Diana back from these beasts and find the source of their evil."

Troy scoffed. "I cannot. I am not worthy. I lost Diana."

Domitia scoffed back at him. "How dare you say such things to me. You saved our lives! If not for you and Mel, we would all be dead."

Troy stepped away from her, shaking his head. He dropped his head in shame. "Forgive me."

Domitia's lips quivered at his face. "You are not a failure! You are a blessing to my family. Both of you. And I want you both with me and the children always." She took his face in her palm, tears streaming down her cheeks at him. "I trust you. Now is the time I need you the most."

She leaned up and took Mel's crying face in her palm, gazing at them both. "I need you both. Diana needs you." Domitia cried with them.

Troy gazed upon her as his eyes teared up. "I am honored."

The Dacians looked upon one another in silence and then turned to Matunaga. He raised a leather-cuffed arm over his head, and a falcon lighted upon it. It had been sitting in the Olive Grove for a few hours now, watching them. But Domitia did not think anything of it because they always had birds throughout the groves, and she assumed it was hunting or drawn to the smell of rotted flesh.

"This is Cotiso, my faithful." Matunaga smiled at it.

Domitia noticed it had a leather string tied on its leg and a small leather shaft attached to it. The Falcon blinked at them with big orange-yellow eyes, eagerly awaiting the command from its master. Its black and white feathers on its chest rippled in the morning breeze. Matunaga pulled a tightly rolled-up parchment from his leather breastplate and pushed it inside the shaft. He closed it off with the cork that had been made for it.

"He's been here the whole time?" Troy asked, astonished.

"He has. We have many faithful friends and animals, if you will. In case the worst should happen, we can get help."

Silence. The bird waited.

"Now it is time for help."

Domitia gasped. "You are sending for help?" She was about to say more, but another Falcon lighted upon a Dacian and then another. Falcons lighted upon them until she counted four. She felt the hair on her arms stand up on edge, and her spine tingled.

Matunaga nodded. "Dacia. Rome. Oltenia."

Troy swallowed. "Why Oltenia?"

"We will warn Brasus and Vasiliki. One will fly ahead for Manius."

Troy swallowed. "And Oltenia…"

Mel felt her back go stiff watching Matunaga and the Dacian's facial expressions. Matunaga lifted his arm, and the Falcon lifted off. The Dacians had put their parchments in the shafts of their birds, and those birds lifted off.

"And Oltenia. Matunaga?" Troy demanded.

Domitia felt the color leave her face. She gripped her daughters around her with shaking arms. But Matunaga sighed, watching the Falcons disappear in different directions in the cloud cover.

"What is in Oltenia?" Domitia demanded.

"The remnant of Nestor's ancestors. More like a relic. He is heading into Dacia, so they must be forewarned. You saw this day coming. I recognized his lineage the moment I saw him."

Domitia's face fell pale, and her eyes widened. "Oh."

Troy thought a moment. "That is not so bad, is it?"

The Dacians murmured amongst themselves, and Domitia gasped, realizing what Matunaga had just done.

She laughed, but it was a nervous trickle. "Out of courtesy, you warn them their heir is coming to the queen of Dacia. War is already here, and now it is too late."

Domitia growled, her jaws hot with anger. "Let them come! Let them wipe out this evil in Dacia, this Fenrir, the son of Loki! Let them come to Rome to help us get Diana back. I implore them to."

Silence filled the space between them as black clouds mingled overhead, a gentle breeze blowing the stench of rotted flesh away from them for a moment. Dia had been buried. The Dacian had been burned on his pyre. The manor sat riddled in blood and demolished. The servants and groundskeepers holed up in their cottages. Domitia glared at Matunaga and then at the Dacians, a half-smile erupting on her pale, firm face, but it suddenly disappeared as reality set in.

"Let us hope Oltenia does not answer." Matunaga sighed, his face long and clenched.

Troy stood there with Mel, still bleeding from wounds that needed mending, watching the birds coast away among the clouds. The Dacian mercenaries stood as a silent haven, but they were shrouded with an endless mercy that would not come now.

"You and I shall be good friends on this journey." Anna poured hot tea into a fancy goblet laden with pink jewels and handed it to Diana.

Diana swallowed, taking it as she was thirsty. The carriage was bumpy, and the horses' hooves echoed around them. The beasts were gone, but men rode the top of the carriage, who Diana was certain were beasts. They were pretending to be human, and she did not like them.

"I want my mama." She said again, her eyes tearing up.

She kept saying it repeatedly, even when the beast handed her to Anna in the carriage and disappeared somewhere in the forest. The beasts were lumpy. They were not soft, and their fur was bristly and stiff, she thought. They smelled funny. Diana had stopped crying when the beast lunged down a rock embankment for the last time in the forest and met a carriage on the trail.

"Oh, Diana. Do not worry. I am taking you to your father. Would you like that?"

Diana's face lit up. "Yes! I want my dada."

Anna smiled at her from ear to ear. "Good. Now let me see. I have baked bread, cheeses, figs and jams. What would you like?"

Diana's mouth watered. "I am hungry."

Anna puckered her pouty lips as her red cloak spilled over her white gown. "Yes, and it is a long journey, little one. Your father will be very pleased to see you."

Diana picked a small loaf of bread, and Anna wiped strawberry jam on it for her. She watched the little girl eat, her tiny face almond-shaped like her mother's. But her eyes were Nestor's. She was thin but resilient. Anna smiled at her.

"I could never have children. I like to think my child would be brave like you." She said, admiring her.

"Dada says I am brave." She took a bite out of the bread.

"Dada is far away with Axius. Will I see him too?"

Anna leaned into her seat, her eyes wide, and her mouth gaped open. "Oh, is he? He will be there waiting for us. He will be happy to see you."

"How long is this journey? Is this an adventure?" Diana giggled.

Anna giggled with her, faking it. "Oh darling, this is the adventure of a lifetime. You shall see."

"The beasts, will they come again?" Diana blurted out, drinking her tea. "They smell funny."

Anna half smiled. "There are many coming, darling. Many."

"They scare me."

"Little one, they do not mean to scare you. They are here to protect you." Anna assures her.

"Dada says they are evil. Are they evil, Anna?"

Anna poured herself some wine and sat there, admiring this little beauty she had taken and her inquisitive nature. "No. They are not evil. They are good. We took you to protect you, and now I am taking you to your father and Axius."

"You are protecting me. Like mama and dada do." She yawned.

"Yes, darling. I am protecting you." Anna leaned over and pulled a wool blanket off the seat.

"What about my sisters? Can they come too?"

"Oh, they are coming, little one. They were meant to come. They will come shortly after us, you will see." She leaned Diana on the seat and covered her up with the blanket.

"Then we will all be together in Dacia!" Diana squealed.

"Rest now. You were up all night. You need sleep, little one."

Diana closed her eyes, sighing. "We will be together again."

Anna kissed her atop her little head, leaning against the seat, sipping her wine. "We will all be together. Dacia wants us all together."

Anna seethed inside. She managed to take one child, but she needed them all.

21

Kilian's One Chance

Kilian smelled the Evergreen forest's crisp hope as they ventured into Pannonia. An open basin and a fishing village lie on the edge of the Drava River there. The Romans knew Thracians inhabited this village, but Kilian knew otherwise. They were Thracians, but Fenrir, the tribal leader, was also there. Kilian felt the hairs raise on his arms and prick him under his cloak.

Once they crossed the river, they would hike into the Dacian Kingdom and closer to the queen Vasiliki. The Drava was a tributary of the Danube, and Titus had his army right where he wanted them, for now. Kilian knew they had made good time. After all, the Romans were very resilient. Titus and his Tesserarius's commanders along with the Centurion, were diligent with the health and well-being of their soldiers.

Past the river where the village lay, forests clawed into the mountains as if the heavens had splayed open emerald jewels. The dense forests crawled up the plains toward the Danube River. Once Titus took over the village, the army would march through the dense forests into Dacia. Kilian feared for them. They would all die if his and Honus's plan failed. He had little time to do this.

About five miles from the river, Kilian became restless and agitated. He could not risk getting any closer to Fenrir's village. He lingered behind Titus and his generals, eying the naïve soldiers surrounding him. He slowly began sinking back into the army until shouting was heard. Titus froze from marching, turning on his horseback to meet Kilian's stare. Honus was pulled to the front through them by a general. Sighing, Titus clenched his jaws at his son.

"We found him coming up on the men in the back." The general scoffed. "He was alone."

Honus grimaced, meeting Kilian's gaze and then scrolling up to his father. Kilian thought Titus looked horrific, like he had just witnessed his son's death before his eyes.

"You disobeyed me. I warned you to stay back."

Honus pulled away from the general and growled. "I told you I was coming. You need me. I am ready, father."

Titus laughed down at him. "Stubborn. Like Axius."

"Stubborn like you." Honus nodded.

Titus lunged down and swiped his cheek with a closed fist. Honus, taken back, fell backward on his bottom, his lip bleeding. Kilian growled inside, his eyes wide as he slunk towards the back further, away from the commotion. The men and soldiers surrounding Honus and Titus became louder until Titus screamed: "Silence!"

Titus lighted off his stallion, pulling his son by his armor and scowling into his face. Honus took it well, holding his breath. "Your disobedience will not go unpunished, Honus. You will ride with me at my side. You will go nowhere else."

Honus licked the blood off his lip and agreed. "I will, father."

Titus seethed at him. "Once we secure this primitive village of fools, you will be given lashes."

The army grew silent as Titus yelled. "Anyone disobeying my command will be given lashes, is that understood?! I am to have order and respect. Without these virtues, Rome is dead!" He yelled.

Honus bit his tongue as the army cheered, agreeing with Titus. He turned his head through the soldiers to see that Kilian had gone. His plan had worked, but not as he had hoped. He would be reprimanded and in pain, but at least he was with his father. He would not be able to fight if he had to with the gashes on his back.

Titus grabbed Honus's leather strap attached to his armor and pulled his face into his face, glaring into his eyes. They were the same height. "Never disobey me again. Is this clear?"

Honus swallowed, nodding. "Yes, commander."

Titus lunged Honus away from him and lighted upon his stallion. "Very well. We have a town to commandeer. This Fenrir is waiting on us."

Honus walked with the men behind his father. "Yes, commander." He shouted with the men, wiping the blood off his face. Gazing over his shoulder, he did not see Kilian. The plan appeared to have worked.

Kilian knew Honus would be reprimanded, and his father would give him lashes. The boy would be unable to fend for himself after being injured that badly. He wished he could take Honus with him, but he also knew the mortal would be unable to keep up with him even if he tried. He pressed up a sloping plateau, watching the Roman army hike to the village, his heart racing.

Hours later, he hiked around the farthest east end of the river to the plain and crossed it, veering miles around the village and the army into the forest. Because he did not know if scouts were in the area, he was cautious about remaining in his human form until he reached the thickness of the dense forest. He was to meet Axius and Nestor and his queen's generals and bring them to her from Lupa's village, the outpost of his people. That was always the plan to get them into the presence of Vasiliki before they were hunted. He just needed to get away from Titus first to do it.

When he reached the forest line, he took a deep breath of mountain air and let the panging fires of transformation in his gut eat at his backbone. He stepped in deeper, gazing around. The canopy of emerald greens flowed into a darkness overhead and looked like tunnels had been dug through the forest. A resonant hunger rose in him, but it was not flesh he needed this time. The desperate quest was seared into his soul, and time ran out. His pupils split into shreds of yellows, blackness filling the void around them as if an eternal pit had opened in his eyes.

He burst through the underbrush, scattering shrubs and shredding the dirt beneath his paws, his elongated fangs snarling out a long snout. As the day fell into night, Kilian galloped full throttle through the wilderness toward the Danube. His heightened senses ate at his innards like a seared fire. His elongated ears perked to the forest noises that had gone silent at his presence. His yellow eyes remained steadfast on the journey ahead, for he had little time to waste. His elongated bulging limbs left indentations into the earth as he lunged into the night, his pitch-black fur blending with the darkness.

As he neared the edge of Dacian territory, it smelled of home, and peace calmed him deep inside. He growled a shriek into the night. It echoed over the mountain plain, and birds catapulted at the sudden break in their silence, their flocks filling the skies like black fingers. Vasiliki's scouts would know he was coming now, but he would not be coming alone. He had little time to get to Axius and the others. As Titus was commandeering Fenrir's village, if Kilian failed to get Vasiliki's help protecting the Romans, everything they ever loved would be lost.

22

The Heirs are Found

"M ama."
 "Mama."

But then a wide gaping mouth full of razor-sharp fangs opened wide on a broad snout and belted out a shrieking roar in her face.

Domitia lunged up from her restless sleep in the carriage. Her eyes were tearing up as her mind kept replaying Diana's screams over and over. She gazed across the bench at Matunaga, who nodded at her, ever watchful yet acknowledging her pain. The older twins were using his lap as a pillow and sleeping soundly, their wool cloaks piled around their little bodies to keep them warm. Domitia pressed her arms tighter around Venus and her youngest. She sniffled and wiped the tear from her cheek, gazing out the window. They would be in Rome by nightfall.

In front of them was her escort. Troy led the carriage on horseback, and Mel sat aside Raoul, who was driving it. The rest of the Dacians were also on horseback, following the carriage and keeping watch. The horses' hoofs on the brick road echoed around them, and birds chirped loudly in the olive trees lining the road. It was a beautiful day, yet lingering pains were evident.

"We will be in Rome soon. Manius should be returned from the Po River by now." Domitia mentioned, taking a deep breath.

"They will not harm her," Matunaga advised her, his dark eyes bright.

Domitia swallowed. "Nestor will kill them all if they do."

Matunaga scowled. "They will bring the queen's wrath down upon them also."

Domitia held her breath, turning her gaze back out the window. "My father told me stories when I was little. I was old enough to understand something terrible had happened when Nestor was brought to our farm but young enough not to comprehend the ramifications of what Rome had done."

Matunaga listened to her.

"Manius was my godfather from birth, and Axius was like a brother to me. We were only eight years old, but then Axius's mother had been stricken with fever and passed, and my father was called off to war at the Black Sea."

Matanuga widened his eyes. "The Dacian wars had become prevalent then."

"Yes, and Rome brought them in. Dacians from the river tribes on the Danube. Dacians from the Black Sea. Rome was filled with the greed of gold, while the streets celebrated this travesty."

"That is how you came to know your husband," Matunaga asked.

Domitia smiled. "He became my best friend, although he is a few years older than me. He became my protector, always watchful over me. I loved him from the moment we began getting to know one another."

"Nestor found a new home then." Matunaga admired.

"I think he had no choice. Something about his homeland always made him uneasy, and as time passed, he did not want to go back. He was taken from a Carpathian tribe on the river at the base of that mountain, journeying into Oltenia. I do not know what my father and

Commander Artgus were doing there. They went out of their way to go there. I remember my mother upset about it."

Domitia sighed. "They were looking for something. Someone, perhaps. My father died shortly after Nestor and I married due to an illness, and I did not get to ask him about his duties for Rome then."

Matunaga narrowed his brows, clenching his jaws. "Perhaps your father and Titus were looking for the beasts?"

Domitia scowled. "I am certain they would have been slaughtered if they had found them! Yet throughout these years, the emperor continues to defy the gods by stealing gold and making wars in a land that keeps spitting Rome out." She whispered, clenching her thin jawline. "Dacia does not deserve to be treated this way."

The carriage came to an abrupt halt. Domitia held her breath, clinging onto her daughters tighter, waking them up.

"Halt!" They heard Troy's voice holler as the horses surrounded the carriage.

Matunaga turned his head to see a horse walking by his window, and one of his mercenaries peeked down at him. "Tracks, going into Rome. Beast tracks."

Matunaga gently tapped the twins and woke them, rising to exit the carriage. "Stay here," he warned them.

Domitia watched him pull his Sickle as he exited the carriage. Ahead of them for miles opened a sprawling olive tree forest dotted with walnut trees and dense shrubbery. They would be going through this small forest for the next few miles. Troy trotted back and forth on his stallion, glaring down at the tracks, several of them. The tracks led into the woods but stopped at the rock outcroppings.

"There is an old road under those rock ledges," Troy warned, glaring through the trees.

Matunaga paraded into the woods, following the tracks, and two of his mercenaries followed him on foot. Troy pressed closer against the carriage, watching their surroundings. He was never leaving Nestor's wife and the children ever again. He pulled his sword, watched, and waited alongside Raoul and Mel with the other mercenaries. They trotted around the field along the forest, watching.

Matanuga froze, gazing down at the wolf tracks. The paws were embedded in the mud from previous storms and had dried as hard as rock. Paw prints were around it, but this one was heavier, as if it had carried something. In one instant, it was walking normally, then it looked like it slipped in the mud and caught itself.

"Whatever you were carrying, you did not want it harmed, did you, beast?" He whispered, eying his men, who noticed the same thing.

They pressed further into the rock outcropping and climbed atop it, peering down to see an old, cracked brick road that needed repair. Wild vines had overtaken a section, springing out from the rocks like gray hair had sprung forth. The paw prints stopped atop the rock, and only the mud-caked prints were noticeable because the clay had dried.

The vines on the road had been smashed down from carriage wheels. He lunged off the rock ledge and slid down a sandy embankment to the road. He stopped at the carriage mark and hunched on his knees, glaring at the prints that suddenly stopped. An elongated knee and leg imprint melted into the vines at the carriage wheel indentations.

Matunaga turned back to the entrance of this wood and glared at the rock outcropping, thinking of the carriage and how it was built. "It leaned down on one knee here at the carriage doors. It handed something to someone inside."

Matunaga stood up and pressed back up the embankment, taking the palm of a mercenary helping him back atop the rocks.

"The child was taken here and then finished the journey in a carriage. A Roman carriage." Matunaga turned to go back to Domitia.

Troy met him and the others at the edge of his horse, his face clenched. "What did you find."

"The child was taken to Rome. Carriage wheel prints are evident on the road. Where does it lead?"

Troy widened his eyes. "Celian Hill. It was always meant as a way for Senators and leaders to escape Rome if the worst should happen. That way, they can get to their villas in the South."

"Ah. And we are going to Celian Hill, where Manius resides." Matunaga marched to the carriage, turning back to the men.

"We must push through and get there before nightfall." He warned them, entering the carriage.

Troy led them on, the mercenaries and horse-drawn carriage galloped behind them through the woods. Only now, a sense of urgency gnawed at them. Domitia bit her lip, scowling.

"She is still alive."

Matunaga agreed. "Yes, she is."

"I will gather my women leaders to the Villa first thing in the morning. I will use all my resources and wealth to track Diana down and hunt whoever has taken her to the ends of the world."

By this time, the children were all awake, wide-eyed and fearful. "Is Diana okay, mama?" Aurora asked, holding her twin sisters' hand aside Matunaga.

"Yes. She is, after all, a Zosime. We are strong and brave." Domitia smiled at them.

Matunaga leered his head at her, realizing what she just said. "Zosime?"

"Yes. That is Nestor's last name."

Matunaga leaned down and pulled up his leather satchel full of books and scrolls. The girls watched him in eager anticipation of what literary works he was digging for. "Zosime." He mumbled to himself.

He pulled out a leather-bound book and opened it to a genealogical tree that splayed across two pages. The girls leaned in, gazing upon it with him. Domitia admired how patient he was with the children. He raked his long-tanned fingers across the branches until one stood out.

"Throughout Rome's History, my people have transcribed and documented bloodlines based on the knowledge people of those bloodlines have given us. Because of the mercenaries brought to me by Senator Opiter and his wife, I learned invaluable knowledge from them."

He stopped at a branch on the painted pages, thinking. "I created a bloodline trail, but the name Zosime stands out."

Domitia fidgeted in her seat, swallowing.

"Here we are." He finished.

Domitia leaned over with her girls and glared at the tree branch silently with him. Matunaga kept going over it, mumbling to himself. Domitia thought his face lost color, and his eyes wavered, which she found unusual because he was so strong.

"What is it, Matunaga?"

He turned the book around so it faced her. She followed his fingers on the branch of the tree that showed Dacian kings and queens, the last one being Vasiliki, the current queen of Dacia. Right beside her, there was a leaf that had an unusual name on it.

Lupescu Zosime.

"I think you have known this for some time, Domitia." He sighed. "Your family would never be able to stay hidden. Nestor bears the family resemblance; I recognized it at Opiters."

Domitia's cheeks flushed, and she swallowed as nervousness rose in her. "Of course you did."

"Nestor is Lupescu, is he not?" Matunaga goaded her. "Nestor chose his new name when Rome made him a freeman."

"What does this mean, mama?" Aurora asked, her eyes wide and bright.

"Are we part wolf mama?" The youngest asked, hugging Domitia tight. Domitia kissed her head, gazing at Matunaga.

"It means Nestor is royalty, nothing more." She added, meeting Matunaga's stare. "He never wanted to go back."

Venus gasped. "The Dacian queen is our aunt?!" The children began muttering amongst one another, excited.

Matunaga sighed, turning the book back around and turning the page. The girls recoiled at the sight of the beast on the page, remnants of Thracian verbiage and Romanian curses written out in faded black ink along the side of the painting.

"Oh yes, children, your father is royalty." He turned the book back to face Domitia, who squirmed in her seat. She did not appreciate being put into a corner this way, especially in front of her children, but she had no choice. Matunaga had proven invaluable to her family, and his expertise had saved their lives.

"Directly from the true bloodline of the Oltenian clan," Matunaga added. "You have known this since he came to Rome."

She glared at him, leaning back into her seat, sighing. "This does not mean they are beasts, Matunaga."

Matunaga closed the book, gazing at her, sighing. "Your husband has been called home to help fight the beasts of his land, Domitia. Your home may never be the hills of Rome anymore when this is all finished."

Domitia swallowed, her eyes tearing up. "Our home will always be where Nestor is."

"Even if he is a beast?" Matunaga questioned her.

Domitia took a deep breath, gazing back out the window, ignoring her daughters' shocked stares. She did not respond to Matunaga either.

She turned her face away from them all, her glassy eyes ever watchful to the woods hanging over them. The horses' hooves beat the bricks, and the birds continued chirping, which told her the beasts were not near them at this time.

23

The Danube

The Danube flowed like a silk goddess under the midday sun as shimmering sparkles of hope broke into a tinge of malice. Axius joined Brasus on the starboard side, waiting. Once they left the Sava River basin, the men sailed due east. Axius pulled his leather cloak over his head as a light misty rain fell upon them, but there was a coldness to the air that made his bones ache. The silence was deafening, aside from the small ship kissing the river waters.

It had been weeks, and sleep fled them like the darkness does when dawn takes over. Axius and Nestor had not shaved and began growing beards. Axius did not care for that, but he felt the facial hair would help him blend in with the mercenaries. Nestor did not shave either but continued to hack his black hair off his head with a dagger.

The men were dispersed atop the deck, with Nestor at the starboard quarter. They had lowered the sail as the Danube flowed briskly. The river was as if a whole new world had spilled before them, only it was lonely, and beautifully dangerous.

Axius pulled at the loose tunic he wore, annoyed that it pulled at his chest. He preferred the Roman army attire and missed his breastplate and shields. At least he kept his leather cuffs and shin protectors over his trousers, and the long wool cloak hid his Falx. He was not giving up his gladius. He had a leather strap around his midsection, an arsenal of arrows protruding over his back, and a long bow in his grip.

A brisk wind belted in at them as the fog dissipated, and Axius admired the Carpathian Mountains in the distance, holding his breath at their grandeur. Axius turned to meet Nestor's glare as the silence overwhelmed them, noticing his dark eyes melted upon the shoreline, slithering closer to the ship.

Nestor met up with Axius, aside from Brasus, and watched it. "At what time do we get off and travel by foot," Axius whispered.

Brasus answered. "Not here. We need to travel some miles yet to get closer to Vasiliki."

Moskin wandered up to them from the port side, whispering. "We stay on the water as long as possible."

Moskin turned to linger at the port side again, gazing at the wooded, hilly shoreline that began to rise above them on either side. Tarbus was unusually quiet. Axius noticed they were watching all around them with caution. Their breathing slowed, and their jaws clenched.

Moskin peered over the side into the forest that seemed to close in on them, darkness playing the shadows like clawed fingers were pressing upon them. "The beasts come soon."

Axius said nothing but watched the wood line at the shore, his ears pricking at the enticing sound of the waters being pushed under the ship. His eyes rested upon the curvy, flowing river that melted into a lush forest of evergreens. The shoreline rose, revealing flowing waterfalls trickling down from rock ledges. Spruce trees dangled over the sides, casting dark shadows upon the waters as the river narrowed in some places and the current roared stronger.

As the current picked up, the men split up and gripped their oars, pushing the Liburna away from rocks at the shoreline. Moments later, the hills rising around them on each side melted to a flat forest bottom. They steered the vessel to stay in the middle of the river, steady sailing for miles until clouds shrouded them in darkness and the current slowed to a dead halt.

The sun started to set behind the mountain, and Axius became impatient. He dropped his oar and marched to the Bow, glaring into the thick underbrush of the forest to his right. He turned as a dark shadow lingered in the path of the wood, watching him. It was hunched down on all fours, then shifted upwards over the brush to stand upright like a man.

Axius lunged around to face it as it dawned on him, his palm pulling his gladius. But when he turned, it was gone. He froze, the hairs on his arms raised, glaring into the forest. Nestor noticed Axius freeze and that he had pulled his Gladius, so he glared into the woods alongside him. He sniffed the air, scowling.

"We are being watched," Nestor whispered, warning the men. "Our weapons do not matter from here on out."

Brasus and the others stopped rowing, eying the woods in silence at the Port side behind Axius and Nestor, who stood at the Starboard.

Silence ate at them like a sickness gnawing their insides while they glared into the wood, and the vessel slowed down to a stop on the waters. A large shadow loomed upon them from the darkness within the forest canopy. A stick snapping made them turn suddenly, but then the men froze as it dawned on them. It catapulted itself from the shoreline across the waters onto the deck, its black ears standing upright on its square head. Claws protruded, and Axius froze at the elongated snout snarling full of fangs, but it was too late. The beast was here.

The ship wavered with the sudden burst of its massive body weight, landing at the bow. Brasus, Moskin, and Tarbus froze, gawking as it steadied itself. It towered above them like a black shadow stretching from storm clouds. It perked its ears atop its head and snarled down at them, gazing at Axius and Nestor.

Axius started to lunge forward and push his Gladius into it, but Nestor pressed his palm into Axius's arm to stop him. "No!" He warned, clenching his jaw. "No weapons!"

Axius froze, his eyes gazing upon this horrendous creature as some dark demon from the pits of hell had opened and met them on the river.

Until it spoke.

When it spoke, another level of hell pierced him. He felt his backbone claw into his brain and chase his toes with shivers carved into his soul.

"We must hurry to Vasiliki." It sounded like a man, but it was deep like a chasm had opened from the depths of the world. It sounded like a bellowing howl erupted from an ice storm stretched across a thick forest, only it filled Axius with a resonating fear instead of coldness.

Axius felt his heart skip a beat. "What is the meaning of this." He mumbled, his lips shaking. "They speak?!"

Nestor huffed, "The wolf of my land." He patted Axius, his palm a firm grip on his shoulder to encourage him, but Axius felt a shiver in Nestor's grip.

"I thought you were dead!" Nestor shouted to it. The beast huffed at him.

"Never dead. Kilian does not die. We feared you were dead too until I found you at the games." He toyed with him. "I knew I had found you."

Nestor swallowed, eying it with a resonating anger that made his eyes sparkle.

Axius took a deep breath. "Kilian."

It let out a malicious trickle of a laugh. "Axius. Come, Roman. We must continue by boat to Vasiliki. We have little time!" It roared at them.

Nestor pulled Axius with him to the oars. Kilian sniffed the air, its eyes in pools of yellows and black. Axius froze watching him, his palm atop his gladius at his side still. Kilian noticed and turned his eyes upon him.

"I will not harm you, Axius. Kilian does not hunt and kill Axius the brave." It said, pressing the men onward upriver.

Axius fretted. "The Kilian I know is a man."

Kilian lunged down into his face, his fangs protruding from his elongated snout. Axius widened his eyes at it, taking in the magnitude of Kilian's size, the snout as large as his head. The fangs were long and piercing, as long as a Roman dagger, lethal. Kilian smelled of pine and evergreens and pressed dirt, a crispness to him that seemed like he had been kissed by nature. Axius met his eyes, large, round black eyes with yellow pupils. He had long lashes and indents over his brows that wrinkled back to his flat, square skull. Kilian was twice as wide as Axius, ripped with finely tuned muscles, and a physique made for hunting.

"You have known what I am or would not have questioned me in your father's presence."

Axius leaned away from it, his face stern. "Kilian, the killer."

Kilian huffed in his face, his breath hot on Axius's cheeks.

"I knew it," Axius mumbled, the truth dawning on him, his voice cracking.

Kilian snarled, pointing a long-clawed finger ahead of them toward the mountain. "We sail through the night; we stay on the water. We will reach the queen faster this way. We are going to war, Axius."

Axius swallowed, sudden realization hitting him. "Where is Titus? How did you get away from him?"

Kilian glanced at Nestor. "The Roman army has reached the settlement in Pannonia and taken it. Titus seeks to kill Vasiliki."

The color drained from Nestor's face. "No! We must stop them." Nestor yelled.

Kilian agreed. "We must reach Vasiliki first. You will need our army to help you fight against Fenrir. His numbers are too great for Romans to fight here. The army will die."

Axius felt anger rise in him. "What is Fenrir?"

Kilian snarled, his fangs dripping slobber. "Beasts, Axius! Beasts are coming for your Titus and your Roman army. They are coming for Rome and coming for my queen."

Axius glared at Nestor, but all he did was swallow.

Nestor huffed. "Damnit!" He cursed.

Kilian pressed the men to their oars and pointed ahead, returning to gaze upon Axius. "Honus is with them now. Stubborn son of Titus."

Axius let out a whimper, narrowing his brows and clenching his jaws. "He was to stay at Pannonia as we commanded! I had him stationed there for his protection."

Kilian sighed. "Yes, that is also what Titus commanded. Yet Honus crept out and joined the army."

Axius felt a desperate pain hit his innards for his godson. "Not Honus. No. I cannot lose my godson."

Nestor shook his head. "They will be slaughtered!"

"The queen is in his debt. It is my duty to help you protect him, Axius. I will keep my word." Kilian assured him.

"What has he done for you to protect him, Kilian?" Axius pleaded, rowing.

Kilian let out a deep, bellowing laugh, and Axius froze at the shrieking sound of it. As he turned to face him, Axius widened his eyes at what he thought was a beast smiling. Either way, it took him off guard, and he almost dropped the oar.

"Honus saved our scouts Vasiliki sent these many years to Rome. We are in his debt."

Axius swallowed, gazing up at this bulky beast with jet-black fur as soft as a morning breeze and eyes with the deepness of a mysterious labyrinth. Its ears portrayed its emotions too, but the broad, long snout with dagger-like fangs set his jaw on edge. Nestor was right, the beasts of these lands were much bigger, but hearing it talk was disturbing. Hearing a beast talk like a man sent shivers up his spine.

Kilian then turned to face Brasus, Moskin, and Tarbus. Axius noticed the men had stayed to themselves at the oars and said nothing. They had put their swords up after Nestor recognized Kilian. "I see the generals have returned. Vasiliki will be pleased. Yet some are missing."

Brasus perked up. "They protect Nestor's family."

Nestor took a deep breath. "They are protecting my family as I have commanded them. Half-breeds attacked my farm and killed many of my workers. We fear they are already in Rome."

Kilian perked his ears up, his eyes wide. "They have come for your family? Vasiliki will be displeased to hear of this."

Nestor scowled. "They will never get to me. They will never touch my family again."

Kilian gazed ahead at the river, the tide ushering them through another hilly wooded plain. "We are at war. Beasts. And man. Let us hope Titus listens to reason."

Nestor stood at his oar, grasping it in his palms but not working it. He glared at Kilian, his eyes narrowed, his jaws clenched, thinking. "We are at war indeed." He mumbled.

Silence pestered the men as they steered the vessel onward deeper into Dacia. Axius gazed upon the backside of Kilian's physique and questioned how his army would kill one. Kilian's muscle-riddled body bulged, and his paws were three times the size of his own. The dagger-like claws were not fully extended, but the tips looked obsidian, glaring, shiny, and deadly sharp. Kilian's back tensed up, and he turned to gaze at Axius as if sensing eyes upon him.

"Do you all look like this?" Axius wondered aloud.

Brasus gasped, gawking at Moskin and Tarbus. "The Roman is sizing up the beast."

Moskin nodded. "He is brave indeed."

"The generals are bigger," Kilian told him.

Axius lunged back, glaring at Brasus, Moskin, and Tarbus. "Bigger, eh? These fools back here are generals?"

Brasus cleared his throat, shaking his head at Axius.

Axius pursed his lips. "Damn."

"The females are not as muscular," Kilian informed him.

"You have women here! Beast women?!" Axius belted out, turning to hear the mercenaries laughing at him.

Nestor rolled his eyes. "I swear, brother, do you know nothing of how procreation works?"

Axius pursed his lips. "I do."

"I do not think he does," Tarsus mumbled from the back of the boat, and the others agreed.

Axius glared back at them. "I do." He thrust his arms in the air and gawked at them.

Nestor sighed at him. "You will see many things. Many things. Keep your wits about you. We must save the army and get back home alive."

Axius agreed, gazing at Kilian again, who met his stare with amusement.

"When you change back to human, are you naked?"

"Not always. We have pelts and change back to our human form, still dressed. It is the power of the curse."

"But you do not have a pelt this time, so..."

"Yes, naked."

"We have extra cloaks." Axius pestered him.

Kilian jerked his gaze down upon Axius and let out a huff.

"It bothers you I am a beast on your boat." Kilian toyed with him. "You have been trained your whole life to kill beasts, and now you see me not as a simple scout in your rich father's house."

Axius drooped the oar to stand aside Kilian, the beast towering over him by feet. He watched the waters split as the boat coasted further into Dacia. Kilian waited for him to speak, watching him swallow and pull at his gladius by his side. Kilian understood, after all, he had pulled at weapons that were not there when he entered Rome.

"My godson is in great danger. The man I love as a father and all my brothers in arms are in danger. We have sustained hard losses, and our streets may soon be filled with more widows and orphans. I fear for Rome." He worried.

Kilian's ears laid flat atop his thick square head, and he nodded. "We are all in danger until Fenrir is dead. Once he is dead, we can hunt their remnant of them and destroy the evil."

They sailed on into the night, a Roman soldier clutching the hope that he could save the people and country he loved, and a beast of Dacia leading them further into uncertain territory.

24

Honus's Punishment

He was not completely heartless. His wife used to say that when she and their daughter were alive, anyway. A part of Titus enveloped mercy and patience with his little blonde-headed miracle, but then, at three years old, she got a fever that never went away. A part of him died that day, too, and his wife, and he sent Honus away for Rome to train in the army.

Titus gripped the flagellum, his short whip that sported three leather straps connected to the handle. He swiped it once in the dirt at his feet and took a breath, glaring with a stone face at the naked back of Honus. The whip left indentations in the ground, resonating an echo like shards of broken glass.

Honus held his breath and closed his eyes, pressing his chest into the pole while his arms were tied above his head. The army had gathered around to watch Titus flog his son for disobedience, a lesson they must learn if Rome is to remain victorious. There can be no rebellion or there will be no mercy. There is no favoritism in Titus's army.

Titus decided that five lashings would be enough. Honus was his son, after all. The generals agreed with Titus a lesson needed to be learned, and the army needed to see it. But Titus knew the villagers there also needed to know Rome was not playing around. If the Roman Commander would flog his own son, he would do worse to anyone else. Titus was known to be methodical in his brutality.

Titus lunged the whip up and catapulted it across Honus's back at his midsection. Honus flared his nostrils and gritted his teeth to the pain as the flesh ripped, searing into his backbone. Honus let out a moan of pain and then braced for another one. Blood drizzled down his back to his legs. Four more to go.

As Titus continued the whipping, Fenrir stood on a hill looking down into the courtyard, watching it. The Roman army had filled the valley at the river, and his villagers were ensuring they had food and drink, serving them. He lowered his cloak hood to reveal a bald head riddled with blue tattoos as if the hottest fire had kissed him from the inside out. Behind him stood four men in the same simple cloaks, trousers, and belted gown to their knees.

The Romans had relieved them of weapons.

They watched with him atop the hill, scowling at the Romans. Fenrir's dark brown eyes sparkled as his villagers lit the torch lights up and down the river banks for miles. The night lit up with fire, and the fire splayed across his face. His clean-shaven face showed a clenched jawline and thin lips under furious black eyebrows that lent a severe definition to his face.

"Let them have their fun," Fenrir whispered, scoffing at Titus whipping Honus.

"What is your order, sire."

Fenrir turned his gaze to his men and nodded. "Once I have the child, then we kill them all."

"What of the other children?"

Fenrir scowled. "One will suffice for now. I need leverage in case Lupescu comes. If one has been secured, we cannot risk taking others and undermining our hope."

"What of Lupescu." Fenrir heard one of them murmur.

He scowled back at them. "The bastard Oltenia heir. He must be the first to die If he is not already dead in Rome. We will continue to hunt him. The child of Lupescu will be leverage."

He turned to walk down the hill because Titus wanted to talk to him after the beating. "Until I have one of his children, we shall pretend the Romans are in control. Got it?!"

The men nodded in agreement, but their eyes sparkled yellow in the night, and deep growls belted out in defiance as Fenrir marched away from them to meet with Titus.

After the beating, Titus commanded two villagers to untie Honus and get him into a house. Two women burst through the crowds to get him. Honus bit his tongue in pain as his flesh was ripped in shreds on his back, and blood pooled down to his feet. He turned his head to glare at his father while the women put his arms over their shoulders, his jaws clenched. But Titus wrapped the whip up and stared at him cold-faced again before his generals approached him.

The women helped him walk through a wooded path to the rear of the village, where a series of river stone square huts lined up through the woods. They paused at the one near the end, peering into the darkness of the woods behind them for a moment. The open, rounded room was lit up with Roman Lamps sitting atop an elongated plank wood table, the fires dancing shadows across the walls, lighting up their faces.

Honus grunted as they pulled him into the open room and onto a bench. A lamp sat in the window, too, but the window had been built to be high, over his head. The women pulled lemon olive oil with herbs from the table and ripped clean fabric to soak in a wooden bowl.

Honus took a deep breath. He was sitting upright on the bench, his back facing them, his fists clenched in pain. He turned his head to stare at the youngest woman, with black hair with green eyes. Her cloaks folded around her as if she had layers of earth on, and her black hair braided down her back in a sloppy knot.

"I told you not to come." He moaned.

Bohdana smirked at him. "Let them try to take me. Ganna, help me with the blood."

The older woman walked around to face Honus and took his face in her palm. "I am so sorry, Honus. You are brave and kind-hearted, not like your wicked father."

Honus's eyes teared up. He grasped her wrist in his shaky palm and grasped it, a tear falling. "Vasiliki will not save my father because of his cruelty. Yet he will not let her live. I fear for him."

Ganna sighed, pushing her long gray hair off her shoulder. She pulled her hand away from his and shoved a sliver of wood plank in his mouth, turning away to help Bohdana clean him up. "Bite down." She warned him.

Honus shifted it so he could bite down better. Then he heard Ganna say, "Get the vinegar." He took a deep breath and held it as they showered his back with it. The stinging blow made him lurch, arching his back in pain. He grunted moans in defiance, gritting his teeth.

When they had cleaned his back of the blood, Ganna painstakingly put lemon balm and St John's Wort on his wounds. They wrapped his midsection and shoulders with the torn fabric soaked in the oil. Honus was still in pain but knew the lemon as an antiseptic would begin healing.

Bohdana bent before him on her knees, taking his hands in her own and kissing his knuckles. Honus leaned his head into her forehead, and they gazed into one another. "I love you. Please go back to Vasiliki." Honus whispered, begging her.

Bohdana smiled at him, tears in her eyes. "I had to come. We met Kilian at the river, so we knew you were successful in coming. We must ensure you are delivered safely before..."

"You know my father will not abandon this." Honus feared.

Bohdana sighed, swallowing. "That is why we have come. If Vasiliki cannot come to save the Romans, I can save you."

Honus sighed against her lips, and Bohdana breathed on his lips, closing her eyes. "I cannot lose you."

Honus leaned in and kissed her, his lips trembling. "Stay cautious while you are here. I will stay to see if Axius comes to warn my father."

"And if Axius does not come?" Bohdana begged him, her green eyes sparkling with worry.

Honus breathed into her face and closed his eyes. "Then I will fight alongside my people. I will not abandon them."

Bohdana swallowed, leaning back to stare at him. "We are your people now, and I will not leave until I know you are safe. You cannot fight injured like this. You cannot fight the beasts at the river."

Ganna stood watch at the doorway, her senses energized since the darkness had come. She sniffed the air and smelled the fires cooking and fish and grains simmering in the pots. She heard the revelry of the Roman army sitting alongside the villagers at the river banks, laughing and drinking. Her ears itched as voices drew nearer, but it was just Romans and the villagers meandering along the torch-lit wood-lined paths, talking about life.

She turned her gaze upon the young couple embracing one another, smiling at them. Honus bent over in pain, putting his weight on Bohdana's shoulders. She pressed her chin into his shoulder and embraced him, still on her knees. Ganna met her stare, shaking her head, frustrated at what Honus had just endured. Bohdana clenched her jaws, her pupils dilating from emerald green to a vibrant yellow for a split second.

Ganna turned away from her and pressed her back into the door jam, allowing the crisp river breezes to calm her nerves. When she turned to stare at Bohdana, Honus had fallen asleep in her arms. "We must get him out of here," Ganna exclaimed.

Bohdana sighed. "Help me put him in bed. We are not leaving until Axius gets here. He is the only one Titus will listen to. I will respect that, for now."

Ganna helped lift Honus into the bed, laying him on his side. The night crept by bitterly. The Roman revelry plagued the air, and a mischievous worry filled the room with dread.

Titus braced his fists behind his back, his red cloak flowing behind him as the wind picked up outside his house overlooking the river. They were not crude huts. They were not barbaric by any standards, for Rome had sent armies here for years to build up this river village's defenses. Fen stood at the end of the table, gazing across the wine vats and the smoked fish. In the middle of the table around the meat platters were grapes from their vines along the river and apples with vats of raspberries.

Titus leaned atop the end of his side of the table, a map strewn across it, thinking. His senior officers lingered by his side, gazing upon the map and questioning their next moves. Fenrir was not a tall man, and Titus towered over him. He met Titus's stare, nodding in submission.

"This wretched queen of yours, Vasiliki, is that her name?"

Titus sneered.

Fenrir scoffed. "She is not my queen. My people are loyal to the Emperor and Rome alone."

Titus bit his bottom lip, looking back at the map. "Her tribe is at the base of these Carpathian Mountains. And yet, in all the years we have worked with you, we cannot seem to penetrate them." Titus pointed to a level flowing plain with rising plateaus, a rocky mountainous terrain between them and Dacia.

Fenrir agreed. "She is cunning, and her generals are violent." He warned Titus. "She has killed many of my people."

Titus pressed his hand out, and one of his generals handed him a scroll. Titus opened it, scanning and inspecting the seal and the signature. As he read it, his face lighted up. "Ah. The Senate has confirmed Vasiliki penned the scrolls your scouts intercepted. The emperor wants her dead, as she is solely responsible for the slaughter of our men. There is no more room for mercy. We will take complete control of Dacia on the Danube there."

The generals agreed with Titus as he continued: "This has been a long journey. We will allow the men a rest and then move forward in the following weeks. By then, Honus will have healed and can accompany me. I cannot send him back to Pannonia now."

Fenrir agreed. "Perfect." He added. "What will happen to Vasiliki's warriors?"

Titus met his stare, his eyes penetrating him, but Fenrir stood still and nodded in respect. "What does Rome do to traitors?"

"Traitors die." Fenrir smiled.

Titus marched up to him and loomed into his face, clenching his jaws, eying him up and down, sneering at him.

"You have been a wise choice for Rome gathering this information against Vasiliki. You will be rewarded once we have this victory. Do not make me regret it."

Fenrir looked him in the eyes and then nodded his head in a bow to him, gritting his teeth. "We are thankful to continue this endeavor for Rome and our people."

Titus cleared his throat, stepping back to look at the map. "Indeed. You understand your people belong on the river and would not do well in Rome." He jested. "You need to stay here with your lowland people."

Fenrir bit his tongue.

"Now leave us. We have planning to do." Titus complained, shooing Fenrir out of the house.

As he turned to go, Titus called after him. "Do not wander off too far, Dacian." Titus's voice was cold, full of malice.

Fenrir felt it. He turned back around and bowed in respect. "I am at your service." He marched out of the house, smiling as he left the trail to head down to the river.

Everything was falling into place, and Titus was right where he wanted him. The unexpected bonus was that he would also get Honus.

25

The Library of Reckoning

Manius and Micah paraded through the streets to the city center to The Bibliotheca Ulpia. It was the most prominent library since the destruction of the Library of Alexandria. Not only did it have archival materials they needed, but Manius was desperate for something else. He needed a particular collection of books not pertaining to public records, and he would use his authority to get to it, with Micah's help.

Micah cleared his throat, hustling through families lingering in the courtyard gardens, smiling at them as he passed behind Manius. The two-story columned library adorned the city square, its white pillars beaming under the early morning sun. Micah paused at the entrance as they meandered in, the desks and chairs lined up from one end to the other, the pillars gracing statues of ethereal beauty.

As they left the long room with the desks, Manius gazed upon a couple of scholars studying and smiled at them. They raised to acknowledge his presence and nodded, going back to their studies.

"This way." Micah then led him through a vast expanse of an open room, circular with windows a story above, screaming in daylight with beams of hope. At the end of that room, it narrowed again to walls of shelves full of books and scrolls from the floor to the ceiling, the light beams kissing the room and the steps down into it.

Manius paused at one shelf, pretending to pull one out and read it, his eyes on Micah. Micah approached a scribe at the back wall who had lighted upon a ladder, and they began whispering. Manius cleared his throat and gazed back to the open round room, the second-story statues watching him as if they knew something he did not. There was no one else in there.

The white-haired old man scribe nodded at Micah and then came down from the ladder. "Follow me, senator." He whispered, and Manius followed him and Micah in haste down a thin passageway between the shelves that opened to a wooden plank door where he had the key.

The scribe gazed behind them to see if anyone was watching, and Manius felt uneasy. As he unlocked the door and let them in, he whispered.

"You can have the time you need. Nothing leaves this collection." He warned them.

Manius agreed. "Thank you."

Micah nodded, agreeing. "Indeed."

He turned one more time. "One final warning, Senator."

Manius froze, swallowing.

"This collection is not in the public record. Be cautious of angering the gods by the knowledge you see here today." He turned and locked the door behind them.

Manius turned to Micah, his eyes wide. "I am certain the gods are already angered."

Micah sighed as he shut them in the library. "He always says that."

"How do we search for this?" Manius pulled out the scroll from Vasiliki, reading the interpretation Micah had penned on it from Matunaga.

Micah gazed around at this dome-shaped private library, with towering shelves filled with thousands of books and scrolls.

"We are looking for a praetorian edict or senatorial decree from the Dacian wars. Trajan, so look for a T. Ah, here it is." Micah bounced over to it, and Manius stood there impressed.

"Let us look for any decree regarding the Dacians. Someone in the Senate is working with these beasts, so I am curious to see what edicts were proclaimed."

"I do not understand why we are looking this far back." Manius pulled an armful of scrolls off the wall and plopped them on the massive table behind them.

"Because there are always planning documented regarding wars. We would be fools to think Rome was unaware of these beasts when Trajan began his campaigns against Dacia." Micah rolled open a book, and his eyes lit up.

"If these are the descendants of Loki, then they have been there for centuries. Rome would have known." Micah added. "A truth is hidden here that has not revealed itself yet."

Micah mumbled outloud, "Trajan's Dacian Wars ended with Decebalus' death, and then Dacia became a Roman province."

"Yes, that is accurate." Manius agreed, reading it with him.

"The Dacians were annihilated. Many Romans were killed. Yet," Micah paused, pulling another book open and then another.

"Much knowledge is lost about the Dacian conquest. It must be here. There must be something about the beasts." He complained, glaring behind him to another wall.

Manius slithered around the round library room, gazing at the domed ceiling in silence, thinking. "The hardest ones to get to are where we need to go." He pointed to the roof and the pillars caressing the dome, the long windows blasting light in at them from all angles.

"You take that ladder, I will take this one, and we will meet in the middle." Micah smiled.

Manius pulled himself up the sliding ladder, his eyes on a sliver of a shelf above the letter D. He pulled one arm through the ladder to prop himself up as he pulled one scroll out at a time to read them from this great height. He heard Micah doing the same under the Trajan column, sighing as he rolled them back up and pulled out another.

Manius coasted to the L section, pulled out one book, and froze reading it. Silence overcame them as they read at the same time, their minds buzzing.

"Lycanthrope," Manius mumbled, whispering the word out loud. Micah paused from reading and stared at him from across the dome, waiting.

"The writings of Trajan, by his scribe. An illness followed my army from Dacia. The scribes and healers call it an illness of the mind. This illness curses the body, making the men stronger and cruel, changing their shape and form so they know not who they once were. Therefore, I declare death to these traitors before this delusion spreads in Rome."

Micah gawked. "The beast curse followed them. I wonder what happened to the army in Dacia for them to get it."

"Rome did not truly overcome Dacia, even during the wars." Manius scowled. "We have been fools this whole time."

Micah chimed in; his eyes melted upon a parchment he had unfolded to read. "Yes, because they were in leads with one another. Between the gold and the silver and the fine jewels and metals. Dacia fed Rome this wealth, and Rome put Dacia's most powerful beasts in the Senate."

"What." Manius blurted out, his eyes wide.

"Vasiliki warned there were traitors in the Senate who bleed like a man. I just found the origin here."

Manius held his breath as Micah read what he had found. "*Hadran, the successor of Trajan, as told by his scribe: Unity of Rome is of utmost importance to our future. Dacia must be colonized, and the beasts there are at peace with us to grow territory and Rome's power in the world. We will continue sending delegates and Senators. In return, Dacia will supply us with riches to fund the expansion of Rome into uncharted territories.*"

They stared at one another from across the dome.

"To rule the world. This whole damn time." Manius clenched his jaws.

"Trace the genealogy of the ones in the Senate, Micah. We must hunt them before we become the hunted." Manius warned him.

"I have my parchment and pen, so it will take me some time to write this down and sneak it out of here." Micah swallowed.

"You have til nightfall. I will stay with you til then. This must be done today. Domitia's children are on the line." He whimpered, climbing back down.

Micah turned back to the shelf, pulling another one down. "The whole world is on the line. And yes, poor Diana." His eyes teared up.

He was, after all, with Manius at his estate when the falcon delivered the painful news. They had not expected to see Domitia show up with the children or the Dacian warriors, but Manius had his servants put straight to work on making them comfortable in their rooms.

Micah lunged down from the ladder and began the tedious work of copying over names. He would access genealogies from the main library, which would take weeks of research. He bit his lip and narrowed his brows, determined.

Meanwhile, Manius kept pulling out parchments and gazing upon the truths that set his teeth on edge. The beasts were always in Dacia, and Rome always sided with them despite all the wars.

26

Lupescu Rising

Seeing her in pain made his heart hurt, so every time Domitia was defiant with her father, Nestor would follow her through the almond groves and watch her try to climb the smaller trees. She would fall every single time, busting a knee open or scratching her elbows. Once, she sprained an ankle, and Nestor had to carry her back to the manor.

"Lupescu, Lupescu!"

She would holler at him as she noticed him watching her on the path. Him, a scrawny boy with blue tattoos on his naked chest and rags for clothing, covered in sweat. His black hair, spiked atop his head, was as sharp as his thin jawline. He was missing a front tooth, but Domitia did not care. He had already told her he pulled it himself for a mercenary to take back to his father, to show he had been taken and was probably dead.

He meandered up to her, a petite, dark-headed beauty with big eyes and olive-toned skin kissed by the sun. Her long, dark hair was braided down her back, and she often had leaves or flowers stuck in it.

"Your father wants you to call me Nestor. Why do you hate your father so?" He would ask, as if he knew the world already, only twelve years old.

Domitia would pause climbing and gawk at him. "I do not hate papa. I hate the ways of men. Telling me what to do."

Nestor laughed at her. "So, rule over them one day. That is your answer. To change the rule of men."

Domitia froze, her eyes wide at him. "You can help me." She smiled.

Nestor gazed into her eyes and swallowed, her beaming face lit up at his own, seeing him for who he was, not from whence he came. He stood below her, gawking at her dangling from the branches precariously, and then she slipped and fell.

Nestor woke to a deafening silence, but inside, he heard Domitia crying. He gripped his heart and took a deep breath, a dull ache in his chest subsiding as he woke. He surveyed the boat and the men. Brasus, Moskin, and Tarbus were at their oars guiding the ship still. It looked as if they had not slept. Nestor understood. He only slept due to exhaustion.

He gazed upon the lowland plain, which became evident as the boat coasted on the Danube. They were miles further inland, closer to the mountains, and he could smell it. He paused and noticed Kilian standing at the bow as a man. The beast was gone. At least he was fully clothed.

Nestor pulled himself up and arched his back, missing his bed and wife. He missed the laughter and tight hugs of his children. He kicked Axius's boot to wake him and smiled as he mumbled something in his sleep. Axius awoke from a groggy but short rest. Nestor joined Kilian to gaze through the darkness as dawn caressed the mountains. Crimson and tangerine hues kissed the horizon, spreading light as if a cloak had been removed from the darkness of these lands.

Miles of open plains and hills rolled like emeralds had been spilled before them. The open rolling hills stopped as they disappeared into a dark, lush forest. Nestor sniffed the air. Kilian noticed and watched him in silence, his eyes turning again to the dense shoreline swallowed in a forest canopy.

Kilian pulled at his cloak. He had raided the men's clothing and dressed in Brasus's pants and tunic. "You miss her. You said her name over and over in your dreams." Kilian mumbled to him.

Nestor gazed behind him to see the men asleep and Axius sitting up, popping his neck.

"I fear for them. I have put them in danger because of who I am." Nestor sighed.

He gazed back at Axius. "Everyone I love is in danger."

"Does she know she married a beast, Lupescu?" Kilian whispered.

Nestor grimaced. "She has always known and loves me anyway. She is the love of my life."

Silence. "My name is Nestor. Lupescu is dead."

Kilian nodded, half smiling at him. "Very well, yet you stayed hidden for years."

"And you came to Rome for years looking for me. Did you not, scout of the queen?"

Killian took in a deep breath, his face flat. "I did."

Nestor sighed. "If anything happens to my family, I will kill them all."

Kilian agreed. "I will join you in killing them."

Nestor turned to see Axius walking up to them. He eyed Kilian and sighed. "No more beast, eh."

Kilian smiled at him. "Not in the moment, no."

"Happy to see you found the clothes." He muttered, gripping Nestor's shoulder, eyeing him. "Brother, you good?"

Nestor nodded but met his face with wavering eyes. "I fear something is not right. I fear for my family."

Axius swallowed. "None of this is right."

Kilian turned to Brasus and the others as the boat coasted into a shoreline and stopped abruptly, but they were already rigid and glaring around them. Movement from the shore made them freeze, and Axius followed their stares, remembering what Nestor said about weapons. They would be of no use here anyway.

A man stood on the shoreline at the tree's edge, fully clothed with a breastplate of metal scales, a wide belt, sporting short swords. His arms and legs were cuffed in leathers. He wore a gray wolf pelt on his head, and the fur cascaded off his shoulders and hung down his back to look like a tail. His face was tattooed in blue symbols like Axius had seen on Nestor's chest and back. He had a long, flowing, dark beard and mustache. His dark eyes sparkled in the dawn as the sun kissed him. He looked as if he had waited for them all morning already.

"We are now in Lupa's village territory," Kilian warned them.

When the Dacians emerged from the wood, Axius froze at the sight of them. Their scabbards were engraved with wolf head symbols, and their arm cuffs had spikes built into them. They had not pulled their long falxes yet, and the scabbards on their backs had long swords sticking up over their heads. They recognized Kilian and tossed a rope to him to tie the boat up. Axius did not recognize their native tongue, but he noticed Nestor perked his ear at them as they conversed with Kilian.

Nestor leaned into Axius. "Stay close to me and me alone, brother."

Axius felt shivers eat his backbone out and followed Nestor and Kilian off the boat through the tribe with Brasus and the others behind. They followed the Dacians in silence under a canopy until it opened to reveal a rolling plain and stone houses surrounding the whole of the round hillside. Fires burned the scent of citrus and fish, and the sounds of waterfalls called to them in a beautiful world Axius had never seen before. He was in awe, but a sense of dread made his chest heavy.

Kilian led the way behind the Dacian and paused when a tall man with red hair dressed in the same body armor met them at the entrance to the village. Kilian bowed to him.

"Ah, the queen's scout has returned alive. Late! But alive." He scowled at him, raising his eyes above Kilian's head to glare at Nestor, Axius, and the others.

"Lupa, high commander." Kilian spoke.

Axius froze at the sight of him. Lupa was indeed spectacular to look upon. His golden, scaly breastplate and body armor were impressive, and Axius studied it. His wolf pelt was off his head and hanging down his back, and he was also fully armed. His auburn beard and mustache were braided down his face, and his long hair was in a thick braid down his back. He was twice the build of Brasus, who was himself a very muscular man.

"Take their weapons," Lupa commanded, crossing his arms at Kilian.

Axius held his breath as the Dacians standing on the path behind them grabbed his weapons, checking his cloak and attire for any others. He clenched his jaws as they prodded at him and grunted, trying to find weapons. When they took his Gladius, he scowled. Nestor nodded to him, letting him know he had no choice. Axius watched all the men get disarmed before the Dacians as more gathered around, and women had joined them. Axius noticed that the women wore body armor, but many wore skirts. They, too, were fully armed.

Once they were disarmed, Lupa huffed at Kilian. "Romans are forbidden here."

Nestor became stiff, clenching his jaws. Axius waited. Would they kill him? A lowly man amongst the beasts?

"He is a brother to Lupescu, Vasiliki's brother," Kilian warned, his eyes bright and changing yellow. "My years-long search for him is now successful."

Axius gasped at Nestor. "What."

Lupa scoffed at Nestor, his green eyes sparkling in malice. "Lupescu is dead." He growled.

Lupa lunged into Nestor's face, leaning down upon him, growling. Nestor did not flinch but met his stare.

"If you are Lupescu, where is it? Transform into the monster we all dread, and I will believe you." Lupa toyed with him.

"My allegiance was never to Lupa." Nestor toyed with him.

Lupa leaned back, scowling at him.

Kilian huffed. "Where is Vasiliki."

"They will not pass, Kilian." Lupa grimaced.

Kilian's eyes began to change as he leaned into Lupa's face and growled. "You will let me pass to my queen, commander."

Lupa did not budge. "They will not pass until the queen gives the command. And right now, I am in command."

Kilian leaned back and pulled at his cloak to remove it just as a voice called out from the crowd. The Dacians split, and Axius noticed Nestor's face drained of color. Brasus, Moskin, and Tarbus fell to their knees and bowed, their heads dropping into their chests. Kilian backed off from Lupa, and everyone bowed except Axius and Nestor.

Axius watched this woman emerge from the wood between the Dacians, and his eyes lit up at her. She and Nestor had similar facial features. Her long wool robes kissed her boots, and her dark hair melted around her face to her chest over the wolf fur hanging down her back. She, too, wore a breastplate in metal scales with a wide belt adorning a short sword and daggers. Over her head were long falxes in sheaths strapped to her chest.

Axius marveled at the twisting blue tattoos snaking around her fingers and wrists and up her finely tuned arms. Her dark eyes narrowed, and she froze at the sight of Nestor, clenching her narrow jaws and pursing her thin lips at him.

As it dawned on her, she took a step back and huffed. "Has Lupescu returned? My brother returned."

Nestor did not bow to her. He stood there aside Axius, clenching his jaws and biting his tongue. "Vasiliki."

"You have brought a Roman here." She sighed. "You know Romans are forbidden in the camp of Lupa and must die."

Nestor scowled at her. "My brother will not die today."

Vasiliki lingered up to Axius, pressing her prowess into him. Axius let her breathe him in, watching her face and how she gazed up and down his body. She then met his eyes, and he stared deep into hers. Unwavering. He felt as if he had kissed the morning sun on her face and held his breath at her blatant fearlessness of him.

"So, you are a brother to my brother, Roman." She breathed into his face, her voice deep as if an ocean had burst forth from the depths.

"Yet you are just a man. We will soon see what type of man you are in the face of the beasts." She leaned away from his lips, still sniffing him. "I can smell you miss your Roman armor since you are dressed in lowly Dacian rags." She huffed, turning away from him.

Axius thrust his hand out to her and opened his palm. She froze, looking at it, confused.

"I bleed the same as you." He whispered into her face. "The beasts bleed as red as my blood."

Vasiliki stepped back from him, her mouth frozen as if she wanted to say something but could not. Axius stood there, holding his palm out to her until she gripped it and pressed it to his side again. She melted into his face, so her breath was hot on his lips. Axius felt her grip as powerful as her stare and his knees went weak at her presence.

She took in a final deep breath of him, closing her eyes. When she opened her eyes, Axius never moved. He stared deep into her, his face stern and hard as if ready for battle. She stepped away from him and half smiled.

"You do, Roman. What is your name."

"Axius."

Then she turned to the mercenaries and scowled. "Where are the other generals? I see many are missing."

Brasus stood up, joined by Moskin and Tarbus. "Protecting Nestor's family from the half-bloods, my queen."

The Dacian crowds suddenly became a mass hysteria of hollering and shouting, and Vasiliki gasped, turning her gaze upon Nestor once more.

"What have you done?" She fretted, her eyes wide at him. And then she shouted, silencing the people.

"Lupescu has returned after being taken by Rome! Fenrir plots to overtake us and use the royal family as pawns!"

Axius turned to Nestor. "You are royalty?"

Lupa laughed, rolling his eyes. "Lupescu is dead."

Silence filled the Dacians once more.

Vasiliki approached Nestor, her eyes tearing up. "Is Lupescu dead, my long-lost brother?"

Nestor swallowed, clenching his jaws. "I am Nestor. I have a wife and five daughters. I will be returning to them."

"Five daughters." Vasiliki grasped her chest. "I have nieces?!" Her eyes teared up.

"And I shall return to them," Nestor warned her. "And Axius, my Roman brother, with me."

Vasiliki sighed. "So be it. Nestor. Then why have you come?" She demanded, her gaze turning back to Axius.

"My commander Titus is coming for you. Rome believes you are at fault for Commander Artgus's army deaths. Rome is coming to avenge the fallen. I am here to warn you and for you to give me time to reach Titus." Axius pleaded with her.

Lupa growled at Axius. "Rome is full of fools."

Vasiliki eyed Lupa and Kilian from the side and then melted back to Axius. "That was not us who killed them. If Titus continues forward, they will all die."

Kilian sighed. "He will not call off the invasion, my queen. Rome has commanded you to die. Titus has joined Fenrir at the river town, and they plan to march."

Vasiliki scoffed. "Is this true, Axius?"

Axius swallowed. "It is true. I must warn Titus to get him to retreat."

"Unless you help them." Nestor butted in, glaring at Vasiliki.

Lupa laughed. "Help the Romans? Ha! It is forbidden."

"It is what is right." Nestor blurted out.

Vasiliki took in a deep breath. "You want me to summon my army to help the Romans survive Fenrir? If I do this, it would be immediate war between the tribes. It will not end well."

"For you?" Axius pondered.

Vasiliki smiled at him, a squint in her eyes as if hope had kissed her soul, but with a malicious intent. "For them, Roman."

"Fenrir must be killed. If we do not stop him now, then the world burns. He wants Rome." Nestor raised his voice.

Vasiliki laughed at him, her voice as piercing as a shrieking howl. "You have no idea how often I sent Kilian into Rome looking for you. You are finally home after lying about being taken as a child. You stand here to tell me my brother Lupescu is dead, yet you talk as if he never left. You want your family safe, Nestor? Then you must stand up and fight here for it first."

Nestor held his breath at her remarks, his face tightening up. "I will never be that beast again. I fight with the Romans."

Vasiliki scoffed at him, growling under her breath. "You and my generals are weak! Weak! You are a burden to us all until you accept it again. We will not help Rome until you do."

The color drained from Nestors face, and he grimaced at her as if a great pain had hit him head-on. She leaned into his face, only an inch shorter than him. She smiled, and Axius noticed her strong jawline and fervent brows over a small nose like Nestor's.

"Lupescu will return when it has no choice but to fight for the ones it loves." She warned him, a sparkle of amber in her eyes.

She stepped away from Nestor, pointing to the mercenaries. "Take them. Purge them of the filth they endured in Rome."

Lupa bowed to her, motioning for other Dacians to take them. "It will be done, my queen." He obeyed.

Lupa motioned for his soldiers to take Brasus, Moskin, and Tarbus. Nestor and Axius watched them being led to the back of the camp, where they disappeared. Axius wondered what the purging meant. Whatever it was, it was too late now.

"Come with me. We have much to discuss." Nestor and Axius turned to follow Vasiliki and Kilian through the camp. When Axius turned one last time to gaze upon Lupa, he narrowed his brows and growled under his breath, crossing his arms at his chest. Axius turned to focus on walking with Nestor.

The grass paths had been trodden down and meandered in and out of the camp. It reminded Axius of a fortress hole within the shadow of a looming mountain. The stone houses danced in the meadow for miles until the Dacians were sparse, and there were only rolling hills and a stone fortress built into them under a cavernous mountain.

The morning sun beat down upon them, and a breeze blasted through the hills with a bite. Axius froze looking at it. Stone houses resembling a city melted into the hills. Axius smelled metal and perked his nose up at it.

"We have an armory. A bakery. Healers. We have a great hall. Houses for all our families. Herbalists. We are nothing like Rome makes us out to be." Vasiliki told Axius. "We are not the killers of Romans."

Axius watched Dacian mothers meander through the fields, picking flowers and herbs with their children. He saw the fathers fishing at the shoreline of a small tributary from the Danube, its crystal waters flowing through the village like diamonds had kissed the valley.

"And all of you are beasts?" Axius questioned, gazing upon the small children playing in the water alongside their fathers while the mothers picked herbs growing by the shores.

Kilian shook his head. "Wolves, all of us, even the little wolfs."

"Why does this Fenrir kill my people?" Axius wondered.

Vasiliki led them past the village, and at the end of the trail, Axius paused at a large two-story house. The smell of hot iron and fires burned, and the window was cracked open to reveal a metalworking shop, the bladesmith. A black wolf blocked his view and then walked away from the window, picking up a forge twice as big as Axius had seen in Rome. It was twice as big for hammering and making weapons for the Dacian wolves.

He widened his eyes as Nestor grabbed him by the cloak and pulled him along the path again. "Bladesmith beast," Axius mumbled.

"Vezina is a scythe smith." Kilian bragged. "He makes our falxes and swords."

"You use scythes?" Axius wondered. "Shit."

"Ah, Axius. You will see." Kilian smiled at him.

Vasiliki stopped at the end of the hill, which turned into a rising rock wall. The wall spilled with engravings, stories, and history.

"When the moon is full, we can see the story of our people here." Vasiliki raised her arm, and Axius thought the wall went up for miles, towering over him.

"We have six weeks until another full moon, Axius. Until then, you must stay in the village." She warned him.

"What happens at the full moon? I know you all are already beasts." He questioned.

She approached him and sighed in his face. Axius never knew a woman as brazen as her. She would get right up in his face as if she was taking in his soul through her eyes. He found himself leaning into her stare, the clenching of his jaws weaker now.

"We are not beasts. That filth will never be one of us."

She reached into her fur and pulled out a scroll, handing it to Axius. He froze at it, recognizing the seal.

"Opiter." Nestor gawked.

"We have a loyal scout who intercepted this. Read it." Vasiliki warned Axius. Nestor leaned in to read it with him.

The gold is en route via carriage. The heart of the paw is at hand. It must be taken before the next full moon. It must be subdued before the heart manifests into its true brutality. We cannot have the Oltenian clan coming into Dacia, for they know nothing of our quests. See to it the heir and its heirs are taken. There is no other way for Rome to grow and take the world. The heir of Fenrinsulfer must succeed and take all.

-Senator Opiter.

Axius gazed upon Vasiliki, his eyes widening as fear grew in hers. Then he turned to Nestor, who had clenched his face so hard blue veins protruded from his temples. Axius saw the same facial features, thin-toned faces, and high cheekbones. The dark hair and eyes, slender, finely tuned bodies, and a fervent passion for life boiling in them now exploded. Axius felt it so thick he could cut it with his Gladius.

"What happens in six weeks?" Axius fretted.

Vasiliki sighed, gazing at Kilian before turning a hard-faced stare at Axius. But she did not have to say anything because Nestor spoke up, his voice harder than Axius had ever heard.

"Any man can become a true blood in the ritual on that night only. So, we better hope Titus and our brothers survive if he is not swayed to abandon this war."

"No!" Axius yelled, his face red. "Roman soldiers will not become beasts."

"If they survive. They will not survive without our help." Kilian warned Vasiliki. "My queen, we must help them."

Axius shook his head, a pounding headache haunting him. "I must go to Titus to warn him. He has a right to know what they are against, please." He begged her. "I must leave straight away. He will listen to me."

Vasiliki shook her head no. "You would be hunted on the way there and killed by Fenrir's scouts. We cannot allow that to happen. Fenrir will not allow anyone to venture to that village and will wait til your commander and the army march to me."

"I must wait until he draws nearer to your territory?" Axius pondered.

Vasiliki nodded yes.

Axius scoffed. "That gives us no time to prepare the army for Fenrir's beasts."

"I told you, man does not survive the beasts at the river," Nestor warned. "They are all dead men unless Vasiliki wars against Fenrir. The only hope is if Titus will listen to you and fall back to Rome before Fenrir comes."

Axius closed his eyes and sighed. Vasiliki watched him in silence.

"You think Roman soldiers cannot defeat these beasts." Axius scoffed. "How does Titus and the army survive there already? Tell me. How does Fenrir allow them to live?" Axius demanded.

Kilian held his breath. "He knows we side with Rome and will try to save them. It will be a weakness for us. Many of us will die protecting your Romans while trying to survive."

Axius huffed.

Vasiliki agreed. "He will kill the Romans and kill your Titus. He will thrust our tribes into a war. Rome will continue sending in more armies to avenge the fallen. Rome will die."

"I must go to Titus." Axius swallowed.

"I will not risk losing any warriors for you to reach Titus right now. Trust me." Vasiliki told him.

Axius flinched at her remark. *Trust me.*

"Can I trust you?" Axius questioned her.

It caught her off guard, and she jerked her gaze to him. "Can I trust you, Roman?! Your people have blamed us for the army's demise for centuries. You will prove I can trust you first, then you will see you can trust me."

A rigid burst of chills rushed up Axius's spine. "So be it." He bent his head and bowed to her, his eyes never leaving hers.

She swallowed, widening her eyes. "You are bold, Axius."

She turned to Nestor. "You have greater fears than Fenrir, dear brother. You have traitors in the court of Aurelian, and they hunt your family." She warned. "My nieces." She scowled, gritting her jaws.

Nestor became rigid as if a sword had gouged him.

She pulled another parchment from her robes and handed it to Nestor. Kilian watched her hand it over to him, his eyes widening. Axius swallowed watching Nestor's face flushed with anger, his eyes narrowing at the revelation. His knees grew weak, and his heart ached watching Nestor's reaction to this news.

"The half-breeds have taken Diana. Domitia and the other children are safe. Dia has been killed. Troy and Mel are injured but still alive. Your farm is in disrepair, and the workers are scattered. We head into Rome at Domitia's command to find Diana and hunt the beasts there. We will work with Manius and Micah to root them out." -Matunaga

Nestor moaned out a growl, gritting his teeth, his eyes changing from dark brown to a dull yellow as his pupils dilated. "I will kill them all!" His shriek howled.

Axius swallowed as he watched Nestor and stepped back in disbelief, his heart pounding. He had no weapons to grab to protect himself and could only lean further against the wall as Nestor raged.

And then Nestor fell to his knees. His tears kissed his eyes in pain. A shrieking growl erupted from somewhere deep inside him that had been oppressed for many years, and a relic of something that was not man burst out.

"I will kill them all!" He clenched his teeth as fangs burst out. He clutched the parchment so tight that dark blue veins popped on the top of his hand and slithered into black lines. While his other hand dug rivets into the dirt at his knees, dagger claws protruded from them.

Vasiliki huffed. "Lupescu is not so lost after all, is it."

A sudden realization hit Axius. He was the only human in a forest of monsters. The worst ones were already in Rome. He backed further away, his shoulder rubbing against the rock wall. As the beast overtook Nestor, Lupescu was born again.

27

The Hunt for the Heirs

Troy stood across the courtyard, leaning into a pillar, while Mel stood across him in the gardens, watching the children play. The girls had a small table with teapots and hand-carved toys across the lawn beside the waterfall. He raised his head to see the Dacians standing or kneeling around the domed courtyard on the roofs, all their backs to the children, their ever-watchful eyes grazing outside the hillside villa to surrounding streets and woods.

The gnarled woods stretched over the villa roofs like fingers prodding at the clay tiles, giving them cover and shade. Troy was restless because Domitia had wandered into the city with Matunaga and Manius but did not like it. Though Matunaga could protect her, he was not sure of Manius's skills with the blade, and if half-breeds were to come after her, she was as good as gone.

So, he stood there, blowing loudly and pursing his lips, nervous until Domitia returned, and he knew she was safe. Meanwhile, the girls played with their dolls in the yard. Manius had his servants create a tea party with fruits, cheeses, and sweet bread. But the girls were not eating. They were not hungry.

Nestor's eldest twins, Aurora and Venus, would stop playing with their dolls to watch him, gazing at Mel. Their faces were drawn, and they were not smiling. Troy wanted to coddle them in his arms, but he could not. He aimed to watch them and keep them safe from the beasts until Nestor returned and they got Diana back. He could not let them down again.

The day faded slowly waiting for Domitia to return. Troy wondered how long it would take her to discover truths from the elderly wealthy women married to the Senators. She would have successfully delivered the parchments by now, so she should be headed back. He sighed and crossed his palms across his groin, his weapons pinging at his sides. The girls pretended to be playing while fully aware that their sister was taken, their mom was now on a desperate mission, their father and Axius were in Dacia somewhere with the beasts, and Rome was in great danger.

When Troy feared his thoughts would drive him insane, a shadow caught his eye to his left, and he froze. Mel popped in his face from around the pillar, laughing at him. "I crept up on you, and you failed the test." She warned him. "You are dead."

Troy scoffed at her, crossing his arms and eyebrows. "You are supposed to be helping me watch them."

"So are you, yet your mind is elsewhere."

Troy sighed in her face.

"I am thinking," Mel added.

Troy rolled his eyes, glaring back at the girls pretending to play in the yard. "Never a good thing with you." He added.

"Let us train the children to fight."

"What!" Troy hollered, triggering the Dacians atop the roofs to glance down at them.

"Nestor would want his daughters to know how to fend for themselves. What do we have to lose?"

Troy glared at her and then jumped when he felt the tug of his tunic by Aurora and the other sisters standing beside her, glaring up at him. "How did you all creep up on me?" He gasped.

"You were not paying attention." Venus chimed in, a mischievous sparkle in her dark eyes much like her father's.

"Teach us how to fight," Aurora added, smiling.

The youngest yelled: "Like Axius! Like Axius!"

They all nodded, smiling, and begged Troy. "Please, Troy. Please, Troy!" They begged, attracting the attention of the Dacians atop the roof even more. Before Troy could respond to them, one of the Dacians had stood up and hollered down, his fist full of thick sticks.

"Eh, Dacian."

Troy gazed up, and the Dacian tossed him the sticks. "Teach them to fight." The Dacian nodded and then turned his back on Troy to continue watching the street below the hill.

The girls were giddy as Mel handed them their sticks, which were more like staffs because they were so petite. Troy marched them to the middle of the yard, his eyes on Mel, who smiled ear to ear.

"Nestor is going to kill me," Troy mumbled to himself.

D omitia gathered her tired wits about her and rode on horseback down the hill past the city, the stacked houses and manors sprawling out over the rolling hillsides. Behind her were Manius and Matunaga, cautious and ever watchful. They had been gone since daybreak and Domitia was more determined than ever after dropping off the parchments with the servants of the houses. The elders were either asleep or had ventured into Rome to conduct their duties for the Senate. Micah had penned copies of many parchments for her, which repeated the same message to her wealthy women friends:

My most trusted friends and sisters, I am calling on you to fulfill an oath to me you made when I supported your husbands and sons for

Senate elections, Magistrates, and consuls. Our families are in danger. I implore you to respond within the week to my pain. A meeting of utmost importance will be at Senator Manius's yard at midday on Saturday. There will be feasting and wine, and we shall discuss this travesty and how we shall help Rome. -Domitia.

Manius had also been conspiring and increased the watch throughout the city of guards to look for the child. By now, all the residents of Rome were made aware that Diana had been taken and for the city to be on the lookout for her. He hoped she would be found if she were still in Rome, and the beasts would be drawn out for the Dacians to kill. That was his hope, anyway.

Domitia slowed down on a brick road at the edge of the valley. The rising hills flowed before them to reveal vineyards and gardens of magnificent displays while the morning sun kissed the emerald fields in the hope of glory. A white stone-stacked house melted into a hill with climbing rose vines brisking its walls and hanging down. The white petals kissed around their feet, wafting in the gentle morning breeze. The wood plank door was wide and inviting, clay pots filled with herbs wafting earthy scents in their faces.

Domitia lighted down off her horse and moseyed up to the door. She paused at first but then knocked. This was the last house they were going to today. She turned to stare back at Manius and Matunaga, who sat atop their steeds, ever watchful. Matunaga had dressed in Roman attire like Micah and wore the robes of the high scribes. The door was answered by an elderly man whose face lit up at Domitia's presence. The door swung open, and Domitia smiled.

"Ah! Peter. How are you?"

Peter laughed, pulling Domitia into his arms and hugging her fiercely. "My child! My child! It has been so long! Please come in." But then he paused, noticing Manius and Matunaga, and his smile faded.

"Ah. I see. You do not come for a visit, do you, old friend?" He nodded. "And carrying weapons? What is ailing you?"

Domitia sighed. "I need your help. Is Freya home?"

Peter swallowed, his long white hair cascading down his back in a long ponytail. His old gray eyes sparkled at her while he pulled on his pristine blue robes. "She is ill, my child. Please come in." He motioned for Manius and Matunaga to join them. "Please come in. You are welcome."

They followed them in, and Peter acknowledged Manius. "Senator. A pleasure. And you are?" He noticed Matunaga.

"Opiter's scribe, Matunaga." Matunaga bowed to him in respect, smiling, but Peter was not smiling at him. "Opiter's scribe." He mumbled.

"Ah. Well then. Come this way." He led them through a great hall in the house that opened to a courtyard brimming with exotic birds. Their caws and spirited colors echoed throughout the home. Domitia smiled at them, admiring their beauty.

"I see you still collect things." She smiled.

Peter stopped and allowed them to admire the birds fluttering the trees in the courtyard. "Ah, yes. Of course, collecting things of beauty has always been a pastime of mine. I did find my wife, after all." He laughed, leading them through another corridor down a hall that ended in a main suite over looking a forest of trees open to the elements.

Domitia paused when she saw Freya huddled on a bed under covers, her frail body thin and pale, her eyes closed. She kneeled beside her, running her fingers through her white hair spilling down her shoulders. Freya opened her eyes, recognition dawning in them.

"Ah, there you are. I had hoped I would see you one final time. What a brave beauty you are, my child." Freya's voice was shaky and weak, and Domitia began tearing up.

Manius stood aside Matunaga and cleared his throat, eying the beauty and looking around everywhere but this old dying woman on the bed. Peter noticed it and smiled at the men. "How about tea? Looks like you all have been traveling a lot today and could use some, eh?"

Manius agreed. "That would be wonderful. Thank you, Peter."

"Very well, you may come with me to prepare it, Senator and scribe, eh?"

Manius gawked at him at first, but then Domitia glared, and he followed orders. She watched both follow Peter down the hall.

Domitia took her hands in her own and sighed. "Peter still has a way of demanding, and leaders follow."

Freya agreed. "Indeed. I love him so."

Silence.

"You are sad. Why are you sad?" Freya asked.

Domitia swallowed. She opened her mouth to speak, sighed, and then blurted it out. "The beasts have come to Rome and taken Diana. Nestor is in Dacia."

Freya took a deep breath and closed her eyes. "Oh." She moaned.

She gripped Domitia's hands, and they shook. "Help me sit up, child." Freya began sitting up while Domitia piled thick pillows behind her back.

"I need to know why my father and Commander Artgus would have taken Nestor from the river as a child. My father died before I found out, and you are only left alive to tell me. I need to know this history to get my daughter back."

Freya took a deep breath and cleared her throat. Her weary blue eyes met Domitia's as wrinkles raced down her beautiful pale face.

"I warned your father that you would come asking questions one day, and he always laughed at me. I assume he thought Nestor would have told you. But then your father died, so I will tell you what I saw. I have no choice."

Domitia sat upright, narrowing her brows to listen to her, her hands still clasped around Freya's.

"You know Nestor is one of them, a king. You knew that as a child."

Domitia felt the blood rush to her head as her heart pounded harder in her chest. "Yes."

"Nestor did not want to be the king, so his sister took the Dacian tribes."

"Vasiliki." Domitia sighed. "He wasn't taken then?"

"Nestor was only taken because he wanted to be. No man could have taken the wolf king otherwise."

"He was but a child." Domitia interrupted, confused.

"Oh, my dear, they are just as powerful when they are children. Size matters not."

"Commander Artgus took a liking to him, brought him to your father, who was on a mission for the Senate to maintain relations since the Dacian wars, and I was with him."

"And no other beasts were with him?" Domitia questioned.

Freya huffed. "Oh, there were Dacian men from his tribe who handed him over. I often thought Nestor forced them into letting him go. Like they had no choice."

"Artgus knew..." Domitia tried to speak, but Freya cut her off.

"...Artgus was a fool. He knew of them, yes. He continued to deny fate and march back into Auvergne, which was his demise. Once the king was out of the way, other beasts rose, shifting the power of the Dacian tribe to an ancient evil. Those poor Romans, what they must have been subjected to when they realized beasts were killing them. Their families left behind." She closed her eyes and sighed. "The horror they must have felt."

"Why was Nestor going there? It seems far away compared to where Vasiliki is now." Domitia pleaded.

"To rule, my child. They had always planned to migrate further away from Rome to save their kind. I know because I talked to them."

"You saw the purebloods?"

Freya smiled, closing her eyes to the memory. "I saw one, Lupa. Fearless and powerful warrior. Wise too. The longer I stayed away on those trips, the more Lupa began to trust me, as I had no ill will toward them. I loved them all."

Domitia smiled at her.

"Nestor is the last of his male bloodline of the remaining relic of the purebloods, bigger, the most powerful. Terrifying, my dear."

"Matunaga sent them a warning when Diana was taken..."

Freya perked up, her eyes wide. "Oh, my child. The relic of them, a few, terrifying, yes. They will come for Nestor and take him for the throne. He will serve his destiny there regardless."

Domitia began tearing up. "What if he still does not want to."

"You will be forced to make a choice, Domitia," Freya warned her, but Domitia shook her head.

Freya glared deep into her eyes. "You are his mate. He chose you, yes, but you also chose him. I watched the both of you grow up together and fall in love. No matter where you go, your love for one another will follow you there, even to the ends of this world."

"I cannot do this." Domitia swallowed.

"He will come for you, Domitia. He will come for you and the family you have made together." She spit.

"Why did he not want to go? Why did he have to come here." Domitia questioned, her heart busting inside.

Freya smiled at her. "Nestor had his reasons. I am sure of it. He does not like strict schedules. Look at what he has done for Rome. He is our hero. Our warrior. He is a carefree soul who cares not for power."

"That is why they took Diana. Because he is powerful." Domitia stuttered out, missing her little girl.

"Now they know who and where you are. They will come for you all. Your family was never meant to stay hidden. Do not give them a chance to take you or your remaining children. They will use your capture as leverage, and Rome will die, then the world."

Domitia clenched her jaws. "You stopped going there after my father brought Nestor back."

Freya agreed. "Something happened in the Senate, and we were commanded not to return. I was made to retire early, and Paul and I settled here. Very happy, I may add. Your father began training you to take over the businesses. He wanted you to be happy and strong. And you are."

"This would not have happened If I had never met him." Domitia cried.

Freya smiled in her face, raising a feeble arm to caress Domitia's chin. "Oh, my child, you cannot control destiny. Nestor was destined to find his mate, and he did. Perhaps that is why he felt led to come. Even if he had not come, Rome would still burn. The beasts would still come. You are better off to have a true blood guard over you than man."

Domitia gasped. "My father did this on purpose..."

She would have said something else, but Manius butted in. She perked up, wiping the tears from her face. It seemed she was crying a lot these days, and it was unlike her. Matunaga stood as a rail watching her, his eyes wide and bright, understanding. Paul emerged from behind the men with a tray of tea and herbal balms for Freya's achy bones.

"Freya, one order is eluding me. Who ordered you and Domitia's father to Auvergne?" Manius concluded, clenching his jaws.

Freya turned her eyes to stare at him, and half smiled, accepting a flower teacup and saucer from Paul with piping hot peppermint tea. "Opiter accompanied us many times on those adventures, even meeting his lovely wife there. He was always giving us missions there." But then she paused, sipping her tea, the hot steam contorting her face.

Manius dropped his jaw, glaring at her.

"Yet, when Aurelian became ruler, the Senate began venturing deeper into Dacia instead and steered clear of Auvergne. Very strange."

Matunaga froze, clenching his jaws, thinking. Manius eyed him, but all he could do was sigh.

"Opiter. It cannot be." Domitia's face looked as if something had stretched it thin, and it was ready to break. She stared at Manius, looking for different answers, but they would not come. Manius did not have any yet.

"Do you have any decree showing this? I know this is not in the archives." Manius asked, his eyes narrowing as he clenched his fists into his robes.

"I do." Paul disappeared out of the room, leaving them all aghast.

"What are you saying, Manius?" Domitia questioned, her face taut.

Manius took a deep breath, but Matunaga spoke for him. "Opiter is conspiring against Rome. All this time."

"Yet you are his scribe," Domitia questioned him.

Matunaga agreed. "Indeed, however, I stayed in the tower watching over the Dacian mercenaries. I studied Dacia and the beasts. I did nothing for Rome."

"Oh, I fear you did more for Rome than you can imagine or were informed about," Manius warned him, pursing his lips.

Manius sighed as Paul brought him a leather-bound box, a miniature chest with iron hinges. "They are all in here. You will not find these in the library."

Manius gasped when he opened it. "Of course, Micah and I knew there were more missing."

He and Matunaga pulled one out each and began reading. Domitia watched their body language change and started to get up to join them before Freya spoke again.

"You see, Rome is good at hiding truths. Before your father died, I was summoned to your house, Paul, and I…" she sipped on her tea.

Manius became weak in the knees at the truths he was reading and sat down on the settee, dropping a parchment to his feet while it clung precariously in his hand.

"…to gather this box of secrets because a scribe was coming to retrieve them for a private archive, and we feared they would be lost forever…"

Manius glared at her, his face tired, his mouth taut as if he wanted to speak but could not. Matunaga continued pulling parchments out, one after another, and comparing them, smiling ear to ear. Manius glanced up at him.

"You were the scribe."

Matunaga beamed ear to ear. "Yes."

Paul huffed. "Well, now you have them, dear scribe of Opiter."

Matunaga paused reading, glaring into the box of the depth of truths there, dropping his smile.

Freya finished, "...we feared Opiter would keep these secrets from the world. The real purpose of why we went into Auvergne was not to take Nestor..."

The room fell quiet, and Matunaga froze, biting his tongue. Manius stood up, the hairs on his neck pricking him.

"We were there to side with the beasts of Auvergne and bring Roman rulers in to reign alongside them," Freya warned. "I was sworn to secrecy by death, but yet I am free lying here on my death bed."

"That cannot happen." Domitia gasped. "Rome cannot rule with beasts."

Freya nodded her head, agreeing with her. "No, it cannot my child. The beasts there refused us. The Dacians did not. When I stopped going in, rumors circulated of Roman soldiers coming back from Dacia infected with madness. The Dacians would never do that."

"They turned into half-breeds," Matunaga exclaimed, picking up another parchment to read. "And the emperor had them killed. Beheaded is the only way."

"These half-breeds have been with us a while, it seems, and the casualties keep piling up," Manius complained.

Paul sneered at him. "I questioned the many journeys of my wife over the years, and now, in the end, we both see many things."

Manius gawked at him, widening his eyes. "Why would a man want to rule alongside beasts? The beast is powerful." He mumbled, thinking. "Man is weak unless trained to fight them."

Matunaga watched him pace back and forth and glanced into the box again, sighing. "It is clear to me now. It is not men who will rule alongside them. The ones we think are men are already beasts. It is all beasts. I was being used this whole time to feed knowledge to Opiter and the traitors the Senate needed."

Manius stopped pacing, the color draining from his face. "I need to check in with Micah. We have a lot of hunting to do, Matunaga."

"Indeed." Matunaga dropped the parchments into the box and slammed the lid shut.

As Domitia stood to leave with them, she froze and turned back to Freya. "Freya. If my father knew what Nestor was when he was brought into Rome, why did he encourage our love for one another?"

The room became a silent haven, and Domitia held her breath. Freya swallowed, her eyes tearing up.

"To protect you from the beasts, my dear. They were always coming. They were always plotting to take Rome. Every journey he took into those lands was to protect you, his family, and those he loved."

Domitia felt shivers chase up and down her spine to her knees. Her eyes were wide with tears, and her face was long as she gasped at this truth.

"They were always coming." She whispered, her lips quivering.

Hours later, Troy had tired himself out instead of the girls. Mel stood alongside, coaching them, egging them on, while Troy taught them to block and strike. It began like chaos and ended with Mel making the girls stand in a row together doing the same movements at the same time. It had worked, but Troy was spent.

Domitia raced into the house with Manius and Matunaga, ready to pull their swords. They paused as Aurora charged. Troy noticed Domitia staring at them wide-eyed. Her face was paler than usual as she watched her girls pretend to fight with swords. As Troy turned to her, Aurora struck him in the groin and then side-swapped his head with the stick. Mel grimaced, watching him fall.

"Ouch," Mel whispered. She turned her face away so he could not see her smile.

Domitia stood there, breathing heavily, glaring at them all. "Is there no end to this Dacian madness?!"

Matunaga watched her disappear past the girls down the hall, her long gown swishing behind her, her steps hard and fast. Manius sighed, plopping the box atop his desk, admiring the girl's perseverance to learn the sword.

"Is she aware they will be joining Nestor in Dacia?" Matunaga turned his face and side-eyed Manius.

Manius sighed, dropping his head into his chest when things bothered him. "She does now."

28

The Library of Deceit

Micah sat at the desk as the afternoon sun beamed in horrendous warm streaks across his face. He had successfully condensed the list on his parchment, which he would roll up and slide into his inner robe. It was forbidden, but he had no choice. He had been working tirelessly for days now and just finished. Lucky for him, the library was brimming with scribes and people coming in this week for research and reading.

He glanced down at the list he had created, based on the genealogy of the decrees of relatives taking office in the Senate since the Dacian wars. He took a deep breath, staring at the tree he had drawn and the many names on the branches. The many, many branches. The top four branches were concerning, and he bent his neck to read the names a final time before leaving.

He rolled the parchment up and stuffed it in his robes, leaning back against the chair and glaring at the mess across the desk. The sunlight kissed his face, lighting up his brown eyes so they were yellow. The door opened, and the elder scribe meandered in, carrying a tray of wine. He shut the door behind him, the echo of it pinging. Micah's hair raised on his arms.

"Wine?" He plopped the tray atop the parchments, staring into Micah's eyes, not wavering. "I see the Senator is not with you today. Is he well?"

Micah opened his mouth to speak but then froze, glancing at the red liquid in the vat. He cleared his throat but did not stand up and began rolling the parchments to put them back. "He is well, thank you for offering. I will take my leave for the day."

As Micah grabbed another one, the scribe lunged down and grabbed Micah's hand. He pulled Micah into his face, his eyes like a steel rod. "Knowledge is powerful scribe. It can be allowed to live, or it can kill."

Micah clutched his fist into a ball while the old man gripped it, meeting his glare with a stern face all his own. "Knowledge is powerful." He clenched his jaws. "My friend."

"Am I your friend, scribe? Renown scribe of Aurelian." The scribe breathed into his face, but Micah just held his breath, his backbone stiff.

"Knowledge is allowing truths to live, old friend," Micah whispered. His eyes narrowed as he yanked his hand from him and stood up. "You have always been my friend."

The scribe smiled into his face, picking the wine tray up. He turned his back to Micah but then paused, side-eying him. "There is a side entrance, just there behind you. Use it. You have a short time."

Micah clenched his jaws, watching him waltz out. He took a deep breath, his right hand atop the hilt of the dagger Manius had given him, which was sheathed at his side under his robe. He narrowed his brows as chills darted up his spine.

"This will not end well for Rome." He mumbled. Micah rolled the parchments up and stuffed them in a crevasse of the bookcase behind him, rolling his eyes. "Forgive me." He complained. He knew he was not putting them in the correct places, but followed the scribe's warning to exit out a secret door behind the desk.

One bookcase was built, sticking out further than the others, and he slid his head behind it. The wall opened to a slim tunnel shrouded in darkness. At the end of it, a wooden plank door loomed in the silence. He gripped his robes and slid behind them as his ear burned to the main door opening. From the view of the desks in the archives, the bookcases were so filled with parchments and books it would take a keen eye to venture past the outcropping like this. It was a perfect door hideaway.

He pressed further down the tunnel toward the door in the darkness, waiting to run, but a familiar voice made him freeze. Micah turned his head toward the front of the trim of the bookcase, listening as the old scribe had burst in again and was not alone. The scribe huffed.

"He was looking for decrees from Trajan. That is all I was privy to. You three know we leave scribes at peace when they are researching or writing. We do not break our oaths or their privacy."

Micah took a deep breath. *He said there were three with him*. He heard Opiter huff. Micah could not risk walking back up there to look at the other two men, but now he feared he needed to redo the list he had on him.

Opiter took a deep breath, admiring the beauty of the domed ceiling shredding light rays against the walls. "Very well. You will continue to advise when they come back. Agreed." Opiter was not asking.

"I will honor the agreement we have, Senator. Scribes do not break oaths." He belted out. "Now, if you will excuse me, there is a section I must correct outside as some history has been misplaced." And with that, the scribe marched out of the room away from them, slamming the door.

Opiter and the two men followed him out, and Micah's heart skipped a beat. He slithered down the darkened tunnel, freezing at the door, when a familiar accent echoed in the domed archives. It was so familiar Micah turned his head to glare back through the darkness at it. It dawned on him he had just heard a Dacian.

29

Diana's Pain

"How long before we reach Papa?" Diana inquired, stuffing figs and cheese into her mouth.

Anna smiled at her, though her patience was wearing thin already on this journey. They sat below the deck on a ship, coasting across the Adriatic Sea.

"A couple weeks, my child. It is a long journey." Anna poured more tea for herself.

"Here is your cloak. Put it on. Autumn is coming, and the air is cooler the closer we come to Dacia. We cannot have you catching ill." She watched Diana sigh, her mouth still full of food, while she slid into the thick, wool cloak.

"Now, child, I must go on deck. You have food and tea, and you have your dolls." Anna leaned over the small table and kissed her atop the head, slithering away from her.

Diana watched her go, a sudden draft making her pull the cloak tighter around her chest while she gripped a doll Anna had given her, although it was not the same as the dolls she had at home. She stood and meandered to the steps leading to the deck. She listened for a moment, trying to hear any conversation. Then she turned around and stared at the small round window over her head, noticing a falcon glaring at her from the ledge.

She walked closer to it. "You are very pretty. I bet you catch a lot of fish here." She smiled at it.

The bird turned its head to face her, plunging its claws over the ledge, where Diana noticed a cylinder attached to one. She turned her head back to the steps and gasped, then faced the bird in anticipation.

Anna pushed herself up the stairs and marched atop the deck of the Trireme. Sailors were spread all over the deck, manning the ship. The Adriatic Sea was a calm turquoise under a clear sky, and she took a deep breath, closed her eyes, and sighed.

"Almost home." She whispered.

She glared at the captain awaiting her command, his wool tunic and long swords strutting over his back in his sheath. "My orders." He asked, his long, dark beard wafting in the sea breezes.

Anna scoffed. "River village. Titus will be going to Vasiliki by then, and we must get the child to the lair before Lupescu finds her."

The man bowed to her. "It will be done."

Anna stood pressed against the railing, her long braided blonde hair spilled down her shoulder. Her regal Roman robes were an enlightening contrast to the drudgery of the men working atop the deck to get them across the Sea. She narrowed her eyes, peering across the sea, clenching her jaws.

"We shall see who wins this final war, Titus." She mumbled, clutching her robes tighter against her chest and then barging back downstairs.

Diana froze at the window, peering out when Anna walked down. "What are you doing?!" Anna demanded.

Diana widened her eyes, her little face in the window, standing atop a chair. She turned her gaze back to her, smiling. "I saw a fish! It jumped out of the water!"

Anna sighed. "Child, come down from there before you get hurt. Yes, there are many fish in the ocean."

Diana let Anna help her down, and she plopped atop the pillows again at the table. "May I draw? I want to draw that fish." She begged.

Anna bit her bottom lip. "Yes, of course you can." Anna turned her back to her to rummage through the table boxes while Diana side-eyed the window again.

Ahead of the ship flew a falcon cresting back to the coast. It would ride the coastline as it was trained to, but now it must return to its master. The cylinder attached to its leg was of utmost importance because now, within it, was a new message from Diana.

30

The Stubborn Heart

Axius stood on the stone wall with one knee up, gazing out over the labyrinth of emerald hillside and rising mountains before him. He had not slept last night. He had been able to shave this morning, and chopped his dark hair off so it stood sloppy atop his head. Kilian had taken him back to the ship to get his clothes, so Axius threw caution to the wind and put his Roman attire back on, breastplate and all. His red cape brisked in the breeze, and Nestor saw it from the narrow path of the stone house where he slept.

Stone houses were built on either side of the path, and a small rock wall ledge was built into the hillside from the slope. Axius took a deep breath but did not turn to look at Nestor.

"I understand." Axius belted out just as Nestor turned to go.

Nestor froze as he said it, his back to Axius.

"I see you have your famed gladius back." Nestor faced him, still not coming closer.

Axius smiled, gazing upon it hanging from his side sheath. "Yes. The Gladius is but a stick to your weapons here, so I cannot harm any of you. That is what Kilian told me."

Nestor nodded, turning to go again.

"And he is correct." Axius belted out, turning his head to face him but not moving from the wall.

Nestor swallowed, his eyes tearing up. "I, Diana..."

Axius held it in. He clenched his jaws. "We will get her back. They will die for this."

"We have sent falcons out. We will find her."

Axius sighed. "Good."

"Come with me." Nestor motioned for him to follow.

Axius stood upright and sighed, following Nestor down the winding path past the stone houses to the end of the glen again. A vast stone house splayed into the hillside, and smoke from multiple chimneys wafted.

"The beast scythe smith," Axius mumbled. "Why here?"

Nestor huffed at him, his eyes brighter than Axius had seen in many years. "You said you understand. I need to know you truly do."

Nestor pushed the double-planked door open that rose above their heads, the smell of annealing iron and steel hot in the air through their noses. The massive cavern-like shop was built entirely in stone, with three fire pits at the end of the wall. There was a half door between them for light and rows of bellows kissing the dirt floor. A room-sized section was open by the bellows for the anvils, with stone pits full of water by each one.

Axius meandered in, gazing around and up to the ceiling as bickerns, forceps, and forging hammers hung from the beams. Chisels, vices, and clamps were strewn atop an elongated table that looked as if it was made from petrified wood. The tools themselves were much larger than a man would use for smithing. This shop was vast and very high.

"How many…" Axius started to say but jerked around at the deep voice answering him.

"Me."

Axius stared at it, his eyes melting to the floor from its clawed paws to the ceiling. It clenched its jaw and snout and glared down at him from the end of an anvil. Its enormous paws clung to a hammer. It wore a leather hyde skirt. Its breastplate was engraved with a roaming wolf head, its mouth wide open full of dagger fangs.

Axius thought he was looking at Nestor in the beast form again. He stepped back, gazing at Nestor.

"He is pure blood," Axius mumbled, uncertain.

"Yes, Vezina is of my clan. I am still bigger than him." Nestor smiled up at him.

Vezina narrowed his eyes at Nestor and huffed. "I am biggest in all village. Bigger than Lupa."

Nestor sighed. "No, you are not."

"Why you bring Roman to my shop?" Vezina complained, pulling a blade out of the water with tongs.

"To make him understand," Nestor warned.

Vezina laughed a bellowing howl. "Ha! A Roman to understand the ways of Dacia wolves. It cannot be done."

Axius glared at the blade. It was enormous and curved and very thick. The beast was making a scythe sword. He found himself wandering closer, watching the process. He froze as the room opened, revealing another part of the shop hidden from the outside.

To the right of him, down a long wall, was a room with Dacian armor and weapons. The scythes, falxes, bows, and arrows dotted the walls. Across the wall was another wall brimming with wolf-head elongated shields and body armor like Vezina's. The wall seemed to stretch a mile, and wolf-heads with gaping snouts filled it.

Nestor followed him, crossing his arms. "Can Rome fight against this?"

Axius stared at him, clenching his jaws. "With the proper training."

Nestor scoffed. "We have mere weeks before Titus marches, Axius. Roman soldiers train for years."

Vezina hammered the blade behind them, and his ears perked up, listening. Axius barged over to him, "Train me to fight you."

Vezina paused from hammering mid-swing. He widened his big, black eyes and snarled, towering over Axius by several feet. "No. Away with you, Roman." He shooed him away from the anvil, his dagger-like claws coming a hair of pressing into Axius's armor.

"What are you doing?" Nestor worried.

"He has created this armor and weapons for your kind. If my people are to fight against Fenrir, I need to know how to take them out. Weak points."

Vezina snorted through his nose and scoffed, raising his snout so Axius saw his fangs. "Fenrir's tribe fights nothing like us."

Nestor sighed, gazing at Vezina, who shook his head. "You do not understand."

"Help me to."

"Men cannot defeat us," Nestor warned him. "The only way to defeat Fenrir is by becoming one of us. Axius, you will have to turn!"

Axius scoffed, walking back to the door. "The Roman Army is made of strong men, not beasts. Beasts have no place in Rome."

Vezina called after Axius as he had turned his back on them to leave. "Eh, Roman."

Axius turned his face to him, one hand on the door frame, his back still to them. Vezina shook his head, closing his eyes, still gripping the hammer. When he raised his broad head to Axius again, his eyes sparkled soft yellow as he spoke.

"Beasts care not for their own, only themselves. We are not beasts here. We are Dacian wolves. Wolves! We are family." He snarled, and with that, Vezina slammed the hammer atop the anvil and barged out a back door between the fire pits.

Axius's heart skipped a beat, his head throbbing. Chills raced up and down his spine, and the hair on his arms stood up. He let go of the door jamb and turned an about-face to look at Nestor, who was still standing in the same place with his arms crossed, glaring at him.

"You hurt his feelings," Nestor warned.

"I still want him to train me to fight." Axius's face was firm.

Nestor growled under his breath at Axius's defiance. As Axius turned and walked into the morning light, a sliver of a shimmering blade grazed his cheek. He froze as the long sword plunked into the wood door jamb mere inches from his face and glared at its origin. Vezina scoffed at him.

"You want me to train you to fight, Roman? Come. You will see."

"Good," Axius answered, following him.

Nestor gawked. "Shit."

Nestor and Axius followed him down the trail into an open, round meadow below the shop. Tall grass swayed in the morning breeze, yellow stalks bending to kiss the ground at their feet.

"You have no weapons." Axius noticed.

Vezina laughed at him. "You do not want me to train you to fight using my weapons, Roman. You cannot carry them. I would cut you in half before you could touch the hilt of that stick you carry." He circled Axius in the meadow, flexing his long arms.

"It is a gladius." Axius sneered at him.

"I will use it to pick fish from my fangs." Vezina snarled, his eyes sparkling.

"So, you allow me to keep my gladius during this?" Axius wondered.

Vezina rushed Axius, picked him up by his stomach, and raised him over his head. Axius scrambled to reach his gladius, holding his breath to the sudden pressure from the clawed paws gripping his mid-section.

Vezina spun him around so his headache hurt worse and his eyes shut, tossing him over his head into the tall grasses, where Axius disappeared in them.

Nestor watched Axius flail through the air yards over the tall grasses before lunging down legs first and sliding, his face wide-eyed and mouth open, gawking at Vezina as he flew. Nestor let out a high-pitched giggle but then cleared his throat.

When he landed, Axius slid through the grass, inhaling a yellow flower up his nose and throat and coughing. He fell head over foot before he stopped rolling, laying there on his stomach with his face in the dirt for a moment. He rolled over with his arms splayed out either side of him. Axius widened his eyes as Vezina loomed over him, picking his fangs with his gladius.

"Damnit," Axius grunted, his face smeared with yellow flowers and dirt.

"This is playing. I am being nice." Vezina scolded him, digging the gladius blade between his front fangs to clean them, his voice muffled a bit.

Nestor sighed. "I am going to find some food." He turned his back on them both and marched back up the hill, bored of them.

Axius stood up slowly as a dull throb ached his back, watching Nestor parade away from them.

"Again." Axius coughed, waving his hands at Vezina's chest, enticing him.

Vezina smiled, showing his fangs, his snout wrinkled back to his black and yellow piercing eyes. His ears stood upright as he slung the gladius into the ground at his feet and punched a fist into his empty palm, grimacing at Axius.

"Very well, Roman."

Nestor marched up the path through the meadow past the shop, pausing mid-step. "I know you follow us, Vasiliki."

Vasiliki stepped out from the side of a house, a dimple on her cheeks. Her eyes lit up. Her gray wolf pelt hung down her back over her tunics of wool and leather. Her black hair was braided on the sides of her head and wrapped into knots at the back of her neck.

"Why did you not acknowledge my presence when the Roman taunted Vezina?"

Nestor sighed, throwing his hands in the air. "He taunts everything, beast or man. He is, Axius."

Vasiliki walked up to him, holding up an apple. Nestor took it and tore a chunk out, enjoying the juicy, sweet bite.

"He taunts the biggest one of us. He must be fearless." She began walking toward the meadow, and Nestor followed.

"He is not the biggest." Nestor griped between bites. "Yes, Axius is brave. Braver than most."

They stood there in silence, Vasiliki watching him eat. "No word yet from the falcons. But soon."

Nestor stopped eating, the apple turning into a lump in his throat. "I fear for them. Domitia, my daughters. My friends. Rome. For them all."

Vasiliki agreed. "I fear for them." Her eyes teared up, and she gripped his shoulder. "You have been missed."

Nestor smiled at her, leaning in and hugging her into his arms. He closed his eyes atop her head, a tear falling on her hair. "Forgive me."

"Nothing to forgive. We were but children." She whispered, gripping him tighter into her arms.

"Our whole world was put on your shoulders to lead after father passed. That must have been painful to bear." Nestor swallowed.

"Yes, but I always had Kilian and Lupa, and they saved me time and again from Rome's foolishness and Fenrir's claws." She smirked.

"This village is small." Nestor glanced around, it dawning on him. "Your kingdom is elsewhere."

"Yes. It will stay that way. We cannot risk Fenrir reaching the heart of our people. Lupa is the keeper of this. He and my warriors are the front line of defense before entering my kingdom. Once Axius has proven he can be trusted, then we shall go there. Not til then." She warned.

Nestor sighed. "Understood."

Nestor's eyes burst open when they heard Axius holler, his echo faint. Nestor let his sister go and rushed down the embankment to the meadow below the shop, apple still in his mouth. Vasiliki watched him go, strolling behind him. Nestor lunged down the hill, but Axius and Vezina were gone. He stood there with apple still in hand, gazing back and forth before Axius catapulted in front of him sideways from across the meadow.

He hollered, and his scream echoed as he passed Nestor at his face in midair. Nestor followed Axius's flailing body roll atop the grass, the once tall stalks now flat in the field. He turned to see Vezina coming out of the wood into the meadow, watching how far Axius flew.

Axius again laid on his back, breathing heavily and thinking, his eyes wide, staring into the blue sky. Nestor appeared over him this time, his face contorted.

"You mock us with your foolish tactics, brother," Nestor demanded, tearing out another bite of apple.

Vezina leaned over him across from Nestor, staring at Axius, who did not move. Axius laid still, sighing heavily as their faces loomed down upon him.

Vezina blinked his eyes, shaking his snout at Axius. "It hurts, yes?" His deep voice had a sarcastic edge of pity but was full of laughter.

Axius took another deep breath, grimacing, suddenly noticing the apple in Nestor's hand. "Did you find food?" He moaned, his eyes widening at the juicy apple.

From the edge of the wood at the meadow, Vasiliki watched Nestor help Axius up. Axius took his hand in his own, and Nestor patted battering hugs on the Roman, his face lit up, laughing at him. She stood at the edge of the wood and watched this Roman meet Nestor's eyes, and then his eyes melted upon Vezina. There was no fear in them, just avid curiosity and passion. The smithy watched him too, his eyes cautious but a glimmer of laughter brimming toward this man who had the nerve to ask a Dacian wolf to teach him to fight.

His scaled metal chest armor plates shimmered in silver, and it was padded beneath that. She could tell he would have been injured by now. His middle section armor did not buckle or dent when he landed, and his leather arm and leg cuffs did not pop off or damage.

His leather boots, laced up to below his knees, kept his footing firm. This Roman had strong brows that were defined above eyes full of power. Axius wore the typical Roman armor, but he had modified it to his arm and leg cuffs. The fact that Axius moved so swiftly in it and did not get injured meant he was vigorous and strong.

Vasiliki watched Nestor and Axius meander up the path to get food while Vezina disappeared into his shop. Her eyes melted upon the back of Axius, his mannerisms, how he handled himself with Nestor. Everything. This was not a typical Roman. Axius had a deep-seated passion burning within him.

From the darkness of the canopy behind her, Lupa emerged and stood beside her. "My queen. No word yet from the Falcons. We expect them within days if the child is indeed on her way here."

Vasiliki took a deep breath, her jaws clenched, her dark eyes narrowed under black brows. "Fenrir, the fool for taking my family."

Lupa scoffed. "Indeed. They will pay. What is your command."

Her pupils changed to pristine yellow kissed with amber. She growled under her breath. "Are my generals prepared?"

"They await your command." He assured her.

"Good. Bring Brasus, Moskin and Tarbus in. We need to break this Roman first before we lose any more of our own. I must test his loyalties, no matter what Lupescu thinks. We have a short time before Rome marches. We have one chance."

Lupa sighed. "You risk the wrath of Lupescu."

Vasiliki scoffed at him. "I have no choice. We must ensure Lupescu is at his full strength before battle. This is one way to do it. They are ordered not to kill him. If they try to kill him, then we shall know."

They stood silently, the trees swaying over them, the flowing river echoing behind them. "This Axius will be commander of the Roman Army if Titus dies. We need to know if Rome will stand with us or die," She whispered. "We have lost enough already."

Lupa nodded in agreement.

She followed Axius and Nestor up the hill into the square where the markets prepared food. She would join them, eventually. Lupa bowed to her and turned back through the canopy, disappearing under a shroud of emerald kisses.

31

The Horde

Darkness can overcome what little light trickles in, but blackness folds in on itself, saturating hope, joy, and peace. There is no peace in the darkness, only brutality. Where light cannot linger or grow, the blackness becomes thick, suffocating souls. Fenrir stood on a cavern ledge, overlooking the blackness. It crawled with yellow eyes and dagger claws gnawing at the rocks in the thousands upon thousands of beasts beyond him, the cavern stretching for miles under the river.

The black pure bloods seethed in the darkness as their shadows stretched like snakes across the cavern walls. The flickering torch lights danced in the breezes from the underground lair. The torches lit up the kingdom , lunging into the blackness where steps were carved from the walls and rooms dug out into the rock.

Hoards of black beasts hunched upon one knee, with one leg up and their arms dug into the rock, perching on the edge of the ledges, their muscle-ridden bodies full of power. Their ears were flat atop their long, square heads, their yellow pupils glowing in the darkness. They howled out retribution, their mouths wide with dagger-length fangs and snouts snarled to their brows furrowed in anticipation. They lined up together as if they were one flesh, snarling and howling in the air at Fenrir, their claws tearing out chunks of rock beneath their knees, sparks of white shards from their claws blinking in the blackness.

The cavern burst open to a labyrinth, the ceiling planked with obsidian spikes. The three scouts of Fenrir stood behind him in their dark robes, half smiling at their army of minions whose growls and shrieks echoed into the labyrinth of this cavern.

"Brothers!" Fenrir raised his hands, and silence became as the darkness was felt, his voice deep and thrusting precedence among them.

"We go to war with the Roman army! They will meet the same fate as Artgus!" He laughed.

"In two weeks, we all march upon the Dacian wolves!" He sneered. "We will take the wretched queen and her fools! We will kill her wolves and take our rightful place on the throne in the heart where our kind began! Giving us the power of our ancestors to turn any man into purebloods!"

Howling shrieks began to echo again, and Fenrir smiled at them. "We will not fail to take the heart of our beasts! Once we take it, then we march upon Rome!"

Fenrir grunted a boiling roar, laughing in the air at his beasts filling the rock ledges and cliffs. They listened to him, their howling roars agreeing with their king. He turned to his scouts awaiting his command, his long robes kissing his feet over a muscle-ridden naked body. His scouts sneered at him, growling but not turning into beasts yet.

"You three will follow me back to the river town. Titus will play with me a bit more. His time is at an end." He laughed, his eyes changing into black, his pupils gone.

"Once they have marched, you will give me cover while I go to Anna, my winch. I know my mate will try to take the child."

"And Honus?" One of them asked, sneering.

Fenrir growled. "Kill him. Make him bleed and suffer. Make Titus watch before he dies."

The three scouts smiled, their fangs protruding over their thin lips. "A pleasure, my king." They bowed to him.

"The beating Titus gave him will slow him down. Humans heal slow." Fenrir warned them, turning to face his hordes as they pierced the cavern with their growls and shrieks.

"Nonetheless, be cautious as he has eluded our grasp for years now and has the favor of Vasiliki." He whispered, sneering.

"And the army, my king?"

Fenrir turned his head to glare at them, his eyes black as coal, his fangs pressing down over his lips. "We march in two weeks, cut them off before taking the wolves. They will not prevail in human form."

"Can we not take the strongest of them to convert? Send them to Rome ahead of us?"

Fenrir laughed. "Half-bloods?! No. From here on out, we take the heart of Dacia to create purebloods. Only the strongest survive in Dacia."

"And the queen?"

Fenrir growled. "Wretched, she wolf. She will accept me as her mate this final time, or I will kill her. Her treachery to our kind will end with me."

He closed his eyes and breathed in the crisp mountain air blowing through the cavern, the rustling of his beasts climbing the rocks around him. "We kill the Romans. We take Dacia. We march on Rome."

He raised his long arms out his sides, smiling as fangs erupted over his lips.

"We take the world." He moaned, facing his cavern of beasts who filled the night cries with howls of endless rage.

Titus stood among his generals, their red cloaks wafting behind them atop the rolling knoll above the river town, the waters sparkling like the sun had melted diamonds in the water. The river twisted and snaked through rolling hills and dense forests, kissing the mountain plains beyond his eyesight.

"I want the army training daily." He commanded.

His generals agreed.

"We march in two weeks. This has been sufficient rest." He added, his palm dangling atop the hilt to his gladius at his side.

They stood, turning their backs to the river and gazing down upon the town. An open field was pressed down where the soldiers were training with their swords, using their shields. Titus crossed his arms and glared at them.

"I want Honus training with them."

"Has he had time to heal from the lashing yet?" One general asked.

Titus scoffed. "He trains, or he will be sent back to Pannonia by an armed guard. He should not have disobeyed my order."

Titus turned to march away and then froze on the path, sneering back at them. "There is no mercy in my army. There is only winning."

His generals followed him back down, the sun blasting the lands in pillars of warmth as black storm clouds loomed beyond the horizon over the forest.

Four hundred twenty miles away, the Olt River ebbed and flowed through Oltenia, frisking the headwaters of the Mures River. Its mountainous plains basked under the rising dawn of a crimson sky, and its forests dotted the world in subtle hues of Autumns early embrace.

Along the pebble-lined river bed, paw prints nearly two feet wide were embedded in the mud trekking south east. Their destination was the Danube. Miles behind them stretched bodies of Roman soldiers, their blood spilling into the river. The blood seemed to follow them on their journey. The stone forts and military roads the Romans had built were empty now, and silence crested the dawn in an eerie splendor.

There were eighteen of them. They were relic bloodlines coming from Oltenia. The wolf commander pulled at his chest straps, his scythe blade sticking over his square head. His pointy ears stood listening, his long snout snarling as he turned to glare at the carnage behind them. They were the greys.

Their grey and white fur blew in the morning breeze, their muscles bulging under body armor of stitched leathers and loin cloths covered with steel plates like scales. They embraced the landscape with crystal clear blue eyes, their ears twitching to the sounds of dead bodies bleeding out behind them for miles.

The Romans had basked too long in their border defenses, too long in their frontier movements. Now, it was time to end it. Now that Kilian had found their king, it was time to bring him home.

The commander glared back at his tribe. The wolves nodded as they gathered behind him on the river, their blue eyes sparkling. Their engraved chest armor of steel sculpted to their bulky chests. Their paws gripped bows and falxes nearly three times the size of the Romans' swords. He pulled up the parchment in the palm of his paw sent to him from Matunaga, gazing upon it again. He snarled in disgust, and a deep bellowing growl erupted from the pits of his fine-tuned muscular body.

"Once Lupescu's child heir is safe, we kill the beast's remnant and any Roman remaining. We bring our king and his family home." He growled.

They moved forward along the river bank into the shallow waters, their paws washed of blood as the Roman carnage flowed behind them in the tide like bloody fingers had prodded an open wound.

32

The Warning

Domitia stood in the private courtyard, watching the table under the Wisteria canopy filled with food, wine, and tea. Manius ensured she would have a private meeting with the elder women of the Senate. Meanwhile, he, Micah, and Matunaga were sitting in his office suite going through the parchments from the archives while the children played in the courtyard within eyeshot of them. Troy, Mel and the mercenaries continued to guard over them.

It would have made Manius feel better about it, but a gnawing itch crawled up his spine since they were given the chest full of iniquities. With every parchment he read, it only grew more pain and uncertainty within him.

He stood at his desk and poured coffee, the steaming brew warming his face. Autumn was coming early. He felt it in his bones. He hoped Axius was alive and well. His mind kept going from the parchment truths to worries about his son.

He could not imagine what Domitia was feeling, especially after Diana had been taken. They did not know where she was and if she was still alive. Manius sighed, turning his face to gaze upon the girls in the yard playing with sticks like they were swords again. He smiled at them, but then his smile faded, and he frowned again.

Micah stood beside him at the opening of the yard, his fists clutching two parchments. "Such brave children they are." He whispered.

Manius turned to him, and half smiled. "Indeed. Very brave."

Matunaga set a parchment down across his lap and sipped coffee, eying them both from behind. "Micah, have you found the person behind the Dacian voice from the archives?"

Manius and Micah turned to him. "No. I have been successful in tracking who the Senators are." He turned to face Manius, his eyes rigid. "With Opiter being one of them, sadly."

Manius scoffed. "Opiter was always plotting things. Many of them have been good for Rome and our people. Many have been questionable, to put it mildly."

The room grew silent before Matunaga sighed. "I stayed too long in that tower. Oblivious to the truths around me."

Matunaga rolled the parchment up and dug into the chest for another one. "Rome has been struggling since the second Dacian War in Oltenia. If Nestor's tribe does indeed come, it will mean death to your people."

Manius turned his head as Matunaga spoke, his eyes narrowing, thinking. "Yes. It will."

"Because the struggles have come from the beasts?" Micah questioned.

"Yes." Matunaga confirmed.

"What happens if they win, Matunaga," Manius asked, crossing his arms over his chest.

Matunaga did not look at him but rolled open another parchment. "They always win." He warned. "They are the strongest."

Micah glanced at Manius and then turned to leave down the great hall to their right. "I have more research to do. I will come to you later with my final findings, and we can move forward from there."

Manius watched Micah disappear down the hall to a study library, facing Micah, but his eyes were focused on Matunaga.

They always win. He replayed that in his head as an ache throbbed his temples, and he sat down on the chair across from Matunaga.

D omitia stood at the head of the table, wisps of lavender Wisteria petals floating around her. Seven women were sitting, looking up at her in eager anticipation. Their robes were a rainbow of colors, their silver and gold jewelry sparkling under the midday sun. A bite in the air made them pull their cloaks tighter over their chests. The women were older than her, but Domitia was no less powerful than them.

The eldest at the end of the table nodded to Domitia, her white hair piled atop her head as if a shimmering crown had grown there, her braids clasped in rings of gold. "In receiving your summons, dear Domitia, you have put fear in all of us," Aneria advised, her wrinkles racing down her face, accentuating a devious frown.

Domitia swallowed but stood fast, her jaws clenched as the women passed around the wine. "Diana has been taken, and I need your help and resources to get her back."

The women gasped, and another one, Dita, spoke up. "Oh, my dear! I am so sorry to hear this! What can we do to help." Her long grey and black hair swiped over her thinning shoulders, her cranberry robes dark against her pale white skin.

The women began chattering amongst themselves and Domitia let them, until Aneria spoke up, her eyes hard. "Taken by what." She demanded.

Domitia took a deep breath, gazing at her, and sat in her chair. "The beasts of Dacia. I do not know if she is still alive."

The table became silent, and the falling of Wisteria petals was felt as if the air itself had become heavy. "She was taken from my home. Beasts attacked my farm, my workers. Many were killed. My business will never be the same again. My home is destroyed."

Another elder spoke up, sitting next to Aneria, her eyes narrowed in furrows of pain. "It cannot be. This cannot be happening in Rome."

The table erupted again, and Domitia sat back and listened to them all bicker and chirp amongst each other, their faces drained of color.

"Told these were but rumors!"

"Beasts, here?! We may all die!"

"My husband promised me none of this was true."

"We have been lied to."

"The Senate must be called."

"Yes, call the Senate. This must be addressed before more children are taken!"

But Aneria sat in cold stone silence, gazing across the table to Domitia, her fingers twitching on the woodtop. Domitia watched her in silence, then her eyes went to the other women's facial expressions and body language. It told her they were panicking. They were afraid for Rome and their own families.

Aneria cleared her throat, and the women silenced, gazing at her. She picked up the wine vat, poured it, and gazed at the pastries, fruit, and cheese. As she plucked figs and cheeses from one tray to put on her plate, she stared at Domitia again, sighing.

"I shall inform my husband to bring together the Senate. This must be addressed before another child is taken. Yes, we must work within our powers to bring Diana home safe." She plopped a block of cheese in her mouth, pulling apart the bread loaf that wafted warm herbs in their faces.

Domitia waited.

"And as for these beasts, who are taking our children..." She sipped her wine.

"They must be hunted. They must die." She finished, her eyes sparkling. "Does Rome have enough brave men to take them?" She questioned, setting her wine down.

Domitia pursed her lips. "I do not know, do we?"

The women gazed back and forth, their eyes wide.

Perhaps the hero for Rome can take them? Perhaps Axius, the elite?" Aneria sneered.

Domitia bit her tongue. "They are already taking them in Dacia."

The women gasped. Aneria widened her eyes, her chest heaving. "What." Domitia stood up, pressing her palms atop the table. "War is coming to our doorsteps. Your children are next. Your grandchildren. The beasts are coming to take us all."

Silence.

"I need you all to get your husbands to call the Senate. We need to increase guards in the streets to hunt these beasts, as they could be any of us." Domitia warned them, her face clenched.

"You mean they turn?" Dita wondered, swallowing.

"Yes. They turn into men and then beasts. If you see one, it is already too late. They are fast. They are strong. They kill with no mercy." Domitia finished.

"You have seen one?" Aneria questioned.

"I have seen many. They left my lands for Rome. They are here, believe me."

Aneria sighed. "So be it." She stood up and turned to go.

Domitia watched her go, but then Aneria turned her face back to the table. "Prepare Manius to be summoned to the Senate. Our men have much to plan for, and we have little time." And with that, she disappeared out the side gate past the courtyard to her carriage on the street below the wall.

Dita turned to Domitia, ignoring the other women's constant jabber. Her face was ashen and drawn, her eyes wide. Domitia nodded at her and then sat back down. She filled her plate with food, but could not eat. She just needed to make it seem like she was hungry, but no one was hungry.

As Aneria disappeared down the brick-lined street, Mel was hunched down. She squatted on her knees, watching her from under a thick brush outside the wall. The hill gently sloped down the street, and steps built into the hillside flowed with flowery gardens and herbs dotting the landscape under gnarled olive trees. A brisk breeze was felt, and Mel turned her head to hear what Aneria was telling the carriage driver.

The carriage driver turned his head, and Mel leaned further into the wall to hide, her eyes wide. She watched his mannerisms and followed his lips move. He spoke in Dacian, and Aneria answered him in Latin. She recognized the distinct single dialect, and chills raced up her arms. Mel had done what Domitia ordered her to do. She turned back up the hill to climb the wall from the trees. Her mind reeled, and her backbone burned with chills that would not go away.

33

Vezina's Warning

"The damn bird should be back with news by now," Nestor complained, his meandering walk sulking into deep anger.

"Agreed, if she was found we would know by now." Axius agreed with him, eying the courtyard. The displays of apples and various baked foods enticed him, his stomach rumbling. The townspeople, or beasts, as Axius called them, were out and about and busy about their duties.

"How will we get her back from them? Open war?" Axius questioned. "Will Vasiliki go to war to save Diana?"

Nestor stopped walking and turned to him, the scruffy beard on his face disheveled just like the black spikes atop his head. "Once we know where she is, I will go get her. Everyone will die."

Axius paused as Nestor continued walking. "As Lupescu? Or Nestor, the hero of Rome."

Nestor clenched his jaws.

"You are not thinking this through. Troy and the mercenaries were outnumbered." Axius warned. "Troy would never have allowed Diana to be taken. The beasts planned it, and now they are in Rome, and our family does not know who to trust."

Nestor swallowed, picking up an apple and tossing it to Axius. "You are right. I did not prepare my home for the beasts. I thought they would never find us. I was a fool, all this time."

"You are royalty. They have taken Diana to use as leverage against you because if you are as feared as they say, then Lupescu is a formidable enemy. I want you to think about this, brother." Axius looked at the apple, but his emotions were toying with him, and he had to confront Nestor first.

"Do you fear they will kill her?" Nestor swallowed, clutching his fists. "I cannot lose my daughter. If something happens to her, I will go mad."

"I think this Fenrir wants you out of the way so he can take Dacia and this heart Vasiliki speaks of. I fear he may lure you to Diana and kill you, then kill her. He wants to rule, after all."

"If they lure me to my daughter, you know I must go." Nestor chirped.

"And I cannot go with you. I cannot go with you because they will overpower me. I am only a man." Axius swallowed, and took a bite of the apple, thinking.

Nestor smirked at him. "You will take the curse of my people then?"

Axius scoffed. "No. I have a short time to discover your weaknesses."

"You think we have weaknesses?" Nestor laughed, continuing to walk.

Axius smiled. "Vezina has already shown me a few. I need new armor, weapons, and time to train Romans with them."

Nestor stopped walking. "You play a fool's game. I promised Manius I would keep you alive. I cannot do that if you continue entertaining foolhardy notions of grandeur for Rome."

"Everything I do here is for Rome. Rome is my home." Axius gritted his teeth.

Nestor snarled. "This was my home! And now I must save it."

"You fled it! You fled to Rome, which is your home!" Axius yelled at him.

"These are not the beasts you are used to hunting, Axius! You have seen some of them! You have not seen them all." Nestor pleaded with him. "You will force my hand on you if you continue your foolishness."

Axius gritted his teeth.

Nestor turned away, blaring his nose. "I will save my daughter, and if you entertain a fool's notion to go on your way, I will not be responsible for your demise."

Axius marched to him and loomed into Nestor's face, his eyes hard. "Tell me, brother, when war comes, whether here or in Rome, will you be the one to turn me, or let me die the cursed death when that time comes?"

Nestor growled in his face, his eyes turning red. "I will do whatever it takes to ensure your survival."

"I need to know your loyalties still lie with our home, Rome." Axius pestered him.

Nestor growled in his face and backed away. Axius watched Nestor storm away from him. Axius finished eating the apple, watching him disappear behind the stone houses of bakeries and horticulturalists. He was still hungry but not in the mood for another apple.

Axius meandered down the street, gazing through the bakeries, the herbalists, and the many houses with families having breakfast or just sitting around talking. He stopped at a meadow at the end of the street and stared upon the Carpathian Mountains rising in the distance. The smell of a brisk storm peltered his face in silence.

He turned his head as the crunching of grass underfoot caught his attention but was met with a fist to his nose by Brasus.

Axius fell on his back, rearing up to grab his Gladius, but it was not there. Brasus had grabbed it. Axius sniffled the pain away, blood dripping from his nose and mouth, and snarled at him. Brasus was emboldened, sniffing the air above Axius like a dog. Brasus dropped the Gladius at his feet, where it lunged in the dirt, sticking up.

"Foolish Roman. A weak fool." He admired the Gladius and huffed at it. "You know, I should have killed you at Opiters."

Axius pulled himself up, facing him. "You would not have killed me, and if so, it would have been short-lived with my father there."

Brasus scoffed at him. "You think I would have allowed them to live also?"

"Would Opiter have allowed you to kill me?"

Brasus laughed. "Opiter. Ah yes. Yes, he would want me to kill you. That is why we are here, Roman."

"To kill me? You could have killed me on the boat. You lie."

Axius froze as Moskin and Tarbus approached behind Brasus, their intent glowing in their eyes. Axius gazed around him, thinking. Nestor had stomped off. Vasiliki was nowhere to be seen, nor Lupa. The townspeople were up the street, and only Axius faced three generals who wanted him dead. And beasts at that. He could not overpower them.

"Why did you return to Dacia, Brasus," Axius demanded.

Brasus scoffed at him, sneering at Moskin and Tarbus. "To get the king back. Back to his demise."

The three of them laughed.

Axius scoffed at them. "You are all fools."

"No one is going to care if a Roman dies here." Moskin laughed.

Axius widened his eyes at them. "What did Vasiliki do to you? Did she put you up to this test?"

Moskin laughed. "She wants to see if you can be trusted, but we have other plans. She is not our queen anymore."

"Who is your queen then?" Axius pressed his boots into the soil.

Brasus scoffed. "We have no queen. And our king is not here."

Chills raced up Axius's spine.

"I want to see how a mere mortal will fight the three of us, the generals of Vasiliki's army." Brasus sneered at him.

"I will fight to the death. Come on, then." Axius stood firm, readying his fists to protect himself. His eyes lit up as if they were on fire.

"Without your little Lupescu?" Tarbus toyed with him.

"You do not want Lupescu here," Axius warned them, but they laughed at him.

Brasus lunged in at Axius, fangs protruding from his gums and his fingernails splaying out black daggered claws. Brasus changed in an instant just as Axius dropped to the grass and rolled between the beasts' legs, yanking his Gladius out of the dirt. Just as Axius turned to face him, Brasus lifted him by his chest to his face and plunged his claws into his chest armor, peeling in to rip out Axius's heart.

Axius held his breath and grimaced into his big snout, his fangs barring in on him. His gaping snout opened, ready to lunge his throat out. Brasus laughed as Axius felt his claws dig in. Axius held his breath and plunged his Gladius through the thick fur in at his heart. Brasus let out a snarling shriek in pain, and Axius continued plunging the blade through him.

Brasus gasped, his eyes wide and black, his ears flat atop his skull. Axius clenched his jaws in his face as blood spewed across his armor. Brasus dropped him and fell to his knees, and Axius yanked the Gladius back out of his heart. Brasus grasped at the hole in his chest, bleeding, snarling. A bellowing howl emerged from somewhere deep inside him that echoed through the town.

Axius swung his Gladius around and swiped Brasus's head clean off. Grimacing, he turned to face Moskin and Tarbus, who became enraged and belted out roars. But it was too late. Brasus was dead at the hand of a man.

Axius pushed the headless corpse down with his boot, leaning away from it to face them. Blood spewed across his face, and he was ready to die. As Moskin changed to lunge in at him, a shadowing blackness overcame the street from the tree line, and Lupescu catapulted onto them both. His size overshadowed them and knocked them down, and he pressed over them. He belted out a roar of rage, snarling in their faces, his snout twice the size of theirs.

Lupescu gripped Moskin's head in his palms and ripped it off his shoulders. The headless body fell limp under his powerful body weight. Lupescu reached over the body and grabbed Tarbus, his claws sinking into his chest. Tarbus had not turned yet, and as Lupescu dug his claws into his chest, a familiar yell from behind them made Lupescu stop suddenly.

"Lupescu!" Vasiliki called.

Vasiliki stood aside Lupa, her eyes wavering between Axius and her brother. Lupescu's eyes glowed a fiery amber when he heard her voice, and he turned his snout to face her, snarling. The black hair raised on his backbone and formed a ridge of spikes down to his tail. Lupescu jumped off Tarbus and lunged across the street into Vasiliki, pressing her back into a stone house. As Tarbus lay on his side, bleeding from his chest, Axius pressed his blade toward him, watching him.

"You will die yet," Axius warned him, blood dripping down his chest and arms.

Lupescu towered over Vasiliki, her eyes glowing in his face like amber on fire. "I am your sister. Lupescu." She pleaded with him, but he pressed harder into her and grasped her throat in his massive paw.

"You allowed your wicked generals to attack my brother. You are a fool." Lupescu howled in her face, pressing his claws into her throat to rip it out.

"They were the fools." But then she changed.

A rage filled the street with an aura of power so thick Axius could cut it with his blade. He watched as she transformed to Lupescu's size. She was pristine white, not black like him. She pushed Lupescu's claws away from her throat, her snout twisting and snarling at his face. She catapulted him off her, where he hit a stone wall across the street, and it crumbled.

She stood tall, raging at him, and snarling in her wolf form. Vasiliki was a white wolf riddled with muscles and elegant form. Her ears perked high atop her square head, her eyes bright and brilliant blue. Lupescu jumped up to face her, his claws engorging his paws, his fangs dripping in saliva. "I will kill you for harming Axius. I warned you all. This is not a game!" Lupescu roared at her, facing her off, his eyes filled with rage.

Axius's heart melted to his knees hearing Lupescu speak. His eyes twitched from him to Vasiliki, two beasts completely opposite one another, but just as powerful.

Lupescu snarled at her, pacing back and forth. He glared into her eyes and craned his snout to Lupa and back to her as more Dacians filled the street to watch the madness. Lupa did not change to help Vasiliki, he stood back on the road and watched them both.

"You play a game here you will not win with me sister."

Vasiliki roared at him. "You left your home and we had to pick up the pieces and fight! You fight for Rome when you will not fight for your own! You come back hoping I will go to war to save Rome!" She bellowed at him, her claws growing longer on her paws.

"I did not command them to kill him!" She belted out. "They came back to me tainted! To undermine my kingdom!"

Lupescu sneered at her, towering over her, clenching his jaws, gripping his paws in fists at her. He stood still and glanced at Axius, then back to her. He huffed, turning away. He paused in the grass when he reached Tarbus, who put his palms over his face to shield himself. Lupescu lunged down and ripped his throat out anyway with his long claws, leaving three dead bodies at Axius's feet.

Vasiliki stood there on her paws, her eyes a raging blue fire, but she did not come after him. Lupa swallowed, taking a deep breath at the carnage.

Lupescu turned to face her again, blood dripping down his snout and chest. "You are three generals short. This is what happens when you betray Rome and Dacia."

Lupescu raced down the hill and disappeared into the forest, leaving Axius gawking at the sibling rivalry, three dead generals, and a sudden tingle carving uncertainty through his backbone. He turned his stare to Vasiliki; his knees trembled a bit gazing upon her wolf form. Her eyes watched him in silence, but she did not come closer. Axius's eyes melted over every inch of her beautiful wolf form, his heart beating faster, his fist clenched tight to his hilt.

She raised higher, staring at him, her crystal blue eyes firm.

"You are a cunning warrior to have killed a beast. I am sorry they came to harm you." Vasiliki dropped her head to her chest in beast form as if her heart had been ripped out and then turned away from him. The crowds disappeared, and only Lupa remained. Axius felt his eyes upon him.

"Do you come to kill me now, Commander?" Axius belted out, breathing heavily.

Lupa cleared his throat, scoffing at him. "Good leaders do not kill another, Axius of Rome. You have done well surviving one. How will you do when thousands are upon you?" He turned, leaving Axius standing there bloodied. He was still gripping his gladius, while the small claw holes in his chest began to bleed through his armor, and a resolute pain made his heart ache.

34

The Reckoning

Axius bathed and marched butt naked to the top of the hill behind the stone house he and Nestor were staying in by the river. He had rubbed his arms and chest in lemon balm to help with the healing on his chest. He needed sunlight and fresh air. This small hill behind the house was perfect.

The Danube's roaring falls and sparkling waters kissed the plains below him, but a nervous energy made him restless. Atop the hill was a level field designed in a circle with views of the rolling hills. The Carpathian Mountains kissed a dusty rose sky among them. He leaned forward into his right knee, his right leg sprawled behind him, and breathed deeply. He closed his eyes and allowed nature around him to arouse his senses.

Axius played things in his mind that were said to him, thinking, plotting deep inside, "*You are a cunning warrior, brave Axius, to have killed a beast.*"

"*You cannot defeat the beasts at the river.*"

"*You must take the curse to defeat them.*"

"*We are a family of wolves here.*"

"*How will you survive when thousands are upon you?*"

He stretched his body further and breathed deeper than he had in a long while. Then, his mind went to what Brasus had told him.

"*We came to send Nestor to his demise.*"

"*We should have killed you at Opiters.*"

"*Our king is not here.*"

Then it hit him. He stopped stretching, turned to peering eyes, and craned his neck to see Vasiliki and Nestor staring at him. His naked backside was brimming in sculpted muscles and round buttocks.

Vasiliki's eyes were lit up watching him. She pursed her lips as dimples caressed her strong face in amusement. "Do you always walk around naked, Roman?" Her lips were flat, fighting a smile, but her eyes told Axius otherwise. She was intrigued with his powerful physique.

Nestor huffed at him. "How many times have I begged you to stop exercising naked? This is Dacia. Not Rome."

Axius stood up and faced them, and Vasiliki's eyes melted upon his sculpted chest, which had claw marks on it. Her eyes then fell to his privates. She raised an eyebrow and held her breath.

"What?" Axius shrugged his shoulders. "Your kind is naked when you turn, what is the difference? I saw your sister naked just this morning."

Nestor glared at his sister, shaking his head. "Hair covers us."

Vasiliki widened her eyes at him, half smiling.

Axius scoffed. "Hair covers mine, too." He smiled at them, his cleanly shaven face a strong definition to his dark brows and eyes shooting laughter at them.

He heard Vasiliki clear her throat but swore a giggle came out. He turned to look at her. "You two forgive one another?" Axius asked, turning to stretch again. "Typical siblings." He rolled his eyes.

"We have received a message from Diana. She is alive!" Nestor's voice was upbeat and encouraged as his face lit up.

Axius stopped, and his eyes lit up. "Good! Where is she?"

Silence. Axius melted upon Nestor, clenching his jaws. He met Vasiliki's stare, which concerned him. He stopped stretching to face them.

"This Anna, the wife of Opiter, has her, and they sail to an inland village off a crest of the Danube."

"Let us go get her." Axius prodded them. "That would be a few day's journey, correct? We can be back before Titus marches. We can meet him on the way here."

Nestor shook his head, his eyes teetering on a dark madness. "Kilian has come back with news. Titus began marching this morning. He is not waiting two weeks as we were advised. We are preparing for war, and..." He paused, staring at Vasiliki.

Vasiliki swallowed, clasping her hands at her groin, her silver bracelets dangling. Axius's eyes melted upon her, and he froze. "You cannot go there. They will take you."

"Nestor cannot go. That is what they want. They will kill him. They will not expect me, and it will be a few of his scouts. I will save my niece, and once we have sounded the horn she is safe, Lupescu comes." She eyed her brother.

Nestor agreed. "I will go into battle to help save the Romans as Lupescu. We will succeed."

Axius gritted his teeth. "Rome will not accept you as Lupescu. Titus will have you killed. This is madness."

"He will accept me or die."

Axius huffed. "So, you send Vasiliki to save Diana?"

"I know of the village, and there are many humans there. Fenrir always needs humans to side with him so it does not look strange to the Roman Empire. With Kilian, we can take the beasts." She nodded.

"There is something else. A truth I saw today." Axius warned them.

"I see a truth, too. Take my cloak and cover up." Nestor tossed Axius his cloak. Vasiliki watched him wrap it around his midsection and cover himself, biting her lip.

Axius half smiled at her, gloating. His eyes craned over her too, and Nestor sighed at them. "Nakedness is beautiful. I do not understand the problem." Axius teased.

Vasiliki smiled at him and then dropped the smile. "Indeed." Her eyes rolled around to the trees.

Nestor widened his eyes at her and sighed. "Go on, Axius."

"Three generals are dead. Brasus told me they came to bring you back to your demise. That they should have killed me at Opiters as if Opiter wanted this. They said their king is not here, meaning this Fenrir was their king all along."

Vasiliki agreed with him. "Yes. And now Anna has my niece. I feared my generals had been corrupted. They never returned home, and they could have."

"Yet the other mercenaries are guarding over Nestor's family. Domitia is like a sister to me, and now they are in my father's house. The mercenaries cannot be trusted. They must be killed." Axius warned, clenching his jaws.

Nestor clenched his jaws, huffing. "Yes, they have all been tainted."

"Opiter trained my father. My father trusted him. My father would have had no one else to go to with these truths. I think Opiter set it up that way knowing one day Nestor would return to Dacia, and the beasts would come for Rome." Axius finished.

"The beasts have been in Rome a long time, Axius. I have been fighting harder and longer battles every year to keep these wars from spilling over the world. Now the full moon comes and war to our doorstep, pulling Fenrir closer to the heart." Vasiliki feared.

"You will send the Falcons to Rome to warn my father and Domitia. Troy and Mel are in great danger." Nestor grieved.

Vasiliki agreed. "It will be done this day."

"You will allow me to go to Titus," Axius commanded.

Vasiliki pursed her lips at him. "I cannot let you go. You have been warned the only way for your soldiers to survive is by taking the curse. Why do you not listen, Axius of Rome?"

"I hear you telling me there is no hope for my people," Axius complained, narrowing his brows at her. "That the only way we will ever survive this is if we take this damn curse."

Vasiliki approached him, their bodies almost touching. But Axius stood there and gazed down into her eyes, holding his breath.

"It is too late for Rome to retreat now." She whispered into his face, her breath hot on his lips. "There is no going back to Rome from here, ever."

Axius swallowed. "Will you allow your army to protect my people while you save Diana? As me and Nestor will be in battle?" Axius pleaded, his eyes wide and bright at her face.

Vasiliki stepped away from him, but he followed her, nearing close to her again. "Even with Kilian and Lupa, Lupescu cannot save you all. So many of you will fall." She warned.

"Yet your army can. This is but a simple village front to your kingdom. I know this. You have an army of wolves somewhere." Axius confronted her. "I know you do."

Nestor gazed at his sister, sighing, but Vasiliki backed away from him. "It will be an act of war upon my people and we have stayed out of it this far. You will risk us killing everything we have ever known."

"What are the numbers?" Axius demanded. "What does his army look like? The numbers."

Nestor gazed at Vasiliki, who closed her eyes and sighed. When she opened them, Axius was in her face breathing on her again, his eyes sharp upon her. She met his stare, gazing up at him, her eyes a glowing amber as if honey had kissed her inside.

"Vasiliki. What are his numbers?"

"His numbers are greater by tens of thousands. We win because of our tactics and weapons, where they are crude beasts. We have never gone into battle and had to protect Romans. Fenrir plots this war to take us all out, using our weakness for man to do it." She paused, her lips hot on his breath.

"It is never too late to do what is right," Axius begged her, breathing in her face. "I need you." He swallowed at her face as she gazed into his firm eyes.

"You are brave," She turned away from him and marched down the hillside, where Lupa awaited her. His hand was pressed atop his scythe at his side, his wolf pelt hanging on his massive body frame as if the mountain had spawned him. Vasiliki turned back to face them. "But you will all die."

Axius watched her go, his eyes lingering on her, his heart beating wildly. She turned to stare at him again, tears in her eyes.

"Lupa will send the Falcons to your family, warning them of the mercenaries. Your warriors there will need all the strength and cunning they must find to defeat them." She marched away from them, leaving Nestor and Axius gazing at her. They stared over the hillside to the sun grazing the horizon in pillars of crimson.

"You cannot protect me in battle." Axius turned to Nestor. "I release you of the burden of doing so. I know my father pestered you."

"What do you want to do?" Nestor looked as if all color had drained from his face.

"I want to go to Titus and you will help me get to Titus. We will warn him so the army will know what they war against, and then we will kill them or die trying to kill them all." Axius belted out.

Just as Nestor opened his mouth to say something, Vezina appeared on the hill on the path at them. "Eh, Roman, come with me." He turned to walk down the hill, pausing, craning his thick neck.

"There is something I must show you."

They followed him into the shop, the smell of hot metal thick in the air, the warmth from the fires kissing their naked arms. Vezina brought them to a table toward the back of the wall, where a Roman cassis, an Imperial-Gallic helmet, sat atop the anvil. Leather straps were tied under the chin and covered with gold sheet metal. The top of the helmet had knobs made of metal and movable cheek visors connected with a thong. A neck protector had been molded to it. The red plume of short feathers starkly contrasted the dark tools and drabness of the shop.

Axius smiled when he saw it. "You made my armor!" He lunged down to pick it up, but his arms could not budge it. He tried to lift it again and sighed. "I cannot lift it."

"The craftsmanship in this tiny thing is the same as our Dacian wolf armor. You cannot lift it because you are not one of us." Vezina warned him. "Your Roman armor will not stand against us in your current state of human."

Axius stepped away from it, his face falling into a hardened reprieve of pain.

"This is what it would take to keep you alive in battle, and you do not have the strength to carry it." Vezina's ears were high atop his head, and his eyes wide and bright.

Axius gazed upon the impressive work of the cassis, gritting his teeth. "If you made me Roman armor, it would break anyway with the beasts' war tactics and strengths?"

"Your armies before you have failed due to this, yes."

Axius stood silent before Vezina spoke again. "Now come with me."

Vezina then led Axius to the end of the room. It opened to a wall of wolf-size Roman armor. Axius was not surprised Vezina had been making this armor, in case the Romans chose to take the curse. It shook him to his core seeing the magnitude of the size difference. He turned to gaze back to the cassis again, and then crossed his arms glaring at the armor three to four times his size.

Roman wolf armor. A weakness hit him at the knees. He opened his mouth to speak, but at first, nothing came out.

"I do not know what to do to save my people. I refuse to accept this curse as our only fate." Axius swallowed, staring at the wall and rows of shields, body armors, and helmets. "They will not be wolves."

Vezina's ears fell flat atop his head, and the wrinkles on his snout raced to his eyes. "Then, they will die," Vezina whispered behind his back.

Axius did not look at him. Instead, he continued to gaze upon the armor and fight back the tears in his eyes. He clenched his jaws as if a silent pain was eating him from the inside out. He kept hearing *we are wolves. We are wolves. We are family*, over and over in his head. He was not ready to accept that.

Vezina sighed. Silence overtook them for moments on end before the big wolf gazed upon the drab cloak wrapped haphazardly around Axius's midsection, and blurted out "Why are you naked?"

Nestor gawked at Axius. "I told you. This is Dacia, not Rome."

35

The Wolves of Dacia

Axius had dressed himself again and meandered to the back cliff wall. The fortress sparkled from the inside as torches and lamps dotted the entrances. He stood there gazing upon it. His eyes tried to understand the carvings, and the ancient language dancing across the stone for miles.

There were wolves riding horses. There was a massive army of wolves carved together as they were one. The wall told a story but he did not understand it, though he did understand the brotherhood of the army standing as one.

A voice sounded behind him, but he did not turn to recognize Vasiliki. "You knew I was coming." She smiled.

"I can smell you." Axius turned his head to side-eye her. "You smell of the vines growing at the river. Sweet, and…"

"Ah." She approached him, her long gown flowing behind her as her wolf cloak hung across her shoulders. "You have more wolf than you realize, Axius of Rome."

She stopped beside him and gazed up. "Do you trust me?"

Axius froze, turning to face her, his brown eyes lit up. "No."

"When I bring Diana back, will you trust me?" She asked, no expression on her face.

Axius clenched his jaws. "No. You are fearful of going to battle with these beasts. I do not know if your army can take them. I have yet to see it. Bringing a child back from their clutches proves nothing."

She turned to walk to the entrance and then faced him. "Come with me, Axius. It is time to show you."

Axius did not hesitate and followed her through the labyrinth of the caverns, both grabbing torch lights in the darkness.

Axius gazed at her backside, her long braided black hair tickled with auburn hues, her flowing gown and fur cloak dragging the stone floor behind her. Her blue-ribbon tattoos snaked up her fingers and slender arms and he noticed the designs on the back of her neck resembled a dragon yet it was a wolf.

She glanced back at him, a twinkle in her amber eyes. "Power and protection."

"The markings?" Axius blurted.

"Yes, the markings you stare at mean power and protection. It is our pride and heritage as Dacian wolves to be marked."

Silence.

"Do you find them ugly?" She whispered.

"On the contrary." Axius complimented her. "They are beautiful. They are strong."

She stopped, turning to face him, their torches lighting up the stone darkness around them. "You will find many beautiful things here." She turned to continue walking. "And many dreadful things."

"Our markings are a small part."

"Why did Nestor leave this place." Axius wondered.

"He never told you?"

"Commander Artgus gave him to Domitia's father. We became best friends, brothers throughout the years." Axius remembered. "My father saw talent in him and made him begin the races for the circus."

"Ah. Nestor to his old tricks, always hunting things." Vasiliki smiled.

She turned and walked on. "Our father was killed in battle. Nestor was in line to rule, and he disappeared on the way to Oltenia to claim the throne. His guards brought us back a front tooth. We thought he had been hunted and killed by Fenrir's tribe. I realize now he pulled it himself to make us think he was dead."

"How did you…"

"Survive?" Vasiliki turned to stare at him, her jaws clenched.

"Kilian and Lupa saved us. Kilian was my father's advisor and very powerful. Still is. Lupa is a brave and cunning Commander. The wolves listen to him. With their help, mother and I protected our kingdom, or what was left of it. She made me queen on her deathbed."

"What is in Oltenia?" Axius wondered.

Vasiliki huffed. "The most powerful Oltenian clan of our bloodline. I kept the heart of Dacia due to my wolves' military tactics. We hope to go home once Fenrir dies and the heart is no longer needed."

"The heart that makes true bloods? Is it a relic?"

She smiled. "It is a place."

Axius froze, listening to her. His eyes craned over her face and rested on her lips.

"Once Fenrir's curse is broken, we can go home."

Axius sighed, his heart skipping a beat. "What happens to the heart once you have gone home?"

She stopped walking, staring ahead, swallowing. "We destroy it. There will be no more purebloods, ever. No need for them."

"You will be the last," Axius whispered, pondering everything.

Vasiliki agreed, taking a deep breath. "We will be the last."

Axius followed her for what seemed like miles. They walked along in the darkness, following a carved-out tunnel in the cavern until it opened to a mammoth-sized cave. Natural light teetered through windows above them, and Axius noticed a large arched opening. He heard echoes the closer they came to the end.

She took his torch from him and dropped them both into a rock basin at the opening. She reached the opening that spread as wide as the cavern wall and motioned for him to come. When Axius walked out into the sunlight, he blinked his eyes, but a reckoning dawned on him.

He froze.

Overlooking a vast plain surrounded by cliffs, the path had carved stone steps down into a kingdom that spread from one side of the mountain to the other. The river kissed it from an underground tributary at the mountain base for miles. The plain stretched miles of roads and stone towers carved into the mountain. A city vibe of villagers meandered about with their children and families. The breadth of the houses and the markets caused Axius to shiver inside. The open plain below them spilled of Dacian men and women warriors in full body armor.

Their curved falxes sprouted over their heads, shimmering under the sun. The women gripped spears or javelins, and Axius counted them as if they numbered the leaves on a Sycamore tree in full bloom. Their helmets were decorated with solid crests, and domed. All the men had long hair, and were rugged with beards. The women had long hair and many of them wore braids with golden adornments in them. But they all looked as if they were one warrior.

Axius recognized Lupa. He was big and burly and built bigger than the others. They were all horseback, and their scaly golden armor kissed their rugged muscular bodies. Lupa gripped his falx facing off the riders across the plain. The first line behind him clasped one-sided battle axes. Riders were behind him, spilling in the field for a mile, and the horses were draped with their own Dacian armor. The horses dug into the dirt and neighed, their eyes melted on the warriors across the plain, rearing to go.

Behind them, rose poles with wolf head flags and gaping snouts on the lines where the populace gathered in the thousands. When the wind blew through them, Axius's ears pricked at the bellowing howl. The Dacian Draco wind instrument sported metal tongues, its shriek echoing through the plain.

Lupa raised his falx, howling at his men, and they charged the other riders. As Lupa neared them, he lunged up from the saddle and transformed into a raging, red wolf. He catapulted midair at them, snarling from a long, broad snout. His wolf body was ripped in muscles from snout to paw, and his tail was like a whip.

His body armor seemed to melt into the wolf pelt on his back. The other riders transformed and plunged into each other, their growling bodies knocking each other off their horses. They pinged their blades against one another, howling into the skies. The horses did not flinch. They kept riding through the chaos even as their riders became wolves.

Lupa pummeled them into the ground with his fists, his sword pinging the others off him to avoid getting hit. The crowds of Dacians standing around the plain screamed and hollered, and many of them raised their fists in victory. When Lupa was done, he helped his comrades up, dusted them off. The horses veered around them back to their side of the plain.

The world froze when Axius watched them transform. The air became heavy like something broke open through the earth like. It was like an ancient relic was discovered, only it was open for a moment and gone again. The awakening pinged his heart and froze his backbone to his soul as chills darted up his legs.

He turned to Vasiliki, who watched him, his face drained of color. She stood there, her robes hugging her thin muscular frame, her face firm. Her pouty small lips were a conscious resolution as she recognized Axius's reaction.

"Rome does not want you to be the last." Axius's voice quivered.

She stared at him, her eyes as firm as her sharp cheekbones. "Now you understand."

36

Darkness likes to Follow

Micah lingered in the market by the vaulted hall. His back pressed into a marble column, the porticoes flanking him like shrouds of mercy. Families and marketkeepers meandered in and out selling and buying. The markets were brimming with life, selling fish and cheeses. The fresh produce held a crisp edge of pureness, and Micah sighed, enjoying the vibe, even for a small moment.

He turned to walk through the porticoes across the market, the cheeses and olive oils enticing him with the spices in the air throughout the busyness of the market. But Micah was not there to shop. He was being followed. So, he picked up a vat of olive oil, smelled it, paid the vendor, and walked on, his back to a darkness pressing upon him.

He meandered past the porticoes and followed the wall to the end of the market, where a lonely street sat. He stopped at the waist high wall, pulled the olive oil up to his nose, and smelled it again, his heart racing. Two shadows stretched across the lawn at him and froze by a pillar. Micah turned to them, his face firm, his eyes wide.

He recognized them as magistrates. The two men sauntered toward him, their white togas kissing the ground at their feet, their fists clenched as hard as their faces. Micah swallowed, confronting them.

"Felix, Atticus. Are you well?" Micah nodded to them, his eyes falling to his feet, waiting.

"We are well, traitor. Faring better than you." Atticus growled at him.

"What is the meaning of this," Micah demanded, his face pale.

"You are to die, as well as your traitorous loved ones." Felix pestered him.

Micah swallowed. "Even the children?"

Atticus rubbed his chin, his blonde hair kissing his tanned face, his eyes as bright as the darkness swelling in him. "No heirs will survive our kings' rule."

"So, at the end of all things, you confront me with the truth of Rome's demise." Micah belted out.

"Rome belongs to the beasts, and we are taking it." Felix sneered and smiled at him. Micah noticed fangs in his mouth and dropped his olive oil at his feet, where it shattered around him.

The men sneered at him, and Micah bent his head up to see the shaft from an arrow plummet through Felix's skull, and his body fell upon its knees. Atticus froze at first, but then his eyes simmered in amber, turning to see who had shot him, his face changing as the fangs burst up from his gums, and a low rumbling growl echoed from somewhere deep inside him.

Troy lunged out from the pillar behind them, his arms flexed, his face clenched. His knuckles drained of color, and he pressed on the grip, an arrow against his cheek at the nocking point. He pulled the string back and fired. The arrow pressed through Atticus's skull, and Micah closed his eyes to the *kerthunk* and the blood spray. Troy slung the bow around his chest, pulling his Spatha. He gripped the handgrip and lunged into the bodies.

Micah gasped as Troy swung the blade around and severed the heads, his eyes roaming from the bodies to the horse-drawn carriage that had stopped in the street. Manius peered around to them from the seat, his hands gripping the reigns.

"Put the bodies in, hurry."

Troy wiped his sword off on one of the bodies, huffing, but Micah sneered at him. "You owe me forty denarii."

Troy paused, yanking on the bodies. "For what."

"The oil I just bought."

"You were to lure them here, not shop." Troy pulled the headless body across the lawn to the wagon, his face clenched.

Micah hopped on the seat next to Manius. "Yes, but I needed the oil."

Troy sighed, his eyes on fire. "I saved your life. We are even. Help me with the body."

Micah gasped. "You owe me for the oil. We are even."

Troy sneered at him as he picked up the head and slung it into the back of the wagon.

Manius jumped down to help Troy. "Hurry. We have little time!" Troy grunted, lifting the bodies into the wagon with Manius. Their faces were clenched, and their desperation as thick as the bloody air around them on the lawn.

Micah watched them load the bodies and heads, turning to Manius when they had finished covering them up with wool cloths Manius bought from the market. "Are you ready for this?" He eyed him as Manius gripped the reigns.

Manius took in a deep breath. "There is no going back now, my friend. No going back."

***Domitia sat with her children in the courtyard. The serenity of the morning did not calm her nerves, even as the gentle streaming water fountains kissed her mind behind them. The girls played with their dolls, and a table of bread, cheeses and fruits was set out for them.

Domitia swallowed, her hand shaking as she poured her coffee, thinking of Dia. She closed her eyes and took a deep breath, controlling her shaking hand.

She sipped her coffee, her eyes folding up to the terrace rolling around them, empty of Dacian mercenaries. They had disappeared at sunrise when Troy and Micah with Manius had crept out. She swallowed the hot drink down even as it formed a lump in her throat, and her chest burned deep inside. Her girls sat atop the blanket behind her, their backs against the stone fountain. Mel walked from one pillar in the garden to another, watching the halls, her bow in her grasp.

"Ready," Mel whispered to her.

Domitia gripped her stomach and nodded. "Ready."

Mel froze as shadows lingered down the hall past Manius's study, and she stepped before Domitia and the children. Domitia stiffened her spine, her eyes wide, her face turning to gaze upon the girls. When she turned around to face Mel, Matunaga slithered out from the study and stood before them in the open, his hand clasping a parchment. Domitia's heart beat her chest to death as she sat there waiting.

Mel grimaced at them, her face still bruised, her leg healing, and she limped back to Domitia. The girls noticed and pressed against the stone wall behind their mother, waiting. Matunaga stepped out with five of the Dacian mercenaries. They stood beside each other, their faces hard, their beards wet with morning dew.

Mel reached in to grab her sword and paused just when the men fell to their knees and bowed. Domitia stood, her mouth open, her eyes watering. Matunaga stepped forward and fell to his knee, pressed out the parchment to her.

His eyes fell upon the ground at his knees. "We serve the queen of Lupescu and the Oltenia heirs." He raised and faced her.

Mel sighed, her chest rearing up and down, her eyes as wide as Domitia's gasp. "Good, because I will die to protect them. Where are the other five."

Matunaga raised, swallowing as Mel took the parchment. "The other four, Domitia…" He paused. "They must be hunted."

Domitia held her breath.

"We need your help to draw them out. It is clear now that although Diana was taken, they wanted you, the mate of Lupescu."

Domitia's knees gave way reading it, and she sat down, a reckoning hitting her as if the stone on the fountain had collided with her. Her eyes watered. "My love. My Lupescu." She gripped her heart, missing him, and then eyed her beautiful daughters, who looked like their whole world was crumbling around them.

Domitia raised back up, standing aside Mel, and huffed at Matunaga. "You will help Manius hunt the others and the other beasts in the Senate." Domitia breathed a sigh of relief, but her hands shook, and her girls huddled behind her on the wall.

Matunaga nodded to her, his eyes lit up as if a fire had been lit within him. "It will be done, my queen."

Domitia watched as Troy emerged, and Manius and Micah lingered behind them. Troy and Manius were covered in blood, and Troy clutched his bow in his palm. Manius nodded to Mel from under the terrace, then grazed a straight face at Domitia.

"Domitia, it is time."

Domitia clasped her shaking hands at her belly, her face drained of color. "It is time to end this." She whispered, but deep inside her mind, she played worst-case scenarios through her heart. "I am ready to go home."

Later that evening, Domitia sat still for a long time while the girls were sleeping. She sipped Ginger tea but could no longer hold it down. The oil lamp flickered as a slight rain moved in, and she sat in a lonely bed herself, re-reading the parchment Matunaga had given her. The parchment was for her and her alone, although two were sent. Matunaga had read the first one to the mercenaries and then handed the other to her.

Tears fell down her face. She turned to see the pillow where Nestor should be, but she did not know if he was still alive. Her heart ached. Her head spun, and she gripped her growing belly and sighed.

"Hello, little one. We will be going to your father soon. He will be so happy to see you."

She smiled at her belly. "He will be surprised because I know you are a son."

She laid the parchment on the pillow where Nestor should be. "After this day, your father can never return to Rome, so we go to him."

She leaned back to try to sleep, although it would elude her again. Instead, she laid face up, grasping her belly, and cried, letting the tears wet her pillow on both sides. Her mind reeled with the parchment Matunaga had given her and what that meant for her family forever.

Our dearest queen, mate of Lupescu, we come to ensure our king is victorious against the beasts who hunt you. We have given Matunaga, the scribe, a proclamation of death to Vasiliki's mercenaries in Rome. They will swear their allegiance or die. If any harm befalls you or the heirs, we shall come upon Rome. Our mission is to ensure you and the Oltenian heirs' survival.

Your most loyal servants, the Oltenia wolves.

37

The Beasts at the River

Axius crept down the narrow stone path from the mountain to get to the field. He lunged across the plain in the tall grasses and froze at the Dacian horse corral, the villages silent so far. Vasiliki and Kilian had gone to get Diana, with Lupa standing along the river watching them go, his face as red as his beard. Axius used that diversion to creep through the caverns because he planned on following them.

He pulled the reigns on a stallion, clicking his tongue at it, caressing its snout. The horse pulled away from him and then gave in to his jesting. As Axius reared up to climb it, Nestor jerked up from behind the other horses. "What do you think you are doing?"

Axius froze, his heart skipping a beat. "Damnit Nestor."

"You are stealing a horse." Nestor stared at him, his face firm.

Axius pulled the reigns anyway. "Yes. Going to help get Diana, and then we go to Titus. As I have said over and over."

"You were going to let me stay here, languishing in my grief for my daughter." Nestor blew out his nose, pulling a horse behind him.

Axius laughed. "You knew I would do this and waited for me."

Nestor cleared his throat. "I promised your father I would guard over you here. That is what I am doing."

"You want to save Diana yourself and kill them all, so do I. You handle the beasts at the river. I will kill the human traitors." They rode side by side together, Axius following Nestor's lead through the gorge out of the city.

"I know you well. You do not listen." Nestor argued. "You were always going to find a way to creep out against Vasiliki's orders."

"Yes. I was." Axius chirped. "I needed her gone first."

Nestor chided him as they trotted out of the ravine along the river. "I want no harm to befall my sister. She has suffered enough."

Axius agreed with him. "I go to help her."

They trotted along, the silence eating at them.

"You fear not the beasts at the river?" Nestor scowled.

Axius huffed. "I fear not beast nor man. They bleed same as me."

Nestor smiled. "You fear my sister."

Axius scoffed at him, his eyes wide. "I do not fear her. She is strong and brave."

"Your loins ache for my sister. Do they not?" Nestor blurted out. "I see how you look at her and how she sees you."

Nestor sighed, gripping his chest. "The way she gazed upon you! It made my heart ache for Domitia. I miss her so! I need my wife."

"Vasiliki gazed upon me when I was naked." Axius pursed his lips, smiling.

Nestor laughed. "When you were naked, indeed. You must be cautious, brother! My sister is veracious."

Axius flexed his forearms gripping the reigns, his jaws clenched. "She is a beast. I cannot love a beast. I will not lie with one."

Nestor laughed at him, roaring his head back. "We are all wolves' brother! Wolves. Her heart is bigger than most." He raced ahead of Axius, picking up speed.

Axius put his head down to follow him as Nestor berated him. "Your loins do ache for her." He laughed. "I give you my blessing if you can handle her!" His laugh was thunderous.

Axius reached him, and they raced one another out of the city. "Shut up." He belted out, but then turned his head and smiled so Nestor could not see his face.

They raced along the river through the plains, following Vasiliki and Kilian. Nestor was good at tracking and hunting. Although his sister and her scout were good at hiding, Nestor could still smell and sense their trail. Axius gripped his chest plate, his wounds still mending, his bow strapped across his chest, his long sword in his sheath over his head, his gladius at his side.

Nestor pressed his head down, squinting his eyes, his black Dacian scale armor accentuating his already fine-tuned body. He, too, was fully armed. His bow was strapped to his back, and two scythes were sticking over his head. On the side of his saddle in a sheath rested a long metal shaft. They chased after Kilian and Vasiliki with only one thing on their mind. To come back alive with everyone, especially Diana.

Anna lunged into the thatched stone house, peering upon Diana, sitting with her feet up pressed against the cold wall. The fire had gone out, and the food they had given here was still uneaten. Anna rolled her eyes, pulling her fur cloak tighter over her shoulders. "Child, you are going to make yourself ill. Cover up."

"I will cover up when mama comes for you."

Anna laughed. "Your mother is not coming for you, silly child."

"Yes, she does." Diana belted out, her face like stone.

Anna tossed her a wool blanket and turned to go back outside. She froze at the child and sneered at her. "Eat your food. You need your strength for what is coming."

Diana swallowed, watching her go. She had been held up in the small hut by the river town for days. She was not allowed to go outside. She was not allowed to draw or paint. She gazed upon the small window opening that let the only light in, watching as dark shadows stretched across the walls to keep her held in.

Anna walked down the road between the houses, and it opened to a plain kissing the river. She took a deep breath and turned to go into her house. Her eyes met a dark figure, taller than her, strong and fierce in his grasp. She froze as his strong hands pinned her against the stone wall, the fire still burning. Fenrir laughed in her face.

His scruffy face breathed into her. She gasped, her blue eyes wide. He raked a palm up her gown and she moaned, a smile beckoning.

"Been a long time since I had the pleasure of your loins." He picked her up by her buttocks and tossed her on the bed.

He pressed atop her and stretched her arms out and held her down. He licked her neck to her bosom and moaned. Then he dove into her neck with his kisses.

Anna's heart was exhilarated. "Yes!"

He raised up and pulled her gown off over her head. He pulled off his long tunic, revealing a ribbed chest and arms swallowed in black tattoos. She helped him rip him out of his clothes and they pummeled each other until nightfall, their growls and roars of passion echoing throughout the day.

Vasiliki peered through the edge of the woods with Kilian, the night rising around them as if a black cloak had been thrust upon them. The river crested like a snake crawling through the plain below them, the ship bobbing up and down in the waters along the shore. The oil lamps had the village lit up well, and Vasiliki sighed, glaring into it.

Men in black armor guarded a small hut, meandering back and forth along the street. Fires were burning in the field aside the town, and five men were sitting around it cooking wild game and talking to one another.

"You take the five. I take the two where my niece is." She whispered.

Kilian narrowed his brows, his bald head shining under the night sky. "Is that so? I think you should take the five, and I get the little wolf."

Vasiliki sneered at him, a half-smile on her face. "You will scare her when you turn. I am her aunt."

Kilian scoffed and rolled his eyes. "So be it. I will let you get the little wolf." He smiled into the darkness, pestering her.

As they begin their hunt down the hill into the village, Kilian whispered. "We must hurry, Axius is well on his way. If we do not beat him, he will never let me forget it."

"I look forward to him jesting you." She mumbled, her eyes changing as amber fire lit her up from the inside out as they crawled through the brush.

As they neared the field in the tall grass across from the five men around the fire, Kilian let out bellowing roar. They plopped back down, watching and waiting. The five men stood, and eleven more rushed from the street to meet them, and then they all turned into beasts.

"You said there were five." Kilian grimaced, his eyes changing into an amber fire.

Vasiliki smiled at him and crawled away to edge around the village. "See you on the other side with my niece."

"You smile at me while you creep away..." Kilian smiled at her, his eyes sparkling.

Kilian took a deep breath, his lungs filling with fire, his back burning into his soul. As the beasts lunged at him from the fire, he catapulted into the air over them. He was twice their size, and for a moment they froze at the sight of him. Kilian landed behind them, pressed into the ground even as it shook beneath the weight of his power.

They pressed together like they had formed a wall, but Kilian raised over them and snarled, his claws engorged like daggers. Vasiliki heard the beasts' bellowing howls of pain as Kilian ripped them apart behind her. She melted into the river bed and followed the water to the small hut where two men stood guarding the door.

They watched a shadow of a feminine form lunge down the street at them from the river. The aura from the oil lamps spread Vasiliki's shadow as if she had melted into the world. A growl came behind them, and they both turned to their left. The man on the left did not have time to pull his sword or turn to his wolf form. She lunged around the bend and yanked him away from the house with her hands.

She ripped out his throat with her fingers and then turned to the other man, gawking at her in silence. As Vasiliki lunged to kill him, a wooden plank plunged through her shoulder and out the front. She froze in pain, turned to see Anna sneering at her. "I knew you would come for the child!"

Vasiliki raised her hand to pull it out and turn into her wolf. A firm, clawed arm rushed her from the darkness and pinned her against the stone house. He lifted her to face his snout, and Fenrir breathed in her face. He growled, his massive, square head wrinkled, and his pointy ears flat. He pressed into her throat as she gasped for air, unable to turn against him.

"Hello, my mated queen." He growled at her face.

Vasiliki was weak with his power over her. She pressed against him with her hand, but he gripped her arm and pushed it over her head. She yelled in pain as the arrow snapped. Fenrir gazed into her with bloodlust, holding her up by her neck off the ground, her life at his mercy.

Another roar echoed over the field and Fenrir scowled at the other beasts coming in to help them. "Kill them! I have her."

Fenrir turned his gaze to Anna and nodded, and Vasiliki watched her disappear down the street toward the river.

Vasiliki watched a dozen more beasts rush the street to meet Kilian in the field. She breathed, her chest beating against Fenrir's massive, black wolf body. She felt his muscles move into her as his chest pressed into hers, his legs holding her up on the wall as he gripped her throat.

"I have waited a long time for you." He leaned into her face, his beast snout pressing against her cheek, breathing on her.

Vasiliki closed her eyes and held her breath.

"You always eluded my grasp, but no more." He kissed her with a broad, wet mouth. His long, black tongue grazed her neck up to her cheek. "You will mate with me. You will bear me pure blood heirs."

Vasiliki's eyes lit up like fire, and she craned her glare to meet his eyes. "I will die first."

She met his black eyes with her glowing amber ones. She held her breath as an arrow plunged through Fenrir's throat and came out the other side. Fenrir dropped her, but another arrow hit him. This time, it went through his shoulder blade and out his back.

Vasiliki fell to her knees, grabbing her throat. Fenrir turned to see Axius standing at the end of the road, another arrow in his thread. His red robe blew behind him, and his golden armor lit up the street with a river of shadows against the oil lamps. His scruffy face was dark, like the shadow of hate under his eyes. Axius clenched his jaws and aimed, his muscles bulging.

"I will gut you alive!" Axius released the arrow, and it found its mark inside Fenrir's throat just as he snarled with an open mouth. Fenrir fell back as the shank protruded out the back of his head. Axius readied another arrow, his hands calm like a hunter had found its prey.

Fenrir stood and yanked the arrow out of his mouth, breaking it off, laughing. "You are a fool of a mortal to think you can take me! She belongs to me." He roared as blood spurt out his snout, snarling at Axius.

Axius aimed, clenching his jaws, his eyes narrowed across his face. "She belongs to no one!" His voice was deep, echoing.

Fenrir growled at his face and bent down to lunge at him just as Axius let the arrow go and dodged out of the way. As Fenrir was in midair to attack him, Lupescu lunged at him through the darkness and knocked him back to the end of the village against the river. As their bodies collided in midair, Fenrir let out a high shriek of pain. Lupescu dug his dagger claws into his chest, catapulting Fenrir away. He pulled the claws back out, spraying blood in midair.

Lupescu raged and roared at him, sliding onto the road while rocks and dirt flew high around him as he skidded to a stop. Lupescu flexed his wolf body and roared where Fenrir had been thrown. His roar echoed over the river and rolling plains.

Axius jumped up and paused at Vasiliki. He pulled her up by her waist, her body tight against his. He gripped her tight and breathed on her lips, and shivers chased Vasiliki's arms. Axius raised a palm against her face and gazed into her eyes.

"Are you well?!" He pleaded with her.

She gripped his palm on her face and sighed into his eyes. "I am well."

Axius lunged a forceful kiss on her forehead and let her go. He turned away to head back into the field. "Get Diana! Get out of here." She watched him chase back up the road into the field. Her heart beat wildly watching him, his bow still in his grasp, his cloak flowing behind him.

She yanked the arrow out of her shoulder and grimaced. Just as she turned to the door for Diana, one more beast came at her from behind the house. She took a deep breath as fire filled her soul, and she transformed, growling shouts of rage.

Axius rushed to Kilian's rage in the field as he tore another two apart, severing their heads from their bodies. As the bodies fell, they changed back to men. Axius gripped his long sword and pulled his gladius, watching as a black shadow loomed over Kilian as he was fighting three more beasts off.

As Kilian lunged up and ripped out the throat of the last beast pressing into him, his eyes caught a shadowy figure looming up from the tall grass. The corner of his eye caught a shimmering gold as Axius sprinted up behind it and jumped. He belted around in midair, swishing his long sword around its neck, and severing its head clean off. As Axius fell, he rolled. He stopped inches from Kilian, who huffed at him.

"Mighty wolf." Kilian pulled him up, turning to go. "I go to help Lupescu!"

"I shall come!" Axius readied his sword again, but Kilian pushed him away. "No! You must wait with Vasiliki and the child."

Axius watched Kilian race off, his heart busting inside. As he craned his neck, he noticed the last beast he had killed changed back to a man. His head laid aside his body. Shivers raced up his spine.

Diana had pinned herself under the table against the fireplace, her eyes wide with fear. She heard two low-moaning howls just outside the door, and it frightened her. She saw blood splatters hit the walls in the shadows and then silence. The door burst open and a big white wolf barged in, blood smeared all over it.

Diana screamed, gasping at it. Vasiliki twisted around, her wolf pelt changing her from the magnificent wolf into a woman again. As her long, black hair spilled over her shoulders, she turned around to face her niece and smiled. She held out her hand.

"Hello, my niece."

Vasiliki bent to her knee at Diana's face, smiling. "You look like your father." Her eyes teared up.

Diana cried. "Papa!"

"I am your aunt Vasiliki. Come, I take you to him, little wolf."

Diana took her hand, and Vasiliki pulled her tight against her chest. Diana gasped as she transformed into the white wolf again with her in her arms. Vasiliki perked her ears up and listened, then bolted out of the hut back up the street. She followed Axius's trail through the field, which was littered with bodies of men now, not beasts. Kilian rushed past her to get to Lupescu at the river, and he moaned recognizing she had the child in her wolf arms.

Lupescu rounded Fenrir at the river, the shallow waters changing to blood, their claws digging at the rocks. Fenrir took a deep breath and pulled another arrow from his shoulder. He stood and glared, his chest bleeding from Lupescu's claw punctures. "You are a fool to have come back! You could have stayed in Rome to spend your days with your family!"

Lupescu growled at him, both the same size, towering, hulking and powerful. "You sent them to my family! There will be no peace as long as you live!"

Fenrir seethed at him and bent down to lunge in, pressing his snout to the rocks. He suddenly stopped as he noticed Kilian lunging through the village onto the street straight at them. Kilian's growl shook the air around them, and Fenrir knew he could not take them both.

Lupescu heard the Dacian horn blow, and his heart melted. Vasiliki had Diana. He could not stay here and continue fighting Fenrir. Fenrir turned away from Lupescu, his eyes red with hate. "I will get your people. Rome will die!" He raced across the river away from them.

As they turned away from one another, Kilian joined Lupescu. They raced back through the village and up the hillside, over the plain to the horses. As Lupescu neared the safe point, he changed back into Nestor, his armor still kissing his body as if the curse had never touched him. Axius was kneeling, holding Diana in his arms, and Vasiliki stood behind them, waiting.

Diana's face lit up when she saw her father, and Nestor fell to his knees crying. She rushed into his arms, crying at his face. Nestor moaned. "I have you! Oh, my beautiful child. I finally have you." He cried atop her head, clutching her tight into him.

"Papa!" Diana clung to him.

Kilian pulled his wolf pelt around his body, eying their surroundings. "We must go now! We have a day's ride and then on to Titus!"

They climbed their horses with Diana in Nestor's lap and began the journey back. Vasiliki gawked at Axius, her shoulder bleeding down her arm. "You mean to continue to Titus?"

Nestor turned to her, sneering. "There were no men at the river, it was all beasts, half-bloods. That means he is sending the pure bloods to Titus. We have no choice."

Vasiliki clenched her face and turned to Kilian, but all he could do was nod, his eyes still on fire, his face smeared with blood. She wondered, "The winch Fenrir kept, did you kill her?"

Nestor gawked at her. "Who?"

Axius turned to them, his eyes wide. "Anna?"

"She has gone then, if you did not kill her." Vasiliki moaned.

"Damnit!" Nestor cursed. "She will return to Rome. We must warn my family."

Vasiliki turned her gaze upon Axius, who rode beside her. He noticed her stare and met her there, their eyes lighting upon one another in silence for endless moments. Axius took a deep breath staring at her, his eyes did not waver.

"Are you well?" He whispered at her, but his face was clenched.

Vasiliki breathed deeply, meeting his stare. "I am well. Axius, the mighty." She smiled at his eyes.

Her eyes lingered on his armor and strong arms. His swords were sheathed at his side, and his face, arms, and chest were sprayed with blood. Axius watched her explore his body, and his eyes lingered up her legs to her hips. They explored one another in the presence of each other and were not ashamed.

Axius cleared his throat suddenly to pester Kilian, who led them. "We were but moments behind you."

Kilian smiled. "I know this, yet you did not beat us there, Axius of Rome."

Nestor laughed, his chin atop Diana's little head as she cuddled into him, his heart full for the moment.

Vasiliki watched Axius, and swallowed, but could not say anything more. So, she turned her gaze away from him to follow the trail home, and they rode in silence side by side together until they neared closer to Titus.

The next night, stars cascaded above them like fireflies, and Vasiliki sat against a log on the forest floor staring into the fire. Diana plopped beside her, and Nestor and Kilian watched them, smiling. Diana sighed, pulling the bread apart.

"You are not a bad wolf." She stuffed it in her mouth.

Axius sat with his legs stretched out across the fire, watching Vasiliki through the flames, his eyes on her beautiful face. Vasiliki laughed at her niece. "No, I am not a bad wolf. Neither are you."

Diana leaned into her, and stretched her arms around her and squeezed her eyes tight. "Thank you for saving me, aunt Vas."

Vasiliki pulled her in, wrapping her in her arms and closing her eyes as she kissed her little head. Then she leaned back up, looked her in the eyes, and touched her chin. "I would do it all over again, little wolf."

Diana gasped. "Your eyes glow like honey."

Vasiliki smiled ear to ear. "So do yours. As you grow to be a woman, you will have my eyes. The women have amber eyes, and then they change to a brilliant clear blue when we are wolves."

Nestor swallowed watching them, missing his wife and daughters. He bent his head down into his drink and sighed. Axius turned to him. "You cannot go back to Rome. Your family must come here. Everything has changed now."

Nestor eyed him, his face lighting up by the fire. "I do not know how Domitia will feel about this. I would be uprooting her whole life and our children to a strange land. Nonetheless, I was wrong to keep my family from my family. Vasiliki loves her very much."

Axius gazed upon Vasiliki, watching how she talked to Diana and doted upon her. When Diana finally got up to snuggle with Nestor again for the night, Axius got up and plopped beside her against the tree. "She loves you. You are her hero now."

"I love her too." She smiled.

Vasiliki stretched her shoulder and moaned. Axius leaned to touch her, but she grabbed his hand. She gripped his palm tight, and he froze as his eyes met her face.

"You were injured. Let me see." He whispered.

She nodded and leaned her neck, and Axius pulled her pelt down off her neck slowly. He pulled it to her bosom, and held his breath. His eyes roved her naked, olive-tanned shoulder. There was no injury, but the blood was still there. It had healed.

She explored his face, and he met her eyes again. His finger caressed her naked skin, and Vasiliki bent up and grabbed his hand. Axius touched the space where the wound was with his fingertips, feeling her skin, as shivers rushed up his arms.

Vasiliki whispered in his face. "These wounds heal. The pain remains for some time."

Axius removed his hand and leaned against the tree with her, his head back, gazing at the stars. "That is good."

Vasiliki leaned in with him. Their shoulders touched as their heads gazed together at the stars, their breaths forming a fog around them. She pressed her head against the tree, joining him.

"Thank you." She whispered.

"For what?" His eyes still on the stars.

"For coming." Vasiliki moaned, her eyes tearing up.

Axius took a deep breath. His muscle armor heaved up and down, and he clenched his jaws. "Do you trust me now." He whispered.

Vasiliki narrowed her brows and held her breath. "I trust you."

"Do you trust me?" She pondered.

Axius craned his neck to meet her stare. He looked in her eyes as she craned to face him. "I trust you, Vasiliki."

He smiled at her face, his eyes lighting up, and she met him with a smile of her own. She leaned her head against his shoulder, and their faces pressed against one another. Axius cupped her face with his palm and closed his eyes, and something burst inside him. Vasiliki clasped her palm atop his as they sat there, intertwining fingers, breathing into one another.

"I will die to save you." Axius whispered against her head.

Vasiliki closed her eyes and swallowed.

Nestor gasped at them from across the fire. "You cannot get naked. My child is here."

Kilian laughed at them, his laughter echoing in the night. Axius and Vasiliki laughed too. They continued leaning against one another gazing into the heavens, their hearts flickering alight as the stars beamed overhead.

At daybreak, they raced over the plain around a rising plateau to get to Titus. Standing on the ledge overlooking the great expanse, Axius bit his tongue. Nestor was bent down explaining to Diana why he had to leave her again, but that Aunt Vasiliki would take her to their city, where she would be safe. Kilian watched this unfold, even as Diana began crying.

Then Kilian bent on a knee to face her, his eyes wide and bright into her teary-eyed face. "Little wolf." He told her.

"Do you know why you are called little wolf?"

Diana rubbed her face. "No. Why?"

Kilian took her hands in his own palm, and smiled into her face. "It is because you are courageous. Look how far you have come, even with the beasts, and you survive. You have a strong heart, like your father."

"Okay." She cried.

"So, with that strong heart, you will go to the city of your father, and our people, your people, will protect you. And other little wolves are there, who will become your friends."

"There are?"

Kilian smiled into her face. "Yes, little wolf. I promise. I never break a promise, and neither does your father. So right now, he must go with Axius to help Rome, and you will come with me and your aunt."

Axius sighed, turning to face Diana. He patted her head and bent down and kissed her atop it. "It will be well, Diana. You will see." He pulled her in and hugged her. "I love you."

Diana smiled at Axius through the tears even as Nestor leaned in again and hugged her tight, his face twisted in pain. "I love you. Kilian and your aunt will get you home safe, and then Axius and I will come later."

As Nestor walked Diana to the horses, Axius stepped in front of Vasiliki, pulling at her arm before she climbed up.

"Titus will not abandon this. I will get his strategy upon the beasts, and not you." He grabbed her hand, and she stared at him.

"When that time comes, Vasiliki..."

She shook her head.

"The archers will be at the back. They will flank you. The infantry will be heavy..."

"Axius." She closed her eyes, and gripped his hand hard. "Your battle tactics will not work with us. You will see the hard way. We will see how disciplined your army is when the beasts show up."

Axius huffed. "You think we cannot survive this?"

"If you survive this, the only end is taking this curse to save Rome."

Axius leaned away from her, and breathed out his nose. "That cannot be the only way."

Vasiliki sighed. "Your stubbornness is the source of your strength. I admire it. You always find a way."

He leaned away from her. "You admire me, or is it because you saw me naked?"

She turned away from him and climbed to get on the saddle, a smile hitting her face so Axius could not see her. "Ask me again when you have lived."

She gripped the reins, and Axius plastered his hand atop hers, their fingers intertwined. "I will ask more of you when that time comes, Vasiliki." He smiled, but inside he was shaking.

She did not smile back at him, but her face lit up at his eyes. "When the beasts come, they will plunge into a bloodthirsty madness, and will be very powerful. They will rip your army apart, Axius. Lupescu will guard over you, but until we come, even he may die…"

Axius clenched his jaws, his eyes narrowed. "If we do not live, you will come with the Dacian wolves and kill them all."

Vasiliki closed her eyes. "So be it."

He stood there with Nestor and watched her leave with Diana in her lap and Kilian leading the way. They had a short time to return to the city and ready their army. They would be headed across the Pannonia plain into Dacia before Titus marched in. It would be too close. By the time Vasiliki assembled her army, Titus would be on the battlefield, with the beasts coming behind them. It may be too late.

Nestor watched them leave as Diana peered around Vasiliki to stare at him. Nestor waved at her, smiling. "Diana is so much like my sister."

Axius huffed. "She is like you."

They stood there readying their horses but Axius paused, gazing at the back of Vasiliki. Her long, black hair whipped behind her as she, Kilian, and Diana raced over the plain.

"You love her," Nestor spoke up, his eyes going from his saddle to Axius all of the sudden.

Axius swallowed but could not speak.

"You better live because if I have to deal with Vasiliki's broken heart, I swear I will pull you back down here and beat the shit out of you first." Nestor sneered at him.

Axius looked at Nestor and pulled his horse to head down the plateau in the opposite direction. Then he turned to face him. "You are of more value than me, brother. You have a wife and children. You are the one who must live."

Nestor followed behind Axius, but a settling fear began to cripple him. He promised Manius he would keep Axius alive. There was only one way the army would survive the beasts at the river, and remaining human was not one of them. Axius refused to listen. Nestor feared something may burst inside him before he could save his human brother, and if they did survive this, he had to make a choice.

When they reached the lower plain of the plateau, they raced side by side to get to Titus's army. Titus would be filling the valley into Dacia from Pannonia, confronting her city. Their engagement would be tactical and an embrace of a massive formation of order as warriors. The central line of heavy infantry would be heavy and outmaneuver the beasts.

Axius believed this with all his heart. He just had to get to Titus first before Fenrir's hoard did. He had to explain to him and the army that beasts were coming to head them off in the valley to kill them all while using them as leverage to kill the Dacian wolves. They had little time to do it. This may not end well for Rome after all. Either way, he and Nestor had to fight the beasts with the army.

38

The Romans Face the Beasts

Titus sat atop his horse, watching from the top of the hill with his Tribunis Laticlavius. His senior officers filled the ranks with him in the lead as if the tree line had bled out over the army, and the only one not there with him was Axius. The Romans marched in waves of four thousand. Before the army, marched the hoplites with their spears and shields. The long shields filled the valley in red like the battle had already started.

The left, center, and right wings filled the plain, and the men looked like dots with red spiky heads. Behind the hoplites came the legionaries, their metal torso scale armor singing under the dawn bursting over the horizon. A finely tuned instrument, their Galea on their heads swimming in crimsons as the feathers wisped in the morning breeze.

Behind the army, legionaries pulled onagers, the catapults forming their line under Titus's ever-watchful eyes. He clenched his fists over his saddle, envisioning the slings helping to bring this battle to a quick end. The onagers would sting and pile drive into the Dacians. Ballistas followed the onagers, their frames pulled behind the legionaries.

The Ballistas would make short work of an invading army with the thrust torque of stones shot at the enemy. The army of twenty thousand marched in several columns, with scouts on horseback veering around them. The Tribune officers flowed with their men, flanking them.

The heavy infantry anchored the defensive center of their battle line march. Titus turned his horse to follow the army, his senior officers melting the line with him. Before him, for miles, filled the endless expanse of mighty Romans. Behind him lay the quiet river town and Fenrir biting his tongue watching them.

Fenrir stood with his generals lingering behind at the river. They had stayed out of the way as the Roman army prepared to march, and their intimidating strategies did not cause him grief. He laughed at their backs as he watched them march toward Dacia. He craned his neck as the ground vibrated under him from the horde coming, following the Romans. They would be miles behind them.

A vast cavern where Fenrir kept his horde was west of the river town. It was where they bred, lived, and breathed. He clenched his scruffy face, his eyes lighting up like a fire had lit him from the inside out. He would wait a while longer so they could flank the Romans from all sides. He needed them to reach Dacia and closer to Vasiliki first.

He still needed Vasiliki. She had done well over the years alluding his grasp, and just when he had her, that fool of a Roman saved her. He would kill that Roman and take the queen, whether she wanted him. If she did not submit this time, he would kill her.

"At dawn, we kill them all. Make a bloody path through the Romans to take the wolves." Fenrir seethed, his pupils dilated to an amber fire, his face stiff and twisted. "The Dacian wolves cannot save them all."

His eyes glowed, filling with black. "Everything will fall."

He turned to gaze back at them, their eyes filling in with blackness, their fangs protruding from their gums. "Vasiliki is mine and mine alone."

The West cavern erupted as the beasts plunged from the caves like a river dam had broken loose under the earth. But it was pitch black and snarling retributions that echoed for miles.

Axius and Nestor raced as they had never raced before, even when in previous battles. Even when Nestor raced in the games. They pressed their faces into the wind and leaned into their horses, the thumping of the horses' hooves pulling them closer and closer to Titus. As the day pressed on til nightfall, Axius had a pressing crush weigh on him, but he pushed harder anyway to get to the army. Time was running out.

Vasiliki plunged into the village with Kilian, their Dacian steeds spent of energy, their minds racing on what was coming. Lupa met them at the road with his warriors, his face broad and bright, and he pointed to the river miles out where the caverns rose.

"The Romans come!" He belted out, seething, but then his eyes fell upon Diana in Vasiliki's lap, and it dawned on him.

"You have the little wolf. Well done! Axius and Lupescu?" He questioned. "Where are they?" He fretted.

Vasiliki closed her eyes and swallowed. "They are headed to Titus." She moaned. "Fen's horde is coming!"

Lupa clenched his jaws at her, gripping a firm hand over the hilt of his Falx. "My queen, what is your command." The warriors stood silent, waiting, and then Vezina popped out to watch.

Vasiliki nodded to Kilian, and he rushed away from them to get to the heart of the kingdom. She turned to face Lupa and her people, her chest heaving. "Prepare the army! We battle to save the Romans. We have little time!"

Lupa's mouth dropped open, but then he paused as his face froze into a scowl, his long red beard blowing in the breeze. He belted out a moan of anger and then popped his fist into the air. "To war!"

The warriors hollered with him and rushed to get to the city, their armor, and their horses. Lupa paused as he turned to go, his face craned into a malicious smile at her. "It is about time!"

Vasiliki sat atop the horse, watching her people race around the village, her arms tight around Diana. She bent down, kissed her head again, and sighed as Diana gazed at her. "My brave niece, it is time I show you who you are."

Diana smiled at her, her face wide with excitement.

Cavernous ravines plunged up around the plains miles away as Titus pushed the army onto it before Dacia, ready for battle. The mountainous caverns rose around them from all sides, their shadows lingering, the Danube flowing like silk ribbons as dawn broke slowly. Titus craned his ear to hear shouts, and then a horn blew of an arrival. He bent his neck to the commotion that turned into echoes saying "Axius" over and over.

"Axius comes, my lord!" Titus heard, and he clenched his teeth watching Axius and Nestor burst through the reserves at the rear of the army. Axius's face was clenched and sweaty, his red cloak bending behind him like it was on fire. He was wearing his Galea, and his eyes lit up on fire under narrowed brows. Nestor was wearing black Dacian scale armor, and Titus froze at the sight of him.

His horse abruptly stopped at Titus's face as Nestor joined him. Titus scowled. "You disobeyed my order!"

Axius took a deep breath. "Damn, it is good to see you!"

Titus smiled briefly at him, his face lighting up, and then rolled his eyes.

"You may flog me if you survive, commander. You may expel me from the army. I will gladly take that!" Axius belted out.

Titus gritted his teeth at Axius, his eyes craning to Nestor. "Nestor, I know Axius put you up to this."

Nestor huffed at him, his naked arms flexing his tattoos around his biceps, his wavy black hair disheveled atop his head. "Commander, the beasts of my land are coming for us." He warned. "They come now! They are but a few miles away."

"What! We go to battle against the queen of Dacia, not beasts."

Nestor huffed. "You go to war with the beasts of my land. The queen wants to help Rome."

"The queen plots against Rome."

"No! That is a lie by this Fen you have just left." Axius warned him.

Titus grimaced at them, eying his senior leaders, their faces as hard as his. "Rome has given proclamation she must die!"

Nestor growled at him. "She will not die, Titus!"

Titus sneered at him. "You do not get to tell me what she is when Rome has deemed she must die! There are consequences for disobeying."

Nestor shook his head. "The beasts are in Rome, Titus! They seek to control." He pushed his long arm out behind them, pointing to the caverns filling with morning fog. "They are coming."

Titus turned with his leaders to look but saw nothing as it was still miles away. Axius roamed his head around, looking for Honus. "Honus, where is he?" He begged, raising on his horse.

Titus scoffed at him. "With the infantry, do not change the subject, Axius. You disobeyed my direct order to stay in Rome and wait for me."

Titus sighed, closed his eyes, and clenched his jaws. "Now you are forced to go to battle with the army. We are at Vasiliki's doorstep."

Axius sneered at him. "Damnit, Titus!" His head craned to find his godson as a deep-seated urge to protect Honus filled him with dread. "You war against the Dacians who wish us no ill will! Our war is with this Fenrir, whom you have kept in Rome's clutches these years, and he betrays us."

"Do not speak to me, Axius!" Titus raged. "It is because of your stubborn tactics that Honus crept in, and Kilian escaped."

Behind them for miles, rageful roars filled the air between the cavern passes on either side of the plain. The rear archers and infantry turned their heads to face it, but the roars belted at them from both sides miles out. Titus heard the roars echo, clutching the reigns tighter, and the twenty thousand soldiers craned their heads toward them.

"What." His eyes lighted upon the plain.

Axius swallowed, his forearms flexing. "Fenrir has betrayed Rome, and the beasts seek to take our Senate and rule. You must believe me! I am not mad. I am trying to save us. My father is fighting this now in Rome, and my family is in danger. Everything we love and know is in danger, Titus!"

Titus let out a moan of anger.

Nestor bit his tongue and closed his eyes, fighting the urge to change into Lupescu before the Romans. Titus craned his neck to listen, his horse spooked. Axius yanked his long sword and held his breath as the shadows grew through the cavern passes surrounding the army, their shrieking howls filling the plain.

"It is too late!" Axius pressed into Titus. He pushed his arm out, his knuckles white on the hilt of his Gladius, and pointed to the passes. "You see what comes to hunt us!"

Titus pulled his long sword, his eyes wide, and his face twisted as if a pain had shot up his backbone. Writhing blackness filled the caverns, flanking them on each side as roars catapulted high around the army. The beasts belted off the cavern walls, snarling as they hit the open plain together. The beasts formed a line to flank the army a mere two miles away from their lines on each side.

Titus's face went as white as his eyes, but he gripped his sword and scowled at them. "Kill the beasts!" He ordered.

"Do I have your blessing to help command?!" Axius pleaded.

Titus bit his tongue. "You may Axius. This does not change that you disobeyed me!"

Axius nodded his head, his face lit up like fire.

They melted with Nestor into the right wing, the army peering at them from behind their shields. The Dacian horse was unafraid of the beasts, but the Roman horses neighed and bucked against the rear line archers' miles back.

Axius pressed into the men and raced to the rear of the right wing with Titus, where the Optio stood, who glared at him as if he were mad. If the army could survive, the Optio kept them in obedience, with the horn feeding them direction. The man clutched his staff and wax tablet in silence, his wide eyes peering at Axius, who confronted him.

"The beasts are coming!"

The Optio pursed his lips, and then he heard the roars belting the skies around them. He clenched his jaws at Axius's face.

Titus commanded him. "They flank the army. Form the Cannae! Invite them in, and we must cut off their heads."

The Optio pulled the Cornu to his lips and blew the command for the army. The sound filled the ranks as it vibrated and buzzed against his lips. The middle and left wings followed, and the plain moved as if it had become one. As Axius and Nestor raced with Titus to the rear, the left wing and centers pulled back and formed a tactical reserve behind a weak center, but Axius knew it was nowhere near weak. It was an illusion to get the beasts into the heart of the army so the sides could kill them with spears and their swords.

The Cornu blew at each left and middle line, with the Optios controlling the army in Titus's order. The army would use its skill of intense fighting, viciously attacking the beasts in bursts. Axius craned up on the horse to see Honus but did not find him. His heart beat erratically in his chest.

"Where are you, Honus?!" He cried inside.

It was too late because the beasts had come, and it was too late for Axius or Nestor to do anything more than help the army survive them until Vasiliki's army showed up. The beasts lunged onto the plain before the Romans, flanking them on either side. Their blackness was as thick as the night as their roars filled the breadth of the armies' defenses.

Titus emerged with vigor to the rear of the lines behind the reserves, eying the Ballistas lined up in precision. Their wood frames sunk firmly into the ground to hold them steady and they stretched for miles on the plain. The soldiers manning them mended together as if they were one. Axius and Nestor sat horseback beside Titus, watching and waiting as chills darted up their spine.

"Take them out!" The soldiers pressed the spears into the slider, standing behind them at the winches where they ratcheted the bowstring back to the firing positions.

"Fire!" Titus commanded, and the air became black as the darting missiles blinded the rising sun.

The pointy shafts darted high in the air and fell, impaling a line of the beasts flanking them. The beasts flailed back, roaring screams of pain. But then a rage filled their eyes as their snouts seethed, and they pulled the shafts out of their bodies and got back up. And they kept coming.

"They will not die that way! It is hand-to-hand combat. That is the only way!" Nestor yelled, his face contorting and fangs pressing through his gums as he raged in pain at Axius. "These are all purebloods, Axius!"

Axius swallowed, his face contorting into a river of pain.

Fenrir stood in his beast form from the plateau overlooking the plain behind the army. His eyes glowed like obsidian, his breath heavy in the morning air. His generals appeared behind him through the woods, snarling. "They are in position, my king."

Fenrir laughed. "Kill them all."

One of these generals pulled up a horn and blew into it, shattering the morning air with cries of brutality. The Romans held their breath, peered through their Galeas, and gripped their elongated Scutums in one arm and their spears pressed out in the other. They melted together in the thousands as the beasts pummeled into them.

The beasts lunged, catapulting atop them and going airborne on their shields. They pried their dagger claws at the edges while the soldiers gritted their teeth to stab at them and hold their weight up. Axius watched in horror as the long red shields flew behind the beasts like a mountain of pain had bled out.

They peeled the shields away from the Romans, pillaging their hearts out of their chests. The beasts ripped the Romans limbs from their bodies. The front line became blood and chunky body parts where humans used to be. Axius yelled at the carnage beside Titus, who narrowed his brows in seething anger. They gazed at the reserves standing before him, waiting while the left and right wings continued getting assaulted, and not one beast had fallen yet.

The line of men behind the first line who were killed thrust their spears out to gore the beasts, but it did not kill them. The beasts dug deeper into the lines. They split the four thousand Roman soldiers in each left and right wings into a rage-filled blood bath, prying their shields away from them as if they were parchments.

Titus gripped his sword, watching the chaos as the beasts ripped into the formations and more shields were flung away from his men, line by line. His face went red. The ballistae continued their relentless firing, but Axius knew these creatures must be beheaded.

"Stay with Titus." Axius turned his horse to go, even as Nestor gawked at him.

Nestor sneered. "Axius, no!"

Axius would not relent. "As they get closer to you, use the archers to slow them down so we can behead them. I am going in!" Axius lunged his horse through the reserve line and straight to the right wing across the plateau. He did not give Titus or Nestor a chance to stop him. Axius could not sit idle any longer watching his men die.

Nestor held his breath, watching Axius leave them, his eyes wide with terror. "Do not die." He worried. "Please, do not die, brother!" He pleaded. "Damnit!" Nestor raged.

The Dacian stallion Axius rode pressed through the back of the line as the beasts rose over the shields. They landed atop the men and pried them apart with their claws. The right-wing split apart, and soldiers screamed at one another in unison, but it only gave the beasts an edge to kill them quicker. The roars filled the hearts of the men and echoed like thunder over the plain as if some evil force had awakened. The evil force raged from a darkness like a veil had been thrust over the plain.

Axius lunged down and grabbed a spear sticking up. He held his breath and grimaced, lunging it into the neck of a beast coming over the line at his men directly at him. Nestor was right. These were bigger. The spear lodged in its throat, pushing it back. It gave Axius a moment to whip up to its snout on horseback and swipe its head off with his long sword. The headless body fell atop the men as they grasped their shields, and they took a deep breath.

"Cut their heads off!" Axius commanded them, pulling the horse back through the fray of madness as the men teamed up two by two to fight. One disables a beast, one to cut its head off.

Axius suddenly knew the value of the Dacian horses. It was fearless in the face of the beasts and gave Axius an edge. But the beasts kept coming, and as the plain filled with them, it became clear they outnumbered the Roman army. The reserves at the back filled the plain behind Axius, their spears darting past him in midair. The Romans still alive lunged in to swipe their heads off as the spears pushed the beasts back for a moment, stalling for time.

Even as the reserves became engaged by force, the archers on horseback began their assault. The beasts breached the rear of the left and right wings, punched through the center, and hit the reserves toward Titus. Axius heard Titus's strong voice commanding the Optios, "Cuneum formate!"

As the horns blew the command, the Romans, not separated by death or beast, pulled together in triangular shapes with the soldier in point headed into the fray of beasts rushing them. Instead of their wide formation diving into the beasts, the soldiers at the back of the triangle split the air open with their spears. As the spears gored the beasts, the soldiers in the middle would rush and cut off their heads, their speed and agility put to the test.

Above Axius, the air became consumed with arrows and spears darting over the army. The beasts continued their assault to wipe them out and rid the Romans of their Scutums. Axius recognized a tall, blonde-headed soldier fighting with a group of Romans. As he turned the horse to get to Honus, he was knocked off. A beast roared into him at his shoulder, and the breath of his lungs came out of him as he hit the ground hard at its feet.

His shoulder pulsed in pain down his arm and was ripped open. His Galea popped off his head. He lay on his back, taking deep breaths to compose himself. The Dacian horse neighed and lunged away from him and the beast.

Nestor did not want to turn to his wolf form before Titus, but they gave him no choice. He planned to stay near his Commander to save his life, just as Axius commanded. The beasts breached the back of the reserve line where Titus sat on horseback. Titus readied his sword, taking a deep breath. Five beasts breached the rear of the army and catapulted over soldiers to get to Titus. Nestor lunged off the horse and ripped into them midair as he transformed.

Titus was thrown off his horse as Nestor transformed beside him. His horse flailed away in terror, leaving Titus on the hill surrounded by the archers and catapults, slinging anything they had into the fray. He leaned up, gazing at the horrific truth of what he had just seen.

Nestor tore into them before Titus, ripping into them with his claws and pulling them apart as if they were nothing. He lunged into their necks with his claws, ripped their throats out, then pulled their heads off. He tossed the heads back into the battle, where they hit other beasts coming at him. They paused, their ears flat on their skulls, their eyes wide as he roared at their faces.

Lupescu had come.

As he raged and roared in the air, his echo carried to Fenrir, who growled, recognizing it. Fenrir split the trees down the hill to enter the battle, his deep hatred following him there as his generals plunged behind him.

Axius tried to get up but was injured. As his men fought for their lives around him, the beast circled him, snarling. Axius had dropped his long sword, and his head spun. Above him, arrows continued filling the skies like night had fallen. The beast bent on all fours, snarling into Axius's face. It dug its claws into the ground to lunge and rip him apart.

Just as the beast lunged at his face, a spear shot through its chest and another one through its stomach. Honus catapulted himself atop it, plunging his blade across its neck, and severing its head. As the head fell, Axius was jerked up by strong grips on his forearms by the men Honus fought with. Two female Dacian wolves seemed to appear out of nowhere to help protect these men.

"Axius! Get up!" Honus called at him as his soldiers lifted him to save his life.

Honus pointed to the hill where Titus was. "Ganna, Bohdana! Make a way for us through." Honus commanded them, and these wolves pressed into the madness.

They melted through the fray and pulled Axius to the back of the line again as the Romans came back together to form walls of soldiers holding out spears. When one beast would lunge into them, it would get gored, and another soldier would drop in, lowering his to face them. It made a wall behind them even as bodies splayed and ripped apart on the plain, and the beasts kept killing them.

"To Titus!" Honus screamed, his face bloodied, his long sword jutted out before him.

As they drug Axius through the madness, Honus led the way running beside these wolves. As they neared the hill, Axius was not prepared for Lupescu killing them, and Titus lunging a spear into Lupescu's shoulder.

Axius screamed. "Noooo!" Even as Lupescu fell to his knees, his eyes upon Titus.

Honus stood before his father, pressed into him. "He is one of us, father! This is Nestor!"

Titus grimaced. "No! He is a beast and must die." He pushed his son off him.

Axius stepped in the way, his arm bleeding down to his fingers. "You will not harm him! He is my brother." Axius pulled his gladius with his uninjured hand.

Titus scowled at the men who stood between him and Lupescu, even as Lupescu raised and pulled the spear out, growling at him. He folded his eyes upon Titus and huffed. "It is me Titus, it is me, Nestor."

"This is witchcraft!" Titus sneered, pulling away from Honus.

"It is not witchcraft. I am a Dacian wolf Titus." Lupescu whispered at him. "I am the rightful king of the Oltenia wolves."

Titus lowered his sword and gazed at Axius and then his son. "That explains things! You knew. You knew this whole time."

Honus sighed. "I knew, father."

Titus pointed the sword at Axius and smiled at him. "And you. You stubborn little boy I trained..."

Axius smiled back at him, and for a moment, although brief, laughter was felt between them.

Axius gripped the gladius at Titus and held his breath just as a shrieking horn bellowed in the distance. Ganna and Bohdana were beating off beasts coming from inside the lines they had breached straight at them.

Vasiliki had arrived.

39

The Dacian Wolves Retribution

The howling shriek filled the plain with uncertainty and rose over the beasts as if a heavy fog had landed in their souls. The beasts stopped killing to acknowledge the Dacian wolves had come. The mist rose over the plain on the outskirts. The gaping mouths of the Draco horns filled the breadth of it as their heads rose above the cloud.

The golden draco heads split the fog as the wind blew through the horns, sounding like the earth had just opened something ancient. The heads stopped bobbing up and down the plain and rested silently. From within the fog, Vasiliki burst out from the center. She gripped her falx sword out from her side as if she had slit the fog wide open with it. Her wolf pelt hung on her scaled body armor down to her feet, and her eyes lit up like the amber was on fire within her. She grimaced at the devastation as her fangs burst out.

She growled, "Save the Romans!" She commanded.

The Dacian wolves burst through the fog by the thousands on their paws the whole length of the plain. Lupa led them, their clawed paws gripping scythe swords and falxes and a hum coming from their throats of endless growls seeking retribution. Their deep-throated growls rolled like thunder had come over the plain.

The wolves riddled the landscape as their hairy, bulky bodies were kissed in armor of golden scales. They hammered into the beasts from behind, blasting into the line of the Romans, still holding their own, miraculously. The Romans were relieved as the Dacian's vengeance lunged into them, cutting the beasts down with their massive weapons. The Romans the wolves saved gawked, their faces pale with tension.

Lupa lunged forward until the beasts were no longer upon them, shouting, "Get up, Romans, you will survive this day!"

Lupa and his wolves pressed atop the beasts as they attacked the Romans, pulling them off the humans and tossing them away from them against one another. Lupa gripped his scythe in his paw and growled as he cut into them. He slashed them in half with his blade and sprayed blood across his fur and the Romans who lived.

He lunged atop the beasts and knocked them down on their backs under his massive paws. With his fist, he ripped their heads from their necks and stood atop the headless bodies. He held them up as trophies and shrieked his roar high in the air on the battlefield.

High-pitched roars echoed on the plain, and Lupa turned his eyes past the Romans still holding their own with the beasts. He growled, seething inside. A wave of blackness came for them at the center of the plain. The beasts writhed toward them like the pits of a deep chasm from the underworld had been unleashed. He gripped his scythe sword and bent atop the dead bodies, howling to his wolves.

All around him, as the Dacian wolves were fighting and cutting the beats down with their blades, their ears perked at Lupa's call. Fenrir's hoard was not done with them yet. They meant to annihilate them all here. Lupa turned to head to the front of the lines again even as the Romans stood together, their Scutum's lifted as a wall before the beasts and their spears straight out to impale them.

The Romans surviving stood neck and neck behind their Scutums and filled the plain with red and uncertainty. The beasts catapulted toward them on the plain, and the dust filled the horizon behind them as the severity of their army became apparent. Fenrir flanked them, sending in the final kill order. Lupa growled and lined up with his wolves behind the Romans, even as the rear of them turned and gasped in horror at these giant wolves with body armor and swords as long as their human bodies.

Lupa gazed down upon them, his eyes bright, and huffed. "Stay strong, soldiers."

As he waited with his wolves, they ducked down. They pressed their paws to the ground and let the vibrations of the beasts call them for just the right moment. They closed their eyes and pressed their snouts to the earth, their ears vibrating from the rush of the beasts coming at them all to wipe them out.

Lupa's snout wrinkled to his closed eyes, and a snarl emerged deep inside him that echoed as a roar. His eyes flew open. All along the line, side by side with him, his wolves burst up behind the Romans.

Lupa and his wolves burst up over the Roman wall of Scutum's as wide as the open plain and pummeled atop the beasts raging in at them. They swung their scythe and falx blades in front of them, slicing beasts in half or beheading them. They pressed into the fold of them and knocked them away from the Roman lines.

The Romans stood there watching the horror unfold, the wolves getting slayed alive and fighting for them. They watched the wolves fall, then get back up, snarling into the face of these monstrous beasts coming at them in droves. The Romans saw an open line where there no beasts on the plain were coming at them as the wolves made a bloody path through them to the end of the valley. They raised their Scutums and pressed in to help the wolves finish them off.

Vasiliki burst around the Romans in her wolf form, with Kilian following her to find Lupescu and Axius, if they were still alive. The plain seemed to go on forever as she lunged into the madness. She pulled beasts off the Romans toward the back of the line and split them wide open with her blade. As the Romans witnessed these new powerful wolves saving them, they began to fight alongside them to kill the beasts. Their shouts of rage continued to fill the horizon around them between the human cries of anguish as they died.

Fenrir had enough. He lunged his head high in the air and let out a shrieking howl. He plunged down the hill into the madness with his generals between his beasts. He killed Romans as he rushed through to the back of the line or what was left of it. His eyes were on Vasiliki, but they had to get the famed Kilian out of the way first.

He moaned, looking for her and pressing harder to gallop through the battle when he recognized her white form. "Vasiliki, I come for you!" He roared.

As they headed off through the blood bath, Fenrir's five generals lunged over the beasts fighting the Romans, who seemed to be surviving. They lunged against Kilian, pushing him off the path of following Vasiliki. Kilian rolled snout over paws away from her, and she paused to see Fenrir chasing after her.

Kilian roared at them, pressing into the dirt to gain traction. "Go!" He roared.

Vasiliki roared as Fenrir chased her, his paw clipping her back legs. She rolled snout over paw and landed atop her back, and Fenrir lunged atop her. She pressed her falx blade into his shoulder, and he belted out a roar as blood spurt across her chest. He lunged his snout down and tore into her left shoulder, ripping it open. Just as she thought he would kill her, Fenrir was catapulted off her with spears. The Romans were helping her.

Vasiliki pushed away from Fenrir and ran on her two paws instead of four, even as he pulled the spears out and eyed her. He pulled the spears out of his shoulders and ripped through the Romans who had helped her, lunging across the bodies to head her off. She galloped to the rear of the line and belted out a roar to Lupescu as she smelled him nearby. The closer she got to the back, her heart fainted to see Axius injured, although he was still alive.

Lupescu jerked to see her rushing at them and noticed two of Fenrir's generals pressing behind her. Lupescu lunged over his sister and hit them head-on in midair. Honus backed away from Axius to Titus and readied their swords as two massive paws slammed into them. The hit knocked them away from Titus, and they went airborne. Ganna and Bohdana could do nothing as they continued to press against the beasts attacking them from all sides.

Axius flew head over foot over Vasiliki. She froze to stop galloping, her paws indenting the ground. Honus flew backward and hit a catapult. The wooden frame stopped him, and he fell flat on his face. As Vasiliki lunged back to catch Axius, Honus pushed himself up to see Titus lifted by the top of his armor in midair by Fenrir.

Titus squirmed in Fenrir's grip as he met his face, their eyes filled with hate upon one another. "I have been waiting years to do this, Titus, so you know the one killing you is Fenrir," Fenrir growled.

Titus grimaced in his face. "You will still die, beast!" Titus raised his gladius to Fenrir's snout and knicked it open, and Fenrir growled.

Vasikili caught Axius in midair the best she could since her arm was torn up. Lupescu raged behind them against the generals, injuring both with his saber claws. Honus hollered at them, screaming for

Axius even as he landed atop Vasiliki. As Axius bent up off her to stand again, his eyes met Fenrir's.

"Noooo! No. No!" Axius raged at him, tears filling his eyes even as he pushed himself off Vasiliki to get to him.

Fenrir plunged his claws through his chest and ripped Titus's heart out. Titus lurched and convulsed, even as Fenrir dropped the heart at his feet and let his body fall.

Honus pressed up, tears filling his eyes. "Nooooo!" He screamed, but it was too late. "Augh!"

Fenrir bolted away from them all as they lunged to get to him. His hairy body was bleeding out, and his remaining generals followed him, sustaining injuries themselves.

Axius melted up the incline at Titus's body, meeting Honus there as he lifted his father in his arms and cried into his face. A weakness he could not describe hit his knees, and Axius fell. He fell, and he could go no further.

"Father. Father!" Honus cried, his bloody hands shaking. "Nooo! Noo! Nooo, please, no." His aching moans filled the hill with his doom.

Axius dropped his gladius and leaned forward, his body convulsing in sobs. He belted out a moaning sob into the air, gripping his heart at his chest as if his own had been ripped out. His face twisted in hot pain, the searing fire of this loss burning him from the inside out. It would not go away, ever. A moan came from Axius that was seeped in hot anger.

"Auggghhh Auggh!" He wailed as his face flooded with tears.

Lupescu railed against the generals as they pummeled him, and then Lupa came with the wolves to the back of the line, pulling them off him. Lupa swung his scythe around the neck of one of them while Bohdana lunged into the other. She kicked him in midair before Lupescu and Kilian grabbed him by the throat and ripped it out. Kilian roared against them, pulling their heads off. Now, two of Fenrir's generals were dead.

Lupa stood gripping his bloody blades aside Kilian as a growl that would not dissipate echoed deep from within him. He stood, breathing heavily as he eyed the death of his wolves along with the Romans. He took a deep breath, fell to his knees, and closed his eyes. Kilian stood beside him, gawking at the plain devastation. They were all bloodied up and injured, but their resolve remained steadfast. Kilian grabbed Lupa's shoulder and pressed into it, his eyes bleeding tears, his snout twisted in pain.

As the reckoning hit them what Fenrir had done, Lupescu turned his gaze upon Axius and Honus. When he recognized Titus's body, he dropped to his knees behind them on the hill.

"Not my Titus." His chest heaved up and down, and he clawed the ground in pain. "Not Titus." He bellowed, and a raging moan echoed out of him as his snout twisted in pain.

He stared at Axius, who had a nasty gash on his arm and bled to his fingers. He was wounded and needed mending. Honus cried against his father, his arms slashed open, his legs and body armor splattered with blood. Both he and Axius had head wounds and busted lips. He breathed out and in on his knees, a raging fire rising within him he had not felt in a long time.

Vasiliki stood behind Lupescu, her snout quivering, watching Honus and Axius grieve. She melted her teary gaze upon the world around her and the loss of life. She moaned as she recognized wolves among the dead. She bent her snout to her chest and growled, moaning for their loss.

Titus was dead. So many were dead.

Behind her for miles, the Dacian wolves had decimated any beasts remaining on the battlefield, but the plain was missing three-quarters of the Roman army. The survivors belted out cries upon their knees or raged where they stood, even as the world was littered with the bodies of humans, beast, and wolf.

Axius and Honus cried, their hearts broken in grief. Their souls ripped to shreds as if the world had broken, and there was no healing it. Kilian and Lupa joined beside Vasiliki, their strong wolf forms lingering over Lupescu, Axius, and Honus. Their body armor was littered with blood sprays, and as they stood snarling inside, they continued clutching their swords. Their breathing became deep and shallow. They let the living mourn the dead, even as their injuries throbbed within them.

Out of twenty thousand Romans, only two thousand six hundred remained. Fenrir tried to kill them all.

He almost succeeded.

Axius rode alongside Honus, following the horse carrying Titus's dead body. Honus held his father's Galea in his hand atop the saddle, his blood plastered all over it. Lupescu followed them in silence while Vasiliki and Lupa with Kilian, led them back to the city.

They all stayed wolves just in case they were attacked again, their paws gripping their brutal blades caked in dried blood still.

Behind Axius for miles were the remainder of his army, with the wolves trailing them to keep them safe. A pressure hit his chest as he was now responsible for them. He gazed back at them, weak and bloodied. Some of the men eyed him with great suspicion, but the pain was still too real to acknowledge what had just happened to them. All they knew was that they were alive and being led further into Dacia by their new commander, Axius.

They marched as one but broken. They marched as survivors, the pain from their loss thick enough to cut it with their swords. Every man walking was bloodied. Everyone had injuries and needed stitches or mending. They carried their swords, their body armor pinged or damaged, but they were still alive.

"Fenrir will come back," Honus mumbled, his eyes gazing at Axius. "He always comes back to finish what he started."

Axius met his godson's glare, and tears filled his eyes again. "I know."

Axius took a deep breath, his lungs filling with a raging fire, and added. "So do I."

"I knew you would come." Honus cleared his throat just as the tears fell down his face again. "You always come."

Axius sniffled as his tears fell again, and he gazed at Honus with a grieved face, "I knew you would survive." His voice cracked as his lips quivered. "Proud of you."

Honus glared at Axius's arm, bleeding down to his hands. "They ripped you open. You need stitches. It looks bad."

Axius moaned in pain, but his heart hurt worse. "One thing at a time today." He could not smile through the pain even if he tried.

"One thing at a time," Axius told himself, even as his lips quivered staring at Titus's body, and the world around him seemed to have caved in to utter despair.

On the edge of the plain, past the decimation of the riddled bodies of humans, wolves, and beasts, Fenrir stood with his horde of tens of thousands. They had met him there from his mountain after this battle. They emptied the mountain of them. The wolves decimated his army, and the Romans proved more diligent in surviving than in his previous battle with Commander Artgus.

But that was just the first wave. He had lost thousands of them, too, but the second wave was just beginning. If this second wave failed, he would launch the final assault. His numbers would decimate the wolves and men. As the day fell into night, the beasts walked the plain into Dacia. Fenrir had one chance to take the heart, and time was running out.

He needed this second wave to draw the Dacian wolves to his horde. If this worked, he would be closer to taking the heart from Vasiliki. He grimaced in his wolf form, still bleeding from battle. He lunged into the darkness, leading his army that filled the plain like a plague bleeding out, and hell's lair was beginning.

40

Where the Heart Breathes

The cool night air held no reprieve as the grief felt was adamant through the village. Axius stood alongside Honus and Nestor as Titus's body lay on the block, ready for the pyre. He lay in the block, the stone wall rising around him to form a ledge for the cremation, as his red cloak spilled over the side. Before them lay an open field, where the fire would burn until dawn. Honus took the burning torch and held his breath.

Axius stood back with Nestor as Honus said goodbye, but inside, he had died. Behind them, for miles, the wolves were burying their dead also. The shrieks and howls filled the valley around them. The two thousand six hundred Romans who survived stood behind them in the open field, paying their respects. The wolves ensured the men would have shelter, blankets, water, and food.

Ganna and Bohdana had been busy rushing into them with medicinal supplies to mend the wounded, and other healers had joined to help. They had stopped to stand to the side of the hill to pay their respects for Honus's sake, and they watched him light Titus on fire and step back.

Bohdana took a deep breath and leaned against her mother as a tear fell down her cheek gazing at the broken Honus. A tall, slender blonde replica of his father Titus, Honus clenched his jaws and sniffled as he stepped back to Axius and Nestor. The fire lunged into the heavens before them, filling the field with dancing embers in the wind.

As Titus burned, there was no more room to breathe through the tears. Axius's arm had been stitched and was in a sling, and he was not happy about it. That meant if they went to war again, he would be nearly useless and only have the use of one arm. He bit his tongue and sighed, even as Nestor scowled ahead of them, thinking. Honus stood between them, towering over Axius and Nestor, his shoulders slumped in defeat.

The fires lit their faces as they bowed on one knee, and the army behind followed. Their bloodied and ripped cloaks spilled on their backs as if the earth had opened and was bleeding out. The men held their Galeas against their chests, their faces battered and bruised, their hearts busting inside. Their faces were clenched and brows narrowed, their eyes set in a fiery stare upon their dead Commander.

As Honus, Nestor, and Axius bent upon one knee and faced Titus, something broke inside them. Axius let the tears fall, pressing his forehead into his closed fist. Honus watched his father burn as tears fell down his face, his mouth shivering as his head raised to the sky. Nestor watched the fires, but he did not cry. He clenched his jaws and took deep breaths through his anger to compose himself. His eyes became as dark as obsidian and then twisted into an amber haze kissed by yellows, his lips in a snarl.

Hours later, Axius could not sleep and hiked to the back of the city under moonlight, gazing upon the wall again. His shoulder throbbed in pain, but Ganna's lemon salve took the edge off. The pain would continue to linger for a while, he feared. He had bathed and changed back into his armor, even though his shoulder cuff had been damaged. He had planned on having Vezina repair it for him in the morning.

He held his breath, gazing upon the wolves like brothers dancing on the wall as a familiar scent tickled his nose. Vasiliki approached him, and his heart lit up. Her long, white robes cascaded down her body, and her furs kissed her shoulders. Her black hair was pulled down her back in a long braid. She had been injured on her shoulder, and although it had healed, she was still in pain.

Axius closed his eyes at her presence. "The white flowers. You smell like hope." He turned to her, but she was not smiling.

"I grieve with you, Axius." She whispered. Axius gazed upon her face filled with tears. She gripped her heart and belted out a moan. "We lost so many. So many!" She cried.

Axius's lips quivered. "You saved us. There would be no Romans left alive if not for you. You became my hope this day."

"Your brave soldiers picked up the pieces on that battlefield and fought with us. I am honored, but my heart hurts." Tears fell down her face as she sighed.

Axius came to her, and she melted against him. He wrapped his good arm around her, holding her tight. He bent his scruffy face into her shoulder, breathing the scent of her in. His lips moaned against her neck and she closed her eyes and let him kiss her. He roamed his open lips up her neck to her chin and roared against her lips, and she kissed him back. He rolled back down to her neck and breathed against her shoulder.

She raised her palm to the back of his head, stroking his scruffy hair. She leaned her face into him, even as her tears kissed his dark hair. She closed her eyes and raised them to the moon above them, taking a deep breath as her eyes lit up.

"It is time to show you the heart of my people." She moaned and pulled away from him. As she turned to go, Axius clutched her hand in his own and squeezed it tight. He did not hesitate to follow her.

He followed her through the caverns to the city where Lupa had practiced sparring with his wolves. She led him past the horse stables and over a hill that opened to a round stone fortress sunk beneath it. It was nearly midnight. He followed her over winding stone steps into the fortress, and they came upon an open circular room carved in runes.

The runes danced on the walls as torch lights lit the space, revealing an expansive cavern carved from the earth. Axius froze at the sight of it. The ceiling rose in massive stone pillars. The walls themselves were a work of art. The floor was round with runes carved, except for a rectangular altar in the middle. The altar was wide and smooth, as if it had been meticulously sculpted and worn down. A line of runes was carved in the middle of the altar. A wolf head was carved in it like the tattoos he had seen on Vasiliki and Nestor.

"What is this place?" He gawked, amazed.

Vasiliki whispered at him. "Where purebloods are made."

Axius paused but found himself meandering toward it, his eyes upon the runes he could not understand. "This is the heart of your people, Fenrir seeks?"

"Yes, he killed many today to get to it. He will not stop."

"No, he will not." Axius stopped near the altar, his gaze upon Vasiliki.

Vasiliki lingered at the altar's edge, her boots touching the runes carved into the massive round cavern. "If Fenrir takes this, he can rule the world, not just Rome. His retribution will be swift and brutal, like the battlefield you witnessed."

Axius froze, clenching his jaws. "You did warn me."

"We lost good warriors, Axius. Strong wolves fell. Imagine what he will do with the world."

Axius felt shivers rush up his arms. "Yet some survived, some Romans survived."

"I lost two hundred wolves today. Two hundred out of thousands. You lost a majority."

Axius dropped his head and sighed.

"He is coming back. Your men are weak now." She warned.

"I know what you say, Vasiliki." Axius stepped closer to the alter and froze, his eyes caressing her body for endless moments.

As he stepped closer to her, his breath left him. Sharp stabbing pains darted up his spine as a blade was shoved through him from his back at his heart.

He looked down at his chest to see a shard of a blade with runes carved in it sticking out of him. Blood poured out of him. He jerked his good arm behind his back to pull it out, but his hand was met with a strong fist he could not bend. He gasped in pain as realization severed him from reality, and Nestor propped him up on the altar.

"Forgive me, brother." Nestor cried at his back, plunging the blade deeper through him. His human hand was steady, even as his voice shook.

Axius convulsed in pain, his knees giving out on him.

"I love you." Nestor's voice was a desperate plea.

Nestor cried behind Axius's back, tears filling his face down his bloody Dacian armor. He pushed the blade so deep the hilt rested against Axius's backbone. Nestor grunted as his lips twisted in grief.

"I warned you I would do what is needed to save you," Nestor whispered into Axius's ear, his breath hot on his neck.

Axius belted out a painful yell and convulsed in pain. Blood spilled out his mouth, his eyes wide at Nestor. "No. No." He begged. He breathed through the pain, even as blood choked his lungs and tears fell down his face, riddled in agony.

"We cannot lose you. We will not lose you as we lost Titus and our brothers." Nestor jerked the shard out of him.

Axius heaved a gasping moan as Nestor lifted him and placed his body on the altar, his blood pooling atop the runes.

Axius turned his head to see Vasiliki crying, her face in her palms as he clutched the edge of the altar in a desperate grasp, his body lunging in pain.

"Forgive me." She cried, falling to her knees, sobbing atop the runes.

Nestor leaned atop Axius's face. His eyes were stricken with grief as his tears fell upon his cheek, and he whispered, "Breathe, mighty wolf." His lips quivered into Axius's face as his fangs burst through. "Breatheeeee."

Axius closed his eyes as a blackness came over him. He fell into a deep place where nothing touched him nor could pull him out of it, and all hope was stripped from his soul. Something ancient breathed inside of that desperation, wanting to be freed. It lunged up from the deep, belting out a vicious roar. It ripped through and burned him from the inside. As he blacked out, his eyes dilated to an amber kissed by fire. Within that fire, he breathed an awakening that seared him to the foundation of his backbone, and something that was not human grew within it.

Nestor pulled Vasiliki up by her forearms and hugged her tight. "This is the only way." He cried with her, then took her face in his palms and stared into her eyes.

"Axius will live, sister. He will live!" He encouraged her.

Vasiliki pulled his hands away and turned to stare at Axius's body. Nestor pulled her out of the heart with him. "Come! We have little time before Fenrir attacks again. Axius must rest before the curse takes hold."

Vasiliki lunged out with Nestor to return to the village, her heart bursting and her head spinning from what they had just done.

Two miles from the river village, Kilian sat hunched down in his Dacian armor on a plateau overlooking the river. His naked arms danced in tattoos under his wolf pelt. He gripped his falx sword, his tanned knuckles white against the hilt. His thin, unshaven face clenched into the wind blowing from the open plains. As he sniffed the air, his backbone grew shivers. He stood up, his eyes twisted into a darkness shrouded with amber light.

Miles out came a wave of blackness; the beasts were coming. He belted out a growl, his face twisting in hot anger, his pupils now red. As Fenrir's second wave hoard neared closer to the river, Kilian blew the shrieking horn bellows to warn the city.

Fenrir had come. It was too late. The Romans would fall.

41

Where Grief Finds Them

Honus sat up in the bed with Bohdana as the horns echoed. He turned his head to the door of their home, his heart beating wildly, and catapulted over her butt naked to get to his armor. Bohdana gasped, yanking her dress to slip it over her head, her face still wild from their passionate lovemaking.

"He comes when your men are weak!" She lunged up to help him fasten the straps, his wounds still fresh.

"Stay back this time." He warned her, strapping his boots on.

Bohdana pulled her cloak over her shoulders and snarled at him. "I will not." She marched to the other side of the room and yanked her falx sword off the wall, but Honus followed her, gripping her wrist.

She paused at his strong face, which looked so much like Titus. "I cannot lose you."

Honus plunged into her, grabbed her face in his palms, and kissed her fiercely. "I love you, but I need you to go and help protect the city and the children if we fail. Please stay back this time." His eyes were on fire, and his face clenched into hers.

She could not tell him anything else because he lunged out the door into the darkness with his swords to join the wolves, who filled the street to the river. Her mother, Ganna, popped into the doorway, clutching her cloak, her face wild with worry.

Bohdana pulled her Dacian armor from the table and slid into it. "Help me, mother."

Ganna helped her daughter strap into the black and gold scale armor, her mouth twisted in pain, her heart breaking.

Lupa stood alongside Kilian as a wolf, and Honus joined them, their swords clutched in their desperate grasps. The wolves melted to the river alongside them, the streets and surrounding hillsides filling with them. They were ready to fight for the city's heart. Kilian's eyes glowed, but he had not turned yet.

Lupa turned to Vezina, who had come ready to fight. "Get the Romans to the city! They are too weak to fight."

"We are stronger than you give us credit for!" Honus hollered at him, his face rigid with grief still.

As Honus turned to go with him, he met Ganna and Bohdana in the street.

"I told you to stay back!" Honus yelled at her, his face clenched in pain.

Bohdana gripped her falx and smiled at him, her long black frocks spilling down her back on her armor. "I only stay when you pull me in the bed. Otherwise, I do not listen." She teased him.

Honus sighed at her as they ran down the street to the plain, his face lighted up at her eyes. "Damn, I love you."

They rushed to the fields together, their hearts racing, their fists clenched into their hilts, even as the bellowing horns continued to sound in the distance.

"Save the Romans!" Vezina cried, his moaning howl racing through the city.

Kilian yelled aside Lupa. "He comes to kill us all and take the heart."

Lupa gripped his falxes in both paws, his red and white fur blowing in the breeze lingering at the river. "His tactic was to draw us out to save the Romans and kill as many of us as he could. He bested two hundred of us." He belted out a roar and raised his scythe swords into the air, his thunderous anger echoing over the village to the city behind them.

Fenrir scowled, leading his second wave hoard across the plain to the river. They heard the bellowing horns blow, so he knew Vasiliki knew he was coming. He turned his neck to the blackness slithering behind him for miles and howled. "Kill them all! Take the city!" They lunged toward the river.

Lupa edged closer to the river as the darkness bled around them from the forest, and the stillness of the night carved uncertainty upon the village. Shadows crawled across the river like a black shroud had been pulled over the land, and Fenrir plunged over the waters with his hoard. Kilian lunged into the black, powerful wolf, his dagger claws protruding from his soul. With the line of fully armed wolves, he and Lupa met the beasts at the water's edge and clashed into them.

The silver edges of the wolves' falxes and scythe blades screeched against the claws of the beasts pressed into them. As Lupa and his line lunged into the fray, they left land and pushed them back across the shallow waters. Dacian wolves were drug into the water and ripped apart by the beasts raging, outnumbering them.

As the river sparkled in blood and beast cries, Fenrir dove into the center with his hoard and pushed Lupa and Kilian back to the village, the river littered with Dacian wolves and beasts.

They meant to outnumber them here at their weakest after saving the Romans. Kilian lunged into the madness as the street behind him filled with beasts and wolves fighting. He was pulled into a frenzy with a dozen beasts tearing into him all at once. They meant to kill him there. As Kilian was pushed down on his back and claws and fangs sank into him, he held his breath and raged.

He lunged into them like a snarling demon had taken hold of him. He got a hold of an arm of one of the beasts attacking him and pulled it off, then used it swipe the others, pushing them back. As they stepped back, he twirled atop them and snaked his way around their heads midair, ripping them from head to limb with his eyes on the streets now filling with beasts.

Fenrir pressed his hoard through the village, his beasts overtaking the wolves ten to one. Although the wolves used their blades to kill and beat them off, their numbers were too great. They pressed through to the fields where the Romans waited in the darkness for them beneath the forest canopy.

Honus peered out from the blackness as the snarling beasts filled the fields before them. The Roman tents were still up. Their Scutums leaned against the hill or splayed against the fires. Many of the Gaeta's were still laid out by the bedding, so the beasts thought the Romans would be there. Honus whistled, and the whole forest at the line lit up in flaming arrows, all two thousand six hundred. They surrounded the fields, their faces still bloodied, their strong arms ready to fire.

The beasts not in the field chased around them to get to the city wall. Honus gave the order and the field lit up like darting flames. The arrows found their mark through the heads, and the beasts were thrown back or paused at the surprise. The headshots pressed them back, and Honus leaped out with half his army flanking them.

Honus lunged out, swinging his long sword through a beast's neck, and swiped off its head. The Romans followed suit and throughout the vast expanse of the field, as the beasts were stunned, they swiped off their heads in short bursts. As the bodies fell, Honus prepared for more.

The street howled in retribution. Honus and his men dunked their blades into the fires throughout the field and stood waiting for the beasts to come at them again. The fires would make the blades cut faster and hotter. In the woods, their whistles carried far and wide. The Romans held their breath with their arrows ready as the field lunged to life with the beasts. Honus pulled his flaming sword from the fire and took a deep breath.

The beasts faced them off, and the line grew stronger. Just as the Romans saw how they were outnumbered, Ganna and Bohdana burst up behind them with Kilian and Vezina and began ripping them apart from behind. As the beasts turned to see the commotion, the Romans fired flaming arrows again over their heads into them. And Honus lunged into them with his soldiers, their hot blades seared by fire.

Fenrir reached the city walls with beasts on his heels, pausing at the shadows looming within the caverns. Lupescu and Vasiliki met him there, their blades in their tight grips, their eyes on fire, snarling into the masses coming at them. He stood over his beasts filling the fields and paths behind him, his power evident and sneered at Vasiliki's white wolf form.

"Fool of a she-wolf." He belted at her, raging.

Lupescu bent down on all fours, snarling into his face with his paws gripped on his falxes. "You will not touch my sister."

Fenrir scoffed at him, pacing back and forth before the caverns. He stopped and bent his snout down, his eyes glowing yellow at him. His laugh echoed with a malicious intent. "She is my mate, Lupescu. She belongs to me and me alone. She dies today if she forsakes me this last time."

Lupescu lunged up from the caverns and roared into them, swinging the blades even as the beasts rounded them to the cavern walls.

Diana sat against the stone wall with her knees into her chest. Her long hair spilled over her petite shoulders, her eyes wide. She sat with rows of other children in the tower at the city, the escape route built into the mountain and cavernous tunnels for them to follow in case the worst should happen.

The Dacian children her age and older huddled together, and Diana saw five boys stand together, nine and ten years old, their ears pressed to the doors, listening. They were petite children, but Diana knew they were strong. One of the boys gazed upon her, his dark eyes sparkling.

Diana scooted over when he sat aside her. "I am Zyraxes. I am ten," He whispered to her. He then took her shaking hand in his and smiled at her face.

"We will protect you, daughter of Lupescu." He promised.

Diana swallowed at him, her eyes tearing up. "Where is my papa?"

Zyraxes clenched his face. "He goes to battle again to save us."

Diana sat there with him, holding her hand and leaning against him, as his eyes spilled in amber haze kissed by sunlight. The children squirmed suddenly, their eyes glowing, and their faces turned to the city center. The howling filled the city plain under the mountain. The beasts had breached it.

Zyraxes stood up, and the boys his age led the children out the door across a tunnel into the mountain. He pulled Diana by her hand, gazing back at her while they ran. "Hurry, Diana, hurry." He beckoned to her.

Behind them the beasts bellowed into the tower. All twenty-nine of the children froze at a wall by the tunnel they needed to go through. They waited in the darkness while the beasts hunted them. Torch lights from the tower danced shadows down the hall, and Zyraxes stood before Diana, breathing deeply. He waited, and Diana widened her eyes noticing his were glowing amber.

Zyraxes stood with his five friends in front of the children. They were cornered. The beasts pressed in at them, their eyes glowing in the dark, rising above them like shadows of mourning. Diana widened her eyes at them and screamed.

There were three of them. They loomed in on the children, and Zyraxes growled, clenching his fists, ready to fight. Another shadow rose over them and filled the cavern with its growl, but it was not a beast. It opened its amber eyes and sneered at them from behind, pulling all three of them away from the children with a swipe of its paws.

The children stepped out together, watching as the looming wolf ripped the beasts apart and then pressed down the corridor at them through the darkness again.

He melted in at them, rose to the tunnel ceiling, and his eyes lit up as he belted out. "Diana." His black fur was so dark purple sang in it, but his snout was lit with power and passion.

Diana gasped. "Axius!"

Axius bent in to the children and lifted her in his paws, and then he turned to the boys and nodded at them. "Protect them." He commanded. He pressed his snout against her head and set her back down next to Zyraxes.

The boys nodded at him, their eyes riddled with power, as they watched Axius lunge back down the corridor into the tower and out into the city. Axius lunged into the caverns, his growls filling the breadth of the city halls, the stone cracking beneath his stride.

Lupescu ripped into them, but even dozens on one were too much. Fenrir beasts were taking the city, and it did not matter how many he lost. They were not killing Lupescu. They wanted him to watch. They pulled him into the street before Vasiliki while Fenrir rounded her.

She stood in a circle with the beasts, watching the spectacle. Lupescu roared and raged at them. Although he continued killing them, they had more standing behind ready to pick up the slack. It was just enough to keep him from helping Vasiliki.

"She wolf." Fenrir stood taller than her, his black hair now glowing as the sun began rising upon them.

He flexed his muscles before her, his body an intimidating specimen. He could overpower her if he wanted, and Vasiliki knew this. He was stronger and bigger than her. Fenrir pressed into her with his stance without touching her. Vasiliki snarled, his motives upon her body evident. Her blue eyes seethed back at him.

As Fenrir scowled to speak, he paused and perked his ears up as other roars suddenly blasted into the city from the mountain pass. The echoing roars gained traction and behind them to the river, the beasts flooding in paused their attack. Fenrir seethed because he did not know how many were coming.

"Oltenia comes!" He paced around Vasiliki as she stood with her blades pressed out at him and the beasts surrounding her because he had no time left.

"I will not tell you again, she-wolf," Fenrir growled at her, standing tall. "We have little time!"

Vasiliki took a deep breath. Her white hair was kissed in crimsons as she faced him. "I do not love you."

He laughed at her, his deep howl echoing.

"I need you to breeeeeedd." He sneered, his fangs drenched in blood. "You are destined to be my mate." He growled and held out a bloody paw to her, twice the size of her own.

"Take me, Vasiliki. I will be your mate for life. You will be mine. Together, we can rule the world with our purebloods." He commanded her.

She stared at the sun slowly rising behind him. Her eyes lit up a pristine blue as she took a deep breath. Her gaze fell upon him. Fenrir gazed upon her beauty, his chest heaving up and down, looking at her with expectation. His eyes grazed over her strong wolf form. The hope of his anticipation thick in the air around them.

"My beautiful Vasiliki." Fenrir whispered to her. "My mate."

Lupescu roared in rage to see his sister lower her blade at Fenrir. As Fenrir towered over her, she gazed through the masses upon her brother. Lupescu pulled against them as they held him down, and he howled at her face. "No, Vasiliki!" He pleaded with her. "No!"

She sighed. It was a deep sigh that burst up from the deep vat of her soul. Then she melted into her human form before Fenrir.

"Nooooo, sister!" Lupescu pleaded, even as rage filled him over and over, and he could not get to her.

Vasiliki gazed at Fenrir with her bright eyes and sneered at his snout. She dropped her blade. She clenched her grieved face into the sunlight as her wolf pelt kissed her muscular body. Then she turned to Lupescu one last time and smiled at his face.

Her eyes met Fenrir. "Never." She whispered at his snout.

Fenrir raged into her, pressing atop her on the grass. He pressed her human body down with his paws and held her arms over her head.

"She wolf." He breathed into her face, his snout clenched and snarling.

She met his eyes as a tear fell down her cheek. "Never."

Vasiliki held her breath and closed her eyes. Fenrir lunged into her throat and ripped it out. Her body jerked up into his mouth, and her blood poured on the grass around her as she bled out. He attacked her so fast she did not moan or convulse. She lay there with her arms splayed out either side of her, her eyes closed, and her blood pooling around her.

Lupescu screamed a moaning howl of pain. He widened his eyes and burst up even as the beasts continued to hold him down. He cried through his rage at them, his body bleeding and ripped open. Fenrir turned to Lupescu next, his snout dripping in blood.

"It is time for the Oltenian heir to die."

As he stood from Vasiliki's body, Axius burst out from the caverns upon them. He matched Lupescu's speed and power and growled into Fenrir's face. He plunged his saber claws into his shoulder, knocking Fenrir in the air over Lupescu. Fenrir landed into the crowd of his beasts, even as Axius ripped into his shoulder midair. The beasts lurched away from them, and Axius flayed Fenrir open from his neck to his wrist.

Lupescu rose above them and plunged through, ripping, and clawing their chests to get to Fenrir. His eyes burned red, even as the

Oltenia wolves lunged into the street behind him and rose over the beasts to back him up. The Oltenia wolves towered over the beasts, and their roars vibrated through the city street. They flayed into them with their falxes, their claws shredding them to pieces even as Lupescu and Axius raged.

Axius pushed himself off Fenrir's bloodied shoulder and landed on the grass with a thud, his paws sinking into the dirt. He flexed his long arms and spread his saber claws, his snout snarling at Fenrir.

"I will gut you alive!" Axius roared at him.

Fenrir scowled. "Roman fool!" He recognized Axius. "You are all dying."

Axius raised and towered over Fenrir to lunge into him just as Lupescu belted over him in midair. Lupescu pressed into Fenrir's neck to pull his head off. Fenrir raged at him just as five beasts catapulted into Lupescu and knocked him off Fenrir. Axius was pulled back into the fray of fighting with the beasts as they overcame him. They pulled him down onto the street by his arms.

The street exploded in more chaos as Lupa and Kilian pile drove through the remnant of them, pulling them off Lupescu and Axius. The beasts fell to their deaths. The gray and white Oltenia wolves lunged into the street fighting, putting themselves between Lupescu and the beasts and cutting them down with their massive Falx blades. The village roared in retribution, the Dacian wolves' howls and shrieks of rage bellowing into the rising dawn.

During the chaos, Fenrir disappeared, fleeing over the hillside away from the Oltenian wolves that had finally arrived. His surviving generals flanked him as his survivors galloped back over the river waters into the forest.

Fenrir laughed. "Prepare the third wave." He growled. "This time, they all die." His beasts followed him retreating, their scowls shredding the forest to the open plains.

Kilian and Lupa met at the field with the surviving Romans as the Oltenian clan burst through the woods over the hills at them. The gray and white wolves rattled the air with their roars of retribution, and their weapons were still caked with blood. They howled into the dawn with their power.

Lupescu stood gazing around, his shoulder ripped open, his neck bleeding down his muscle-riveted wolf stomach. Any beast remaining was cut down swiftly and beheaded. The bodies fell and filled the river village with malice. Fenrir was unsuccessful in taking the city, but they had sustained more losses, and their queen was now dead.

Lupescu turned to see Axius, a powerful black wolf like himself. His back was to him, and he had fallen on his knees before Vasiliki. He watched grief melt over Axius again, his powerful wolf form heaving and broken. His lungs heaved in and out realizing she had been killed.

"No." He bellowed, his pain never ending.

Lupescu stood behind him, weak and bloodied, his heart breaking all over again. Axius bent over the body of Vasiliki and moaned against her head. This big wolf leaned over her chest, his arms splayed out over her palms, and cried into her blood.

"I love you." Axius cried, his snout quivering. "I love you, Vasiliki."

Lupescu stood there, his knees weak but too angry to fall upon them, his body bloodied and torn. "I saved you for her."

He leaned his head back and closed his eyes as a growl belted up from his guts. "I saved you for herrrrrrr!" He moaned into the sunrise, clamping his clawed paws together.

Behind him, shadows lingered and a presence he had not felt in many years pulled at him. He froze at first, ignoring the Oltenia wolves who surrounded him from behind. But as they bowed, Lupescu felt their presence sear a mark in his backbone, and it called him. He turned to face sixteen of them. "You are too late. My sister is dead. My commander is dead."

Their head commander glared at the other wolves, then back to Nestor, meeting him with blue eyes. "Sire, what commander? I am here."

Nestor took a deep breath as realization hit him. "The Romans are my brothers. You will not harm them." He commanded. "Is that clear? I know you hunt Romans."

The Oltenia wolves sighed, bent their snouts to their knees, and agreed. "So be it." The commander sneered. "We shall not harm them, my king."

"What is your name?" Lupescu demanded.

The commander gazed upon him, even as the sun kissed Lupescu's magnificent wolf form. "Istros, my king. We have come for you, my king."

Lupescu dropped his head at his hairy chest and turned to his sister and Axius. "They will be back. Fenrir is still alive."

Istros growled, his eyes glowing yellow. "He will die and his hoard with him."

Lupescu sneered at them through his tears. "Yes."

Then Lupescu turned to his Oltenia wolves, even as Kilian and Lupa crept up behind them on the road. Honus stood even more bloodied than before but still alive. The beasts' headless bodies riddled the landscape around them. Lupescu grimaced, his snout breaking into a grief-stricken pain of unending sorrows through his snarls. He stood tall in the sunrise, clenching his fists to see the survivors ahead of him for miles. Something burst inside him, and it lit up, and ravaged him from the inside out.

He towered over all the wolves. He towered over the Oltenian clan. His eyes lit up with fire and then cascaded into a pristine blue, and that something that broke inside him unleashed the worst parts of Lupescu. He clenched his snout tight and snarled as a roar belted up from him that had finally attached to his backbone, and the fire would not go away. His roar chased the rising sun. Lupescu stood above his own, the sun kissing his powerful backside like a crimson tide washed over him.

When Lupa and Kilian noticed Axius leaning over Vasiliki, they froze. Lupa bowed his head and moaned. "No! Not my queen."

Kilian cried, which he never did. He fell to his knees, his eyes wide with pain, and bellowed into the dirt. "Vasiliki."

Lupescu ignored their grief and pointed a long, hairy, muscular arm past the Oltenian clan to the Romans in the fields who survived. "They take the curse or die." His voice was deeper than before. "Fenrir will try again, this time the remaining hoard."

"We take our kingdoms back." His fangs protruded from his snout as he said that, his eyes filled with loathing hate. "We march to them. Not one shall live from that wretched mountain." He snarled.

Istros snarled at Lupescu. "It will be done, my king."

Lupescu eyed them, his snout fierce. "Call all the Oltenians to come. It is time we ended this, and the head of Fenrir is on a spike." He turned away from them to join Axius.

"Sire." He called out, and Lupescu turned to face them.

"We have two of us going to Rome as we speak to care for your mate and heirs. We know the mercenaries hunt them. That is why we have come. Matunaga sent us warning."

Lupescu froze as if the wind had been knocked out of him. He pressed his paw against his heart. "Have them bring my family to me.

I need my wife at my side. This war will soon end. We shall finally be free."

He turned away from them. "There is no going back now." He closed his eyes and gripped his heart as if a deep pain hit him. "My Domitia. We come for you and our little ones, my beauty." He bellowed deep inside.

"It will be done, my king." Istros turned to his wolves, and they nodded. "Send the falcons. We prepare our king for war to take the kingdom back from Fenrir."

Lupescu melted across from Axius at his sister's body. Axius raised to face him, his snout hard.

"Mighty wolf. Do you want to kill me?" Lupescu fretted.

Axius took a deep breath and gazed at Lupescu, matching one another in prowess and power although Lupescu was taller. "I want to kill the beasts who took her from me. I want to kill them all and wipe the world of their filth."

Lupescu sighed. "We will kill them all, brother. We kill them together."

They sat on the bloody field together, hoovering over Vasiliki's body. The sun rose upon their powerful wolf forms like a field of hope had spilled upon them. Lupescu turned his gaze into the rising sun, tears in his eyes.

"Forgive me." He begged Axius, his snout quivering at his face. "Please."

Axius nodded, leaned his long wolf arm atop Lupescu's bloody shoulder, and glared at him. "You will always be my brother."

Lupescu grasped his paw in his own, his face ripped in pain. Axius could say nothing more. All he could do was stare at Lupescu while realization continued to set in what he and Vasiliki had done to him. He was a wolf now. There was no going back.

Lupescu leaned over Axius to pull Vasiliki's body into his arms.

"What are you doing with her?" Axius pleaded.

Lupescu stood up with her, and the Oltenia wolves followed him. "Resting her on the altar, brother. That is our custom."

He turned away from Axius, and the wolves followed him to the heart. Axius watched them disappear in the caverns, and when he turned around, he was faced with the carnage of what he had missed because of his transformation. Honus approached him from the street, stepping over beast bodies, not surprised by his wolf form.

"Look at you, mighty wolf." Honus approved.

"Honus, my godson. Fearless leader." Axius commended him.

Axius stretched his powerful shoulders and neck into the sun, his strength empowering him.

"We lost more Axius. Hundreds more looks like."

Axius sneered into the air. "Aughhhh!" He roared, flexing his arms.

"What is your command," Honus asked, his face hard and bloodied.

Axius pressed into Honus's shoulder, gripping it gently with his paw. Honus met his snout with his eyes, not flinching. "Call the survivors together. This ends today with our weakness. We take the curse or die. We are at war until these beasts are dead."

Honus clenched his face, nodding, his eyes as cold as ice. "About damn time." He marched away from Axius, his step a little lighter.

Axius stood there watching Honus march away from him. His eyes melted upon the bodies littering the village behind him for miles. Again, Roman's bodies melted under the beasts, and Dacian wolves had taken losses. He stood there, gritting his face through his pain, even as his eyes were lit on fire with a vengeance and his heart ached like the sorrow from his losses would never end.

There would be no going back now, ever.

42

Oltenia Comes

Domitia walked in Suburra, the hollow between the slopes of the hills evident as she lunged further into the valley. The insulas rose around her in the streets, surrounding the city block of these dwellings, their dark stone shadowing over her. Roman men and women lingered in the street around her, pressed against the walls, talking, trading, or complaining.

She pulled her cloak tight around her shoulders, wrapped it over her belly, and clasped her hands into her chest. Shouts from citizens in the street cawed at her as she pressed through them. She cupped her palms over her belly and swallowed down the sickness that had been keeping her up all night, only now it haunted her in the day, too. All the pregnancies she had with the girls were different than this one. This child growing inside her was like something had carved itself into her backbone and sprouted something she could not put her finger on.

She passed a tabernae, and smelled herbs. People lingered in and out, buying and selling. As the sun crested further down around her and the insula's shoddy construction towered around her, chills darted up her spine. She paused at the tabernae, eying the sellers and counting down from twenty.

As she turned to go again, and the stone houses rose around her through the street, shadows lingered closer to her that were not the inhabitants there. She walked on until she reached the Suburra wall. She pressed her palm against the ashlar stone, the coldness of it calming the nervous twitch in her palm. It towered over her even as shadows filled the street, and she pressed her back against it.

She craned her neck to see the setting. Its crimson kisses bathed the brick streets in warmth. She closed her eyes, her mind going to Nestor. Her heart ached, missing him. As she breathed deeply, thinking of him, shadows loomed on either side of her in the darkness, and she turned slowly to face it. The mercenaries slithered to her from the side streets, two on each side. Their dark eyes rested upon her belly.

She swallowed as realization hit her. They wanted her. Her face grieved with precision as the sun lingered lower, and the bricks turned dark as night came. Darkness filled the streets on either side of her as if hope had been snuffed out.

"You betray Lupescu." She craned to stare at them back and forth, her face clenched. "You betray all of Rome and Dacia."

The mercenaries scoffed at her, and one by one, they pulled their falx blades.

"Do you mean to kill me?"

They laughed as one slithered closest to her, scoffing at her face. "We mean to take you to our king. You and that little Lupescu growing inside you." He pointed the tip of his blade at her belly, and Domitia gripped it in her palm.

Domitia held her breath and waited as they neared closer. Her eyes were gaping wide on her face as shadows rose behind them on each side of her in the darkness. The shadows rising in the darkness behind the mercenaries had sparkling blue eyes. Their sharp, pointy ears sat atop broad heads and long snouts.

The outline of their form was massive and vicious, and their behavior was as if a wolf goddess had empowered them. A humming roar echoed through the street against the walls, and the mercenaries turned to face them. The wolves pulled the mercenaries into the darkness with them on either side of her.

Their legs lunged out in midair from the swiftness of the attacks. She turned her head and closed her eyes to them being ripped apart, even as blood splattered along the walls down the alleys. When she opened her eyes again, two Oltenian wolves pressed into the street at her, emerging from the darkness shrouding over them.

She craned her eyes up to them, her neck stiff against the wall. Her heart beat wildly in her chest as they approached her from both sides in silence. They slid their falxes in their sheaths when they were but feet from her. Her eyes went from their paws, body armor, and massive muscle-riddled gray wolf bodies to their eyes.

She held her breath at them as they dropped to one knee and bowed to her. A shard of something she thought would never exist plunged through her soul. Chills raced up her spine as a tear fell down her cheek. She gazed upon their power, her lips quivering. The first one who approached her kept his head down to her feet even as he raised his massive paw and spread it out for her. She saw the pads riddled with scars and the claws it had retracted for her.

"I knew you would come one day." Her voice shook.

Domitia pushed her arm out, her fingers lighting upon the tufts of hair, and pressed her shaking hand within his paw on the leathery pads. Her chest beat wildly, her face wide with terror. The wolf raised his broad head to face her. His blue eyes beamed into her soul, and his ears perked straight to acknowledge that she had touched him.

"My queen and heir of Lupescu." He whispered, his voice deep and echoing, even as he gazed upon her growing belly.

Domitia let him take her shaking hand in his own. He cupped his strong paw over hers, his breadth engulfing her human hand. He breathed a voracious empathy at her, and his eyes lit up as recognition dawned this was his queen.

"Lupescu calls you and the heirs home." He whispered at her face.

Her body was stiff in fear at their mighty presence, towering over her. As she breathed them in, the baby kicked. She let out a breath of air, gripping her belly in their presence.

"What are you called?" She whispered.

The one holding her hand nodded. "I am Rholes, one of the commanding generals of Lupescu."

The other wolf raised his head. "I am Scorylo, your majesty."

Rholes let her hand go, and they stood up. They led her out through the darkness, but a strange wind made her stop walking. They belted out a low growl, and Domitia witnessed their transformation back to human. They changed from wolves to Oltenia warriors. The strange wind blowing over them made shivers chase Domitia's spine, and the baby kicked.

She bit her tongue, watching them change, and her mind went to Nestor. She took a deep breath as they led her back to safety. She held her breath as the baby's kicks were profound and rolling. She gripped her belly and swallowed down the sickness hitting her all of a sudden.

From behind them, Matunaga emerged with Troy. They followed them from the street together, their faces stern and determined. It had gone better than they had planned, although putting Domitia in these situations would make Nestor furious.

"Now the hunt begins," Matunaga warned.

43

The Survivors

Axius stood on the hill in his human form where Titus was cremated. Honus stood beside him. The bodies of their dead filled the field behind them, and the fires burned. Three hundred more had fallen to the beasts. Axius did not grip his gladius nor wear his Gateau. His body armor had been ripped and damaged beyond repair. He stood there with the survivors of his army and bled his soul into them as their new Commander.

"You have seen the beasts that took our beloved Commander Artgus and his army! You fought with and survived the beasts that took our beloved Titus!"

The Romans gazed at Axius, their eyes wide.

"They will not stop with Rome! They want the world! They will take it if we do not stop it here." Axius warned them, stretching a bloody arm toward the river. "We stop it here in Dacia!"

"Those who want to return home may go, but you leave today. This must be done for your safety. For after this day, if you do not do as I say, you will die."

The Romans stood amass, the breadth of them filling the village fields before the burning bodies of their fallen. There were only two thousand three hundred left of them.

"Those of you who want to stay and fight against these beasts must take this curse to defeat them!" His voice was deep and echoing. "It will be painful. You will die! But you will be reborn. You will be mighty and strong!"

The Romans eyed one another, their faces folding back to Axius. "If you choose to stay and do this, you can never return to Rome. Your families must defect to be with you!"

Behind the Romans stood Vezina and Lupa, watching alongside Kilian. Bohdana joined them, gazing upon her love Honus, who stood firm as Axius.

Honus spoke up. "They have taken our brothers, and the bodies still lay where they died! They took my father!" Honus cleared his throat, fighting back tears.

"We are brothers still, even in death!" He cried at them, raising his fist.

"I stay to avenge my fallen! I stay to avenge the Rome I know and love. I will stay to end this war with these beasts so the world can live!"

The Romans began murmuring amongst one another, and their whispers filled the air around them.

"What say you?" Axius commanded, his eyes on fire. "Stay or go! If you stay, you will be dead to Rome."

Honus stood with Axius, his face clenched staring at the remnant of them. Survivors. He took a deep breath and watched everyone left alive bow the knee to Axius. Not one backed out. Their red cloaks spilled behind them, still torn and blood-stained. The bodies burned in the field, and the fires rose into the heavens behind Axius and Honus. Axius pressed his face into his army and clenched his jaws. His eyes lit up into their faces of strength, something screaming inside them to come out.

Lupa sighed. "This will be a long night."

Axius pressed a leg up on the wall overlooking the village and plain, the river kissing the horizon under the late-day sun. He clenched his fist atop his knee and glared with a grieved face over the horizon. He closed his eyes, remembering Titus and Vasiliki. He pressed his forehead into his fist atop his knee and sighed inside. He turned his head as Nestor approached him from behind.

"Axius, come!"

Axius pulled his leg from the wall and glared at him.

"What is wrong?"

Nestor rushed away from him, motioning him to come. "Come. Hurry!" He pleaded.

The urgency in his voice made Axius pause, but then he followed him down the road to the end of the village. A stone house was built into the hill, and as he walked in, he noticed Lupa, Kilian, and the Oltenia wolves standing at the entrance. They turned when they recognized him and split apart to let him through.

Axius's knees grew weak, and his eyes wide when they separated for him as he entered. The room opened to reveal stone pillars, a straw floor piled high with cloaks and furs, and Vasiliki standing in the middle. Her white robes danced on her body like heaven had kissed her. Her face lit up seeing him, and a smile burst from her lips.

When Axius's eyes lighted upon her, his strength gave out. He fell to his knees as if the world had taken his breath out of his soul.

"How." He moaned out, and then his voice broke.

"The power of the heart of our people, Axius!" Nestor blurted out, his face a full smile, his eyes teared up. "My sister lives!" Nestor cried.

Axius's mouth dropped open, and he gripped his chest. His face twisted with the shock of pain and shock of her survival all at once. He blew out a moan as tears filled his eyes. Vasiliki came to him and pressed a hand to his face.

He grabbed her hand, kissed it with an open mouth, and lunged up to face her. He enveloped her in his arms and pulled her against his throbbing heart. He breathed against her face, his whole body tense.

"I lost you today." He moaned at her face. His mouth contorted and shivered as tears fell down his cheek.

"But I did not leave you." She wiped his tears, even as hers fell. She cupped his face in her palms, her lips quivering for his kiss.

Axius lunged into her lips with an open mouth, and she met him there. They kissed in heated passion in front of everyone, their tears falling on each other. Vasiliki dove into his mouth, the fire of him burning through her. When Axius stopped, he moaned in her breath.

"You live, and I breathe again!" He cried.

Nestor smiled at them, turning his head to hear Lupa clearing his throat. Lupa coughed and cleared his throat again, his eyes teary. "I am fine. I am fine."

Kilian laughed at him, but he also had teary eyes.

"I said I am fine." Lupa coughed and sniffled.

Nestor turned to them all. "Prepare the Romans. We have little time before Fenrir sends another hoard. This time, we take them all out."

As they all walked out, Nestor swallowed. He watched Axius kiss his sister, and a smile rested on his face. "They are beautiful together." He pulled the door closed behind him as everyone left.

Axius stared into her eyes, clutching her tight against him. "Do you remember before the first battle? I told you if I survived, I would ask more of you..." He stared into her eyes.

Vasiliki smiled. "I do. What do you ask of me?"

He breathed against her lips and moaned. "Everything." He kissed her, grabbed her backside, and pressed her harder against him.

"All that you are. And all that I am. Together."

She met his kisses again, her heart beating wildly, her legs weakening. "I will give you everything."

"I will not stop Vasiliki." He breathed into her. "I will never stop loving you."

"I do not want you to stop." She begged him. "I love you."

He bent his head and pressed against hers, and they stood there, clutched in their embrace.

"I love you." He breathed in her face. "With all I am, with every breath in me."

"Does this mean I get to see you naked again, mighty wolf?" She teased him, smiling, a dimple on her cheek.

Axius pressed his forehead against her and smiled into her face. A happy laughter blew out of him as they clutched their palms together tightly at his chest. They stood there and kissed each other, pulling each other tight together to fall inside one another.

The surviving Romans followed Lupa and Kilian through the caverns into the city. The Oltenia wolves were behind them, with Nestor leading. The torch lights filled the cavernous pass with their shadows. They marched in the darkness, the silence felt on their breaths, in awe of the mysterious city. Kilian led them with Lupa past the plain, the stables, and into the heart. The round room-like cavern was big enough for one hundred at a time, so one hundred Romans were brought in.

The wolves made them kneel atop the runes surrounding the altar. One hundred wolves were waiting on them, pressed against the walls, their Dacian armor belted on their massive bodies. They gripped a shard of stone carved like daggers from the mountain in their paws.

Shards of the runes kissed the blades, waiting to spill blood. The wolves stood behind each Roman, and the men bowed their heads and held their breaths, waiting.

The Romans were still bloodied from battle. Their faces needed to be shaved, and they all needed to bathe. They clenched their fists at their sides and flexed their muscles. Their Lorica segmented plate armor was dinged, and the metal strips had been ripped off many of them. The hooks and leather straps hung down their battered arms, and they were but remnants of themselves.

The wolves shoved the rune shards through their backbones and out their hearts, and the cavern became filled with a mighty splendor.

Axius pressed atop Vasiliki on the furs as night drowned the roaming hillsides around them. Shadows of the trees blowing danced along the walls. They met with open-mouthed kisses, breathing into each other. They moaned in gasps riddled with passion as Axius plunged inside her, his thrusting deep, slow, and steady. He dove into her kisses, their lips aching and on fire.

Vasiliki gripped his muscular back, digging her fingers in as he thrust her. He grabbed her with firm palms, sinking his fingers into the tattoos at her sides. Axius raked his palms up her side, spreading his fingers out and exploring her curves. He roved his open mouth from her lips to her neck, his breath hot on her skin.

She lunged her head back as he caressed the long part of her neck to her bosom. She raked her palms into his shoulders, digging her legs around his waist. She rode her hands down his back, squeezing his tight buttocks in her palms, and pulled him harder inside her. Axius raised over her, pressing his fists into the ground by her arms.

He leaned up over her, lunging inside her hard, their bodies writhing together. He gazed at her face, and his eyes lingered over her body. They smiled, and their eyes breathed each other.

Her fingers grazed his chest and slithered up his neck to the stubbly hair on his chin. His eyes filled with a fire of amber meeting hers. He took a deep breath, raised his head, and closed his eyes atop her. He stretched out deep inside her. As he pressed down atop her again, he devoured her. Again and again.

As the Romans fell and their blood spilled upon the runes, Kilian, Lupa, and the Oltenian wolves carried them out. The passage beyond the cavern revealed a massive lair with alters spreading under the mountain. The alters filled the expanse of the mountain, and the pillars carved to the ceiling glowed in the darkness. The runes cast soft amber hues as if oil lamps had been lit inside them.

The bodies were laid on the altars beginning in the back. They would continue until dawn when the cavern was full of Roman wolves. Their eyes rolled in their heads, and their bodies bled out as the runes carved the wolves through their souls. Blood filled the floor in the cavern, even to the luminescent rune pillars.

Nestor watched as the first hundred were brought in. He stood in the darkness among the rune pillars, his strong face blasting his surroundings. He took a deep breath, gripped his hand to his heart, and closed his eyes. When he opened them again, they were crystal blue, brutal, and vicious.

He pushed his slender arms out at his sides and whispered, even as fangs burst up from his gums. "Breathe, brother wolves. Breatth-heeee." He closed his eyes again and craned his head around as if he were singing into the night. The echo of his deep voice filled the cavern. One by one, the men awoke to a pillar of raging power that had clawed itself deep inside them and burst out, their eyes lighting up as if their souls had been lit on fire.

Vezina bent over, his hammer in his paw, his snout sneering as a growl burst out. He had his tools laid out on the table, ready. His metal armor protected his chest and arms from burns. He knew their designs by heart as he had been making swords for a long time, but these were different. He gripped the steel with his tongs and heated it in the forge until the color of the steel turned yellow. The fires burned around him and filled the shop with a sweltering purpose.

He pulled it out and set it on the flat of his anvil, shaping the corner with his hammer. His thick paws clenched the hammer like the world was ending, and his chest burned, pushing himself to get it done. He tapered both sides to make it even, beveling the edges, his ears flat on his head. He flipped the sword over and pressed the hammer upon both sides until they were even.

He raised it and huffed. A wolf-sized gladius. Axius would be pleased. He pushed it back into the fire, gripping the steel with his tongs. He would follow his process multiple times until the sword was perfect. Vezina then built the capulus of the Roman Gladius with a knobbed hilt and ridges for their pawlike fingers.

His back door was wide open to let in the cool night air as he toiled away through the night. Hundreds of wolves building gladiuses were behind him, filling the valley floor where he and Axius had trained. Their rumbles and clanking rose around the village, even as dawn crested over the mountain.

Aside from them grew walls of wolf-size Scutums, their large, rectangular curves kissing the hillsides. The piles of Roman helmets grew, too, with a ridge of crests running vertically, bleeding in red. Vezina had used old Roman armor to create patterns for these. He raised, eying the gladius he had just made, huffing to himself and nodding.

He turned back and peered out the door as the sun kissed his snout, his eyes lighting up in the valley at the wolves still working. Then he turned his head to the wall aside from his workspace, filled with wolf-size golden Roman Lorica-scale armor, and he laughed, happy with his work.

"Welcome, Roman brothers." He muttered.

He slung the finished gladius in the pile and went back to work. All around him rose the banging and roars of wolves, helping Vezina make the Roman wolves' new armor and swords.

44

Manius forces the Senate's Hand

Manius stood amid the Senate, his toga strapped around his broad shoulders. A golden ring sparkled on his finger as shards of dawn light filtered in at them. He gripped a parchment sent to him by Nestor. The Senate rolled around him like a field of white, their togas with their purple like a seduction of irretrievable forces. Four hundred and thirty-two men peered down at him and waited.

He needed to call them this morning because Matunaga and Troy were hunting the lot of them. Micah sat in the back on the stone, his white robes flowing at his feet. His eyes were wide and observant, and he craned his neck to see Opiter slither in. The Senator rested on the first row alongside other Senators. His long beard was kissed in golden rings, and his eyes narrowed in a firm stare under his eyes.

The seats filled up quickly with consuls and censors along the Senators. Manius took a deep breath and gripped his palm at his toga.

Manius watched as the powerful men stood up, lashing out across the vast floor upon one another. He held his breath, but his eyes were on Opiter, who sat still and watched everyone argue around him.

"We have found yet another body ripped up! What is this madness in Rome?"

Another one hollered. "We must have order! We are a nation of laws!"

"We still war with Dacia! We will wait to hear from Titus. We should be talking about that."

"Yes, war takes precedence over this bear ripping our citizens up in the streets."

"What say you, Manius." Opiter calmed them, and a silence fell like a silk ribbon had been pulled out of a smooth place.

"Titus was killed warring in Dacia." Manius belted out, clenching his jaws, fighting tears.

Opiter's face became pale, and then a sinister calm overcame him. The room exploded again, and some men cried in terror. Manius held up the parchment. "Rome cannot take Dacia. That is clear. The emperor has been informed of this travesty."

The Senate fell silent around him again, and Manius raised his chin and sighed. "The bodies we are finding are being killed by the beasts of the land there. The beasts are here, and we must make a choice." He tested them.

"Yes, my wife talked about a beast!" One Senator piped up. "These horrors keep her up at night."

"So, I recommend we pull out of Dacia," Manius told them, his face hard.

Opiter gasped, his face red.

The men erupted again, and Manius pressed his palms in the air and yelled. "Silence!"

"Twenty thousand men were sent in, yet a fraction remains! Our beloved Titus is gone! And you sit here with your wealth playing in Rome while our people are hunted by these beasts infiltrating our lives!" Manius sneered at them.

"A decision must be made today to end this or send more Romans to die. We cannot afford to lose more. We cannot afford to have our streets filled with widows and orphans unless you will use your wealth to care for them." Manius added.

The room fell silent again, and the men gazed at one another, their fists clenched, their faces hard.

Manius held up the parchment. "I, for one, will not stand idly by as beasts ravish our elite soldiers. Men trained since childhood to be strong and brave! I call for a vote to go to the emperor. This must be done today."

As shouts and debates echoed in the chamber, Manius met Opiter's stare. He nodded at him, sighing inside for this day to be over.

By the time the sun had set, the Senate had sent a bill to the emperor to pull Rome out of Dacia due to this recent loss of life and expense. Manius stood outside with Micah ready to go, his butt firmly planted in the saddle. He watched the men pile out, some lingering to talk, some making plans with their families. He craned his neck as Opiter approached him, and Manius clenched the reigns tight in his palm.

"Manius, where is Matunaga and the mercenaries." He demanded.

"They are with me. You may retrieve them after we dine next Sunday."

Opiter sighed. "Ah, very well then." He paused as if a weight had been lifted from his shoulder and then pressed into him again. "You know why we must continue in Dacia, old friend. Why do you go against me." Opiter pressed into him.

"Everything I do here is for Rome." Manius gripped his shoulder and smiled at his face.

Opiter gripped his toga and took in a deep breath. "Careful Manius. Many here do not agree with you today, even though you got the vote."

Manius held his breath as Opiter said it. He met his stare with a firm, tanned face, his eyes intense under his black brows. He clenched his jaws. "I love you, my teacher, but Rome cannot stay there. You know the beasts are relentless in assaulting us."

"Yes, yes, they are," Opiter stated.

Manius turned his face to his saddle and eyed Micah, his brows furrowed. "Sunday, next weekend, we dine. That gives us time to finish our duties. We shall dine at midday. We still have much to discuss, and with this pressing news of this travesty about Titus..."

"Yes, and if Axius has survived, that makes him the new Commander," Opiter mumbled.

Manius climbed into the saddle. "Bring Anna. I know she has much insight about Dacia as well. Her vast knowledge can be a breath of fresh air."

Opiter went to leave and then paused, raising a finger at him. "Oh, Manius. Axius and Nestor? Are they?"

Manius took a deep breath before him, his face clenched. "No word yet. I fear the worst. We should have received news by now." He turned away on horseback with Micah, and as they left, he craned his neck back to holler at him.

"My home for a feast next Sunday, my friend!"

Opiter huffed. "Of course, I will come. I am a man of my word."

Manius clenched his strong jawline. "So am I." His eyes were as hard stones.

Opiter stood staring at them while they trotted off, a smile on his wrinkly face, even as several Senators joined him in watching them leave.

Micah turned to Manius, his whole body tense. "Did you see them there?" He whispered. "We have one hundred thirty-five beasts in the Senate if my research is correct."

Manius scowled. "I saw them all. The Senate is becoming overrun with beasts while everyone is oblivious. We must be cautious until they are hunted. This ends soon, Micah."

Micah swallowed as Manius sneered at him. "Keep that dagger I gave you close. Keep it close, Micah."

Manius pressed his palm atop the hilt of his long sword, his heart soaring and every fiber in the bones of his body sending an uneasy twitch through him.

Manius,

Titus has been killed. Three-quarters of the army is dead. Honus is well. Axius is injured and will not have the use of his arm as the beasts stalk us still. I will make a choice for him, Manius. The survivors will never go back. You are now faced with a choice.

Anna has escaped us, and I know she travels to Rome. You know what must be done. Stay safe and be diligent over my wife and children until they come to me -Lupescu

Manius pressed a hand to his heart, feeling the parchment Nestor had sent him. He felt Axius was closer to him if he clung to that. Micah gazed at Manius as the sun cast crimson shadows on their faces. Even as they were being followed home, they paced themselves for good reason.

As the sun set over the hills, shadows lingered closer to them from behind. Pine and cypress trees bent and kissed the air in the night breeze, and Manius and Micah paused on the road under a grove of them on the hill. They turned their horses to see the road fill with Senators from within the darkness, their eyes lighting a fire upon them, their purple togas still wrapped around their frames.

Manius watched and waited, but Micah held his breath as they became surrounded on either side of the road by darting arrows. Growls emerged as they were hit, and Manius dropped from his horse, handing his reigns to Micah. The five mercenaries with Troy and Matunaga surrounded them, swinging their blades. Their heads rolled in the road as the bodies fell and their togas filled with blood.

The air upon the hill became roaring hollers, filling the plain with echoes. Manius walked up the road to face them, even as Troy had gored one through with his sword. The old Senator sat on his knees, bleeding out, but even Manius knew he would heal. Manius pulled his long sword.

The senator eyed him, scowling. "You will not win this Manius. The beasts are already here. This is just the beginning."

Manius gazed around at the mercenaries standing with Matunaga and Troy, who held his head back to face him. The mercenaries sported their Dacian-scale armor, and Matunaga matched them, though he still wore his wolf pelt. Their faces were worn and hard except Matunaga, who clean shaven. Their eyes were hard and determined. They gripped their falx blades, their knuckles white over their hilts, ready.

He gazed upon Troy, who still had bruises and cuts on his face and head, but his zeal remained strong. Manius gripped his hilt and sighed, clenching his face. "You do not belong here. You will not take over the world."

Manius lunged up and swiped his head off, and Troy stood standing with it dangling in his hand as blood spewed over his legs and the dirt. Manius turned to his horse, still gripping his bloody blade, and they followed him. They had killed twenty-two, but there were still many more.

The hunt would continue.

The Oltenia warriors smiled at the children as they were curious of them. Domitia let Mel help her pack satchels, her eyes craning back and forth between them and the girls. Even as men, they were big and burly, with blue eyes and intimidating beards. Their black, scaly body armor hugged their rugged frames, and their weapons were formidable.

Mel giggled at the girls as she watched the warriors in silence, even as a cautious reprieve hit her as she gazed upon them. The girls surrounded them, pulling at their body armor and laughing. These big, strong men wolves were gentle with the children.

The eldest twins approached Rholes, pulling at his armor. He bent down upon one knee to be at her level. Venus held a long stick to him, and his blue eyes widened at her.

"Can you sharpen this for me?" She asked, a front tooth missing.

"Sharpen it for what." He smiled, his big red beard filling his face.

"To make it a sword!"

He widened his eyes at her. "What shall I sharpen it with, little wolf."

She pointed to his falx blades jutted up over his head. "Those."

He lunged his head over her and glared at Scorylo, who laughed. "She is like Lupescu."

"Indeed. They are all little Lupescu's." Rholes laughed, and the children laughed with them.

Domitia found herself smiling at these men and how they handled her daughters. A nervous jitter hit her as she noticed a Peregrine Falcon land on Rhole's shoulder. He stood up and pulled a parchment from its claws. Domitia shook all over, meeting Mel at the entranceway to the yard, waiting. Rholes approached her and handed it to her, bowing his head. Domitia rolled it open, her eyes crying for hope.

My love, I have Diana. She is well.

Domitia pressed her palm over her mouth and cried. "Diana is with Nestor! She was taken to Dacia?!" She yelled.

"My daughter taken to Dacia!" She sneered.

The wolves sighed as the girls cheered. Liv's eyes teared up as Domitia continued reading aloud.

We went to war to help Titus, my love. He was killed by Fenrir. Honus is well. Manius was sent this news. Vasiliki saved a remnant of the Roman army, but we have lost three-quarters. Axius was injured. I must make a choice to save him. As we war against the beasts, please know I love you and our children with my whole soul.

We will be successful in taking Fenrir and his hoards. I need you to be diligent and cautious with the beasts there hunting you. Stay clear of Anna, Opiter, and any other Senator coming for you. You know what I say, my love.

My heart calls to you, Domitia. I need you by my side. I ache for you all day as you are seared into my heart. I call you and our children to me. I call you home to be at my side. Please come to me, my beauty. -Lupescu

Domitia gazed upon her beautiful daughters, who clung to the Oltenia warriors, everyone's eyes on her. "It is time we went home."

Rholes and Scorylo nodded, their faces lit up and a smile on their lips.

Mel took a deep breath, clutching her palm atop the hilt of her sword at her side. "The backroad is safest. From there, we will go to Po, where Manius has ships. Will be long journey…"

"Will be a long journey, my queen, as you are with child." Rholes cautioned her.

Mel froze. "Domitia?"

The girls widened their eyes, gasped, and gawked at her. Everyone gazed upon Domitia, who pressed her hands atop her belly. "Perhaps he will be born in Dacia."

"Domitia, does Nestor know?" Liv pleaded.

Domitia's lip quivered. "No."

Rholes and Scorylo eyed one another, swallowing.

"Domitia, what do we do if war still rages there?"

Domitia glared at her, but Liv huffed. "If you think for one moment I am not coming to help protect you or the children, you are ill! I have bled from these beasts and will bleed again if it keeps you all safe, and I will hunt them and kill them just the same."

Rholes gazed at Mel and huffed. "Dacian warrior, brave." He raised an auburn eyebrow.

Mel heard and gawked, eying him up and down before gazing upon Domitia again.

Domitia stared at them. "Lupescu says to come, so we go. I know he and Axius will end this war swiftly. We will meet with Manius when he returns from the Senate tonight."

She turned to begin packing and paused. "My husband does not need to worry about me being with our child. He has a war to fight." She turned away from them and disappeared down the hall.

Mel met Rhole's gaze again and crossed her arms over her chest. "Stop it." She raised a brow to him and pursed her lips.

"Stop what, brave Dacian warrior." His voice was deep and echoing as he smiled at her and leaned into the pillar facing her. His bulky arms were crossed, and all Mel could do was meet his stare, smiling back at him, a twinkle in her eyes. She walked past him and paused, raising her chin to stare at his face. His eyes grazed over her face and met her eyes.

"You know what, you Oltenian barbarian." She pressed her shoulder into his chest armor, pushed him back into the pillar, and turned away to follow the children into the yard.

Rholes watched her storm past him, his eyes on her and the children. Scorylo ran his long-tattooed fingers through his black beard and laughed at him from the opposite pillar. "She will kill you."

But Rholes smiled. "I like her."

Mel stood watching the girls play, a spring in their step with the news Diana was alive and well. She turned her back to the men but craned her neck to stare at Rholes as she heard him say that. A half smile hit her lips, and she turned away from him so he would not see her full-on face crack wide open with a smile or see her face flushed.

Domitia shut the suite door behind her and clutched the parchment to her heart. She fell to her knees, pressed her head against the door and sobbed. She sobbed because she missed her husband. She sobbed because Diana was safe and felt relieved and terrified for her still. She sobbed for Titus and Axius because Titus was like a father to him. She sobbed for Rome. She sobbed for everything she was fixing to have to leave behind and for the woman she knew she had to become to help save the world.

45
Roman Wolves

Axius stared at the mounds of wolf-size Roman Scutums, Galea's, and metal-scale body armor against the massive wall in Vezina's shop. He took a deep breath, smiled, and crossed his arms at his chest. The same was in piles against the hillside outback, with the anvils and fires burning hot. He gazed up at Vezina and nodded, his eyes bright. His face was cleanly shaved, and he had a wool tunic wrap on him that skirted to his knees. His naked torso flexed in excitement at the wall.

Axius's eyes melted upon the Couters, the Cuisses, and the Gauntlets. Even the greaves were designed to be Roman yet powerful wolf armor. Every part of their wolf bodies would be fully armed, even the Sabaton's for the feet, as the wolves and beasts trekked barefoot, their paws a powerful leverage.

The Scutum had a rounded spike in the middle to gore the beasts, and its golden wings stretched to each corner. Axius felt the breath go out gazing at all this. The human Scutum for Rome was four feet tall, but these stretched over Axius's head, and he was considered tall, at five feet eleven.

"It is time to train them to fight like wolves." Axius huffed.

Vezina's ears perked up, and he growled, agreeing. "Good."

As Axius turned to go, Vezina called him. "Eh, Axius."

Axius stared at him, waiting, but Vezina sighed. "I was right, you too stubborn to listen."

Axius paused, even as Vezina continued. "You must be a wolf to defeat the beasts at the river."

Axius swallowed. "Thank you for making this for my people. We will feel like Rome is still with us."

Vezina craned his thick neck and snout at him. "We are all brothers now, mighty wolf. Rome will always be with you."

Axius turned to go and then paused. "Just because you are bigger does not mean you were right." He smirked at him.

Vezina turned to walk out to the hill and picked up a hammer. He slung it at Axius, lodging it against the wall by the door. "Get out, you stubborn wolf." He laughed.

Axius dodged it and watched Vezina go, his face lit up in a smile. His eyes lit upon the majestic power of the body armor he and his Romans would soon wear. He smiled at Vezina's back and turned his head again to gawk at the power before him.

"It is time to end this."

Axius marched out like a fire had ignited under his feet. On the road, his soldiers met him there, their faces refreshed and their wounds healed. They were naked from their waists up, their tunics wrapped around their midsections. As Axius marched up the road to the city, they spilled out to follow him, their eyes lit up at his presence. The remnant of them filled the street back to the river.

Honus followed alongside him. His eyes were lit up, and his fists clenched, ready to fight.

"Ready, son of Titus?" Axius turned his gaze upon his godson. Honus took a deep breath, clenched his face, and then exhaled, nodding. "Ready."

Axius pulled them with him to the plain where they would train briefly with Lupa, first as humans and then as wolves. They had little time because they would be marching to the mountain, where the hoard filled its black caverns with the beasts of the river. To stop them from spilling throughout the world, they must stop them there. The Romans followed Axius and Honus down the street through the village, their faces clenched with resolve, and their souls lit afire in perseverance.

Hours later, Nestor walked the plain chomping an apple. The juices dripped down his chin, and his black Dacian armor glowed under the morning sun. He paused as two Romans flew across him midair at his midsection. His eyes followed them to the straw piles at the edge of the sparring ring. They grunted and hollered, their legs swinging behind them as if they weighed nothing.

The Romans huffed and grimaced but got back up again. On the other side stood Lupa in his wolf form, laughing at them. Masses of wolves had assembled on Lupas' side and stood behind him, their laughter roaring off the horizon.

He was testing them. Nestor took another bite of the apple and marched through the sparring ring straight at Axius, ignoring the bodies of Romans flying around him as Lupa tested their endurance and fighting skills as humans. He crossed his arms and sighed, watching them spar one another with the wolves. His head craned suddenly to Bohdana, who had Diana. Ganna and Bohdana were watching the children until the war was over.

She pulled Diana out to him and sighed. Diana had been crying. "Forgive me, she demands you. She would not relent."

Nestor gawked at first but then knelt to her face and pulled her in his arms as tears fell on her cheeks. "What is it, little wolf?"

The morning sun kissed down on them, but a crisp breeze blew in the air. Diana wiped her face. "I miss mama. I want you, papa."

Nestor put her face in his palm and stared into her eyes, wiping her tears. "They are coming to us, Diana. I have called them home. I swear it."

"Okay," She whispered. Then, she noticed Axius coming to her from behind Nestor and smiled.

Axius lunged around him, picked her up in his arms, and tossed her up in the air. She giggled at him, her legs going limp, her face bright and glowing in laughter. He pressed her into his chest and kissed her head. She hugged him tight around his neck and giggled.

"Diana, have you seen your father as Lupescu." Axius smiled.

Nestor lunged up, his face wide with terror. "Axius, no. Now is not the time for this."

Axius held Diana in his arms. "She is your daughter. Do you think it is time she sees her father, Lupescu? You cannot hide who you are from her forever, brother."

Nestor sighed and closed his eyes as Vasiliki approached from behind them. "Go on, brother. Diana needs to see her heritage."

Nestor backed away from them and raised his chin. "Very well. Axius, hold on to her in case she gets fearful."

A force built around him from the earth like something ancient pried itself loose from the depths and froze upon them. Diana's eyes widened watching her father go from a scrappy, black-headed, scrawny warrior to a towering black wolf. Her eyes melted to the sky as Lupescu's blue eyes beamed down at her, his chest heaving to see her reaction.

Her little hands gripped around Axius's neck. Her face was pale, and her eyes were wide as lemons. She opened her mouth to scream but then paused, swallowing. Axius gripped her tight in his arms until she pressed away from him to let her down slowly. She stepped toward her father as Lupescu knelt to her face, holding his breath.

She grazed her shaking hand over his snout and gulped at his dagger fangs. She stopped at his cheek, pushing her hand into the dense black fur. Lupescu took a deep breath as his little girl stared into his eyes. Her eyes lit up with recognition of him. "Papa."

"Little wolf." He whispered, although his voice was deep and bellowing.

Lupescu pulled up a paw wider than her face, and she grabbed the tip end of his finger and then pressed her fingers against the leathery pads. She spread her hand out in his paw, her heart beating wildly as it engulfed her. She pressed her finger against the claw and huffed, her eyes still wide at him.

Then she met his eyes again and fell into the fur at his chest, trying to put her arms around him. Lupescu closed his eyes, engulfing her in his arms. He picked her up at her legs and stood up slowly. She grasped at his neck, her eyes gazing all around her. She towered over the men and wolves in the sparring ring and smiled into the sun.

She stared at Axius and Vasiliki, who smiled up at her. "I am taller than you now, Axius." She boasted.

Axius belted out, laughing at her. "Indeed, you are!"

Lupescu turned to watch the Romans continue to fight the wolves, cradling his daughter in his arms.

Axius turned his gaze to Vasiliki, and her face lit up in a smile at her beautiful niece. Axius lingered his eyes over her and lunged her into him by her waist. He pressed a firm hand on her lower back and dropped her by his knees. He pestered her lips and neck with kisses.

"I will ravish you tonight." He whispered into her kisses. "All night."

"Not if I do it first." She smiled.

He pulled her upright again and let her go. "I like being in control." He smiled, a laugh belting out.

She punched his forearm. Axius pressed a hand where she hit him.

"Damn." He smiled at her. "Save that energy for tonight." He laughed.

Lupescu turned to him. "Axius, it is time."

Axius took a deep breath, his turn to fight in the sparring ring with Lupa. As he turned to go, he swatted Vasiliki's behind with his palm. She gawked at him, sneering, a smile erupting from her lips. She gazed up at Lupescu and Diana, who stared at her. Lupescu belted a low laugh and turned his snout to face the ring again.

Vasiliki widened her eyes. "Vigorous Roman." She smiled, her face blushing.

The Romans stood on one side with the wolves on the other, and their howls echoed in Axius's ears as he entered the sparring ring. He stretched his neck and muscular arms out and took a deep breath, his naked chest shining under the sun, his groin wrapped in a skirt. He pushed his sandals into the dirt and watched as Lupa crested the ring, pulling his fur pelt off his naked human body. His tattoos kissed his bulky frame, and he looked like a giant compared to Axius.

Axius was tossed a tall wooden stake to simulate combat. He glared at it. "You fight me as human today, eh?"

Lupa cracked a vast smile. "For the moment."

Axius circled Lupa in the ring, gripping his stake as a weapon. "You must hit me with that in the parts that can take me down. Once you do this, you will then fight the wolf."

"I have fought beasts, so what is the difference?" He hunched down even as Lupa circled with him, his eyes on him.

"The hoard is coming, Axius. There will be dozens upon you. If you can take one of us down, you can take a dozen of them down. We are bigger, faster, and stronger than them. Remember this."

"Ah. So be it." Axius took a deep breath and lunged in at him, catapulting the stake into Lupa's chest at his heart.

The Romans stood quietly watching. Their naked muscle-riddled bodies were covered in sweat, and their eyes were hard watching their Roman commander spar with the Dacian commander.

Lupa grabbed the stake at its end, stopping it abruptly. Axius pressed into him, gritting his teeth. Lupa pushed it off before it touched him, catapulting Axius back to the sideline. Axius landed in the straw piles, his elbow cracking the stake in half as he hit. He clenched his teeth and sneered, lunging upright from the straw as if a hand pulled him up.

He gripped both pieces in each palm, twirled them around, and rushed to face Lupa. As he neared him, Lupa bent down, and the wolf burst up. Axius froze momentarily as Lupa catapulted over his head in the ring. He clipped Axius with his claws and knocked him into the air again.

This time, Axius landed on his feet and pressed down with a knee on the ground. When he bent up again, his eyes glittered amber. He lunged into Lupa as he turned to face him. Lupa growled at his face, his claws slung out like blades. Axius dropped below Lupa's swipe and pressed one piece of the stake between his legs, sliding under him. Lupa huffed, his eyes wide.

Axius pressed up from his back and twisted around to hit Lupa with the other stake at his back where his heart would be. He pressed into the dirt, his face clenched. "I got you."

When Lupa twisted around to smack him with his paws, Axius dropped down again and pressed his arm out, pushing the tip end of the stake under Lupa's snout. So, if he were in battle, the blade would plunge from his chin through his head. Axius froze, the dust rising around them, and Lupa scowling his snout in his face.

Axius had one stake under his chin and the other pressed to his heart. The Romans cheered, but the wolves did not laugh anymore. Three more stepped in the ring, and Lupa laughed in Axius's face.

"It is time, Axius," He snarled, stepping away from him.

Axius stood upright and widened his eyes, twirling the stakes in each palm as if they were extensions of himself. "Come on then." He teased them.

As the four wolves rounded him out, Nestor leaned to watch. His snout twisted, his eyes rolling back to Axius and the wolves taunting him. Axius took a deep breath, and then six more wolves stepped out. He stood as a dot among their powerful presence, and the Romans began hollering their grievances toward the wolves.

Vasiliki gazed at Lupescu. "Brother, what are you doing?"

Lupescu did not look at her but continued holding Diana and gazing at Axius in the ring. "Axius must hold his own as a leader here..." He then eyed her from the side, "and as your mate."

"The Romans will learn the ways of Lupa. They must be our brothers if we are to win this war."

Vasiliki did not argue with him further, but her eyes were impressed. A smile hit her face, watching the cold, methodical way Axius waited.

Axius twisted round and round, eying the wolves surrounding him. They towered over him as his fists were still clutched to the planks. He froze, waiting for one of them to move first, and it was Lupa. Axius dropped the planks and transformed as Lupa lunged in at him. The ring became a whirlwind of dirt and dust flying high around them all.

Axius rose from the dirt as the black wolf he was and stopped Lupa's fist from hitting his face. He snarled at it, clamping it in his massive paws. He lunged up, jerked his long arm out, and gripped underneath Lupa's forearm. He picked him up and spun him around in midair. He used Lupa to hit the other wolves, his paws clobbering them while he was in midair. Lupa raged at him as Axius knocked them back.

He let Lupa go, flinging him across the ring back into his wolves. As Lupa hit, he knocked a line of them down together. Then Axius raised higher and roared at them. The wolves left in the ring stood to face Axius, and the Romans entered the ring behind him. Honus led them out, himself a muscle-ridden black wolf. When the dust settled, they stood as Roman and Dacian wolves, facing off. Lupa pressed back into the fray, standing before his wolves. He laughed.

"Well done, Axius. Now it is time to fight." He sneered at them.

The Roman wolves growled behind Axius as they stood as one, their black fur cascading the field together like blackness had fallen upon it. Lupa's red wolf fur kissed his own as if the sun had bred him. His black wolves bent their heads down and growled at the Romans. They lunged into one another in the ring and sparred together, the field filling with dust again and the sky echoing in shouts of roars.

Lupescu stood with Diana and Vasiliki, watching the ring transform into sparring battles between them, and he laughed at them. His laugh was a thunderous roar. He watched Axius and the Romans, well pleased. He nodded in approval of how Lupa had taught them.

Diana squeezed him to get down, and he set her aside Vasiliki. She held Vasiliki's hand and sighed as her aunt gazed down upon her, smiling.

"I am hungry." Diana belted out, the fighting unamusing to her now.

"Come, we shall eat, little wolf." Vasiliki led her out of the sparring field, nodding to Lupescu.

"Do you have cobbler?" Diana asked.

"What is cobbler?"

"How do you not know this?" Diana pestered her. Vasiliki laughed as they walked hand in hand together.

Behind them, the field flowed in wolves' paw-to-paw close combat as the Dacian wolves tested their endurance and speed. Lupa put to test their accuracy and aggression. Their confidence in themselves bridged the gap, as their newfound energy fed their morale. The Roman wolves lived the fire now breathing within them.

46

The Hope of War

By morning, the fires still burned from beast bodies throughout the village to the river. The smoke cast the dawn in an eerie haze. The pyres still smoked from the Dacian wolves and the three hundred Romans who did not survive. They had taken losses, which breathed like fire in their souls.

The Dacian wolves marched out of the city, two thousand on horseback as humans and ten thousand on foot as wolves. They were still outnumbered, but their eyes lit fervently, even as the ground quaked beneath them. Their bulky, hairy bodies spilled in blacks, and some were gray and white. They gripped their oval shields. The wolf head protruded from the middle, gaping fanged snouts as if they were all alive and clawing their way out of them. Strapped to their backs were longbows and arrows in sheaths.

Sticking up over their heads were spears and double-edged swords. They gripped their long-curved falx blades in their paws, the weapon as long as themselves. Their black and golden-scaled armor kissed their massive bodies as they marched out, their plate armor fitted to every part of their body.

Lupa led them out on foot, his red and white hair glowing even in the haze rising from the fires. He growled under his breath, pushing his army alongside Vasiliki. Both marched side by side as if they were an impenetrable force.

Behind them spilled the Roman wolves, kissing the fields and flanking them, their eyes glowing amber. Honus on one side, Axius on the other. They split up around the Dacian wolves and headed into the forest. They gripped their Scutum in one arm, their gladius strapped to their sides. Their Galeas filled the city's edge to the river as lines of red spilled atop the feathers sticking up on their massive heads. Their armor kissed their bodies as golden metal scales hugged their newfound strength. Their long swords stuck over their heads in their sheaths, and their javelins crisscrossed the sword on their backs.

Lupescu stood on the hill, eying them aside from his Oltenia clan. He watched Vasiliki march out with Lupa and took in a deep breath. "We have you, sister. We have you."

He turned to his wolves and nodded. "You know what to do. When the others come, not one beast enters." They nodded at him, their eyes afire in blue perseverance.

Kilian lingered aside Lupescu, his mighty wolf form eying the army formation. "Fenrir is a fool."

Lupescu huffed. "I know the remnant we did not kill lingers for us. We will meet them there and rid the world of them."

Kilian nodded, agreeing. "His numbers are great, but we are stronger."

Lupescu huffed. "Beasts with no good purpose."

"Once this war is over, my family will come home." Lupescu sighed.

Diana grasped the tip of one of Lupescu's fingers, and he bent down to her face. Her eyes lighted upon his weapons and armor, his body armor pitch black like him. She gulped, her eyes gazing around at the wolves looming around her.

"Papa." She worried, noticing that Bohdana had brought up Zyraxes behind them to join watching.

Lupescu gazed down at her. "You are not a little wolf, you know." Lupescu dropped to one knee and stared into her eyes.

"Why not." Diana gulped.

"You are in no way little. You are brave and strong, Diana. You are big and powerful. I need you to know this." He raised a paw, and she pressed her hand atop the leathery pads, her eyes meeting his. "I am proud of you, my daughter, and I love you very much. Always remember this."

He bent his neck to cradle it over her, and she wallowed in his fur, sticking out from the armor. "I know, papa. I love you." Lupescu closed his eyes and sighed over her, his heart busting inside.

He then turned to gaze at Zyraxes, the scrappy black-headed boy who reminded him of himself. "Zyraxes will protect you. He is a mighty wolf, like his father."

Zyraxes stood aside from them and smiled down at Diana. "I want my father to come back, too." He whispered.

She widened her eyes at him. "Who is your father?"

He gazed at the army and smiled. "Lupa." He pointed at him.

Diana gasped, gazing up at Lupescu. He stood up and let her grasp his black finger. They stood there and watched the armies filter out from the city to the river and to an appointed end. They were drawing Fenrir to them, but this time, it was intentional. Once he was dead, they would be free.

Fenrir failed to take the city, but he still devastated it. The Romans, led by Axius and Honus, had proven stronger than anticipated against the beasts. Their resilience was a powerful testament to the rigor of the Romans'.

Lupescu turned his gaze upon his daughter again, his ears straight up. His snout was resolute, watching her eyes and facial expressions take in the power of the massive armies. A mellow sigh emerged as he watched her. She looked just like Domitia but had his black hair. He turned his snout to face the army again, empowered and proud of his offspring. Uncertainty was coming, but they marched together, their vigorous force filling the horizon. If they did not stop Fenrir now, then his children would never be able to live.

The southern Carpathian Mountains stretched across the Danube River, east of the village. Evergreen trees tower through them, opening to rolling plains at the foothills. Lowland forests engorge the land, flowing to alpine meadows. Oak trees and Linden sprawl and form thick canopies of darkness, while the Spruce trees tower like looming shadows.

Within these shadows, Fenrir lurked with his third wave. This would be his final attack. His beast minions had burst from the hoard, following their king slowly after the last battle. They waited in throngs of darkness, basking in their shadows of glory. They waited along the crystal springs under the canopy, hoovering over the rocky plateaus at the edge of the mountain pass.

They waited to wipe out the remnant of the Dacian wolves and rip apart the Romans who had so foolishly taken the curse of the mountain that belonged to them. They should succeed. After all, Fenrir had finally killed Vasiliki, and they now outnumbered the wolves twenty to one.

47

Domitia's Power

Domitia took a deep breath, but the morning sickness made her weak at the knees. She gripped her belly and sighed, her face pale and lips held no color. She was staying sicker and sicker with this pregnancy. Rholes and Scorylo stood beside her against the pillars to the courtyard. They watched her and the children with aggressive precision, their eyes always on them, their fists ready at their sides atop their hilts.

"Ready, my queen," Rholes asked, his human form towering over her.

Domitia peered at his thick-waisted armor, gazing upon a leather sheath. Her daughters were ready behind her. "May I use that dagger?"

Rholes widened his eyes, untied it, pulled the sheath off, and handed it to her. Domitia tied it around her growing waistline, tossing her cloak over it so it was not seen.

"I will give it back." She smiled at him. "I promise." Her eyes twinkled.

Rholes watched her march out with the children in tow, his eyes craning from her to Scorylo. The Oltenian warriors took a deep breath, eying one another. Lupescu would kill them if this plan of hers did not work. It had to work.

Manius peered out at them and nodded, his palm atop the hilt of his long sword, his eyes going from Troy to Mel. "It is time." He told them. "We have one chance." He warned everyone.

As he turned to go, he craned his neck at Micah. Micah stood aside Matunaga and the remaining five mercenaries, and they nodded at him. Manius turned to march out the front with Mel and Troy, where horses were saddled, ready to go, and two carriages were waiting. Raoul would be driving one, Troy the other.

Domitia entered with the children and turned her head one last time to gaze upon the beautiful sprawling manor, her heart flittering inside. This would be the last time they would see it. Rholes shut them in, and Manius led them over Caelin Hill to the backroad that would take them through the forest out of Rome.

The carriages split up, one traveling down Caelin Hill and Raoul driving it, and Domitia's carriage with Troy leading on the backroad.

She was taking her family to Nestor, her beloved. She closed her eyes and held onto her girls tight as the wagon lunged forward, the horse's hooves echoing around them. An endless eerie silence followed them. The silence stretched within her until her guts twitched and chills chased her legs.

Hours later, as the girls had fallen asleep, she leaned her head back to listen. The carriage came to a complete stop within the forest. Her heart lunged in her chest, and then she craned her head to hear Troy talking. But then she froze, and her rage rose as she recognized Anna's voice. Domitia clenched her jaws. Her brows furrowed on her firm face as she stepped out of the carriage.

Anna stood alone under the canopy blocking them, her body wrapped in long red robes. She sneered as Domitia stepped out. Troy sat atop the seat on the carriage, his tanned, scruffy face glaring at

Anna, but he did not move. He eyed Domitia from the side as she stepped out, took a deep breath, and waited.

Anna sneered at Domitia, twisting her mouth at her, even as Beasts filled the space between them under the wooded canopy. Domitia stood aside from the carriage and held her breath, seeing them. She counted twenty-six. They loomed over Anna, growling and snarling at Domitia. Their claws engorged their paws, and their lanky forms melted as one on the road.

"You want me badly, Anna. You want me so badly that you took my child." Domitia warned, her voice cold and calculating.

Anna laughed. "I took your child, and now Fenrir has her. Your Lupescu will be next. All your children will be coming with me."

Domitia did not answer. She just blinked her eyes and lit up a half smile. Anna was not aware of what happened after Lupescu and Axius, with Vasiliki, had saved Diana. Domitia clutched her palms together at her belly and glared at her.

The beasts rose over Anna and snarled at the carriage and Domitia. They lurched lower to the ground, ready to lunge in at her and the children. They filled the breadth of the vast expanse of the road into the forest. Troy breathed them in slowly, meticulously watching them.

Domitia took a step toward them. "Come and take them from me." She gritted her teeth, her lips snarling at Anna.

Anna belted out a roaring laughter and shook her head. "You are a fool, Domitia. Troy cannot protect you from them." She stepped forward, and the beasts lunged around her to get to the carriage.

From the thick canopy overhead, the Oltenia wolves catapulted down through the trees onto the road. They pressed upon a knee bent over. They rose, towering above the beasts, their falx swords in their paws. The beasts snarled and froze at their presence, freezing their attack upon Domitia. They huddled together as a pack, uncertain and cautious of these wolves. Troy yanked his bow and readied to fire, but he did not need to.

Rholes and Scorylo flayed atop the beasts and ripped their heads off, spraying blood at the feet of Anna. They danced atop them in midair, swinging their long falx blades and cutting them down two at a time. Anna hollered in panic, freezing at this battle in her face.

The beasts could not match Rholes and Scorylo's speed, size, or strength. These half-breed beasts looked like mangy dogs compared to the Oltenian wolves. As they flayed them in half and severed their heads with their falx blades, their growls bellowed through the forest as they died. Troy sighed, rolling his eyes, gazing upon Domitia. He was relieved.

Domitia stood still against the carriage door, her girls crying inside from the commotion. The wolves flung the headless bodies into the woods, and they changed back to men. More Senators. Domitia took a deep breath and marched over the blood and body parts to face Anna, who stood shaking at the sudden carnage.

"Turn winch," Domitia commanded her.

Anna stood there with Rholes and Scorylo looming behind her, and Troy was ready with an arrow aimed at her head. Anna scowled at her.

"I said turn. Winch." Domitia clenched her jaws in her face, her dark eyes rigid, her voice cold, and her eyes level with Anna's forehead.

Anna huffed, her eyes lighting up like fire and fangs protruding from her gums.

"Good." Domitia lunged the dagger up from the sheath and straight out at her, slitting Anna's throat wide open.

Anna gasped, grabbing her throat, her face pale and wide in terror. Her eyes stopped glowing, and her fangs sunk. Domitia watched her fall to her knees and roll to her side, bleeding out. Domitia kicked her in the side and rolled Anna over to her back, gazing into her lifeless eyes.

"Nothing hunts my family." Domitia gripped the bloody hilt in her palm and turned back to the carriage to calm her children. Behind her, Scorylo lunged over and chopped Anna's head off.

Troy lowered the bow, his eyes wide. "Damn, the plan worked." He mumbled.

Domitia then turned to Rholes and handed him the dagger. His ears fell flat upon his head, and he huffed. "I would be honored if my queen kept it."

Domitia smiled up at him and slid it back into the sheath, blood and all. "I would be honored to keep it." And then she bent over and vomited, grasping her belly. "This is the last child I am having." She moaned.

Rholes and Scorylo followed her to the carriage once she finished. They gripped their falx blades, eying one another in awe. They still had a long journey to travel, but the beasts hunting Domitia were dead. The blood filling the dirt would disappear as soon as the rains came. The bodies would be ravished by wildlife. And all would be well.

Manius rode horseback alongside Raoul, sitting atop the carriage. They traveled through Caelin Hill, racing the carriage and horses as if a fire had been lit beneath them. The Colosseum rose in the distance, its shadow pressing like fingers upon the road.

They raced to the western bank of the hill near Palatine, a junction near the Aurelian Wall. When they reached the wall, they turned to the Tiber River. They headed to Insula, the island there. Manius kept his head down in his horse's mane and followed Raoul and the carriage, his heart beating his chest to death, his mind on Axius.

As they neared the boat-shaped island, the carriage slowed down. The river crested around it, forming a tributary, flowing and singing in the evening air as the sun began to drop behind the hills. Raoul stopped the carriage as they neared the Cestian Bridge, craning his neck to gaze over the woods sprawling before them.

As they galloped over the bridge, a torch light met them there, and Manius froze aside Raoul. A familiar voice sounded behind him, and his hair stood on end.

"I'm afraid I will not make it to your feast," Opiter called to him. "I have other plans, old friend."

Manius craned his neck to glare at him from behind, his tall frame glimmering in his white and blue robes, his fish clenched over a roaring torch light.

"Of course you do." Manius sneered.

The light cascaded shadows through the woods around them, and from within those shadows emerged darker ones that rose to the trees and growled down at them. Raoul swallowed, his eyes wide.

Opiter stepped closer to the back of the carriage from the road next to the bridge. "You see, I need Domitia. The children are an added blessing, but Lupescu's mate is worth more. The mate of the true king can pivot these wars to our bidding so we can take the world."

Manius pulled his long sword and clenched his face. His eyes were wild with anger as he turned his horse to face him. "You will not touch my goddaughter or her family. This choice is your demise this night."

Opiter huffed at him, his long white beard glimmering in gold, his wrinkly old face lit up in a smile. "I do not think you are one to scold me, seeing how I command the beasts in Rome."

"Ah, is that it? You admit to conspiring against Rome now." Manius huffed, struggling to keep his horse steady as the beasts loomed in on them.

Opiter smiled. "I conspire against the world."

Manius craned his neck and counted dozens of beasts, and his heart shivered, thinking what this night might mean for them as they sacrificed to get Domitia and the children out.

Manius shook his head. "I will not let you take Rome. You will not take the world." He took a deep breath, his face lit up by fire.

Opiter let out a raspy laugh, scoffing at him. "Then die, old friend."

Manius held his breath as the air over his head became consumed with flying arrows. They shrieked, plunging through six beast skulls. The six that were hit flailed as they were knocked down, and more arrows filled the expanse between them at the river and the woods where the beasts stood. Matunaga, with the mercenaries, lunged up from the water and pummeled into them.

The beasts rushed the carriage on Raoul's side, and he dropped below the seat and covered his head with his hands as he had been told to do. Two beasts reached the door on the left side and jerked it off. Mel fired her arrow straight through them, lodging their skulls together. As they fell, she lunged out from the carriage, pulling her long sword, and swiped their heads off.

"Bastards!" She grunted as their heads rolled. "Nothing touches my family!"

The air around Manius became consumed with arrows, and the hacking echoes of beast heads chopping off. He turned to Opiter, who stood behind him still, wide-eyed. Manius slid from his horse to confront him, even as the mercenaries and Matunaga were beating the beasts behind them in the woods, and Mel had joined to help.

Manius clenched his long sword and pressed toward Opiter, but he turned and ran to the river, dropping the torch into the water. Manius chased him to the bridge at the river's edge, and then Opiter turned to face him. The air froze around them like a thick veil had been thrust over the world. Manius held his breath, pulled his gladius, and pressed his long sword at Opiter as he transformed into a beast.

Just as Manius was about to plunge the sword through him, Opiter growled in his face and swiped his forearm at his chest. He lunged down and gripped the hilt over Manius's hand. Manius clenched his face, not able to stab Opiter in his heart, and met the beast Opiter's snout. While his black eyes were sneering over him to take his throat, Manius shoved the gladius up through his chin. As Opiter gasped, Manius pushed the blade out the top of his head.

Opiter pressed back, his paws in the water, letting go of Manius's long sword. Manius swung around and swiped his head off. The headless body lingered at the edge for moments before the current took it. Manius stood there bleeding down his arm and chest as Mel came up behind him. He craned his neck to her and sighed.

He gripped the long sword as blood poured off it. He closed his eyes as the sun set like a blood bath had blessed them. Behind Mel stood Matunaga and the five mercenaries, all bloodied. One of them dropped the head of a beast at his feet. Manius watched it roll down and land near him at the water's edge. He pushed it into the river with the blade of his bloody sword.

"Ready," Manius commanded them.

They nodded, their faces streaming in blood, their body armor sinking upon them as if the Dacians were one flesh. Matunaga smiled. "Well done, Manius. Well done."

Mel smiled at him. "Not bad for an old man."

Manius walked back up to her and shook his head as laughter filled the air around them. "I am not old. Do not believe everything Axius tells you." He smiled at her through the pain, his eyes twinkling.

As they headed back to the carriage and Raoul, Matunaga nodded. "Now, the library."

Manius agreed, hopping on his horse, even as he pulled at his bloody arm. "We finish this tonight."

They followed Manius back over the bridge to get to Micah.

Micah sat at a desk in the Ulpian Library but was in the open in the central Forum. Scrolls splayed over the top, but he was not reading them. He sighed, gazing upon the parchments that showed the names of the city's population. He sat back in the chair and stared at the pillars even as shadows slithered from the Forum.

A familiar voice sounded behind him, and Micah raised his head to acknowledge it but did not turn.

"The famed linguist and scholar comes to study the names of the beasts in Rome." Aneria chimed.

Micah slowly stood up and turned to face her. "I knew that was you."

Aneria smiled at him and turned as other Senators joined her, their eyes lit up dark. Micah gazed upon the men and stopped counting at fifty as they filtered in. There would still be some to hunt after tonight. Micah took a deep breath and faced them, his dark brows furrowed on his strong face.

"I know you wanted Domitia. That is why you conspired with Opiter and Anna to take the child." Micah began the conversation with her.

Aneria sneered at him. "You are wise, Micah. I am saddened Rome will lose such a gifted, strong mind as yours. Unless..." She paused. "You join us, of course."

Micah watched her hold her hand out, and chills rushed up his arms. He folded his hands at his groin and clasped his palms together, and then his eyes met hers.

"I will die before I become a beast." His young face was stern and clenched.

Aneria pulled her hand back in and sighed. "Pity."

The Senators surrounded him in the Forum, and Micah craned his neck to face them all, his eyes taking in their strategy. "Tell me, Aneria, does Aurelian know you plot against him?"

She balked. "Plot against the emperor? No. This is not what we are doing, dear Micah."

"Tell me before I die what you plot, Aneria," Micah demanded.

Aneria coasted back and forth before him, the Senators' eyes filling in more with black, their faces clenched around him. Micah watched them, recognizing them all, and his heart fluttered. He was disappointed, but he had a plan.

She gazed up to the pillars and eyed him from the side. "Fenrir cannot rule if Lupescu and his mate and heirs live. So, they will die. His sister, Queen Vasiliki, must also die before she mates unless she accepts Fenrir. Their union of purebloods will be of great value to the world once we rule."

Micah gasped. "Lupescu."

"Oh, you know Lupescu because he is Nestor, our famed hero. He has done well hiding here these many years. Pity he took a wife."

Micah took in a deep breath and glared at her. "Pity you go after a king who will be your demise. All of you."

Aneria laughed. "You are the one surrounded, Micah. You are alone here, and no one to hear you scream."

The lamp lights lit up Micah's firm face as he clenched his jaws. "You die first."

Just when Aneria went to scoff at him, the forum became engulfed by Roman soldiers from the yard shooting their arrows into the Senator's heads. They hollered at the Senators and flayed into them, more than doubling them. Behind them came Manius, and the mercenaries with Matunaga and Mel dove into them, cutting their heads off alongside the soldiers.

And then it was just Aneria left. And Micah glared at her, his fists still clenched.

Manius nodded at her, his arm bleeding down his robes. He huffed at her face. "You dared to take Rome with these beasts. You failed to see I control the Romans patrolling the streets at night to keep us safe."

Aneria sneered at him. "You will die, Manius. Perhaps not by my hands, but the beasts will get you."

Manius gazed around and nodded to the soldiers who had come to his aid. The mercenaries caught her eye, and she gawked at them. Manius bent to her face and glared into her eyes.

"This week, I ensured my patrols are aware of the beasts stalking Rome. So, whoever is left on this list dies tonight." He breathed in her face.

Then he stepped back from her and pulled his long sword. He lunged up and swiped off her head. Micah was still standing there calmly, his eyes wide, his face flat. He sighed heavily as the head rolled to his feet.

"I am so tired of seeing heads coming off." He rolled his eyes.

Manius turned to his soldiers and pointed back outside. "You have the names on you. They die tonight, or Rome will never see peace."

The soldiers nodded to him and rushed back out, leaving Matunaga and Mel with the mercenaries, staring into the silence with Micah.

Manius sighed. "I am ready to see my son." He raised his head and closed his eyes. "I miss my son."

Matunaga gripped his shoulder. "It is almost over, my friend. Now, we need to get you some stitches. Come."

Manius followed everyone out, his arm aching and his heart burning.

48

The Desperate Hour

The Dacian wolf army paused marching as they reached the lowland forest plain at the mountain's base. Around them rose gently sloping rock walls and plateaus brimming with forest. They were miles from the city but still close enough. The majestic peaks loomed over them like they were small insects to the world. Vasiliki stepped away from the army and galloped out in front for two miles, gazing at the magnificence of the mighty mountain. When she stopped, she took a deep breath. She was waiting on Fenrir and his hoard. She stood up, her back tense, her white hair standing on her back to form a ridgeline of spikes.

Her golden-scaled body armor sung to her majestic wolf form, her pristine blue eyes cold and calculating. She sneered her snout in the air and sniffed, and then growled from deep inside, the noise from her rumble echoing. She roamed her eyes around, raised her snout, and roared. She roared again and again until her eyes caught a powerful black beast lingering atop a ledge two miles out.

Fenrir stood high on the plateau as the sun set, craning his pointy ears to a familiar roar. He rose slowly, his eyes widening as he peered out. He sneered, recognizing the pristine white wolf, her body armor kissing her majestic form. His massive, muscular body flexed, and he froze at the sight of her. He clenched his paws into fists, snarling.

Vasiliki was still alive, and his blood boiled to get her. His snout wrinkled, the shock of her survival making his spine rigid. He belted a snarl before his beasts, clipping the rocks beneath him with his claws. His eyes darted to a bellowing yellow as he took a deep breath, eying her beneath them.

"She wolfffff!" He roared.

He catapulted across the plateau's ridge to cut her off. His hoard was behind him on both sides of the plateaus, meeting her on the plain.

Vasiliki heard his roar and galloped back to the pass. The vast expanse of it craned open to reveal her army with the horse riders in the rear, ready. Fenrir caught up to her on the ridge plateau ridge and slid down the hill to cut her off before she reached the pass to her army. On either side of her, the beasts slid down the rocky hillsides. Vasiliki craned her neck down and galloped, her muscles burning. She needed to draw as many out as possible.

As she cleared the pass to the plain, the beasts filled the expanse behind her in a seething, snarling blackness, following her. They slid down the rocky hills from the plateaus, giving chase. Fenrir still wanted her, no matter what. Vasiliki pushed herself harder than ever before. As she reached the army filling the plain, the beasts were but breaths behind her.

The beasts lunged behind her, and their darkness filled the span behind her for miles. As they gained traction, they pried out their long claws to clip her back paws and knock her over. Fenrir stopped chasing her as he noticed the army and clawed his way back up the plateau.

Lupa snarled, watching his queen run from them. The wolves bent down and readied themselves. "Ready yourselves!" He ordered. They pressed into their wolf head shields, their ears back, their snouts growling.

Vasiliki catapulted over Lupa and the first line as they were bent on one knee. She lunged in midair to get away from them as they jumped up to grab her from behind before the shields. As she jumped into the folds of her army, Lupescu catapulted up over them. He met them midair with his shield. He plunged his falx blade straight out and swiped, goring them alive or cutting them in half.

Lupescu landed atop them as they filled the plain and pummeled through them with his blade. He seethed and roared in rage, cutting through them. The plain was filled with beasts as blackness enveloped the land. The battle had started.

Lupa and Lupescu pummeled them as the first line of defense. The beasts pressed into them like a mountain wall, hitting them head-on. The wolves shoved their Dacian shields into their chests, goring them alive. The beasts ricocheted off the wolf head shields. They were tossed in the air away from the wolves back into their army, flailing and getting stomped among them.

The wolves tossed them airborne, goring them alive. Their bodies filled the air over the beast army with flailing limbs and snarling howls. Lupescu landed in the throes of them with his falx steady, and Lupa, with the first line followed him, swinging their falxes. They beat into them still with their Dacian shields, the gaping wolf mouths tearing into them.

The beasts filled the plain before the wolves. They pressed Lupa back onto the plain, the beasts folding into them still. Lupa let them beat his wolves back for another two miles before the air became thick with different roars the beasts had never heard.

Echoing roars filled the air and vibrated off the mountain pass from the tree line. The roar filled the expanse of heaven and vibrated the air. Axius raised his snout to the canopy and seethed out a moaning roar. He then clenched his snout and waited with his Roman wolves under the canopy of the trees. On the other side, Honus waited with his thousand fifty Roman wolves. The Romans smacked their Gladius hilts on their Scutums, and the air over the plain roared like a thrumming drum.

They waited to ambush the beasts out in the open, gripping their Gladius's in one paw and their Scutum's in the other. They formed a wall under the canopy as if the mountain had bled out, their Galea's adorned with the red feathers atop their heads. They gripped their weapons with firm paws, their eyes roaring and inflamed with vengeance.

When the plain pass was full of beasts plummeting into Lupa, they jumped off the hillside and flanked the horde on both sides. When Axius landed, he roared in their snouts. He lunged his long arm out, flinging beasts away from him with his Scutum. As they pressed in, he and his Roman wolves tossed them back midair upon one another.

The Roman wolves met his roar, and their snouts were lit on fire, their scowls intimidating as the red mohawk atop their Galeas. The Roman wolves pressed upon them, and the beasts turned to both sides instead of assaulting Lupa's wolves directly. Axius throttled into them, using the Scutum as a wall to press them into Lupa.

As the Romans met walls of beasts, their gladius's severed limbs and heads. They attacked them in short bursts of precision and drove them to Lupa. Lupa and his wolves pressed into them to finish them off as Axius and Honus led the Romans, ambushing them on either side.

As the Romans pressed the beasts into the kill zone directly at Lupa, the air over them into the pass became consumed by darting arrows. The darkness plunging over the army fell into the beasts as they continued to descend the plateau and slide down the hillside at them. Fenrir ducked behind a boulder, snarling, and lunged back up the ridgeline to crest around the plateau. He would get Vasililki again one way or the other.

The Dacian archers continued firing blows into the beasts' heads to slow them down as the Romans hacked them down from the sides. When their arrows were spent, they plunged into the battle on horseback from behind Lupa. As the beasts continued to fill the plain from the plateaus, the horses pressed into them around the wolves and lunged into the fray.

The archers pressed up from the saddles and transformed in midair. They pressed their falxes straight out and hit the beasts as they jumped in at them, swiping off their heads. The beasts fell as their headless bodies rattled the earth. The wolves snarled in midair as they hit the wall of beasts meeting them there.

Axius pushed his Scutum into a wall of them beside his Romans, with Honus following on the opposite side. They pushed the hoard into the center to Lupa and his wolves. The Romans made a wall with their shields and attacked them in short bursts with their gladius. Axius belted outrages at them, his eyes steady, his wolf body enraged with power and vengeance. The beasts were pinned in and dying.

It was working, but they were not done yet. Axius met Honus as they pile-drove the beasts into the center for Lupa and his wolves to kill them. The Roman wolves began dispersing up the hills to the plateaus to hunt the beasts.

"Go!" Honus roared at him. "Hurry!"

Axius turned and raced back up the hillside, digging his massive claws into the rock to climb.

Fenrir growled in seething hate as he clawed to the plateau ridge. Below him, his hoard was being hacked apart, and the Romans were following the ones trying to get away up the hillsides. The Roman wolves flayed into them with precision, their roaring howls a fitting retribution.

When Fenrir reached the top, Vasiliki stood waiting on him. She stood on the ledge, her back to the drop, scores of beheaded beasts lying at her feet strewn around the ground. Around them, the wolves joined the Romans on the plateaus and began their ascent to hunt the beasts. The raging howls and growls echoed around them as they died.

"You have lost this day, Fenrir." She seethed at him.

The sun started to set over the mountain, and tangerine shadows touched Vasiliki's white fur. She stood there, her whole body tense, glaring at him through her pristine blue eyes. She gripped her falx in her paw and scowled at him.

"Fool of a she-wolf! My hoard goes to the city to take it while you are here. This was to draw you out!" He clipped a rock with his claws, and sparks flew.

"They will not take the city! You die today." Vasiliki sneered at him, her snout snarling under her blue eyes, her body armor ripped in places on her chest, and blood splattered on her head. "You are foolish to think we would not have prepared after your last attack upon us."

Fenrir stood taller and loomed over her, taking a deep breath. He arched his shoulders back and twisted his neck, closing his eyes. And then he stepped toward her, his breathing easy and strong.

Vasiliki pressed her blade out to him. "Careful beast." Her eyes followed him.

Fenrir laughed at her, his fangs showing. His laugh was deep and harrowing. "We are alone here," He scoffed. "I do not fear your blade. I overpower you easily, she-wolf."

He stepped closer. "You should fear meeeee." He warned her, his deep voice a scowling echo.

Vasiliki pressed her blade further until Fenrir played with its edges on his claws as if sharpening them. Vasiliki pressed her ears back as the screeching echoed. Fenrir danced his claws up her blade and then smacked the edge, and she lowered it to her side. Vasiliki raised her snout to him and held her breath, waiting.

Lupescu rose behind Fenrir from the sloping incline. He plunged his falx blade through Fenrir's back and it erupted out his front chest. "You should fear meeeeeee." Lupescu moaned behind him, his seething growl as thick as his blade.

Lupescu pushed the blade through so the hilt touched Fenrir's backbone. "I warned you never to touch my sister," Lupescu growled.

Fenrir belted out a howl of pain and jerked around to fight him. As he lunged forward to come off the blade, he swiped at Vasiliki's shoulder. She slid backward off the plateau. As she fell, Axius reached out from the wall he had climbed, and they grabbed one another's paws midair.

He pulled her into him, grunted, and held her weight. "Hello, beautiful." He shoved her straight back up to the ledge.

Vasiliki readied her blade in midair as Axius shoved her upright. As she blasted straight up, she met Fenrir's scowl. Lupescu pushed Fenrir toward the ledge to face her, and Vasiliki swiped her blade through his neck. As she severed his head, Lupescu grabbed the head and turned with it in his paw. He lunged to the highest pillar of the plateau they were on. He pushed his long arm out, holding the head, and roared so the world heard him.

Fenrir was dead.

Below them, for miles, Lupa continued to kill them with his wolves while the Romans squeezed them into the kill zone. Vasiliki reached down and pulled Axius up as he was still climbing. He pulled her into him by her powerful waist, and she breathed a sigh of relief into his neck. Axius growled and raised his snout into the sky, breathing heavily. "Let us finish this."

Lupescu crawled down from the rock outcropping with Fenrir's head. "Come! Let us show the hoard their leader is dead."

They slid down the hill into the final throes of the battle, the beasts retreating as Lupescu sported Fenrir's head at them. Lupescu stood above them all, his height overpowering every wolf and beast. He jumped into his army, standing in the midst, and roared with Fenrir's head in his grasp. He held the head up to show the beasts still lingering along the plateaus as his blue eyes lit on fire.

"I come for you all!" Lupescu raged at them, his towering frame and power shadowing the beasts still on the plain.

"I come for you allllllllll!" He roared, his growl a thunderous terror over the plain.

The rising plateaus on either side of them became engulfed with wolves hunting the beasts, and their moaning howls of death echoed through the mountain. When the wolves were done, the Dacian and Roman wolves turned an about-face and trekked back to the city. Their hearts were on fire, and their bodies were still enraged to take out the final horde coming for their home. Only this time, they were energized because Fenrir was dead.

49
Retribution

Kilian waited in his wolf form on the river's edge and stood in the darkness, watching the remainder of Fenrir's hoard slither toward him. He was hunched down on all fours, his claws sunk into the mud on the bank, his amber eyes peering on the vast expanse of beasts coming to take the city.

They moved as one, their ears pricking the air around them. Their elongated limbs and massive bodies flowed like the river waters. As they reached the edge to lunge over, Kilian raised up and roared at them. He turned up the road to draw them through the village. He pulled a torch from a house and lit the torches at every house to guide them on. The flickering lights lit the village, and the shadow of Kilian pressed onward to the city wall.

A creeping itch pestered Bohdana as she stood with Ganna, gazing out of the tower room in their wolf forms. The roars echoed off the river and into the caverns at them. Bohdana and Ganna were armed in their wolf forms, but an eerie silence hit them as they heard the ground shake in the village. Bohdana readied her falx sword and growled.

Zyraxes stood up to see out, too. He and the other children with Diana were back in the tower while Bohdana and Ganna watched over them. He gazed out of the open window, peering above the city plain, his amber eyes glowing to see in the dark. Dawn was nearly approaching again, and he turned to stare behind him at Diana, who was asleep on her fur. He was commanded to guard over the Lupescu heir, so he turned and woke her up.

"Diana, the beasts are here. Wake up." He whispered.

She opened her big brown eyes, and he smiled down at her. "Again?" She rolled her eyes. She froze as her ears caught vicious growls and roars outside the city wall. The beasts were coming from the village and the river.

She sat up and stood at the window gazing into the darkness with him. "I hope our papas are coming back."

Zyraxes caught Bohdana and Ganna glaring at one another, and Bohdana sighed.

"If they do not come back, I will protect you."

Diana narrowed her brows at him. "I can protect you too, you know! I am mighty."

Zyraxes pursed his lips and smiled at her. "Good. You should know how to protect yourself."

Bohdana laughed at them. "Spoken like the child of Lupa, who trains daughters to be warriors." She rubbed his black hair with her paw, proud of him.

They stood there listening into the darkness together, waiting for Bohdana and Ganna to usher them into the mountain pass if the worst should happen.

The village flooded with beasts, the river waters full of them crossing. Torch lights burned up and down the streets to the rising cavern city walls. But it was silent, and no wolf waited for them. The beasts lingered together in herds by the thousands, scowling and growling into the quietness of their surroundings. They reached the city walls, filling the expanse of fields before the cavern pass. As they flooded the cavern pass to get to the city, shadows waited there.

Blue eyes peered at them through the darkness behind pillars of stone or boulders, waiting. They waited until the beasts filled the cavern pass at the city wall in the labyrinth of tunnel. When the beasts numbered in the hundreds and filled the span of cavern pass, the Oltenia wolves pulled them into the darkness with them. The beasts roared moans of shock, and as more beasts entered, they heard them.

All along paths leading to the city, wolves drug the beasts into the darkness between the stones, ripping them apart. Then they would lunge out to pull more in with them. The Oltenia wolves numbered in the hundreds. As beasts filled the village field before the wall, they paused at the cavern. They paused at the moaning screeches of death from their own.

From the rising cavern walls where the carved-out openings were, beast heads littered atop them. The Oltenia wolves tossed the decapitated heads at them from the darkness, and invited them back in to die. They slung their heads out the narrow windows, screaming roars of rage. But then the field lit up behind them in torch lights, surrounding the village to the river.

They turned around to face the flaming lights, meeting Lupescu. The aura from the lights danced off his magnificent wolf form as his eyes glowed down at them. Behind the beasts, Kilian clawed back down the wall and rose to face them.

Lupescu towered over them, holding Fenrir's head. Behind him stood Vasiliki, Axius, and Lupa, aside from Honus. They gripped their falxes or gladius's, their armor bloodied, their snouts snarling at their faces. The wolf army spilled behind them to the river as beasts were being slaughtered in between. Lupescu sneered at them, scoffing.

While the remaining beasts turned to face Lupescu, the Oltenia wolves spilled out behind them from the cavern pass and stood alongside Kilian. They stood against the wall facing the back of the beasts, filling the space with their mighty presence. They pinned them all in.

Lupescu pressed his bloody falx blade at them, and his eyes changed to a fiery blue. His snout growled, wrinkling to his firm eyes. He seethed at them, shaking his broad head in disgust.

"Kill them all," Lupescu commanded.

Axius and Lupa, with the army, lunged into them, and the beasts fell. The Oltenia wolves did not let them enter the city. Fenrir was dead. Lupescu pulled up Fenrir's head again and pressed it upon a spike. He handed it to Lupa. "Put this at the village entrance by the river."

Lupa gladly took it, laughing as he went.

Lupescu sighed, closing his eyes into the darkness, even as the torch lights danced off his thick fur. He stood towering over his wolves, closing his eyes as the sun sparkled. He took in a deep breath and raised his snout to the heavens.

"I am ready for my family to come home." He moaned, gripping his heart.

Axius approached him with Vasiliki, and he smiled at them with his eyes. Vasiliki gazed at Axius, their snouts as powerful on their presence as their gripping body armor and majestic, muscular forms.

"We rest," Axius said, sliding his gladius into his sheath.

Lupescu huffed deep inside, nodding. "I will rest when my family is home." Then he turned to Axius and Honus and grunted at them his approval.

"Brave Roman brothers. All of you." He turned away from them to get to Diana.

Honus watched as Bohdana lunged out to see him, her wolf face desperate. Honus opened his arms wide, and she jumped into them, knocking him over.

Axius watched her knock him down, and he and Vasiliki laughed at them.

"It is a good thing you are still alive!" Bohdana moaned, pinning him down and straddling his wolf body.

"Of course, I am still alive." Honus eyed her beautiful wolf form.

Bohdana's amber wolf eyes sparkled at him. "Marry me, Honus of Rome."

Honus widened his eyes, rolled her over, and pinned her down. "Yessssss!"

Axius and Vasiliki walked away from them, laughing as they rolled atop one another, playing, thankful they were still alive. Axius gazed down at Vasiliki, their wolf forms accentuating one another, their body armor opposite one another.

"I love you, Vasiliki of Dacia." His voice was deep and echoed through her.

She met his handsome wolf snout, her eyes sparkling. "I love you, Axius of Rome."

"I am in control when I ravish you tonight." He eyed her up and down and then marched away from her to help clean up the bodies.

Vasiliki scoffed at him. "We shall see."

She pressed her snout to her chest and joined him in cleaning up, their eyes upon one another as oppression had finally been lifted around them.

50

The Arrival

Manius stood aside Domitia and the girls on the bow at the Po River. They watched the banks disappear and felt Rome die behind them. The Oltenia wolves, the five remaining mercenaries, and Matunaga were ready to go. Troy and Mel watched the stern and starboard sides with keen vision, but they had nothing to fear anymore. Micah swallowed and sighed heavily, but he felt led to come and stay with Manius.

They were defecting from Rome. They had killed the beasts in the Senate. They had hunted the others on Micah's list, and he found they were beasts also. Manius took a deep breath and then eyed Domitia's stomach.

"He certainly is growing. Nestor will be happy."

Domitia smiled and pressed her palm on it, and the baby kicked. "He grows more active by the day."

Manius wrapped his long arm around Domitia, pulled her into him, and kissed the top of her head. "I love you, my daughter. You are the bravest woman I know." He stared into her eyes, his eyes watering. "I am sorry you and the children must leave the home you have always known."

Domitia met his stare and wrapped her arms around him, hugging him back. "Our home is where Nestor is."

"I will live my days with my son and watch your children grow." Manius sighed.

They stood there on the bow of the ship and watched Rome disappear forever. They all stood there in silence, even as the dawn fled before them and darkness shrouded them with endless mercies.

Nestor and Axius had spent many weeks cleaning the village and repairing houses and stone walls. They had burned the headless beasts' bodies along with the heads. Falls' crisp bite was in the air fully, and soon Winter would bring with it storms and brutal temperatures. Bohdana and Vasiliki, with the women wolves, had gathered the last of their herbs and harvests in the city. Time paused there, and daily life was enjoyed once more.

In the heart, Axius stood gazing at the altar Nestor had put him on to save his life. He stood in his human form, admiring the room where his surviving army became wolves. He stood in his Dacian robes and cloak, his fur skins hanging on his muscular frame. He marched through the corridor to the cavern where a river of alters lay, and a part of him broke inside. He gripped his heart, staring at this massive cavern space. The rune pillars towered over him, and a bitter breeze blew in from the mountain.

"It is magic." Vasiliki emerged from the heart and joined him. Her long black hair flowed down her back, and her face lit up at his presence. She pulled her fur pelt tighter over her shoulders. "I knew I would find you here."

Axius admired her and peered around again, his eyes facing the cavern ceiling. The magnitude of its splendor made him hold his breath. "It truly is."

"How do we destroy it." He asked flatly.

Vasiliki sighed, glaring around. "Vezina and Lupa will break the pillars at the alters. Once the rune pillars are broken, we are done."

She grabbed his hand, and they stood together under the pillars, clasping palms into one another. "There is one thing I want to do before we destroy it."

Axius pressed his head against hers, closed his eyes, and whispered against her lips. "What?"

"I want you here. Take me here."

He opened his eyes. "I love you, Vasiliki." He breathed against her lips.

She smiled.

He kissed her with an open mouth, breathing into her. "Will you be my wife?" He pressed her back against a pillar.

Axius moaned. "I promise to love you with all I am, forever." He begged her, clutching her hands in his own at his chest.

Vasiliki gasped. "I would be honored, mighty wolf."

He stared into her eyes and sunk into her lips. He pulled her tight into him. She met his kisses as they raised their clothing up on each other, and he lifted her as she straddled him. Their mouths were open and moaning into one another as Axius lunged inside her against the pillar. They ravished one another until dawn kissed the mountain again.

Lupescu lifted the last of the rocks to help Vezina fix the wall outside his shop, and he froze when Kilian hollered at him. "Lupescu, your family comes!"

Lupescu dropped the rocks as his heart sank to his knees, perking his ears straight up. He took a heaving breath and lunged down the road through the morning fog at them.

Domitia took a deep breath as Rholes, Scorylo, and the mercenaries pressed them up the Danube as Troy and Mel helped with the boat. Her eyes craned up to the woods and the rolling hills and settled upon the Carpathian Mountains in the distance. It was fall, and the leaves had bled out in crimsons and bright oranges, kissed in yellows. The morning fog was so heavy they could not see the waters. Her heart fluttered when they coasted to shore, and Lupa met them there. He was not in his wolf form. None of the Dacians were.

Manius watched the children with Mel and Troy and whispered, "Go, Domitia. He will want to see you first."

Echoes of shouts hollered through the village, and Domitia let Rholes help her out of the boat. She grasped her round belly as Rholes let Kilian pull her through the fog.

"My queen!" Kilian bowed to her.

Domitia swallowed, looking at him. "You came to Rome and found my husband."

Kilian's eyes met hers, and he nodded. "I did, my queen." He raised to face her, motioning her to follow him. "I will take you to him."

Domitia's knees grew weak as he led her alone on the road, and then turned to stop her. "Please wait here, he is coming for you." Kilian bowed his head again and disappeared.

She was left alone gazing upon village's beauty, even as a dark shadow loomed above her through the fog.

Domitia had her back to him, and as chills darted up her spine, she craned her neck to face Lupescu. Her eyes grazed the fog and lifted to his powerful snout. She froze as his pristine blue eyes beamed upon her and widened her eyes up at him. She took a deep breath as if the air had been sucked from her. Her mouth craned open as she realized this was her husband.

Lupescu took a deep breath, seeing her for the first time in months. His eyes roamed over her beautiful, strong face and body. As his eyes lingered, he craned his snout at her growing belly and froze, staring at it. Lupescu moaned and dropped to his knees before her. Domitia held her breath as his big paw stretched out to touch her belly, his eyes lingering upon it. His paw shook, and when he touched her, the baby kicked him.

Lupescu moaned again. "My son." Tears filled his eyes as his voice broke.

Domitia cried when she heard Lupescu's powerful, deep voice for the first time. She gazed down at his massive square head as his ears perked straight up, feeling their baby. She pressed her hand atop his paw and squeezed into it, feeling the power of him.

Lupescu raised his snout to stare up at her, and within the fog at her belly, he lunged up as Nestor. He took her face in his palms. "My love!" He cried.

Domitia gasped. "Lupesc..." But she could not finish saying his name because Nestor lunged into her lips.

He kissed her with a ferocious hunger, their mouths open to inviting passions. Their mouths cried into one another as if they had spent a lifetime apart. Nestor rested his open palm on her belly and rubbed it, leaning his forehead against hers as he closed his eyes. He enveloped her with his strong arms and sighed against her lips.

"My love. I missed you!" He pecked kisses all over her face and leaned into her neck. "I left you with child! Domitia, forgive me."

"I could not tell you." Domitia moaned in his face.

"Forgive me." He cried.

Nestor pressed his lips upon her forehead and held her against him. He enveloped her with his arms, his Dacian armor squeaking. She melted into him and sighed as he moaned. "You are home. My family is home. And we are safe."

Kilian led Nestor's girls to them, and Bohdana had brought Diana out. Domitia fell to her knees as the girls enveloped Nestor, and Diana rushed to her. She took Diana in her arms, crying atop her head. "Diana!" She squeezed Diana tight as tears fell on her hair.

"Oh, Diana!" Domitia cried and looked at Diana in her face with tears. "You are so brave!" Diana cried in her mother's arms as Domitia cuddled her into her chest.

Nestor fell to his knees beside Domitia, tears running down his face as he enveloped his daughters in his arms. "My beauties! My family." He cried, kissing their little heads and squeezing them so tight he felt his world had burst inside. And they lingered in one another's arms, embracing the family they had fought to keep alive.

Lupa stood aside his son Zyraxes, watching the beautiful family of Nestor huddled together on the ground. He rubbed his head, and Zyraxes patted his hand off. "You did well son. Proud of you. Your mother would be proud, too."

Kilian walked up to them and watched Nestor cry with his wife and children back together.

Zyraxes sighed. "Diana is strong like Lupescu, but she looks like her mother. She is beautiful." And then he raced off to join the other kids playing in the fields as the Romans and Dacians worked.

Kilian took a deep breath and eyed Lupa. His dark eyes beamed as his furs kissed his muscular frame. "You have not told him he will guard over her and become her mate if she chooses."

Lupa cleared his throat. "One thing at a time today, Kilian."

Kilian laughed. "Ah, yes! That will be fun when the day comes." He marched off, leaving Lupa watching Diana melt into her mother's arms. "She is strong indeed." Lupa smiled at her and then craned his head to smile at his son playing behind him.

Axius walked up the road with Vasiliki to see this spectacle, sighing inside. Manius cleared his throat behind him and waited. When Axius noticed his father standing beside Micah, he ran to him and lunged a hug around his waist, picking him up. Manius took Axius's face in his palms when he dropped him and leaned against his forehead.

"My brave, brave son!"

Axius laughed. "I heard you killed beasts. Not bad for an old man."

Mel laughed at them, standing aside Troy. "That is what I said."

Manius gripped Axius's face hard in his palms and glared in his eyes, smiling. "I am not old, you little shit." And they all laughed with each other.

Vasiliki stood watching behind them as Nestor and Domitia held their children. She wiped her tears. "Look at my beautiful family. Look at them!" Tears fell down her cheeks.

Axius joined her, gazing at them, and Manius smiled watching them. "They are finally together and safe," he sighed.

"They are beautiful. Look at how many nieces I have!" She smiled through her tears, her heart busting inside. She pulled on Axius's arm. "Look at them, Axius. They are lovely."

Axius gazed at her, his eyes lingering on her happy face. "Yes, it is beautiful." He smiled.

Vasiliki met his stare and leaned into his chest, and Axius pressed his lips on her forehead. Manius cleared his throat again, gazing at them both. "You have found the one now, son. Right?" He hoped.

Vasiliki smiled at Manius, and he bowed to her. "Manius, Axius's father. Pleasure."

"I see the handsome resemblance." She smiled. "So happy to finally meet you!" She lunged across Axius and hugged him.

Manius pressed his palm atop her head and smiled, hugging her back. "Finally."

Axius smiled at Manius, his face lit up. "I am happy you are safe, father."

They stood silently before Axius blurted, "I was right to come to Dacia. You can admit it now."

Manius scoffed at him. "I sent you here. It was my idea."

Axius glared at him. "It was not."

They stood there picking on one another while Micah smiled. "Oh, I have so missed this." He sighed. "I am not certain how I feel about the wolves yet." His eyes went around watching for them as Matunaga approached him.

Matunaga patted Micah on the shoulder. "These wolves are friendly, I promise you."

They stood there lingering in the morning fog together and watched as Nestor motioned for Vasiliki to come. "Vasiliki, come!"

She melted to them, her nieces hugging her, and then her eyes froze at Domitia's belly. Domitia went to bow, but Vasiliki gasped, "No, no. You do not bow to me, my sister."

Vasiliki leaned into her and hugged her. Domitia accepted her loving embrace and hugged her back. They stood around laughing and talking to one another as the morning fog dissipated and warmth touched them by the midday sun.

Axius stood beside his father, a joyous laughter on his face. Their stance was strong together, and their faces clenched into the future of whatever awaited them. Behind them, the Romans filled the fields, building homes and cutting firewood. They worked alongside the Dacians to get ready for Winter. Before them lay a vast city and a new beginning. They had survived the beasts and were together.

51

6 months later

Nestor lay in bed naked with Domitia, his tattoos kissing his muscular body aside her pale, smooth skin. Outside, the snow fell as the city became a haven for silence and beauty. Their girls slept soundly under fur covers in the other room as a roaring fire warmed their stone house. The long table was filled with bread and a vat full of honeycomb and dried fruits. Their table was full of goodness, and so was their home. The fire crackled, and the soft bellowing howl of snow flying in filled them with rest.

Nestor reached over and ran his fingers over Domitia's naked arm to her side, his heart filled with pride. He caressed her nakedness with his powerful grasp, his eyes filling up with her beauty. He pulled her body against his and fell into her kisses, his strong arms gripping her backside tight against him.

"My beautiful Domitia." He moaned. "My brave wife."

She stared into his eyes and smiled, and then the baby cried. Nestor turned to see their son moving in his fur-lined cradle behind him. "I have him my beauty."

Nestor leaned over, picked up his son, and smiled at him as tears filled his eyes. He held him out in his palms. He kissed his little nose and then his cheek and his forehead. "Hello, Titus. My mighty wolf. You get bigger every day."

Then he turned and laid Titus between them. Nestor smiled at his son. The infant had thick, black hair, and was the spitting image of Nestor. Domitia gazed into Nestor's eyes and smiled, holding the baby's fingers. Nestor caressed his son's forehead and cheek with his finger. His eyes lighted upon his wife, who had birthed their sixth child, and he finally got a son. He had come earlier than anticipated, but Nestor knew his son was ready.

"You did well, my beauty. You did well." He whispered in her face, resting his tattooed hand upon his son's little belly as he slept.

Domitia gazed at him. "He is beautiful." She closed her eyes as she said that, falling asleep in exhaustion. Nestor pulled the fur over her shoulders. "Rest, my love. Rest." Nestor whispered into her face, kissing her cheek.

The infant opened his eyes and gazed at Nestor, and a smile burst on his lips. Nestor smiled at him, his laugh lines stretching down his face. "Today is a big day, my son. We have a wedding! You will get an uncle. He is mighty and brave, my son. You will learn much from him."

Domitia fell to sleep, and Nestor smiled at her. He leaned over his son and grazed her cheek and lips with his fingers. His eyes explored her face and skin, his heart breathing to life again. "You are my whole world."

At midday, when the sun was the warmest, Nestor officiated the wedding. His face lit up like the beauty of the snow surrounding them. On the side stood Domitia with their children, and Mel held the baby with Troy smiling at him. The world was brimmed in pristine white, and the city gathered around them at the edge of the woods. Manius stood beside Matunaga and Micah, watching as Axius finally married Vasiliki. He gripped his heart and watched them stand together, holding hands, gazing into one another's eyes.

Their white robes cascaded in gray and white furs to their boots, and Vasiliki's hair was piled atop her head in a crown. Snow fell gently, touching everyone's heads with glory and hope. It was not an elaborate fancy wedding like Manius would have given his son in Rome, but this was simple and perfect nonetheless.

"Axius and Vasiliki are now husband and wife." Nestor smiled at them, and before he let them kiss, he pressed a firm palm on Axius's shoulder. Axius met his stare.

"I would tell you to go and be vigorous, you have my blessing, but you are already with child." He laughed.

Axius widened his eyes, and a smile cracked across his cleanly shaven face. Vasiliki laughed and the whole crowd roared in laughter at them. Axius turned to see Manius with a wide smile and then turned to face Vasiliki. He lunged into her lips, kissing her ferociously as everyone cheered for them.

"About damn time!" Honus hollered alongside his wife, Bohdana, and laughter filled the air.

Nestor held out his arms and hollered. "Let the feasting begin!"

The day bled into the night, and as the fires burned around the campfire celebrations, the city feasted. They enjoyed stuffed cabbage leaves with walnuts. They passed around roasted leeks, carrots, and mushrooms. The veal stew simmered over the fires, and the tables filled with roasted wild pigeons. The honeycomb kissed the tables along their baked bread. Aromatic wines filled the space on the tables between the grapes and pears.

The night was filled with laughter and hope until finally, in the still of the darkness, Nestor sat atop the log around the roaring fire. His wife and children were covered in their furs, surrounding him. Nestor gazed around at his people, and the fire beckoned everyone to come. His Oltenia clan were mingled throughout the city, and people sat around their own fires, telling stories and feasting.

Mel and Troy joined Nestor, aside from Domitia. Mel pressed into Troy's arms as he leaned over and kissed her face. They had survived together.

Axius held his nephew, Titus, and gazed at him, sitting beside Nestor. He kissed his little head as Vasiliki pulled the baby's hand into hers. "Hello, Titus." Axius smiled. "You honor us by taking his name. He was a brave man."

"He is beautiful." Vasiliki smiled. "Yes, Titus was brave."

Axius stared at her face. "You are beautiful." Vasiliki leaned into him, and they kissed. "My beautiful wife," Axius whispered, staring at her growing belly and excited for their little one.

Honus and Bohdana crept along the fire and sat down against the log with Ganna. They had food in their hands and wine in their vats, and they had enjoyed the day and the wedding.

Manius and Micah waited alongside Vasiliki, Kilian, and Lupa, with his son having joined. The city's children sat around Nestor's daughters as their parents mingled around the other fires. They were busy eating and chatting about their way of life, and Nestor's daughters were telling them stories about Rome.

Peace filled Nestor's heart and overflowed from a vat deep inside him he thought would never come. He gazed around the city and then up as snow gently fell upon them again. He took a deep breath and smiled at his daughters playing with the other children and his wife, who was the love of his life. She sipped her hot tea and smiled at him. Her face lit up by the fire and her heart was full.

Nestor jerked his head as the baby cried in Axius's arms. He leaned his hands toward him. "Hand me my son." He smiled. His eyes lit up as Axius bent the baby to him. Titus stretched out, his mouth wide, crying.

Nestor held Titus up in his palms and sighed at his face, kissing his nose. "Why do you cry my son? You were fed before Axius took you, and your mother needs a rest."

As Nestor held Titus up to his face, the baby gazed at him. He smiled back at Nestor, and his eyes beamed a clear blue. Nestor smiled at him from ear to ear, pulling the wool blanket tighter around him to keep him warm. Nestor raised his voice so everyone could hear as the fire lit upon their faces and warmed them in the cold.

He smiled at Titus, "Mighty wolf, let me tell you a story."

The fire embers rose throughout the city as a gentle snow cascaded upon them. Hope filled the air of both Dacians and Romans. As Nestor told stories around the fire, the wolves rested the powerful fires lit within them, and they feasted.

Dacia was abandoned under Emperor Aurelian by 275 AD. After the withdrawal, survivors of the war with the beasts defected to Oltenia.

The End.